Vagabonds, Renegade

Erik Kreinbrink

ISBN: 978-0-9861915-1-0

CHAPTER 1

Jericho hurried through the streets of Gheistmar with the wooden box in his arms. The arrow inside the box would change everything. No longer would they have to be afraid of the Brutes. With this arrow, they could get past the protective armor the Brutes wore.

He rushed to the palace, eager to tell Duke.

He passed the reflective pool where he had killed Edict and several other Brutes. The pool had been drained and cleaned and refilled since then. The bodies had been removed and burned and Edict's special armor was kept inside the palace where Duke and Cinder studied it, searching for a weakness or a way to replicate it. So far they had been unsuccessful. Jericho couldn't wait to show them what he had discovered.

When he walked up the palace steps, two guards blocked his path. More of Duke's soldiers. Irons, they were called now. They wore a gray uniform with shiny steel armor and were all equipped with a short sword and shield. Some of them were veterans of the fight against the Brutes, but many more were new. They had arrived in Gheistmar later. Duke had been recruiting more and more soldiers for his Irons.

The two guards blocking his path looked like veterans. They

had eyes like dull metal and one had a scar on his face.

"I need to see Duke," Jericho said.

"He isn't seeing anyone right now," said the Iron with a scar.

"This is important. It's urgent." Jericho held out the box. "He needs to see this."

"We have our orders." The guards remained standing there, blocking his path.

"I didn't come across the city to be turned away," Jericho said. He stoked his ghosts. He had five ghosts now, and each was far stronger than the ghosts of the guards. "You're either going to let me pass, or I'm going to force my way through."

Of the two possibilities, Jericho was fairly certain they would fight him. The Irons were absolutely loyal to Duke. Duke had recruited them from his gym and brought them here. He turned them from haunted social outcasts to people with riches and reputation.

The Irons used to view Jericho as a warrior savior. They knew he had saved them in the battle against the Brutes, and that they could never have taken Gheistmar without him. But after Jericho had gone against Duke's orders and opened the clock tower, the Irons began to dislike him. Even hate him. So these two Irons might be stupid enough to try and fight him.

Jericho didn't want to hurt them too badly. He planned to have Domnul knock one guard aside while Orion threw the other. Soot could shove open the palace doors. He'd keep Susha and Leo close to him, just in case some pesky other spirits tried to attack him. He was about to send his ghosts rushing out when the Iron with the scar raised his hands.

"Wait," the Iron said. "There's another way."

While Duke and Cinder had taken up residence in the palace, the rest of the Vagabonds were scattered throughout the city. Flint and Thera had moved to Gheistmar recently. They had set up a forge where they made and sold relics. They had helped Jericho create the special arrows. Flint was standing outside the door when Jericho returned from the palace. He looked more excited than Jericho had seen him in a long time.

"How did it go?" Flint said.

"It didn't." Jericho pushed past him and entered the forge. The light from the fire beat and pulsed like the heart of a star. It's ability to create or destroy had always awed him. He wished he was more talented as a smith. He should have been, as Soot had been a blacksmith when alive.

Perhaps due in part to Soot, the forge was a comforting place for Jericho. He liked the smell of leather and smoke and heated metal. He enjoyed the ring of the anvil and hammer playing their song while the fire crackled. This was a place where things happened. Where things were made.

The new arrows were lined in careful rows on top of a table. They were magnetic, so none of them could be too close to each other. To keep the needed space between each arrow, Flint and Jericho had designed a quiver to hold them. The quiver separated each arrow by a sheath of leather so they didn't touch and stick together. Jericho picked up the quiver and began sliding the arrows inside it, one by one.

"You're going to have to explain this better," Flint said as he followed Jericho inside. "Did Duke like the arrow or not?"

"He didn't see it," Jericho said. "He didn't see me. He was too busy, they said. So I left the arrow with the guards and wrote a quick letter explaining how it worked."

"I can't believe Duke turned you away."

"I'm afraid I'm not much loved in this city," Jericho said. "Not anymore."

"You think opening the clock tower was a mistake?"

Jericho was still for a moment as he contemplated the question. Then he resumed sliding the arrows into the quiver.

"Maybe," he said. "But it was a mistake I had to make."

"There was a heavy price to pay ... "

"I know," Jericho said. "I feel bad about that. Especially about Mira. I think about that a lot."

Two months ago, he had opened the tower.

Night after night the bells had tolled. They rang every hour, which was impressive because it meant that the ghost in the tower was not only strong enough the ring the massive bells, but it could also keep time.

The bells would also ring when Jericho walked past the tower. That was not only impressive, but damned interesting. It was like the ghost was daring him to open the tower. Perhaps the ghost wanted to be bonded to him. Or maybe it wanted to kill him. Either way, it intrigued him. With his four ghosts bonded to him, not much frightened Jericho. He didn't think any spirit could harm him.

Still, he was cautious.

He had brought little Claire to the tower to see what she thought about it. Claire could sense things in the ether far better than anyone else. Jericho had watched as she closed her eyes and focused on the tower.

It had been that moment when he realized that Claire was no longer little. She had grown up over the last two years. She was nearly as tall as he was, and her face was leaner than when he had met her. She had let her hair revert to its natural color of sandy blond instead of dyeing it black, and she wore it pulled back in a pony tail. The scars on her face had faded, but they were still noticeable. Sometimes the light would catch on them and flash and make it look as if she had tears streaming down her face.

She was pretty, though. A woman now. Jericho was immensely proud of her. She was a talented Vagabond, especially for her age.

"There's a lot of silver behind these boards," Claire said. "There's silver and plenty of strong spirits."

Jericho looked at the tower. Tall, dark and imposing, it was like a fortress of all its own.

"You think it's relics?" Jericho said. "Maybe weapons?" He was constantly on the lookout for some way to counter the special armor that Stone had found within the city.

"It might be," Claire said. "I have no way to be sure."

There was a storm that night. It was chilly and raining, all of which suited Jericho just fine. He was warm in his wire-lined and heated coat, and his ghosts always seemed stronger in that kind of inclement weather.

Despite it being cold and wet, several people gathered around him. They had sensed his waves in the ether and crowded around to watch. He hadn't thought much about it then. He hadn't considered that they might be in danger. At the time, he had been too busy thinking about what might be inside the tower.

He had grabbed hold of one of the boards that was nailed across the doorway and pulled it free. It fell on the cobblestones with clatter. Several skeleton keys had been nailed to the inside of the board.

"That's a lot of relics," Claire said.

"Probably meant to keep people and ghosts out of the clock tower," Jericho said. "To protect the treasure inside."

Two other boards were nailed across the entrance. They bowed as something pressed against them from inside the tower. The wood creaked and began to splinter as whatever was inside pushed and struggled to get free.

"No," Claire said. "Those relics were there to contain whatever is in there. We should get out of here."

The boards snapped and the ghosts burst from the tower in an explosion of splinters, howling as they swarmed towards Jericho.

"Keep your ghosts close to you!" he called to Claire. His own ghosts charged and met the tower ghosts in a clash of wailing and mist and lightning. As the spirits battled, the dark street was washed with flashes of light as if a thunderstorm was raging in the sky above. The ghosts from the tower were strong, but not strong enough to get past Jericho's own spirits. They broke away suddenly, seeking weaker prey.

They found it.

One of the women in the crowd was yanked through the air and into the tower. She screamed as she was pulled into the absolute blackness of the tower's interior. Her screaming grew quieter—more distant—as the ghosts carried her high up inside. Her voice sounded faint. Like she was very far away. Claire took a couple steps forward, like she wanted to go and help the woman, but she stopped before entering the tower.

"There still more ghosts inside," Claire said. "And one of them is much stronger than the any of the ones that just came out."

"That's the one that rings the bells," Jericho said. "It has to be."

"That poor woman ... "

"I'll get her." Jericho walked into the stygian blackness of the tower.

"Wait!" Claire called. "I think the ghost is using that woman as bait. It wants you enter."

Without turning back, he said, "Go get Lilith." And he let the darkness of the tower swallow him.

CHAPTER 2

Electricity snapped between the wires of Jericho's coat, making shadows leap and flutter around him like bats. That was the only light inside the tower and his progress was slow. By that dim, flickering light he found a staircase and he began to climb.

The steps were wooden and surprisingly solid for how old they must have been. They ran along the wall, turning at each corner. The air was musty and thick with disembodied whispers. None of the ghosts attacked him, but they were certainly aware of his presence. Somewhere high above, the woman sobbed.

He kept his ghosts stoked and kept climbing the stairs with one hand gripping the railing and the other on the hilt of his kilij. The sword wouldn't help him against malicious spirits, but it still brought him some measure of comfort.

As he climbed, the tick-tock of the clock tower's gears became audible. Which was strange, because the clock was stopped. The bells rang, but the time on the clock face never changed. Some sort of machinery was operating, though. That was clear.

He kept climbing. Then the stairs ended, and he moved quickly away from the top of the stairs. Cruel ghosts seemed to love pushing people off of high places, and it was a long, long way down. Only a wooden railing separated him from the fall, and he didn't want to be anywhere near it. So he went deeper into the room despite being unsure of what was in there.

He saw the woman first. She was tall and pale and wearing a white dress, so she was the easiest thing to see in the light. She was standing rigidly and her eyes were rolled back in her head like she was possessed. Which she was, most likely. No one with their senses about them would be just standing there while evil ghosts flew around them.

And it was loud in the room. Unpleasantly so. The clack of the clock's gears reverberated through his body like the pumping of a second heart. He had the vague impression of being surrounded by machinery, but he couldn't see anything beyond jagged shadows.

He stoked his ghosts, urging them to create more electricity so he could see better. It wasn't their specialty, but they managed to make enough sparks to light the room in brief, uncertain flashes.

He was indeed surrounded by machinery. There were gears as tall as a man, weights hanging from chains, and numerous bells that were truly massive. And they were all motionless and silent.

The clock in the tower wasn't moving at all. The noise came not from the huge clock, but from countless other clocks strewn around the room. Grandfather clocks were stationed along each wall like grim sentries. Smaller clocks were perched upon shelves and tables. They all had pendulums. The swinging metal flashed through the guts of the clocks like quick fish. And each and every clock was perfectly timed with the others, creating the synchronous tic-tock that felt like one giant clock.

Deeper in the room was the lord of the tower. As strong as any of the ghosts that he had bonded, even Jericho could easily sense its presence in the ether.

"You wanted me to come inside," Jericho yelled. "Well I'm here."

The ghost came closer. Though he couldn't see it well, Jericho had the impression of a man with a beard and flowing robes.

Yes, the ghost sent. I wanted you to come here.

The numerous other ghosts slid through the darkness like stalking panthers. Jericho figured that if the bearded ghost gave the command, the others would attack. When dealing with dangerous groups of people or ghosts, Jericho had found that the best strategy was to take down the leader as fast and as brutally as possible. Otherwise the mob would win by numbers alone.

Somewhere in the darkness, one of the ghosts hissed. Another muttered angry words in a language Jericho didn't recognize. They all seemed to be growing agitated by his presence. Things were about to become violent. Jericho prepared to strike out at the ghost with the beard. There were too many ghosts in the tower. Taking out their leader was the only way he was going to get out of this.

I wanted you to come here so you could free me, the ghost sent.

"Free you?"

They enticed me here with all of these clocks, and trapped me in the tower to ring their bells for them.

By "they", Jericho guessed that the ghost meant the Elders of Gheistmar. Sometimes ghosts could be lured somewhere by items they had liked or been interested in when alive. It was nearly impossible to bring in one specific ghost—that'd be like trying to catch one specific fish in the ocean—but it was feasible to attract a certain type of ghost. One that was intelligent and interested in accurate time keeping, for instance.

I need your help, the ghost continued. For as you can see, my jailors are quite formidable.

Which changed everything. Instead of the bearded ghost being the leader of the mob, he was their captive.

Jericho had to figure out the leader of the mob, and fast. They looked like they were screwing up their courage to attack him. He managed to discern a hulking beast of a ghost. Maybe he should attack that one first. Sometimes taking out the biggest person in a group as nearly as good as taking out the leader. Then he noticed a ghost that was impossibly tall. Its head seemed to be stretched into long oval. Ghosts often dressed themselves in the garb of the time period in which they had lived, so maybe that ghost was just wearing a peculiar hat.

Jericho kept turning in a slow circle, waiting and trying to decide where to strike.

Then, like a rush of black water, the ghosts surged toward him and clashed with his own ghosts.

CHAPTER 3

The fight was brief and violent.

Jericho sent Domnul and Susha toward the tall ghost with the hat. Domnul was his strongest ghost and Susha was his quickest, and he hoped they'd be able to banish that spirit fast. Orion took on the hulking ghost, while Soot stayed close to protect Jericho. The spirits all collided with a boom. It was like a tornado had been unleashed inside the tower. Small clocks were swept off the shelves. The tall grandfather clocks fell over like dominos, their wood cracking and metal components springing loose as they hit the floor. Even the heavy bells swayed to much that they began to ring with deep, sonorous tones.

Phantom fingers clawed at Jericho. One ghost bit his arm. It hurt, even through the leather of his coat. They pulled him off his feet and tried to drag him to the railing so they could throw him over the edge.

Soot was a good protector, though. He smashed the ghosts, one by one, like a big man stomping on rats. Soon no more invisible hands were clutching at Jericho, and he was able to scramble away from the railing.

Then it was over. The remaining evil spirits fled and the air grew still. The bells ceased to ring, thankfully. Many of the clocks were silent now, their delicate parts scattered across the floor. Others struggled on, ticking or making wounded metallic clangs as they tried to tick. The woman was no longer standing there. The cacophony had probably snapped her out of her possession and she had run like hell.

Jericho's four ghosts came back to him. He was impressed: not one of them had been banished.

I want to leave, the bearded ghost sent as he drifted closer.

"So leave," Jericho said. "Your jailors are gone."

They might come back. Which was true. A banished ghost might be gone for minutes or days, but if they were anchored to an item or person, they would indeed return.

And I fear I would also come back, the ghost continued. *I was drawn here in the first place. I might be drawn here again. I want to leave this tower and see the world.*

"You're asking me to bond you."

I am.

"I have four ghosts bonded to me. And as you just witnessed, they are powerful."

As am I. And I can help you see the world differently. More completely. The ghost moved closer still, and Jericho caught flashes diagrams and mathematics and heard music of a stringed instrument that might have been a guitar or a lute. He saw the graceful arc of parabolas and pendulums swinging in perfect time and the white light of stars viewed through a telescope.

"Very well," Jericho said. "I will bond you." He wasn't sure if he could bond another ghost or not. Most Vagabonds went insane after bonding three. Five ghosts was a lot of voices to have in his head. But this ghost seemed worth it. Intelligent and strong, it would be a worthy addition.

The music grew louder. It was from a lute, he suddenly knew. He could almost feel the smooth wood of the instrument in his hands. The sensation faded and he was in the lecture hall of a university, speaking, debating, arguing. Then that too was eclipsed and he was suddenly alone, staring into the starry night, taking measurements and making notations as the cold light of countless stars slowly rotated in the heavens above.

Later, they told Jericho that they had found him staring straight up at the roof of the clock tower, like he was intently watching something. Nothing was above him but beams and wood, but still he stared. He had been there all night, alone. Standing. Raving.

The others hadn't dared enter the clock tower at night. Some of the evil ghosts had still been lurking near the entrance, and even Lilith was too frightened to fight past them. When dawn came, Lilith and Claire and Flint and Thera had all gone into the tower to find Jericho. After climbing the stairs, they did find him. The broken clocks and bells all around him were covered with a fine, white frost. Jericho had looked at them with glazed eyes and said,

"I have bonded a great ghost. His name is Leo." Happy about it, he had smiled.

Lilith had looked at him and said, "My god, I don't think he knows."

It was an odd thing for her to say, Jericho thought. With the sudden burst of the new ghost's knowledge rushing through his head, he felt he knew almost everything. Geometry, astronomy, physics; he wanted to stand in front of a crowd and deliver a fascinating lecture. He had the urge to tell Lilith all about the tides of the ocean and what caused them.

Lilith reached out and put a hand on his arm.

"Jericho," she said, pronouncing his name slowly and clearly like she thought he might have trouble hearing her. "Some people are dead."

Which helped pull him free of the fading rave.

"The Brutes!" he said. "Did they attack the city?" He drew his kilij and everyone moved back a step.

"No," Lilith said. She shook her head slowly. She seemed

sad. She walked over to the wooden railing and pointed down.

Jericho followed her and looked. The body of the woman in the white dress was laying on the ground, motionless and surrounded by a spray of blood. One of the ghosts must have thrown her over the railing.

"There's more in the city," Lilith said. Her voice was flat. "At least three more dead."

"How?" he said, confused. "Who killed them?"

"Duke is outside with a lot of soldiers," she said. "And he's furious. Be careful what you say. I don't think they're going to hurt us, but ... "

"Are you saying they blame me?" The pieces came clicking together. "The ghosts of the clock tower killed those people, didn't they? And they blame me for opening the tower."

Lilith gave a solemn nod.

Now fully free of his rave, he was able to hear the murmurs of a crowd outside. One by one, he looked at Lilith and Claire and Flint and Thera, meeting their eyes.

"You should all leave," he said, and sheathed his sword.

No one answered him. No one left. Instead, the group of them descended the stairs. They paused by the body of the woman in white.

"Her name was Mira," Thera said. "I talked to her a couple of times at the market."

"Mira." He said the name aloud, memorizing it. He had never spoken to her, and found himself wondering what she had been like. It was peculiar, feeling sorrow for someone he had never met.

The people outside grew louder; they had seen Jericho and his friends. Jericho breathed in, and breathed out. They all left the clock tower together.

The sunlight was dazzling and hurt Jericho's eyes. Duke, bright in his gold plated armor, looked like a pillar of light. The armor of the Irons flashed like white fire. They had the tower surrounded. Maybe it was to make sure no more evil ghosts came out. Or maybe it was to make sure Jericho didn't get away.

"What were you thinking!" Duke roared at Jericho. "I told you not to open the tower. A total of six people died because you disobeyed my orders."

Jericho wasn't sure what to say. He wasn't all that good at arguing. Should he challenge Duke's authority and tell him his orders meant nothing? He looked out at the faces of the Irons. Many of their expressions were outright hostile. Perhaps they had known the people who had been killed.

While he was still deciding how to respond, Claire spoke.

She said, "He didn't mean for anyone to get hurt. He was looking for something to help us against the Brutes."

"Tell that to the friends of the six Vagabonds who died," Duke said.

"A lot more will die if the Brutes come here," Claire said. "If they bring their special armor, we're screwed."

"Justice must be ... " Duke trailed off, and Jericho knew that he had been about to command his Irons to arrest Jericho, but he had stopped. Because Jericho was stoking his ghosts and getting ready to fight. The power of his five ghosts rippled through the ether, and even though the sky was clear, the day seemed to darken as though clouds had covered the sun.

Lilith was ready to fight, too. Electricity snapped between the relics in her hair. The others had their ghosts stoked as well. Their little group, against an army.

"You damned ... renegades," Duke finally said. He waved his hands to dismiss the Irons. "If you open any other buildings without my consent, there will be serious consequences."

The name stuck. Renegades. Jericho and anyone close to him became known as "the Renegades", and the tension between them and the rest of the city was palpable. It continued to grow worse, with Jericho wondering if soldiers would come for them. It was ridiculous, really. They were all on the same side. He had hoped the magnet arrows would bridge the divide between the two groups. Had hoped Duke and the Irons would be grateful for a way to defend against the Brutes. But if Duke refused to even see him, that possibility seemed remote.

Now, as Jericho slid the rest of the magnet arrows into his quiver, Flint grabbed his shoulder.

"I don't like that look in your eyes," Flint said. "You get that look when you're about to do something crazy."

"I'm going hunting for Brutes," he said. "Hopefully I'll find one of their raiding parties. From the reports we have, it sounds like they sometimes wear that armor when they attack coven houses. Killing a Brute while he's wearing his armor is the only way we'll know for sure that these arrows work."

A woman's voice said, "I'm going, too." It was Claire. That girl could be as quiet as smoke. She had entered the forge without making as sound. "You know I'm the best as tracking people through the ether."

Jericho thought about it. She was right, of course. She was the best at feeling through the ether. And she would probably be safer with him than she would be in the city.

"Alright," he said.

"And I want Peter to come with us," she said.

Jericho was at a loss for a moment as he struggled to figure out who Peter was. Then a face connected with the name. Yes. Peter. A young Vagabond who lived nearby. He worked with Flint at the forge and was learning to fight with a sword. Other than that, Jericho didn't know a thing about him. Why would Claire be asking to bring him?

"Will this kid get in the way?" he asked.

Claire's expression darkened. She suddenly looked older. Grown up and serious.

"I won't let that happen," she said.

Jericho thought about trying to find Lilith and ask her if she wanted to go. But she had grown continually more distant from him since the clock tower. She seemed more interested in mixing ghosts with technology, something in which Jericho had little interest. His ghosts didn't care for much modern stuff, and neither did he. So while Lilith had one foot in the past and one foot in the present, the gap between them grew and they spoke less and less.

No, he decided. He wasn't going to ask her.

"Go get your stuff," he told Claire. "And Peter. We'll leave within the hour."

The three of them left the city without incident, and headed West. If they went West for a few days, they'd reach the Brutes' stronghold, the Lourde's Den. But Jericho had no intention to go that far. Going to the Lourde's Den without a full army would be nothing short of suicide. The Brutes were dug in and well fortified, and they would fight like cornered animals if attacked there. He didn't want to take on all of the Brutes, just a raiding party.

So they headed toward a coven house a day's walk away from Gheistmar. It was a decent sized house. Around a dozen Vagabonds tended to stay there at any given time, so it was typically safe. Yet a few months ago, the Brutes had attacked, killing four people and taking as much as they could carry. Jericho figured that he and Claire and Peter could stay at the house for a few days, and if a raiding party ventured into the area, he could go confront them.

Claire disagreed.

When they were nearly to the coven house, she told him it wouldn't work.

"The Brutes won't come anywhere near this place," she said. "They'll sense you and all the other Vagabonds in that house, and they'll stay far away. They're cowards like that. If we want to fight them, we'll have to do something more aggressive."

"We're not going to the Lourde's Den," Jericho told her. "Not just the three of us."

"No," Claire said. "Not there. I mean we should go somewhere closer, and with fewer people. Like ... how about our old home? Flint and Thera's house?"

Back when Flint and Thera lived there, the house had been reasonably safe from Brutes. There had been other coven houses between them and the Lourde's Den, and the Brutes had plenty of other targets to choose from. Now, though, the Brutes had been on a raiding spree for over a year, and many of the Vagabond homes had been abandoned. In some cases, the people there had all been killed. Hell, Jericho didn't know if their home was still standing.

But Claire had a point. That house was the closest Vagabond home to the Lourde's Den. There was a good chance that a raiding party would pass within a few miles, and Claire would be able to sense them. If the party was small enough, Jericho could go attack them. If it was too large, they would have plenty of time to get out of there.

"Okay," Jericho said. "Let's go home."

Because it seemed like a good idea ...

CHAPTER 4

The bell rang, signaling that Jericho was nearly out of time.

This was a new situation to him. It was entirely unexpected and his ghosts were of no help. He had asked them for guidance, hoping that they could assist him with their knowledge.

Don't kill Peter, Susha had sent. *He seems nice.*

Which wasn't much help at all, because even Jericho knew not to kill Peter. It had been a mystery to him why Claire had asked for Peter to accompany them on this trip. It hadn't made sense. The kid was nice, certainly, but he was no great asset to their team. Claire could track Vagabonds. Jericho could fight. Peter ...

Peter could feel through the ether and he was learning how to fight with a sword, but he was young—especially for a Vagabond—and he had long way to go before he could be considered a proficient warrior. So why had Claire asked for him to come along? It hadn't been apparent to Jericho. Not at first.

It should have been obvious. Why else would a young woman want to spend time in the company of a young man? She liked him, of course. And Peter liked her back, which put Jericho in a position. Because he had become a sort of father to Claire, and talking to a daughter's suitors was something fathers did.

The setting sun bloomed red in the western sky. He and Peter had been out in the field for over an hour, shooting the new arrows. Jericho had said he wanted to test the arrows and make sure they flew straight, but Flint had made the arrows and Jericho was certain that they would fly flawlessly. What he really wanted was to say something to Peter. Now he just needed to figure out what it was that he had to say.

He wished Lilith were here. She would have known what to do. He wished a Brute raiding party would come by. That would be easier to deal with than having this talk.

The bell rang again, its sound rippling through the dusky air. Claire was ringing the bell on the front porch. The dinner bell. It was time to eat. It was time for Jericho to say something.

"Peter," he said. "Claire ... she's a good person."

Peter nodded. He did it with no trace of a smile. Like he understood the weight of the moment.

"She is," he said.

"Okay, then." Jericho slipped his bow into the leather case on his back and they went inside.

The small army was miles away from the target, but that was perfect. They wanted to arrive right before dawn and set fire to the house while everyone was asleep.

Setting fire to a place wasn't that easy, of course. Buildings didn't burst into flame just by having a torch touched to them. They needed some help. That help came in the form of pitch.

The pitch was truly nasty stuff. The thick liquid was sticky and highly flammable. It clung to whatever it landed on and just burned right through it. Wood, cloth, flesh—the pitch would set it all aflame. They had to be especially cautious when transporting the pitch. They used thick clay vases with tight fitting lids. They filled the vases and sealed them with wax and meticulously wiped down the outside of the vases to remove any errant drops that might have escaped. While marching, they carried the vases in net-like backpacks. They carried one vase per pack, one pack per man. Nobody wanted vases smacking together and breaking.

They were going to surround the house and hurl the vases of pitch against its sides, covering each wall to set it all ablaze. After that, all they had to do was wait. When the house's occupants came running outside, screaming with their clothes and hair on fire, they would put them out of their misery. No one was to be left alive.

"Did your new arrows work?" Claire asked as Jericho and Peter entered the kitchen. Several dishes heaping with food were on the table. Steam leaped and curled off the hot food. Duck and vegetables and gravy; Claire was becoming an excellent cook. In contrast to the delicious food were the serving utensils, which were made of iron and terribly crude. The prongs on the serving fork were uneven and bent, and the serving spoon looked more like a miniature shovel. Jericho had made them. He had wanted to try his hand at blacksmithing. Soot had been a blacksmith while alive, so Jericho should have possessed some smithing skills. He just didn't have a talent for it, apparently. Or maybe Soot hadn't been a good blacksmith.

That's why Flint had made the arrows, not Jericho.

"They fly fine," Jericho said as he sat down. "And I'm confident that they'll work. Stone's armor won't be able to protect him from these."

The mystery of the Brutes' armor had obsessed him. He had thought about it constantly, searching for a weak point. The battle with Edict had nearly killed Jericho. It still gave him nightmares. Edict's armor had ghosts bonded to it that had knocked aside Jericho's sword. They had blocked arrows from reaching Edict, too. They protected him in every way, ensuring that no harm would come to him. Jericho had managed to kill Edict, but just barely. He couldn't count on being that lucky with Stone. And for all he knew, Stone's armor was even better than Edict's had been.

"Now we just need a raiding party to come close," Peter said. He took a bite of mashed potatoes and his face registered surprise, like it didn't taste how he expected it would.

"What's wrong?" Claire said. "Do they taste weird?" She spooned mashed potatoes onto her plate. The ugly spoon looked huge and awkward in her small hand. She took a bite and chewed slowly with a frown on her face. She swallowed and set down the spoon and bit her lip. Her eyes looked glassy like she was fighting back tears. She took a deep breath, inhaling and exhaling audibly. "I worked really hard on this dinner," she said. "And now look at it."

It was all there. All untouched. It still looked delicious. Except now there was no steam rising up from any of the food. It had all gone cold.

Jericho didn't know what to say. It was his fault. Entirely his fault. He had been thinking about Stone and his ghosts had gotten worked up and he wasn't paying close enough attention and keeping them held tightly to him. They were dense, physical spirits who dropped the temperature with their very presence, and now that he had bonded yet another ghost, they were stronger than ever. This wasn't the first dinner they had ruined.

He felt terrible. Claire had gone through all the trouble to make a nice dinner for Peter, and Jericho had ruined it. He stood to leave the room and let the two of them be. As he left, he passed the empty aquarium. Years ago, he had gone down the creek and caught fish to put in the aquarium. Those had been good days. Now the tank stood empty.

He left the kitchen and went up to Lilith's old room. Most of her stuff was still there. The painting he had given to her was on the wall. Without her ghosts to play with the lights behind the frame, the painting was dark and dull. The boat looked like it was nothing more than a charred piece of wood resting on a sea of ash.

He missed Lilith. He remembered the night they had spent playing checkers while a rain storm battered the house. There was so much he wished he had said, so much he wished he could say. He wondered if he would see her again, or if the time spent with her was now firmly in the past, existing only in memories that would eventually fade like the brief, bright light of a shooting star.

He stood there for a long time, thinking.

Go to bed, Susha sent to him. *Things will seem better in the morning.*

Or they will not, Domnul sent grimly.

Which made Jericho smile as he went off toward his room.

CHAPTER 5

It was about thirty minutes before dawn when they
surrounded the house. It was the perfect time for an attack.
Everyone in the house would probably be asleep and it was still
dark. And yet, they were cautious. They stayed a hundred yards
away from the house as they positioned themselves. One of the
men had a spyglass. He looked at the house for some time.

"One of them is awake," he said. "The girl. She's downstairs."

"Kill her first."

Claire sat at the kitchen table. She was reading an old book
with pages as delicate as dried leaves. The leather cover was split
and cracked. It was neat to be reading such an old tome, even
more so because it was in Old French. The ghost she had most
recently bonded had lived in Paris nearly eight hundred years ago
and, since the ghost was fluent in the language, so too was Claire.
It had been a difficult rave for her, but the knowledge she had
gained was well worth it.

She set the book down. It was hard to concentrate on the
book. She kept thinking about Peter. They had talked about
moving in together. There were plenty of empty houses in

Gheistmar. Or, if they decided to have children, they would look for a nice quiet coven house in the country somewhere. Later, of course. Their relationship was still young, and Claire wasn't ready to be a mother.

She leaned back in her chair and reached for her smoking pipe. She lit it and inhaled and then breathed out the sweet smelling smoke, watching as it rolled and tumbled through the air. She half expected to hear Thera's voice, scolding her for smoking inside.

Something bumped against the outside of the house, and Claire smiled. The ghosts in this house were always noisy. Many of them were as strong as the ghosts in Gheistmar.

The kitchen window shattered as a man came tumbling through. He landed hard on the floor in front of Claire. Her breath caught in her lungs and her heart seemed to stop. Where the hell had he come from? An instant later, the front door burst open and a second man entered the kitchen behind her. He held an axe in his hand. Not a battle axe, but an axe made for chopping wood.

The first man got up from the floor. He clutched a shovel with both hands, holding it like he would hold a club. The edges of the shovel flashed brightly like they had been newly sharpened.

Claire was on her feet without even thinking. As a reflex, her hands flew to her belt and she was suddenly holding her hatchet.

Both men approached her, one from the front and the other from behind.

"Jericho!" Claire screamed.

The night always had a certain rhythm to it. The crickets' chirping, the night birds' songs, and the deep bass of croaking bullfrogs all possessed a relaxing cadence. When they went silent, something dangerous was nearby. A predator, an approaching storm — something.

A small part of Jericho was always expecting a Brute attack, so when the crickets and the night birds and the bullfrogs all fell silent, he snapped awake. He struggled into his clothes and scooped up his weapons. He had his sword on his belt, his bow in his hand, and the quiver of arrows slung over his shoulder as he ran from his room.

He was already halfway down the stairs when Claire called his name.

Jericho had an arrow nocked and the string of his bow pulled back as he stepped into the kitchen.

Jericho's bow was a present from Lilith. He had been using a long bow, but it was cumbersome and difficult to use. This bow was much different. It was a modern bow, made from some kind of material Jericho didn't recognize. With the help of Flint, she had adorned the grip area of the bow with silver. The silver was shaped into a wolf's head. Its mouth was open, like it spat out arrows. The wolf's eyes were two sapphires, each of them with a tiny light bulb behind them. The electricity that Jericho's ghosts put out made the eyes glow.

Jericho loved the bow. Not only did it look amazing, but it was extremely efficient. It had two pulleys on it. One of the pulleys was like a misshapen oval, and it allowed Jericho to pull the bow back all the way and hold it easily. The weapon was light and easy to use and Jericho had practiced with it relentlessly. He had a flat leather case for it that he wore slung across his back. The case made it effortless to carry the bow, and he never went anywhere without the weapon. It was more like a part of him. And he was damned good with it.

As he entered the kitchen, he took in the sight with cold calculation. Claire was between two Brutes. The ghosts bonded to them must have been weak, because Jericho couldn't even sense them. Both of the Brutes were armed with rudimentary weapons. One with a shovel, the other with a wood axe. Typical of the Brutes: they grabbed anything that was handy. Basic weapons, but they had a longer reach than Claire's hatchet. They posed no problem for Jericho's bow, however.

Jericho shot the Brute who was farther away, the one with the shovel. The arrow slammed into the man's chest, sinking deep. The man's legs gave out and he fell down. He was dead before he hit the floor. The man with the axe leapt toward Claire. She danced backward and then Jericho's second arrow was in flight. It hit the man in the back, tearing skin and muscle before piercing some vital organ and dropping him.

A large object was hurled through the open window. It nearly hit Claire. She ducked just in time and the object—it looked like a clay vase—crashed against the wall. It shattered and spilled a foul black liquid everywhere, coating the wall ... and Claire. The liquid had splashed all over her, covering her from her hair down to her boots.

Jericho recognized the smell of the liquid. He knew what it was. From the look in her eyes, so did Claire.

Pitch.

Time seemed to freeze. Claire stared at Jericho, her eyes full of fear and despair and desperate pleading. The lines of scars around her eyes flashed silver in the light, making it look like she was crying. Jericho held Claire's gaze. She was like a daughter to him. A lot passed between them in that one long moment.

A burning torch sailed in through the open window, leaving an orange trail of color behind it as it flew through the air. It hit the wall with a dull thud, and the pitch burst into flame.

CHAPTER 6

No survivors. That was the mantra that had been drilled into them over and over. This entire endeavor might prove worthless if even one of the Vagabonds escaped. To achieve this goal, they had devised a specific battle plan.

Like most good plans, their plan was a simple one: Set the house on fire and slaughter anyone who came out. They had experimented with another house of a similar size, setting it ablaze and timing the flames. The structure had been completely on fire under thirty minutes. Within an hour, the roof had fallen in and two of the walls had crumbled. Of course, they figured the house would be untenable much sooner. Ten minutes, they guessed, was all the time it would take before the smoke and heat forced the house's occupants to flee.

He took out his pocket watch and looked at the time as they started flinging the clay pots of pitch. They launched their pots with almost mechanical precision. On all sides of the house, the pots crashed through windows and they threw burning torches in after them. Soon the interior of the house pulsed with the orange glow of hungry flames.

Ten minutes before the Jericho and his friends would be

forced out of their home. That was the maximum. They might come out sooner, of course. They might group together, assess their situation, and decide to rush out. They'd gather their weapons, choose which side of the house from which to make their exit, and try to take the offensive.

Doing that would just make them die quicker. They would be back-lit by the flames, highly visible and easy targets. They were completely surrounded and their time was short. Ten minutes, before they'd be dead.

From the side of the house came the unmistakable sound of arrows hissing through the air. He started to run over to see what was happening, but then one of the Vagabonds tumbled out of a front downstairs window. It was a young man, hardly more than a boy. Someone leapt forward and chopped down with a sharpened shovel, hacking into the boy with such savage ferocity that the impact of the blade cracking through his skull was audible over the crackling of the flames.

This was going much better than they had hoped.

There was quite a bit of commotion on the side of the house. And fire. Fire that was in the completely wrong place.

He ran to the side of the house and saw that he had been wrong. Things weren't going well at all.

Jericho watched in horror as the torch set the pitch aflame. The fire surged across the wall and floor and Claire.

"Pull your ghosts to you!" Jericho shouted as he unsheathed his kilij and swung it, smacking the flat of the blade against her and pushing his ghosts' energy into the blade. He hoped her ghosts could protect her against the freezing chill of the weapon. Which, it seemed, they did. The flames covering her shrank and died, leaving her standing there stunned. Her hair was singed and her face covered in soot, but she was alive.

"We need to go," Jericho said. Claire was still covered in pitch and fire was all around them and spreading fast. It wasn't safe to stay inside the house. He didn't know where Peter was, and he had no way to warn him. Jericho could only hope that Peter would realize that he had to get out. The place was going to burn to the ground. The best chance of survival was to attack.

The kitchen table was made of solid oak. Flaming pitch had splashed across the top of it, but the fire hadn't eaten far into the wood yet. Jericho flipped the table onto its side and picked it up by its legs, holding it in front of him like a flaming shield.

"Follow me," he told Claire.

He heaved it through the broken kitchen window and leapt out after it.

The table landed on its top and Jericho yanked on the legs to put it on its side again and ducked behind it. Claire jumped out the window and crouched beside him, both of them using the table as cover. Rocks and shovels drummed against the table, none of it piercing the dense oak.

The table wouldn't protect them for long, though. The Brutes were closing in from all sides. Jericho figured he'd be able to rush them and fight his way free. His ghosts could propel him fast enough that they wouldn't be able to catch him. Or he could rain arrows upon them and give Claire a chance to escape. He didn't think they could both get away. It was either him or her.

Easy decision.

"I'm going to shoot some of them and open a hole in their lines," he said. "When that gap opens, you need to run fast and keep running. Do you understand?"

Claire didn't respond. The fumes of the pitch radiated from her.

He grabbed her shoulder and shook her.

"You need to focus," he told her.

"Peter ... "

"If I can help him, I will. Right now, I've got to get you out of here. Run, and shroud your ghosts so they can't find you. Okay?"

She nodded.

"Okay?" he asked again, louder.

"Okay," she said.

"All right. Get ready." Jericho nocked an arrow and leaned to the side. He picked out a man-shaped shadow and loosed his arrow. It hit, dropping the man. He shot another. Then another. The Brutes in that area went scurrying for cover.

"Go!" he shouted.

Claire ran. Two Brutes rushed toward her. One carried a shovel and the other ran after her with his arms outstretched like he wanted to rip her apart with his bare hands. Jericho shot the one with the shovel, and he fell and rolled in the grass. The other Brute was just about to grab Claire when Jericho's next arrow slammed into his side, dropping him.

Then Claire was free, disappearing into the night. Jericho was worried about her, but he had faith that she would escape. She was very good at shrouding her ghosts and slipping past other Vagabonds undetected.

Besides, the Brutes would be too busy fighting him to go after her.

He shot another one. He reached back and checked how many arrows he had left. Not enough. More Brutes seemed to be arriving. He didn't think he could fight through them. And he couldn't stay crouched behind the table. If they rushed him, he wouldn't stand a chance.

One of the Brutes ran forward with a vase in his hands. His arm started to cock back for the throw.

It became a race, a contest of pure speed. Jericho already held his next arrow. He swabbed it across the top of the table. The sticky, flaming pitch clung to its tip. In a motion practiced and exercised through countless repetitions, Jericho nocked the arrow and drew back the string of his bow and loosed it. The arrow drew a bold, bright line through the night air and shattered the vase just as the man was bringing his arm forward. The pitch ignited, covering the man and everything around him in liquid fire. He was doused in flame and ran toward his fellow Brutes like they could help him. They ran from him. There was nothing they could do to save him and they didn't want to be set on fire too.

Jericho ran. He aimed right for the fire, right for the middle of all the chaos. They threw weapons at him, but he was a moving target. A fast moving target. His ghosts propelled him forward, turning each of his strides into gigantic leaps. It was like having a tremendous wind at his back, moving him in whichever direction he chose. He jumped over the fire and ran past the Brutes and into the shadows of the night.

He spared a moment to glimpse back. The house was a towering inferno whose light spiked high against the black night sky. Peter's body was on the ground. His head was cracked open.

Jericho gritted his teeth and debated what to do.

The Brutes were coming for him, their footfall a thundering rumble that reverberated through the soil. He considered trying to find Claire, but didn't want to lead the Brutes to her. It might be best if they met back in Gheistmar. He turned away and started running.

He ran relentlessly, his body propelled by his ghosts and his mind fueled by rage. The countryside slid by. Woods were replaced by empty fields studded with the occasional lonely house. Then it was back to woods again. The branches stretched over the road, forming a sort of tunnel that shut out the moonlight. He kept running, never thinking too hard. He focused only on putting one foot in front of the other.

We should go back. Domnul sent. *We should go back and kill as many as we can.*

No, Jericho sent. *I want them all dead. Each and every one of them.*

Gheistmar was many miles ahead, and Jericho tried to think of nothing but the simple action of running. Yet, something kept sparking in his mind. A small thought, a puzzlement that wouldn't fade. Like a stubborn ember that wouldn't die, it burned in his head. The Brutes shouldn't have been able to approach without them knowing. Claire was the best at feeling waves in the ether. No one could sneak up on her. It just didn't make sense. How had such a large group surprised them?

CHAPTER 7

Jericho didn't know how many Vagabonds had died trying to enter Gheistmar, but he knew the number was fairly high.

The main gates were the only entrance. Gheistmar was set deep in the woods far away from any civilization. The city had been built in a circle, and it was ringed by high stone walls. In front of the walls was the moat. There was a drop of at least fifteen feet before the surface of the brackish water. Countless relics were scattered along the bottom of the water, each relic containing a powerful and malicious spirit. Those ghosts were some of the most vile that Jericho had ever witnessed. They seemed to exist for the sole purpose of hurting people.

To enter the city, a person had to walk across the bridge and through the gates. It was best to stay in the middle of the bridge and not look to either side. Many of the ghosts were quite capable of yanking a person right off the bridge. Other moat ghosts were like sirens. They insinuated themselves into the Vagabond's mind, possessing them and making them turn and step off the bridge. Once they fell into the water, the person was either torn to pieces or drowned, whichever came first. It was a nasty death and a strong deterrent that served to keep weaker Vagabonds away. Jericho thought it was a good deterrent to have, though. For if a Vagabond wasn't strong enough to pass by the moat, they would surely die later within the city.

For a while, there had always been a handful of Vagabonds stationed on the grass before the bridge. They had a checker set with them. Any Vagabond wishing to enter the city had to play a game of checkers without using their hands. The pieces were rooks, the silver coins used by the Vagabonds, and the person wishing to enter Gheistmar had to use his ghosts to move the pieces. They didn't have to win the game, they just had to show that they were capable of using their ghosts in an intelligent fashion. It had been an effective means of determining the skill level of new Vagabonds.

As Jericho approached the city now, though, there were no Vagabonds challenging him to checkers. Instead, there were four Irons guarding the bridge. They all had swords on their belts. One of them had a rope.

The rope was Duke's answer to the dangers of the moat. Instead of a Vagabond proving they were strong enough to enter Gheistmar by moving rooks with their ghosts, now each and every Vagabond crossed the bridge with a rope tied around their waist and a group of Irons protecting them. If the moat ghosts got past the Vagabond's own spirits, then the Irons would simply pull on the rope and drag the poor Vagabond into the city.

It worked, mostly. No one died from the moat, but an increasing number of Vagabonds inside the city were dying from ghost attacks. Dying, or having their minds shattered by a possession and becoming insane.

Still, Duke claimed the process was a success. He said it allowed many more Vagabonds into the city than previously possible. It also let Crossbreeds enter the city, allowing them to trade their goods at the market. Since Crossbreeds brought all sorts of supplies from the human world, their presence was encouraged. They weren't normally strong enough to stay inside the city long, though. Duke had talked about housing all the

Crossbreeds and weak Vagabonds near the entrance of the city. Hopefully the ghosts would be less dangerous there."

Maybe it would work, maybe not. Jericho didn't much care. His only thought was getting past the guards and into the city.

Since they had to walk across the bridge several times each day, the Iron guards chosen for the position had to be stronger than most other Vagabonds. These four were stout guys, each with two ghosts bonded to them. As Jericho approached, they clumped together, blocking Jericho's path and keeping him from walking across the bridge unprotected.

His first instinct was to bull through them. He could, certainly. He could push past them and be into the city with seconds.

The guard with the rope stepped forward and held it up. "We're supposed to tie this around every Vagabond crossing the bridge. Those are our orders." He spoke like it was an apology.

Jericho clenched his teeth. He had no reason to be angry with these men. Besides, if things went as he hoped they would, these very Vagabonds might be fighting beside him. They might die because of him. The least he could do was allow them to follow protocol.

"Fine," he said.

The Iron tied the rope around his waist. With Jericho leading and the Irons holding the rope as they walked behind him, they crossed the bridge.

It was a humiliating experience. Jericho felt like a child.

It was obvious the safety rope was unnecessary. While the moat ghosts howled and raged, none of them came even close to him. His own bonded ghosts kept them at a distance. The Irons marching behind him were at far greater risk of being grabbed and pulled off.

They passed through the massive gates and into Gheistmar. As soon as he stepped off the bridge, he took out his sword and the guards stopped and stared. Flint, probably the most talented Vagabond blacksmith alive, had forged the weapon. It was a gently curved, single edged sword called a kilij. The kilij was made from Damascus steel. Also known as "wootz steel", it was good, hard steel that kept its edge and was yet flexible enough not to break. Its watermarked finish was unique. The dark rippled lines along the blade made the blade look almost black.

Just as impressive as the sword was the ghost anchored to it. For an anchored ghost, it was very powerful. The ghost specialized in dropping the temperature, and it always kept the sword very cold.

Icy mist streamed off the blade as Jericho held it in front of him. He cut through the rope and walked away without looking at the guards.

He shouldn't have cut through their rope. He was being cruel and petty, but he couldn't help it. They were wasting his time.

His ghosts fed off his anger, and they whipped themselves into a fury. Other Vagabonds stopped and stared at him in amazement. A man with five ghosts bonded to him? It was a sight that most of them had never seen. Just as astonishing was the raw power of the ghosts. His ghosts loomed over the others like oak trees standing over weeds. People practically dove to get out of his way.

The citizens of Gheistmar were a motley lot. Vagabonds often dressed in the style that their bonded ghosts had dressed when they had been alive, and the streets of Gheistmar were full of historical contradictions. Knights and Vikings and Samurai and ancient Greek helots and countless other cultures all coexisted. Vagabonds with ghosts from similar eras usually grouped together. The city had districts divided by centuries and cultures. There were numerous factions inside the city, and sometimes the Irons had to work pretty hard to keep the peace.

There was a new building just inside the gates. Duke wanted it built, which confused Jericho. Gheistmar had several buildings that were empty. Why build a new structure when so many empty ones were available?

As Jericho strode through the cobblestone streets, he remembered the vicious battle they had fought against the Brutes in the streets. The Brutes had outnumbered them, and it had been

Flint who came up with the solution. Duke's Vagabonds had formed a shield wall. The undisciplined Brutes had dashed themselves against the overlapping shields and broken like a wave against a rock.

They needed to do that again. They needed to form phalanxes and go march into the Brutes' own territory and end their threat permanently.

The sun had just dipped below the horizon and Vagabonds were out lighting the gas lamps that lined the streets. The lighted lamps made Gheistmar look almost like a real city—a place where people actually lived—and not some ruins of a dead civilization.

He approached the palace from the front, passing the long rectangular pool where he had faced and killed a mob of Brutes. The pool was only two or three feet deep. The motionless water was like a mirror. It reflected the palace on its perfect surface until the water clouded with a thin coat of ice from his ghosts.

He strode past the frozen pool toward the palace. The palace itself was one of the finest works in Gheistmar. It was made of white stone and had a triangular roof and Doric pillars, giving it the look of an ancient Greek temple. Wide marble steps led to stout wooden double doors. The doors were closed and two guards stood by them, one on each side.

Jericho walked up the steps toward the closed doors to the palace. The two Irons stood in front of him, blocking his progress.

"Duke doesn't want anyone to see him," one of the Irons said. "He's busy."

"It's urgent," Jericho said. "He'll see me. Tell him Jericho needs to talk to him ..."

"I know who you are," said one of the guards. He hawked and spat on the front of Jericho's coat. "Now get out of here, you damned Renegade."

CHAPTER 8

Sitting at the head of the table, Duke looked like he was made
of gold. The palace dining room was lit with braziers and the
gold he wore flashed with light. And he wore a great amount of
gold. His leather gauntlets were strapped with thick bands of the
yellow metal, the buckles on his heavy boots were gold, and
several gold chains hung from his neck. On each chain dangled a
skeleton key. The keys were relics, each with a strong spirit. He
had taken one of the keys from Edict's body. It was a relic from
the Elders, and the ghost bonded to it was a powerful protective
ghost. It allowed Duke, or any Vagabond possessing the relic, to
walk across the moat bridge without any chance of being attacked
by the moat ghosts. Duke didn't need to worry about that. His
ghosts could fend off the ones in the moat easily. He wore the
relic because it was a symbol of his leadership. He just wished it
was gold.

Gold was a good conductor of electricity. Silver was better,
but gold was still very good. More than adequate for almost any
level of spirit manipulation. And, unlike silver, gold didn't
tarnish. It always flashed bright and cheery. In this gloomy city

full of ghosts, a little brightness went a long way.

Duke was tall and even more physically fit than most Vagabonds. He had the physique of a statue, and wasn't shy about showing it. He rarely wore a shirt, opting instead for a flowing purple coat.

One of his ghosts hissed in his mind. The ghost was upset about something. There were abnormal waves in ether, and the ghost wasn't sure why.

He frowned. He didn't want this night ruined. He was throwing a feast in honor of some Vagabonds who had just arrived in Gheistmar. They were strong, and would be excellent additions to the citizen population if they decided to stay. This dinner was to welcome them and show them that living in the Haunted City was as pleasurable as it could be terrifying.

The new Vagabonds had experienced the terror aspect of the city already, that was for certain. It was impossible to go anywhere in Gheistmar without phantom fingers sliding through your hair or witnessing apparitions appearing and disappearing at all hours of the day and night. And no doubt these new arrivals had already been regaled of the perils of going to certain areas of the city alone. Duke wanted to counterbalance that. He wanted to show these Vagabonds how wonderful it was to live in Gheistmar.

His ghost hissed again. All four of his spirits suddenly began clamoring.

Quiet, Duke sent. *One at a time.*

He wasn't worried. They were safe enough from any problem. Six Irons were stationed around the room. The guards weren't there because Duke feared an attack from some Vagabond tribe, but rather because the ghosts bonded to the Irons would help keep away malicious spirits. If some larger problem occurred, these men could handle it easily. Duke was curious why his ghosts were upset, but he wasn't concerned.

Then the door to the dining room was flung open and Duke suddenly found himself wishing he had a dozen extra guards.

———————

Jericho's ghost, Susha, had been an assassin in ancient Japan. She was quick and strong and even though she had been dead for centuries, she could still kill a man in several different ways. Old habits died hard, and she preferred to kill people silently.

There were basically two ways for a ghost to get past a Vagabond's electrical aura and harm them. The first was to bull their way through the aura and through any ghosts the Vagabond had bonded. The second was to move quickly enough to dodge the bonded ghosts and use speed to penetrate the aura like an arrow.

Susha was able to do it the second way. She was so fast that the ghosts of the Iron who had spat on Jericho's coat had no chance to react before she slipped past them and attacked the man.

The guard clutched at his throat. He couldn't breath. He was drowning, to be specific. Ghosts were composed of water and energy and Susha silenced people by collecting enough moisture from the air and condensing it and shoving it down their throat.

The other guard was frozen in terror. Jericho didn't give him a chance to recover. He grabbed him with one arm and flung him down the steps. Jericho stopped Susha from killing the spitting guard and instead sent her and the rest of his ghosts crashing against the doors. With a deafening crack of wood, the doors burst open and he strode into the palace like he owned it.

Jericho marched down the long hall. The palace was a particularly haunted place and his ghosts loved it. They played with everything they could get their pale little hands on. Heavy wooden doors slammed shut. Others swung open so hard they rebounded against the wall behind them. One of his ghosts tossed a vase of flowers down the hall. Somewhere a pane of glass shattered.

He did his best to ignore the antics of his ghosts and focus on the ether. Even though he wasn't talented at reading waves in the ether, Jericho was still able to sense Duke's rough location in the palace. He was somewhere near the left side of the palace. Given the hour, Jericho figured Duke would be in the dining room. The guards at the palace doors had probably sounded the alarm by now, so Jericho hurried through the halls to his destination.

A set of thick wooden double doors barred the entrance to the dining room. They were ripped open by his ghosts before he could even touch them. Several people were seated at the table. Most were fairly strong Vagabonds. At the head of the table was Duke.

Guards rushed at Jericho. Six of them, all with swords drawn.

He jumped.

His ghosts took hold of him and hoisted him up so that his single bound carried him over the heads of the guards and down onto the center of the table.

Jericho landed hard, his legs bending so much he knelt down. Ghosts flew from him, knocking serving dishes and glasses off the table. It was as if a shock wave radiated out from him, clearing the table of everything. Gravy and wine and sauce were flung everywhere and people screamed and toppled over in their chairs as they were suddenly covered in their dinner. With the people wet and squirming on the floor, the scene resembled a brightly colored massacre.

Duke bounded up from his seat and smashed his heavy fist upon the table. His eyes burned with fury.

"Damn you, Jericho!" Duke boomed. He was a tall man, and he was intimidating even from half a table length away. The table cloth fluttered and his chair was flung aside as Duke's own ghosts were stirred to anger.

But Duke's anger was nothing compared to Jericho's. Might as well compare a match to the roaring fire of a pitch-soaked city gate.

"The Brutes attacked my home," Jericho said. His voice was a roar compressed into a hiss. "We need to fight the Brutes again, and this time kill each and every one of them."

The entire room grew silent. Whether Jericho's anger caused it or the very mention of the dreaded Brutes, people ceased to speak or even move. Jericho met Duke's blazing eyes and waited.

Duke didn't blink or look away. Jericho imagined he could see Duke's mind processing this information, grinding it up and sifting through it for anything of value. Duke was nothing if not longsighted.

"We can talk," Duke finally said. "But get off my damn table."

Duke's mind churned furiously. Jericho was here. That development was unexpected, to say the least. Jericho had said he'd be back in Gheistmar in a few weeks, and Duke certainly hadn't thought he'd be making an appearance any time soon.

"I'm sorry the Brutes attacked your home," Duke said. "But what do you expect me to do about it?"

They were alone now, walking through the halls of the palace. As they passed by windows, their ghosts made the curtains flutter and glass panes frost over.

"We need to go to war," Jericho said. "Just like we did when we fought the Brutes for this city. This time, though, we need to destroy the Lourde's Den."

Duke coughed. He stared at Jericho. The man was crazy.

"Their coven house?" Duke said. "You want to assault their coven house?"

"If we don't, they'll just keep coming back. One day, they may even mount an attack here, on Gheistmar."

Duke waved that concern away. "The Brutes have that strange armor they stole from here. Surely you remember how weapons couldn't hurt them? I don't understand how you think we could go against them on their own turf and win."

"Simple," Jericho said. "This time we have a way to get past that armor. Remember how even our arrows were deflected? I've found a solution to that."

"Yes," Duke said. "I received the letter you sent me about your magnet arrows. But even so, taking the Den would be costly in lives. Gods! You remember how those savages fought!"

"We can do it," Jericho said. There was urgency in his voice and desperation. "We know more now and we're better armed and better prepared and we can go and kill those filthy bastards in their own home. Let us bring the war to them. Let them see their loved ones dying in front of their own eyes. Let their eyes glaze over in death as their own home burns in front of them."

"You're angry now," Duke said. "You're being reckless."

"I'll still be angry in a week or a year or a decade. And, according to you, I've always been reckless."

They walked in silence for a few long moments. Duke thought about it. He thought hard, considering all the angles and problems. In a way, this was a major opportunity.

"There are some soldiers I can spare," Duke finally said. "But you won't like it."

"I don't have to like it," Jericho said. "Can these men kill Brutes?"

"Oh, they can kill Brutes. But 'men' might not be the word I'd use."

CHAPTER 9

Jericho walked out of the palace alone. The Irons at the door glared at him as he passed, but they didn't say anything and he ignored them. He was still trying to puzzle out his conversation with Duke.

Duke had promised to show him these mysterious soldiers the next day. He wanted to attend to his guests. He wanted to sooth them and convince them that, despite the violent intrusion on their dinner, Gheistmar was still a great place to live. Duke didn't want Jericho anywhere around for that.

"Besides," Duke had said. "Lilith is in the city right now. I'm sure you'll want to speak to her before we march on the Brutes. Spend some time with Lilith, and then meet me here at the palace tomorrow afternoon. I'll take you to see the army."

Lilith lived in an apartment located in the ancient Grecian district. He hurried through the streets.

He passed the Tombs, the massive building where many of the Elders had been laid to rest. The building's walls were made of black stone and lined with red stained glass windows. At night the Tombs was particularly impressive. The stone blended in with the night sky while the oil lamps inside made the windows glow like the eyes of devils.

While many of the compartments in the Tombs were filled, there were still plenty available for any Vagabonds who desired to be laid to rest there when they finally died. Jericho had actually purchased a compartment for himself and a sarcophagus. It seemed as good a place as any for his dead body.

Several blocks later, Jericho walked through the geographical center of the city. The exact center of Gheistmar was pinpointed by a large, round fountain. It had low walls a few feet high. In its center was a statue of a man with his arms upraised and his hands with the palms turned up. His hands collected rain and fed it through tubes down his arm to his wrists. His wrists had ragged holes torn in them so that the water issued forth in thick streams. Red gems lined the holes, coloring the water red like blood.

The statue's wounds made Jericho smile. From all appearances, the Elders had been much more powerful Vagabonds than anyone alive currently. But, judging from the statue, it appeared that some of the Elders had also ripped open their own wrists with their teeth. It showed Jericho that they too had encountered similar dangers and difficulties while exploring the supernatural world.

Jericho kept walking, moving past the fountain and into the Grecian district. The Vagabonds he saw on the streets wore cloaks that would have fit in ancient Athens or Sparta. They carried short swords and spears made of ashwood. A handful of them even wore the Spartan helmet. Flute music floated out of the open windows of an apartment. Soon he was standing in front of Lilith's door. He knocked and waited.

Nothing. He kept waiting. Then he knocked again, harder this time.

Still no answer. Lilith wasn't home. There were about a hundred places in the city that she could be. Jericho didn't know the first place to look for her. There were no lights burning in Flint and Thera's home. He guessed they were out somewhere, too.

He walked aimlessly through the streets, hoping to encounter one of his friends by mere chance. They might sense him in the ether and come and find him.

No luck. No one came to greet him, and he had no idea where they might be.

What he did know was that he needed rest. The Brutes' attack, his run to Gheistmar, and forcing his way into the palace had exhausted him. He was finally coming down off his adrenaline and it all hit him at once. He could have fallen asleep right there in the street.

Let's go home, his new ghost, Leo, sent.

By "home", the spirit meant the clock tower. After banishing the ghosts from there, Jericho had adopted the building as his own residence. Like a trophy, of sorts. He thought about heading there, but he was hungry, too. A hot meal sounded like a great idea.

He found an inn. "The Iron Anchor" it was called according to the sign out front. It was a decently sized building. Its walls were made of rounded gray stones. He hadn't been there before, but he knew what the inside would be like. It would be the same as just about every inn over the centuries: there would be a large fire in the common room, tables full of customers eating food and drinking beer and mulled wine, and hurried serving girls attending to the customers.

Jericho pushed open the door and went inside.

The common room was full. There were two long tables, and both of them had every seat occupied. The room quieted as Jericho entered it. Vagabonds bent over mugs of ale glared sullenly at Jericho. A large fireplace with a roaring fire filled the room with glowing orange light.

A man was standing behind the bar with a half filled mug of ale. He was frozen in place, staring at Jericho. Perhaps he had never seen someone with so many ghosts bonded to them. Or perhaps he had recognized Jericho. It didn't matter, really. The guy looked like he was the person to talk to for placing orders. Jericho went over to him.

"I'd like dinner," Jericho said. "Whatever is hot."

The man hesitated. Then he swallowed, and said, "One rook, please."

Jericho took out one of the silver coins. Some people considered it poor etiquette in Gheistmar to offer someone a rook with the skull side up. He made sure the coin was showing the raven as he placed it on top of the bar and slid it forward.

The man had a sheen of sweat on his face. He took the coin with obvious reluctance, then turned went into the kitchen.

The Vagabonds in the common room were still glaring. They were all men, and all fairly strong Vagabonds. They wore soldier's clothing. Gray soldier's clothing.

Jericho realized his mistake. "The Iron Anchor" ... as in a place for Irons to gather and drink. A place for Irons only. Jericho wasn't an Iron, and he wasn't welcome here. Worse, he was a Renegade.

Not wanting any problems, he walked over to the fireplace and crouched in front of it like he was a cold traveler warming himself. He had his back to the room so he wouldn't make eye contact with anyone and provoke them.

It didn't work.

One of the Irons scraped back his chair and stood. He walked over to Jericho. He left his mug of ale on the table. That wasn't good. It meant the man wanted to have both hands free for whatever he was about to do.

"Are you Jericho?" the man said. "Jericho Toller?" The man had long red hair braided into a ponytail that fell past his shoulders. He had bright blue eyes that he squinted into a glare. His speech wasn't slurred, so he wasn't very drunk, if at all. He had a dagger on his belt. The hilt of a knife stuck out of the top of his boot.

"Well, are you?" the man said. "Are you the prick Renegade who insisted on opening up that haunted clocktower? The ghosts that came out of that place killed six people, you know. One of them was my brother."

The room had grown quiet when the man walked over to Jericho. Now it went dead silent. No one spoke, no one moved.

The only sound to be heard was the crackle of the fire.

"Did you hear me?" the man said. He put his hand on the hilt of his dagger. Several men stood.

There were perhaps twenty people in the room. All of them were Irons. All of them would help this man. Not one would come to Jericho's aid.

Jericho had his bow and his kilij and a dagger. If he got enough space, he could shoot a fair number of these men. Then it would be blade work. If he was able to make it to the stairs, they would be able to attack him only two at a time in that narrow space. It would be ugly and messy, but he would survive.

He didn't want to fight these men, though. If things went well, they would be marching with him against the Brutes tomorrow. Besides, the man's brother had died because of what Jericho had done. How could he blame the man for being angry? So he wanted to resolve this without bloodshed. He figured the best way to do that would be to show them that they couldn't win. He figured he should show them precisely who and what he was.

Each of Jericho's bonded ghosts had a specialty. His newest ghost, Leo, had an ability that, as far as Jericho knew, no other ghost had. Leo was able to make time slow for a brief period.

Leo didn't slow time itself, of course. He just made it seem that way to Jericho. He could make a single second stretch to what felt like a half a minute. The first time it had happened had been in a rainstorm. Jericho was sparing with Flint and he had slipped. Flint's wooden blade had been streaking toward him and Jericho was sure he was about to get smacked hard.

Leo must have sensed Jericho's distress and worked his magic. Time had stretched. The rain had slowed and then nearly stopped, the drops quivering in the air like thousands of tiny frozen stars. Jericho was able to easily discern the path of Flint's blade. He was able to lean just enough to allow it to sweep past him without so much as grazing him. It was like dodging an attack from someone who was underwater.

Then time had snapped back. The rain started falling again and Flint went back to moving at full speed. Since then, Leo slowed time whenever Jericho was in trouble.

Jericho and Lilith had talked about it at length, hypothesizing how the ghost was able to do it. Lilith guessed that Leo added his own tiny bursts of electricity to Jericho's brain, amplifying Jericho's own sensory perception. It was just a guess, though, she had said. When he asked Leo about it, the ghost had kept quiet about how he did it. Jericho didn't care. He just cared that Leo was able to do it consistently when Jericho asked him to.

He asked him now, and Leo obliged.

The flames in the fireplace slowed and then froze in place. The fire looked like it was made of solid glass. The men in the room were motionless.

Jericho was not. He was spinning on the ball of his foot and turning. One hand was reaching down for his kilij and the other for the man's long ponytail. With time slowed like this, his movements seemed to take forever to complete, but he was able to do them with a great degree of precision. He was just grabbing the man's ponytail and pulling when time snapped back to normal.

In what now seemed to be hyper speed, Jericho pulled the man's ponytail and sliced through it with his kilij and tossed the hair into the fireplace. He kicked the man away. The man stumbled and fell on the floor. Before his friends could help him, Jericho ordered his blacksmith ghost, Soot, to throw a table against the wall.

Soot was a very physical ghost, and the best of his spirits at moving things. Although the table was long and heavy, Soot flipped it into the air and hurled it against the wall. The table shattered into pieces against the stone wall. The sound of the wood splintering was astonishingly loud. The sheer violence of the act was stunning.

No one moved. The stench of burning hair wafted through the air.

"I'm sorry for your brother," Jericho said to the man on the floor. He went to the door and left the inn. No one followed him outside.

CHAPTER 10

Jericho was furious with himself. He was making trouble with people whom he needed as allies. He went to the clocktower.

Flint had helped him install a heavy door with a decent lock. Jericho unlocked the door and went in, climbing the wooden steps that spiraled upward. The steps creaked and ghosts whispered in the shadows.

He had made the area at the top of the stairs into his living quarters. Most of the clocks were still there. After throwing away the ones that had been utterly destroyed, he had placed the small clocks on shelves and stood the tall grandfather clocks along the walls. Only one of the clocks still worked. It was a sturdy grandfather clock that had somehow escaped the destruction. He laid down and listened to its rhythmic ticking, his thoughts swirling over the recent events.

So Duke had soldiers who were not men. Jericho fell asleep trying to figure out what they might be.

When Jericho awoke, daylight was prying its way around the curtains of the window. It was time to go see Duke. Still half asleep, he stumbled down the stairs and out into the street.

The city was bright with sunshine, and he didn't care for it. Gheistmar was a city of the night. Its true beauty came out during the hours of dark, particularly with a thunderstorm. Its beauty, like most of its slumbering citizens, was hidden.

The palace, though, gleamed in the light. Its stones were bright and polished. The long pool in front of the palace flashed bright in the sun. Duke came out of the palace and met Jericho on the steps.

"How do you feel?" Duke asked.

Jericho didn't reply. He was too numb to feel much of anything.

"Right," Duke said. "Follow me."

Jericho followed Duke through the streets of Gheistmar. They went to the back edge of the city.

Gheistmar was circular. It followed a very simple design: the best things were in the center of the city. The palace and the big fountain and the nicest houses were all near the center. Well-off citizens and high class businesses were close by. As the streets radiated out, the conditions worsened. The lower class Vagabonds and taverns of ill repute were closer to the outside walls.

The very worst of the city resided along the back edge.

Thieves, robbers, and cutthroats lurked here. Yet Duke and Jericho walked through the streets without a second thought. They were both veteran warriors with multiple powerful ghosts bonded to them. Ominous figures searching for an easy victim slid deeper into the shadows as they passed.

Broken Vagabonds resided here, too. Gheistmar was a dangerous place, and there were plenty of empty-eyed Vagabonds slumped in doorways. Victims of a rave that had broken their minds, these people were often derogatorily referred to as "shards" because they had only part of a mind left.

Duke and Jericho headed toward a dingy stone structure that was next to the city wall itself. It was the jail.

Many of the buildings in Gheistmar utilized ancient artistic methods to produce breath-taking beauty. The jail was not one of those. It looked like a giant toad squatting on the ground. Its walls were made of large brown stones stacked unevenly on top of one another and its roof was composed of rough timber. The jail had thick oaken double doors that were braced with steel. Duke opened the door. Tendrils of fog slithered out to curl and twist and die in the daylight.

"We keep it cold in there," Duke said. "We have about a dozen ghosts who do nothing but fly around in there and cool the air. It helps preserve things."

They went in. Jericho could feel the presence of numerous ghosts. But what really hit him was the feeling of rage. Ancient rage and hate permeated the atmosphere, tainting the air with a dirty oily feeling. The ghosts here were more than the normal angry spirit.

The temperature drop was sharp. He could see his breath. His eyes had to adjust before he could see much else, the light was so dim. They were in a long corridor. On each side of the corridor were doors leading to cells.

Jericho went to the door to the first cell on the right. He peered in through the bars. It was empty. A metallic gleam caught his eye, though. He squinted. There was a large metal hook hanging from the ceiling. The hook dangled from a chain about seven feet off the ground.

"What is this?" Jericho asked. "A butcher shop?"

Duke laughed. His voice boomed and echoed through the building. His loud voice was out of place, like a sunbeam pushing its way into a tomb.

"It looks like pigs should be hanging from those hooks, doesn't it?" Duke said. "Well, you're not far off. We call this the Charnel House."

It's probably people, then, thought Jericho. He could read the grim amusement in Duke's voice. He braced himself for the grisly sight of hanging corpses. He had witnessed plenty of death in his many years. A few more bodies wouldn't unnerve him.

But when they went deeper into the building and Duke

directed his gaze to a cell that was occupied, Jericho turned and vomited onto the grimy floor.

"This is the future of Gheistmar," Duke said with a sweep of his hand. "We call them 'The Wretched'."

Jericho wiped the vomit from his lips and stared through the bars in horror. As he had guessed, there was a corpse hanging from the hook. The hook was imbedded in the back of the body, and the corpse hung facing them. It was relatively healthy looking. Pale and slightly decayed, perhaps, but overall it was in good shape. Except for its face, that is. The face of the corpse had been cut off. The eyes, nose, and skin had been raggedly cut away, leaving only bone.

That was ugly, but what had made Jericho sick was when the corpse turned to look at him. Its empty black sockets fixed upon him and the lipless teeth chattered at him like it was trying to speak.

"How ... how is this alive?" Jericho stammered.

"Technically speaking," Duke said. "It isn't." Duke didn't say anymore. Jericho took a closer look, carefully observing the corpse. He let his ghosts run over it, using them to feel like a blind man would use his fingers. With his ghosts, he felt the angry spirit within the corpse.

"Unbelievable," Jericho muttered. "You've forced a spirit into a dead body." Bringing the dead to life had been tried in almost every culture. To see the dream—or nightmare—finally realized was amazing to behold.

"We didn't force spirit to do anything," the Duke said calmly. "We just gave it what it wanted: flesh of its own."

"But how?"

Duke smiled. He used a key on his belt to open the cell door. He took out his knife and marched up to the corpse and made an incision on its arm. Red liquid laced with silver seeped out. The creature didn't seem to mind.

"Originally we tried putting chains inside the body. We thought ghosts would be able to manipulate the metal. But it wasn't nearly precise enough. It needed to be more lifelike, if you will. So we decided to give them special blood. We pumped the body's veins full of a mixture of blood, silver, and liquid mercury. It took a great deal of experimentation to get the ratios right, but once we had it, the ghosts were able to control the bodies. The ghosts use the silver as a conductor that allows them to travel instantly everywhere through the body and control each muscle. Just as our muscles are controlled by electrical pulses sent from our brain, their bodies respond the electrical pulses the ghosts create.

"We keep them on these hooks because, let's be honest, it just wouldn't do to have these things running around the city. The ghosts that control these are greedy evil bastards who enjoy hurting the living. And now that they have flesh, there's all sorts of mayhem they could create. We don't trust them much. Hanging them up like this keeps them out of trouble."

Jericho eyed the blood and silver that oozed from the cut on the corpse's arm.

"Do they die like normal humans?" Jericho asked.

"They can bleed out eventually, making the ghost lose its hold on the body. Think of the body as a puppet and the blood is the strings that allows the ghost to control it. A damaged puppet can still be manipulated. It's only when the strings are cut that the puppet master loses control. But it takes an immense degree of bodily trauma to make them bleed enough for the ghosts to lose control. Even chopping off the head doesn't guarantee death. We're working on creating a relic with a healing ghost bonded to it. With a relic like that, they'll be pretty much immortal."

"How long have you been working on this?" Jericho said. "I haven't heard a thing about it."

"We felt secrecy was important," Duke said. "We didn't want anyone hearing about this and trying to counter it with some other weapon. And it worked. Now we have an invincible army that can kill the Brutes without a single Iron risking his life."

Jericho should have been happy, but he was too unsettled to feel any joy.

"Who did all this?" he said. Duke was a talented Vagabond, but there was no way he could have figured it all out on his own.

A low chuckle slithered through the air. The cell brightened as if a fire had been lit inside of it.

"Hello, Jericho," a man said as he entered the cell. He had no hair. The skin on his head and face had been badly burned. His features had been melted and the skin stretched tightly over the bone. His eyes were undamaged, though. They stood out, bright white, against the reddish tint of his face.

What stood out even more was the robe he wore underneath his dark gray cowl. The robe was made from a reflective fabric and had a myriad of tiny rubies and pieces of amber attached to it with silver wire. His ghosts flashed through the silver in his robe, making it look like he was a walking fire. In one hand he carried an ashwood spear. The tip was a flat black blade that didn't reflect any light at all.

"Cinder," Jericho said. Cinder had once lived at the house with Thera, Flint, and Jericho. Cinder liked to focus on possession, an area in which Jericho had little interest. Jericho was disappointed that Cinder was the one who had accomplished this great feat. Of all the Vagabonds, Cinder had always made Jericho uneasy. Spirits who possessed people were the most malicious and greedy spirits of them all, and Jericho found it difficult to like a person who spent all of their time among such spirits.

"This took us a long time," Cinder said. His voice was raspy from his burned vocal cords. "It's been a lot of work. To finally be successful brings me joy beyond words."

"And these ... men will fight the Brutes?" Jericho asked.

"Oh yes," Cinder said. "They obey us without question. They'll do anything we ask."

"How can you control them? How can you be sure that they don't turn on you?"

Duke and Cinder exchanged a look. Duke smiled.

"We have our ways," Duke said.

There was a vibration in the floor. Jericho could feel the tremors even through the thick soles of his boots. It was like a small earthquake. An earthquake with a steady beat. Like footsteps. Like something very large and very heavy approaching.

"Jericho," Duke said, clearly enjoying the moment. "I'd like you to meet Colossus."

From the gloom emerged a hulking form. Good god! This was more of a beast than a man! As tall as a normal human, it was twice as thick. Muscle was layered upon muscle. Steel cables were used as stitching to help hold the monster together. Its face was hidden behind a steel mask that looked like a skull. The mask was held on with leather straps that wrapped around its head. It had no hair and only black sockets gaping in the holes in the mask where its eyes would be. Yet it saw Jericho clearly enough. It turned its masked face toward him. Jericho instinctively took a step back.

"This revenant is a very special one," Cinder said. "We augmented his bones with steel plates and rods and, as you can see, we used steel cables to stitch parts of him together. The spirit that controls him is very powerful as well. It has learned to manipulate this body with a high degree of skill. Colossus is like a walking fortress."

"That mask ... Is that armor to protect his face in battle?" Jericho asked.

Cinder laughed. "Yes, that will protect him in battle. But he needed it before that. His face is ruined. All of the Wretcheds' faces are. We cut them away. Sometimes the original spirit tries to get back into the body and the Wretched can't properly function as the two spirits fight. Cutting away their faces seems to help hide the body from its ghost."

Jericho studied the hanging corpse.

"Where do you get these bodies?" Jericho asked.

"Graveyards," Cinder said. "We steal them from human graveyards."

"I'll be fully honest with you, Jericho," Duke said. "Another reason we cut away the faces and hide them behind masks is so that people don't see someone they know walking around as a

Wretched. We try to get the bodies from graveyards that are far away, but there's still a chance that could happen, and we don't want that. When we unveil the Wretched to the public, we want people to appreciate these warriors for what they are. They need to recognize what an accomplishment it is, and understand how much safer our city is for it." He was silent for a moment. "I think after they destroy the Lourde's Den, there won't be a single Vagabond who doesn't love these Wretched. You know, 'The enemy of my enemy is my friend' type of thing."

"How soon can we march on the Brutes?" Jericho asked. All of this was crazy, but if it was a way to destroy the Lourde's Den, it was well worth it.

"These warriors live to serve," Cinder said. "They can leave this very moment if need be."

"Let's march tomorrow at sunset," Duke said. "That will give me time to announce to the citizens of Gheistmar what we're planning to do. We'll have a formal display of the Wretched and march off with the city watching."

They exited the building and began walking back toward the palace. They didn't make it far before Duke stopped. He grabbed Jericho's shoulder.

"Do you feel that?" Duke asked.

"I feel your hand on my shoulder," Jericho said.

"No, you fool. The ether. There's a very strong Vagabond nearby." Duke closed his eyes. He pointed down a dark street. "Somewhere over there."

Jericho couldn't feel anything in the ether. Or, to be more precise, he felt too much. The ether in Gheistmar was constantly agitated by the large number of Vagabonds gathered in one place. There were too many waves for Jericho to make any sense out of.

Then came the distinctive sound of a horse's hooves clopping on stone.

They hadn't been able to bring horses into Gheistmar. Not at first. The animals were too skittish to lead across the moat bridge. It had taken an inventive person to figure out how to get horses into the Haunted City.

Because of its high buildings and narrow streets, the city was a tangled garden of shadows even in the day. Until it came closer, the horse was just one dark shape among many. Then it happened to pass through a slice of sunlight, and Jericho got a good look at it ... and its rider.

Jericho didn't speak. He waited until the Vagabond stopped the horse in front of them and dismounted.

"Hello, Lilith," Jericho finally said.

CHAPTER 11

Lilith wore riding breeches and a simple shirt that were both covered in mud and she was still shockingly beautiful. Her electric blue eyes contrasted brightly against her pale skin. Her long, dark hair was braided into tight, thin braids and decorated with several silver relics. Tucked into her belt was her whip and a dagger. She was wearing her favorite boots. They were black leather and came up nearly to her knees. They were studded with silver buckles and each one had skeleton keys dangling from the laces. The boots had always looked too big for her. Her "kitten stompers" Claire had termed the boots, though Lilith loved animals and would have been about the last person in the world to squish a kitten.

"Hello, Jericho," she said back. "Hello, Duke." Her eyes didn't leave Jericho's as she spoke. Jericho's ghosts murmured happily amongst themselves. They recognized Lilith. Their murmurs were the equivalent of a jungle cat purring.

"I'm sure you two Renegades have a lot to speak about," Duke said. "I'm heading back to the palace. Jericho, you still want to leave tomorrow to march against the Brutes?"

Jericho nodded.

"Fine," Duke said. "We'll meet tomorrow, then." He strode off toward the palace.

"Who's marching against the Brutes?" Lilith asked. "And why?"

"I'm afraid I have some very bad news," Jericho said.

Jericho told her. Right there, standing in the street, he told her about the attack.

"Poor Claire," Lilith said. "Peter was her first real relationship. Maybe even her first love. She must be devestated."

"If she's alive," Jericho said.

Lilith took a step back like he had slapped her.

"Claire is fine," Lilith said. "I'm sure of it. Maybe not emotionally, but physically, she's fine. You trained her well. She'll either come here or go to her human home. A group of plodding Brutes aren't going to catch her."

"She"ll either come here or hide out somewhere. A group of plodding Brutes aren't going to catch her."

"You believe that?"

"Yes," she said. "Without any doubt." She rubbed the horse on its nose. It was a large horse the color of fog. Thick leather straps crisscrossed its chest. The straps were studded with skeleton keys. The spirits anchored to the relics protected the horse by keeping the city's ghosts from tormenting the poor animal.

"Let me take Wisp back to the stables," she said. "Then we'll go to my apartment and you can tell me everything."

They didn't speak on the walk over to the stables. They moved quietly, ghosts in a city of ghosts. The only sound was the clopping of Wisp's hooves.

The stables had been built by the Elders who had apparently owned plenty of horses. There were enough stalls for hundreds of horses. Nearly all of them were empty. Counting Wisp's stall, there were nine stalls that were occupied. The other horses were bigger than Wisp. They had black coats that shined like polished obsidian.

All the horses were young. They had been raised from birth in the city, so that they grew up around ghosts and became accustomed to them.

She took off Wisp's saddle. Then she removed the bit from his mouth and rubbed him down. Jericho just watched. He made no move to help. Lilith's ghost Abigail had been an acrobat and an equestrian in the early days of the circus, so she knew her way around horses. Jericho, though, didn't know a thing about them. Domnul, his soldier ghost, had been in a battle on foot against a cavalry. Whenever Jericho saw a horse, a spike of fear shot through him as he recalled Domnul's memories of the cavalry thundering down upon them. He had never ridden a horse, and he didn't intend to ever make an attempt.

Once Wisp was stabled, they set off towards Lilith's apartment. They passed through several different districts, and each was like its own city. It was like opening a history book to a random page, reading a chapter, and then choosing another random page. There was no planned sequence to the cultures, no adherence either to geography or chronology. Some of the areas were heavily populated. Others were desolate.

The Grecian district was a fairly popular district. They had to thread their way through people crowded in the streets. When they came to Lilith's apartment, she used the palm of her hand to push open the door and walked in and started up the stairs. Jericho followed her and closed the door behind them.

"Aren't you going to lock it?" he asked.

Lilith looked back toward the door. There was an audible click.

Jericho stared at her, then at the door.

"Did your ghosts ... " He tugged on the door. It didn't open. "Your ghosts just locked the door! How did you manage to teach them that trick?" Jericho was amazed and a little jealous that she was able to do that.

"I've learned a lot here in Gheistmar," Lilith said. She continued walking up the stairs.

"You were always a quick study," Jericho said. He followed her up the stairs into the darkness above.

"I miss my family," Lilith said. She struck a match and moved about the apartment, touching the match to oil lanterns and bathing the place in a warm glow. "But I've learned so much being a Vagabond. A doctor here showed me how to use ghosts to help people, to heal them. If someone had a bad cut, I could use my ghosts to hold their flesh and skin together so they didn't bleed out. I could hold them together until they were able to get proper care. I miss my old life, but I'm glad I came here."

Lilith's apartment was small but nice. Despite living in the Grecian District, she had furnished and decorated it mainly with items from the Victorian Era. Her two ghosts, Abigail and Niko, had lived during the Victorian Era. The decorations were probably to make them happy.

She poured honeyed wine into two clay cups and gave one to Jericho. They both sat down.

"So the Brutes set fire to our home," Lilith said. Her voice was quiet and it wavered a little. "And then they killed Peter."

Jericho was touched that she called the house "home".

"They snuck up on us right before dawn," Jericho said. "I'm surprised Claire didn't feel them through the ether." He paused, unsure how to phrase what he had to say next. When he began speaking again, he pronounced the words slowly.

"And the Brutes came very, very close to burning Claire alive," he said.

He described the scene for Lilith. He described the pot of pitch that had been flung through the window and doused Claire in the flammable liquid and how the torch had been thrown in right after and set the pitch alight.

"She was staring at me, thinking she was about to die," Jericho said. "If I hadn't had my kilij with me, she would have burned to death right in front of me ... " He went quiet.

Lilith didn't say anything. Her eyes were unfocused. Glazed, like she was staring far off into the distance or way back into the past. They sat there in silence for a long time. Finally Lilith spoke.

"That's horrible," she said. "If she had died, I don't know what we would have done."

They went quiet again.

"The Brutes have to pay for this," Lilith said.

"They will. Duke and I are going to march on the Lourde's Den. A big group of Irons is coming with us. We're also taking the Wretched."

Lilith smiled sadly.

"So you've seen them, then? Our warrior Revenants."

"You know about them?" Jericho was surprised she had known, but he hadn't.

"Duke and Cinder showed them to me a little after you and Claire left the city," she said. "The Wretched worry me. Some of the spirits that operate the bodies are so malicious. I think I'd even use the word 'evil'. I don't trust them and I don't understand how Cinder controls them." She took a sip of her wine. Her wet lips gleamed in the lamplight.

"They don't make waves in the ether, you know," Lilith continued. "Or, at least waves large enough for us to detect. It makes me uneasy seeing something walking around right in front of me without me feeling it in the ether. But I guess my biggest worry is the Wretched going rogue for some reason. That'd be horrible if it happened at the Lourde's Den. I mean, then we'd be caught between the Brutes and the Wretched. It wouldn't be a good thing."

"What do you mean, 'we'?" Jericho said.

"You expect me to stay here, safe behind the walls of Gheistmar while you get revenge? Not a chance. Hell no." Her blue eyes burned with cold fire.

Jericho smiled weakly.

"I understand," he said.

"So you don't have a problem with me coming along, right?"

"I doubt it would matter if I do," Jericho said.

Lilith gave him a little grin.

"I'd listen to you," she said. "You've taught me so much. If you gave me a really good reason and you honestly didn't want me to go with you, I'd listen."

Jericho drank from his cup. Of course he didn't want Lilith to be exposed to any danger. But it wouldn't be fair to her. It'd almost be an insult, in fact.

"You deserve to watch the Brutes die for what they've done," he said. "Besides, you're tough as hell and I trust you."

"I'm glad we agree," she said. Then she went quiet. Lilith stared into her cup for a long time. It was like she was trying to see something at the bottom of the dark liquid. When she finally looked up, her eyes were large. "Jericho, how are we going to do this?" she asked. "I mean, can we even do this? I remember that special armor that Stone wore. Nothing we did hurt him at all."

"Let me show you the arrows," Jericho said.

CHAPTER 12

Jericho reached back and slid off his quiver of arrows. The quiver was similar to the case for his bow. It was leather and had a flap on the top of it that kept his arrows contained and protected them from the elements. Even after shooting the Brutes, he still several arrows left. He removed a few of the arrows and laid them on the table. The tips of the arrows looked like dull black stone.

Lilith inhaled sharply.

"My ghosts don't like those arrows at all," she said. "I just tried to move one with Abigail, and she couldn't touch it."

"They're magnet arrows. I took magnets, weighed them, and sharpened them into points to make the arrowhead. Flint used them to make the arrows."

Lilith picked one up with her hand. She held it at eye level, rotating it.

"Yeah, my ghosts really hate these things."

"So do mine," Jericho said. "It interferes with their electrical field."

"Why make arrows like these, then?" Lilith said. "Upsetting your bonded ghosts isn't a great idea."

"If our ghosts can't touch these, neither can the ghosts bonded to the armor. These arrows will pass right through the protective barrier the ghosts create. One of these arrows can kill Stone as easily as if he were wearing a thin cloth shirt."

Jericho sat on the couch and watched Lilith pack for the trip. She darted around her apartment like a bee going flower to flower.

"How long do you think we'll be gone?" she asked.

"Probably no more than six days. Two days to walk there, three days to walk back. We'll have injured with us, so we'll be moving slower. I imagine we'll spend the majority of one day at the Lourde's Den."

"One day of absolute hell. I wish there was another way to do this."

Jericho agreed with her, but he didn't know of any other way. He drank from his cup of wine.

Lilith opened one of the drawers in her dresser and her face lit with a sudden smile. She slammed the drawer shut and looked at him mischievously.

"I have a present for you, by the way," she said.

He set down his cup. She had given him a present before: his bow. Both he and his ghosts had been skeptical of the bow, as it wasn't made from wood and had strange wheels on it. But Lilith and Flint had crafted silver to it to please his ghosts and the bow's wheels and its material made it much better to shoot than his old longbow. It had been the best present he had ever received.

"What is it?" he asked.

"I can't tell you. Not yet. That's part of the fun. But I think you'll love it. It's something you've wanted for a long time." She opened another drawer and took out some clothes and rolled them into a tight cylinder that she stuffed into her backpack. Her smile faded. "Today is not a good day for gifts, though. And right now I want to get out of these muddy clothes and bathe and go to sleep."

"At least tell me how you unlocked the door with your ghost."

In spite of everything, this intrigued him greatly.

"I just practiced," Lilith said. "Abigail was good at picking locks when she was alive. And now she's good with using moisture to move things. So I got some locks and practiced using her to move the tumblers." She opened a drawer and took out a lock. She put it on the table.

"This is what I practiced with," she said. "Once I was able to open it, most locks were pretty easy. Play with it, if you like." She gave him a half a smile like she used to in the old days. "In fact, let's make a deal. If you can open it by the time the sun comes up, I'll give you your present. If you don't, you'll have to wait until we return to the city."

"The Brutes are tough," Jericho said. "There's a decent chance we'll never return."

Lilith didn't say anything.

Jericho looked at the lock. It was a heavy, old thing as big as his fist. It had a little rust on it but it still looked strong enough to protect a king's vault.

"Fine," Jericho said. "It's a deal. Go to bed. When you wake up, you're going to find an open lock laying on your table."

CHAPTER 13

The next day, the sun was just beginning its decent into the western horizon when Jericho and Lilith went to the palace. The platoon of Irons stood in front of the steps. Arrayed in full armor, they looked like pieces of an efficient killing machine.

A man wearing an old fashioned gas mask stood in front of them. The gas mask wouldn't work, though. That was plain. The portion covering the man's mouth was gone. His lips had been chewed away, exposing teeth that were filed into points.

The man was Beetle, one of Duke's most trusted soldiers.

"You know," Lilith told Jericho as they approached the palace. "I'm pretty sure Beetle would never cheat on a bet."

"I didn't cheat ... " Jericho said without conviction. Maybe he had cheated with the lock, but he hadn't meant to.

Beetle either saw them or sensed them through the ether. He stared at them a moment. He said something to the platoon, then walked over to them.

"Hello, Lilith," Beetle said. Despite having no lips and pointed teeth, his speech was remarkably unaffected. The injuries had happened a long time ago. He looked at Jericho but didn't say anything. He looked back to Lilith. "Are you ready to march?"

"Where are the Wretched?," Lilith said. "I thought they were going to be with us."

"They're meeting us there," Beetle said.

Jericho and Lilith exchanged looks.

"That wasn't the deal," Jericho said.

The palace doors swung open and Duke stepped out. His gold-plated armor winked in the light as he descended the steps toward them.

"Why aren't the Wretched going with us?" Jericho asked Duke. "I thought they were supposed to be the ones fighting the Brutes."

"They will fight the Brutes," Duke said. "Nothing's changed. But you have to realize, the Wretched can't march like normal soldiers. Remember, we don't trust them. They obey out of fear, not out of allegiance or love. On a long trip, they'd have many opportunities to run. We have a carriage we'll use to get them there. The road to the Lourde's Den is in fairly good shape, and I know we can count on you to clear any fallen trees or other obstacles."

"Bring the wagon with us," Jericho said.

"The horses need to run when they pull the wagon. They aren't fond of the scent of the Wretched. It'd be impossible to force them to move at a slow pace."

"You want us to bumble along into hostile territory and just hope that you'll come and save us?"

"You'll have a full phalanx of Irons," Duke said. "And you and Lilith aren't exactly helpless. Besides, I don't think the Brutes will attack you. They'll probably create defensive positions at their home, not run out offensively."

"But what if they do attack before then?" Lilith asked.

"I'm sure you'll be able to fend them off. Though, as I said, you shouldn't be concerned about them taking any aggressive action until we arrive on their doorstep. Just march until you get about an hour or so away from the Den. Then make camp and wait for me."

"And what if you don't show up?" Jericho said.

Duke shook his head.

"We'll be there," he said.

It was like marching at the head of an avalanche. The Irons stomped along on the road, their boots pounding against the cobblestones. Their pace was startlingly quick. Jericho had expected the city soldiers to be softer and weaker. Instead, they were like Roman legionnaires marching at a fast and disciplined pace. Despite the cool spring air, sweat streamed down everyone's face.

Jericho and Lilith and Beetle were at the head of the column. It had been an unspoken agreement that the Renegades would be next to Beetle. If the captain of the Irons minded, he didn't give any sign of it. Beetle didn't speak much, and he hardly said anything at all to Jericho. Apparently the man still harbored some hard feelings from the clock tower incident. Jericho neither liked nor minded Beetle.

Further back in the column was a Vagabond that Jericho kept turning around to look at. He was fairly certain he had never seen the Vagabond before, yet there was something unmistakably familiar about him. The man was a knight in all black armor. He was huge. Taller than Duke and twice as wide, he was as big as Colossus. He wore full armor, including a helmet. All of the armor was black and polished to a mirror shine. *Who the hell marches in full plate armor?* Jericho thought. It was impressive, to say the least.

Even more impressive was the buzz of ghosts emanating from the man. He had three ghosts whirling around him, and the spirits were quite strong. Jericho wondered if the ghosts helped carry the plate armor, floating it along as the man walked. The knight's weapon was a harpoon. A damn harpoon! Affixed to the harpoon was a long chain. The chain dangled nearly to the ground before running back up and looping around the knight's wrist.

"Who's the knight?" Jericho asked Beetle.

"That would be Cull," Beetle replied. "He arrived in Gheistmar over the winter. He doesn't say much and we're not sure where he came from, but he's one tough bastard. The Irons had a sparring tournament a few months ago. It was a big deal. Everyone competed because the prize was some amazing armor. Cull not only won the tournament, but he won it easily."

The armor ... that's what was familiar about the man. Jericho had seen that breastplate before. It had haunted him in his sleep many times.

"That's the breastplate the Brute Edict wore," Jericho said. "Except it wasn't painted black."

"Yeah," Beetle said. "Duke figured the armor wasn't doing us much good just sitting in the palace. He figured he might was well give it to our best soldier. I think it was a good decision. Between the armor and Cull's fighting skills, he's unstoppable."

""I'm glad he's on our side ... " Jericho trailed off as something in the woods moved. Off to the right, about a hundred yards away, a figure jumped from one shadow to another. "There's someone tracking us."

"It's just one of them," Lilith said. She had her eyes closed, like she often did when she was paying close attention to the ether. "A scout, probably. Should we go after him?"

Jericho considered it. They'd most likely be able to catch the scout, but it might be a trick. The scout might have let himself be seen on purpose so he could lead them into an ambush.

"No," Jericho said. "Let's stick to the plan. We'll wait for the Wretched. The Brutes will know we're here soon enough anyway."

The air felt charged. It felt just like the quiet moments before a big thunderstorm when the sky was about to split and dump torrents of rain and lightning upon the earth.

"The clearing is less than an hour ahead," Jericho said. "We'll set up camp and post guards and wait for Duke."

"What if he doesn't come?" Lilith said.

Jericho didn't answer.

The sun had set by the time they arrived at the clearing. They
ringed the perimeter of the clearing with guards. The night was
cold and they gathered wood and started fires. They ate and laid
out sleeping mats. No one could sleep, though. Not with
knowing they were going to the Lourde's Den when morning
came. Instead, they gathered around the fires. Some Irons stared
silently at the flames. Others told jokes and strived to be as
lighthearted as possible. Still others simply sharpened their
swords.

Jericho and Lilith sat with Beetle near one of the fires. Despite
being deep in Brute territory, Jericho felt safe enough. Nearly a
third of the Irons were standing watch and the clearing was well
lit. The Brutes weren't going to sneak up on them.

Lilith looked particularly radiant in the glow of the fire.
Jericho had a hard time looking at anything but her. She must
have felt him looking at her because she glanced over. Her face
was expressionless. Jericho had no idea what she was thinking.
Lilith held his gaze for a long time. Then she turned to Beetle.

"Beetle, you need to be the judge," Lilith said. She went into
her pack and took out a cloth sack. "I bet Jericho that he wouldn't
be able to open this lock. What do you think? Does this lock look
open to you?" She handed Beetle the sack.

Beetle held it open and looked down inside. The fire turned
the goggles on his mask into circles of bright orange.

"What the hell happened to it?" Beetle asked.

Jericho had spent quite a while trying to pick those locks.
Lilith had made it seem so easy when she had done it, but
Jericho's ghosts just weren't able to do it. Both they and Jericho
had grown frustrated. They poured their strength into the task,
yanking on the tumblers and trying to force the lock open. The
lock had bent and twisted under the immense pressure. Then it
exploded. Pieces had ricocheted around Lilith's apartment,
whistling and ringing as they bounced off the walls and floor and

furniture. Lilith had come stumbling out of her bedroom with her hair disheveled and her whip in hand.

"What happened?" she had screamed at him.

"I got the lock open," Jericho had said.

Lilith had looked around the room, staring at the pieces of the lock still spinning and rocking where they had finally landed.

"Cheater," she had said. And gone back to bed.

Jericho watched as Beetle upended the sack and dumped out the remains of the lock. The pieces chimed as they bumped against each other and formed a little pile of metal scrap. They all stared at the pieces for a long moment.

"I don't know if it's open," Beetle said. "But it sure as hell ain't closed."

"Beetle agrees that the lock is open," Jericho said. "Now give me the present you promised."

"You don't deserve this, you know," Lilith said as she reached into her pack again. She took out a dagger and handed it to him.

Jericho unsheathed the dagger. It was well made and had a good balance. The hilt was wood wrapped with leather.

"Stab something with it," Lilith said.

Jericho jabbed the dagger into a log. Instantly, the blade crackled with electricity.

"Flint forged the dagger," Lilith said. "And the ghost that Thera bonded to it is terrific at generating electricity. She taught the ghost to send out voltage whenever the dagger strikes something." She grinned. "I know how you've always wanted a ghost that could send out bolts of lightning."

When it came to dropping the temperature or moving physical objects, Jericho's ghosts were unparalleled. They were never able to produce much electricity, though. Jericho had always envisioned being able to send out bolts of lighting. It was possible ... it *had* to be possible.

Jericho stabbed the log again and watched the electric current surge through the knife.

"I love it," he said. He looked up at Lilith and stared into her eyes. She had always been his best student, but there had been more to it than that. At least for him. He had never said a word to her about feeling anything for her, however. She was his student, and it wouldn't have been appropriate.

"There's one problem with it, though," Lilith said. "The blade can get very hot. So be carefu—"

She never finished her sentence.

CHAPTER 14

Jericho always loved to watch approaching thunderstorms. He liked to watch the towers of clouds rise up and collapse, muscling against each other like wrestling giants. He liked the rumble of thunder and the way the breeze would sometimes weaken and fade away like the final breath of a dying man. Whenever a storm passed by, he liked to go outside and watch.

Once, lightning had hit a tall oak tree nearby. The storm had just been arriving and Jericho hadn't expected any lightning so soon. The speed with which it had happened astonished him. One moment the oak tree had been standing tall and majestic, and a fraction of a second later the tree had burst apart in a flash of flame. The tree was in pieces even before the crack of sound reached him.

He had never seen anything else happen that fast, but Lilith was close. One moment she was casually talking about the dagger she had just given him, and the next instant she was a blur of motion. Only because of Leo working his magic could Jericho even follow her movement. She leapt to her feet and twisted her hips and her right hand shot down to her whip. She must have stoked her ghosts because sparks of electricity suddenly covered her and her whip looked like lightning itself. With a twitch of her wrist, she uncoiled her whip and then lashed out with it ... right towards Jericho.

The whip passed so close that its electricity singed him and the electrical current hummed and crackled in his ear. Then there was a loud crack directly behind him. He spun to his feet to see an Iron clutching his own throat with one hand. The Iron's other hand held a knife. Blood streamed from the man's throat and ran down his chest. He dropped to his knees and his hand fell away from his throat. His throat had been ripped open by Lilith's whip. The Iron toppled into the dirt.

"He was coming up behind you with his knife raised," Lilith said. "He was going to stab you."

"I don' t understand why he'd do that," Beetle said. He looked confused. "Did you know that man, Jericho?"

Jericho knelt and examined the dead Iron's face.

"No," Jericho said. "I've never even seen him before."

"So why would he do that?" Lilith asked. She coiled her whip and tucked it back into her belt.

"Maybe he was ordered to," Jericho said. He looked evenly at Beetle.

Beetle met his gaze without flinching. "If I wanted you dead, I'd fight you myself," Beetle said. "I would never order one of my men to knife you in the back while you sat next to me."

"For what it's worth," Lilith said. "I believe him."

"Maybe this man harbored a grudge against me for the Clock Tower. Or maybe ... " Jericho trailed off.

"Or maybe he was possessed," Lilith finished.

They all sat in silence as they thought about that. Some Vagabonds were masters of possession. They could control strong and insidious ghosts that were capable of forcing someone to do their bidding for a short time. Maybe the Brutes had a Vagabond who had bonded spirits like that. He could be out there in the woods, slipping his ghosts into their camp and making them fight one another.

"We're not going to get much sleep tonight," Beetle said.

Beetle was right. None of them slept during the night. He passed word to all the Irons to be on the alert for spirits possessing people, and everyone eyed each other with suspicion, awaiting the first signs that a person had been possessed. Using the wrong language, not knowing someone's name, mispronouncing a word, or just plain acting strangely were all common indicators of a possession. The problem was, when they were so worried about possession, everyone started behaving oddly and it became all but impossible to discern who had been taken over by a malevolent spirit.

Jericho and Lilith sat with their backs pressed together so no one could sneak up on them. Even through his coat, he could feel her warmth.

"Thank you," Jericho said.

"For what?"

"For saving my life. For the lightning dagger. For ... everything."

"You're welcome," she said.

They were quiet for a long time. All of the fires in the camp had been built high, and the burning wood snapped and popped. Now and then a breeze blew, making the trees sway and their leaves clap like the applause of a phantom crowd.

Lilith tensed. Leaning against her, Jericho felt her muscles tighten like something had just frightened her.

"There's someone coming," she whispered. "And they're making some pretty big waves in the ether."

"It's too early for Duke," Jericho said. "Daylight isn't for another couple of hours."

They jumped to their feet. Lilith uncoiled her whip and Jericho unsheathed his kilij. All around the camp, Irons stood up and took out their weapons as they felt the waves in the ether. Finally, Jericho felt them too. They were some pretty damn large waves.

The fires in the camp shrank as everyone unleashed their

ghosts. The air was filled with eerie moans and hissing voices.

"They're using the road," Lilith said. "And they're coming fast."

The night air was damp, and it carried sound well. Despite the shuffling of the Irons in the camp and the crackle of the fires and the wind rustling through the trees, the noise from the approaching Vagabond was audible. The noise was also distinctive.

When Jericho and Lilith heard it, they looked at each other in confusion.

There wasn't another noise that Jericho could liken it to. The closest thing might have been the sound of several muskets firing in the distance.

Horses. Several of them, all running at a fast pace on the cobblestone road. Jericho sheathed his kilij.

"Duke's early," he said.

The clop of the horses' hooves grew louder and louder. The noise seemed out of place in the otherwise quiet night. Then the horses were there, snorting and shaking their heads and tossing their manes. There were eight of them, all sleek and heavily muscled. They were paired up, so they made four rows. They pulled a massive black wagon. Duke sat on the driver's seat of the wagon with the reins in his hands.

"Whoa!" Duke cried out as he pulled back on the reins. The horses didn't want to stop. They kept running and the wagon passed the clearing. Duke kept working the reins, and the wagon slowed and finally stopped about a hundred yards past the campsite.

Jericho, Lilith, Beetle, and a handful of Irons walked down the road to meet Duke. The wagon looked more like a rolling fortress. Everything on it was reinforced. It was made of black wood and steel, and it looked like it needed all eight horses to pull it. The windows of the carriage were covered with wood and behind metal bars.

No, Jericho amended. The wagon wasn't like a fortress. It

was more like a prison. The door on the side of the wagon was barred from the outside.

"The horses really hate the Wretched," Duke said. He stayed on the wagon with the reins clutched in his hands. "They ran hard the entire way."

Jericho eyed the wagon. It wasn't rocking or shifting in any way that would indicate someone moving around inside.

"So you have the Wretched in there?" Jericho asked.

"Yes I do," Duke said. "Cinder is in there, too. He's making sure they behave." He looked around at everyone. His face was grave. "Well, shall we do this?"

The Irons formed up. With the wagon leading the way, they all set off towards the Lourde's Den.

CHAPTER 15

Quill entered the room and found Stone sitting in a chair in front of the fireplace. There was no fire lit and for an instant Quill was afraid that Stone was raving as he stared at the empty fireplace. If he was raving, they were in serious trouble.

"I miss Pest," Stone said without turning. "Sometimes I still think I hear her speak." His voice was clear. He wasn't raving. That was good. But Quill didn't know what to say about Stone's sister. Jericho had killed her almost two years ago.

"The Vagabonds from Gheistmar are coming," Quill said instead. "I saw them myself. At least a phalanx worth of soldiers, maybe more. Jericho's with them, too."

Stone didn't reply. He just kept staring into the fireplace like he was deep in the past.

"Did you hear me?" Quill said. "They're coming. They'll be here soon." He was considering his options, trying to figure out if it would be better to run or to stay with Stone and the rest of the Brutes.

"We knew this would happen eventually," Stone said. He stood and faced Quill. His pity and sorrow seemed to fall away from him, and he was once again the hardened leader of the Brutes. "We planned for this. Put on your special armor. Make sure everyone has two or three spears. And check that the trees are ready. That's going to be a nasty surprise for them."

They arrived at the Lourde's Den just as dawn was breaking. Sunlight washed the sky with bright pastels, but the light was filtered through the leaves and branches of the trees and their little army was still covered in shadow as if the night's gloom had clung to them in wet rags. They stood on the edge of the woods and stared. None of them had ever been there, but they had heard the stories of a mansion so haunted no one could enter it.

The mansion rose up in front of them. Perhaps it had once been the country home of a prosperous family. It was huge. Three stories high and very wide, it was a magnificent structure. Tall arched windows lined each floor. A smaller building, the servants' quarters, was off to the right. In the front of the mansion, there was the problem.

Between the army and the mansion was a large graveyard. Thick mist blanketed the ground and all but the tallest tombstones were visible only by their very tops. The mist swirled as if people were moving beneath it. And they were. The Brutes were hiding there, crouching beneath the mist. Which was strange, because it was pointless. Even Jericho could sense them in the ether.

"They're up to no good," Duke said. He still sat on the driver's seat of the wagon, pulling the reins to keep the horses stationary. "That fog could be hiding anything."

"What could they possibly have?" Beetle said. "We know they haven't found any more special weapons from Gheistmar."

The woods were quiet in a noisy way. Leaves rasped against each other and the rush of the river behind the mansion was constant sibilant hiss, but no birds chirped, no squirrels leaped from branch to branch. The animals seemed to have fled the area, if they ever came there at all.

"This is a bad place," Lilith said. "I think the ghosts here are even more dangerous than those in Gheistmar."

Duke laughed.

"I think that's the understatement of the year," he said. "Jericho, will you do the honors of opening the wagon? If I let go of these reins, the horses will bolt."

Jericho went to the side of the wagon. He slid the bar out of the way and opened the door. It was dark inside the wagon, too dark to see anything. Then the butt of Cinder's ashwood spear pierced through the darkness. The pale wood seemed as bright as a moonbeam. Cinder himself emerged next. His cowl was wrapped tightly around him, hiding his bright robe. He stepped down and stretched like he had been in a cramped position for hours. He rapped his spear against the side of the wagon and the Wretched began to come out.

Jericho had only seen the Wretched wearing rags and hanging from hooks in their cells. Now they wore black quilted shirts and pants overlaid with polished steel armor. Their steel masks flashed in the sun. They all carried the Roman gladius, a short sword perfect for thrusting and killing in close quarters. They didn't carry shields of any kind. Jericho supposed that if he were invincible, he wouldn't bother with a shield either.

"Form up," Cinder said to the Wretched. "Battle lines."

Without hesitation, they obeyed like well-trained troops. Jericho was surprised to see how naturally they moved, how smoothly. He had expected them to be more awkward. Instead, they looked just like living people would have.

With the Wretched out of the wagon, Duke was able to finally let go of the reins. He stepped down and stood next to Jericho.

"We'll let the Wretched go first," Duke said. "But we don't want to get too far away from them, so we'll follow close behind."

"Fine," Jericho said. He nocked one of his magnet arrows onto the string of his bow.

Jericho and Lilith and Duke and Beetle got right behind the Wretched and the Irons arrayed themselves in lines behind them. Cinder was closer to the rear so he could watch the battle and direct the Wretched as needed. Everyone had their ghosts unleashed and the air was cool and laced with disembodied voices. Jericho looked at Lilith. She met his gaze evenly. Neither of them said anything.

"Wretched," Cinder called out. "Advance!"

In perfect step, the Wretched moved forward and everyone else followed. They went ten steps, and nothing happened. Their footsteps were deep booms that reverberated through the damp soil. Filled with liquid metal, the Wretched were extremely heavy. They kept rumbling forward. Fifteen steps. Twenty. Still nothing.

The Wretched descended into the fog. It was up to their chests and made it look like they were swimming. Then Jericho was in the fog. It was cool and damp. It made the grip on his bow slippery.

Something squirmed beneath his foot. A snake? He jumped aside and looked down. No. Not a snake. It was a rope.

The rope jerked taut. It ran from the fog out to a tree behind them. Two other ropes snapped up off of the ground and quivered, waist high, in the air. The ropes were pulled and chunks were ripped out from each of the trees' trunks.

In a moment of awful clarity, Jericho understood. The trees' trunks had been skillfully chopped away, supported by a block of wood, and then chopped some more. Ropes had been looped around the blocks and the trap covered with bark and mud. When the blocks were pulled out, the trees would come down.

Right onto the Gheistmar soldiers.

Wood cracked and groaned as the trees leaned and began to fall.

"Run!" Jericho called out. The only way to go was into the graveyard. The army surged forward.

The Brute warriors suddenly appeared. They rose up from beneath the fog, dropping the ropes they had been holding and picking up their weapons. Many held crude spears made from branches with knives tied to them. They threw the spears. With their targets so close, they couldn't miss. The sound of so many spears piercing flesh was like that of a wave smacking hard into wet sand.

The trees crashed down upon them. Small branches clawed at Jericho and the ground shook with the impact of the trees hitting the ground. Jericho was far enough away that only the utmost branches reached him. Many of the ranks behind him were not so fortunate. Heavy limbs descended on the men like clubs wielded by giants, breaking bones and smashing soldiers down into the soft earth.

There was no where to run. The Brutes would casually stab them in the back if they tried to scramble through the prison of branches that was now behind them. The only way was forward, into the mist, into the merciless barrage of the Brutes.

Jericho was filled with despair. In seconds, their army had been thrown into disorder. So many men had died in the space of a few heartbeats that he felt certain they were all going to die here.

With Leo slowing time, Jericho watched clearly as the Brute ranks hurled yet more weapons. The air itself seemed to become solid as the spears flew. The weapons were a black wall that rushed at them, blotting out the sight of the Brutes who had thrown them.

Again, that awful sound of blades slamming into flesh. Men were spun around from the impact and dropped, dead before they ever hit the ground.

But many more didn't drop. The Brutes' spears hit them and they staggered backward a step or two and then kept going. Jericho had forgotten about the Wretched.

The first volley of weapons had largely been absorbed by them. They bristled with spears, yet that didn't even seem to slow them. Nothing was hurting them.

The Brutes saw this. They kept throwing their spears with growing panic. The blades slammed into the Wretched, piercing hearts and ripping through throats and smashing through metal masks into their faces. At best, a perfectly placed spear knocked a Wretched soldier back a step or two. More often, the Wretched didn't even seem to notice it had been hit.

Cinder truly had created invincible warriors.

A Brute climbed on top of a gravestone. Jericho had seen him before. The man with green eyes and red hair. He wore the special protective armor, too. It looked like exactly the same kind that Edict had worn. The ghosts of the mail swirled around him, pulling in the mist so that it looked like a translucent cocoon.

It was time to see if his magnet arrows worked.

Jericho pulled back the string of his bow and took aim.

And loosed his arrow.

CHAPTER 16

When Orion was a boy, he used to enjoy watching the farmers harvest their grain. They swung their scythes tirelessly, the blades glinting in the sun as they arced through the air. Orion would station himself alongside the field and use his bow and arrows to shoot the rats and snakes that scurried out, rousted from their homes by the approaching line of farmers.

Jericho's ghost offered this memory as the Wretched battled. They were a lot like harvesters. The Wretched worked in an almost businesslike fashion. There was no rage, no blood lust. Just work to do. They hacked into the Brutes and either ignored or didn't notice the Brutes' attacks upon them. Most of the Wretched bristled with so many spears that they looked like quilpigs. The shafts wagged back and forth as the Wretched marched steadfastly forward.

Jericho's magnet arrow flew above the Wretched and above the battle and was just beginning to descend in its arc when it slammed into chest of the Brute standing on the gravestone. The Brute clutched at the arrow, probably astonished that something had pierced his barrier of ghosts. Probably wondering how it had happened. He fell from the top of the gravestone and into the fog.

Jericho's arrows worked! He wanted to tell Lilith. He looked around for her. Where was she? Jericho climbed on top of a gravestone to get a better view. It made him a perfect target, but he didn't care. He couldn't find her. Was she beneath the fog, wounded? Had she been crushed by one of the trees? All sorts of unpleasant scenarios flashed through his mind.

He almost didn't see her. It was her whip that caught his eye. It was glowing brightly with electricity as she lashed out with it from behind the Wretched. The whip was long enough that she was able to reach the Brutes even from behind the undead warriors. The Brutes yelled as the whip tore into their flesh and scorched them with electricity.

The mass of Brutes churned as so many of them died. One Brute caught his attention by standing perfectly still as if he had just witnessed something shocking. Something he couldn't believe. It was Stone, and he was looking at the gravestone where the man in the special armor had been standing. He was wearing that same armor. He and Jericho made eye contact.

Stone ran, pushing through the Brute ranks until he broke free and made a dash for the servants' house.

Jericho shoved his way through the Irons and ran through the mist, striving to reach the building before Stone did.

The battling Brutes didn't see him. They were far too busy being hacked to bits by the Wretched.

And Cull. The huge knight had waded into the fray. He threw his harpoon and speared a Brute in the center of his chest. Cull gave a mighty heave on the chain and the harpoon was ripped out of the Brute's chest in an explosion of blood and bone. Cull caught the harpoon one-handed and swung it like a club, bashing in the skull of another Brute. The spears and blades of the Brutes were batted aside by the ghosts bonded to Cull's special armor.

Yes, Jericho was certainly glad Cull was on their side.

Stone was much closer to the servants' house, and he made inside first.

Jericho followed. His steps were steady and his kilij was in his hand as he entered the house.

The first room was empty aside from furniture and a cold fireplace. Before he could move deeper into the house, two Brutes came rushing out at him with sharpened shovels. His ghost Leo kicked in and suddenly time stretched. The one wore a necklace made with beer caps on a string and, to Jericho's eye, the necklace seemed to float as it was jostled by the running Brute.

If Leo slowed time by adding his own electricity to the connections in Jericho's brain, he also must have done something similar to Jericho's muscles, for Jericho was able to move quicker than his enemies.

His free hand slipped out the dagger Lilith had given him. With his kilij in one hand and the dagger in the other, he lunged and stabbed. He buried a blade in the throat of each warrior and ripped out the blades in a spray of blood. The blood seemed to hang in the air, quivering, until time snapped back to normal. Then the warriors fell, collapsing into unnatural positions as their bodies jerked with their death throes. Jericho's dagger crackled with electricity, cooking the blood on the blade. It smelled like meat roasting. He shook some of the blood from his blades and tucked the dagger back into his belt.

Where was Stone hiding? The house was a decent size. There were plenty of rooms he could be in. Jericho went door to door, opening each one. Stairs were behind one door. The stairs went down, leading to a basement was so dark it was nearly black. Would Stone have gone down there? Probably not, as there would be no way to escape from the basement. Stone wouldn't go someplace where he would be trapped.

Jericho was just about to close the door when he heard a sound. Someone was tapping on a wall down there. Maybe Stone. Maybe just a ghost. Only one way to find out. He went down the stairs slowly. Sinking into the blackness felt like being swallowed by dark water. In that kind of lightless place, the dark seemed to press against his chest.

It was foolish to chase Stone down there. This could be a

trap. For all Jericho knew, there could be an entire army of Brute warriors hiding the basement.

He tightened his grip on his kilij and kept descending into the blackness. With every step he took, he expected a Brute to lunge out at him.

But he made it all the way down okay. And the basement wasn't lightless. Not completely. Stone was holding a candle. He was in the corner of the basement facing the wall. When he sensed Jericho, he spun around. He bared his teeth in a feral grin and unsheathed the long crowbar he carried on his back.

"You killed my sister," Stone said. He was trying to sound mean, but the fear was evident in his voice.

"She was trying to kill me," Jericho said. He sheathed his kilij and unslung his bow and nocked one of his arrows. "And you attacked and burned my home."

He loosed the arrow. The magnet arrow flew through the armor's ghosts like they weren't even there and rammed into Stones chest. Stone grunted and staggered backward.

"Didn't ... burn ... anything." Stone said through gritted teeth. He bumped his back against the wall and that simple collision seemed to take all the fight from him. He fell to the floor and lay there with eyes wide and white as he died.

Blood roared in Beetle's ears. His breathing came in shallow gasps. His back burned from a deep gouge that a tree branch had left and a spear had cut his shoulder, but he was happy. When the trees had toppled down on them and the Brutes had started throwing their spears, he had been certain all was lost.

As the battle wore on, though, he realized that they were winning. The Wretched were cutting down the Brutes with ease. Nothing the Brutes did could even slow the undead warriors.

Cull was dealing massive damage, too. Beetle watched him harpoon a man and then bash another's head in.

The Brutes were brave. Beetle had to give them that. They dashed themselves against the Wretched, trying to win through numbers and sheer ferocity.

It didn't work. The Brutes were being cut down with almost monotonous regularity. Like a giant machine, the Wretcheds' blades rose and fell, leaving behind mangled lifeless bodies. Cinder was right there along with the Wretched. He shouted orders and gestured violently with his spear. Where he pointed, the Wretched went.

The Brutes were being compressed. The front ranks were being pushed back while the rear struggled forward. How could anyone in the middle even breath?

Suddenly it was too much. The Brutes broke ranks and fled. It was like watching a fissure in a dam. First a trickle as a few ran, and then more and more until it was a torrent of retreating warriors. They washed over the ground and streamed into the building that had once been the servants' quarters. Men poured through the open front door and many even dove inside through open windows.

It was a retreat, but a tactical one. Brute warriors appeared in the second-story windows and hurled rocks and bottles and spears down. The front door to the building was slammed shut and doubtlessly barricaded from the other side. The building was a defensible position, and the Brutes would be able to make a good stand there. Beetle swore. With the Brutes digging in like that, it was going to be dangerous and tedious to wipe them out.

"Retrieve the pots of pitch!" Cinder cried out. About half of the Wretched ran back to the wagon. They went inside the wagon and came out with rounded clay pots. The pots had tight-fitting lids that allowed them to even be turned upside-down without a single drop spilling. This was particularly convenient because the Wretched carried each pot in a kind of net sack.

While most of the Wretched took clay pots out of the wagon, a few of them took branches. The branches had their ends wrapped in cloth and looked like they had been soaked in something. Oil, maybe. It looked like they had made torches.

The Wretched with the torches ran to Cinder. Using one of the modern lighters, Cinder lit a flame and touched it to each torch. The torches caught on fire immediately.

"Burn them!" Cinder yelled. He removed an antique pocket watch from the folds on his robe and looked at it and nodded as if he were calculating something. The Wretched ran toward the servants' building. The Brutes threw all sorts of stuff down upon them with no effect. It might as well have been a soft spring rain shower as far as the Wretched were concerned.

They hurled the pots at the building. Upon impact, the clay shattered and each pot burst apart in a ball of wet, black goo that clung to the building. The Wretched with the torches used them to ignite the pitch. Within seconds, the side of the servant's quarters was painted with flame. A few of the pots went through windows. Soon, the interior of the building was glowing as fires started inside.

Someone was running around by the Wretched. It looked like Lilith. She was grabbing Wretched by their arms and trying to pull them away. It looked like she was trying to stop them from setting the building on fire. If so, she was far too late.

The liquid fire was gnawing away at the outside walls of the building. The interior flickered with the light of the growing fires inside. The fire was spreading quickly. Towers of smoke rose up from the windows.

Brutes started to try to escape. They slipped out of side doors and ground floor windows ... right into the waiting blades of the Wretched. Cinder directed the undead to completely surround the building. Not a single warrior could slip through their vigilant lines. This was it. The war against the Brutes was going to be over soon.

Relief rushed through Beetle. His body was fatigued but he was so happy that it was finally over that he needed to find somebody to celebrate with.

Beetle found Cull. The giant knight was standing perfectly still as he watched the building burn. The flames were reflected in the black mirror of his armor. Cull wasn't much for idle conversation, so Beetle didn't say anything.

Beetle took out a flask. His victory flask, he called it. He held it out to Cull. Cull didn't move to take it. Beetle clinked it against his armor in a cheers and drank. Cull turned to look at Beetle and though Beetle couldn't see his face, he could swear that the knight was glaring at him.

"Oh, don't take yourself so seriously," Beetle said. "We won."

Lilith grabbed the arm of one of the Wretched and pulled with all her strength. It didn't pay her any mind.

"Stop!" she cried out. "Stop! Jericho's inside! I saw him run inside the house!" She grabbed some of the Wretched and tried to physically make them stop. It was no use. The unfeeling Wretched continued to fling their pots and the building was hopelessly on fire in less than a minute.

Duke stood next to the Irons. They were all watching the building burn. Lilith ran over to him.

"Jericho's inside there!" she told him.

"What would you have me do?" he asked. He gestured toward the house. Flames covered the entire outside. Inside was more fire and the remnants of the Brute army. The Brutes were screaming now. Maybe they had been for a while and Lilith had just noticed.

"I don't know," she said. "Maybe we can ... " But no idea came to her. She stood next to Duke, helplessly watching as the building burned. She furiously sought some way to rescue Jericho.

Ghosts could lower the temperature. Perhaps they could put out some of the flames ... No, that wouldn't work. Ghosts couldn't lower the temperature enough to put out a fire of that magnitude. Maybe the Wretched could hack through the walls and pull Jericho out. That could be feasible ... if they knew where Jericho was, precisely. It was a large building and he could be anywhere inside.

A loud creaking of wood ripped through the air. Lilith's heart seemed to stop beating for an instant and she gasped, certain that more trees were about to crash down upon them. But it wasn't trees falling, it was the house. Its once straight lines were warped and it was sagging in upon itself. Then, with a groan, the building collapsed. A myriad of sparks took to the air, forming twisting constellations against thick black smoke.

A few years ago, Lilith would have cried. Terrible sorrow thrashed in her breast, trying to crawl up her throat and choke her. But she was a Vagabond. A Renegade. She had experienced lifetimes of pain and loss. She stood next to Duke and watched the flames devour what was left of the building. There were no screams from inside now. The only sound was the steady crackle of the fire and the occasional dry scraping as the wood shifted. Some small, unreasonable part of her kept hoping to see Jericho push his way out of the burning wreckage. Miracles sometimes happened, after all.

Just not today.

"The main mansion is completely deserted," Cinder told Duke. "I scanned it with my ghosts. No one is inside." His robe seemed to pulse in time with the glow of the fire. Lilith still stood beside Duke, silently watching the flames.

"So the mansion really is too dangerous to enter," Duke said. "Should we torch it?"

"I wouldn't. The ghosts in there are incredibly strong. They're not things we want to upset and have follow us back to Gheistmar."

Duke nodded. He looked to the sky. The day's light was fading.

"Let's form up the army and get out of here," he said. "We don't want to be near this damn graveyard when the sun goes down." He put his hand on Lilith's shoulder. "I'll send men back tomorrow. When the wreckage is finally cooled, they'll dig through it and find Jericho. Then we'll have the biggest funeral celebration Gheistmar has ever seen."

Lilith dipped her head once and turned away from the fire. She walked back into the army's ranks with her chin high and steady. A tough woman, Duke thought. He looked back toward the mansion.

In the backyard there looked to be an orchard. It was

overgrown, but the rows of trees were evident. Some of the trees were in bloom. The white flowers bobbed up and down as a breeze moved through the branches. A tall man was standing in the orchard. He looked huge. Nearly as big as Cull. Was he one of the Brutes? The man was staring right back at Duke. His facial features were too far away to discern, but he didn't appear the least bit friendly. Maybe the guy was an Elder. Maybe he had been living in the mansion and no one knew.

Something was off about the man. Duke didn't know what. Not at first. Only when the next gust of wind sent the white flowers into motion did he realize the man's clothes didn't react to the wind. Was it possible the man was a ghost? Yes! Duke now saw how the edges of the man's outline were blurred slightly. That ghost was extraordinarily powerful and physical to be standing fully visible in the day like that. He had never seen a ghost that strong. Not even Jericho's ghosts.

"Let's get out of here," Duke said. The Gheistmar army formed up quickly. They collected the injured and the dead that they could find—dammed fog!—and marched hastily. No one wanted to be around the Lourde's Den at nightfall.

CHAPTER 17

A week later they held a mass funeral for everyone who had died fighting the Brutes. The funeral ceremony was a heady spectacle of celebration and mourning. Vagabonds filled the courtyard outside the palace. The crowd wrapped around the shallow pool and streamed into the gardens. As the sun set, they drank, roasted food over open fires, sang, and played games.

The most popular game was called "fishing". They would put a lit candle on a piece of wood and set it afloat on the pond. One Vagabond used a ghost to move it around while another Vagabond shot arrows at it. It was a great night game. The candle zipping along the pond's surface was a bright target and it was obvious when an arrow hit the candle and drowned the flame in the dark water.

Other candles surrounded the collection of coffins outside the palace doors. Nearly fifty coffins, each occupied by an Iron who had fallen during the attack on the Lourde's Den; it was the most death the city had seen since they fought the Brutes in the streets.

The center coffin was the largest. It had extravagant carvings in the wood. No lit candles were near it. Each time a lit candle came too close, angry ghosts snuffed it out. The ghosts were upset that the Vagabond to whom they were bonded had died. They might linger around that body for days or even years depending on their whimsy. Duke guessed it'd be years in this case. These ghosts were strong. The body, of course, was Jericho's.

It had been surprisingly easy to retrieve Jericho's body. They had returned to the Lourde's Den in the day and Cinder had used his ghosts to feel through the wreckage of the servants' quarters. Cinder had his ghosts search for powerful ghosts clustered together. Normally, such ghosts would keep a comfortable distance from each other. The exception would be if they had been bonded.

So Cinder just searched for strong, bonded ghosts and when he found them he had the Wretched dig and sort through the mess of ashes and bodies and scorched wood. They had found Jericho's body in the cellar of the building.

"You're sure it's him?" Duke asked as he looked down at the coffins from a palace window. He clutched a tankard of wine.

"You've asked me that five times already," Cinder replied. "Yes, it is him. It's Jericho."

Duke watched the funeral. It was informal. Vagabonds had so many memories of various traditions for celebrating and caring for the dead that it was impossible to settle on one template. Instead, they just set the coffins in front of the palace and provided more food and drink than the citizens could possibly consume.

Jericho's coffin moved! Duke blinked. Was he imagining things? He stared, intently focused. It moved again! The coffin shuddered and rocked back and forth.

"He's alive!" Duke yelled. "Look at the coffin!"

Lilith ghosted through the crowd and approached Jericho's casket. She opened the lid and looked inside and winced. The body was barely recognizable. Jericho's kilij was there, though. There was no mistaking that steel or the ghost bonded to it. And he was wearing his special coat. The metal wires jutted out from the scorched leather like bones poking through decaying flesh. She closed the casket and walked away. She would try to remember him alive instead as that burnt husk of a human.

Lilith watched the revelry of the funeral. A loud cheer went up from the crowd as an archer hit the floating candle. So many people ... were they here for Jericho? No, surely not. He wasn't loved after loosing the ghosts in the clock tower. The majority of the crowd was probably here for the Irons who had died. She didn't know any of those dead soldiers. She had little contact with the Irons in general. She was here only for Jericho.

She selected a glass of wine from a table and took a sip. She wasn't going to get blind drunk like so many of the other Vagabonds here. She would have a glass or two of wine. Maybe later she would cry. Maybe not.

For some reason she found herself thinking of Jericho catching the fish for Claire's aquarium. He had spent hours down at the creek trying to find the perfect fish for Claire. It had been such a tender gesture from a cold blooded Vagabond warrior, and it had surprised her. Life with Jericho had been full of surprises. The time she had spent with him had been a mixture of horror, revelation, and happiness. She raised her glass of wine in the direction of the coffin. Cheers. Hope you find peace in the afterlife. Or, knowing you, hope you find a way to come back and haunt us all.

Lilith took a sip from her wine and was about to turn away and go home when movement snagged her gaze. Jericho's coffin was moving! It shuddered like someone was struggling to get out! Her heart leapt up to her throat. She wanted to run up to it and rip open the lid. She also wanted to run far, far away. Frankly, she was terrified. She envisioned that scorched corpse thrashing inside the coffin, somehow still alive. The conflicting emotions of joy and terror rooted her to the spot. She couldn't move, couldn't think. She could only watch as the corpse in the coffin struggled to get out.

"Jericho's alive!" Duke yelled. He grabbed Cinder by the shoulder. The man felt like he was nothing but a withered corpse beneath his robes. Duke let go.

Cinder didn't even look out the window. His mouth twitched in what looked like amusement.

"Alive? I doubt that," Cinder said in a flat voice. He left the room.

Duke watched from the window as Cinder emerged below with a brazier of incense. The brazier swung gently at the end of a chain that dangled from Cinder's burnt hands. Blue-gray smoke puffed out of the brazier, leaving a haze in its wake.

Cinder walked around Jericho's shaking coffin, spreading the smoke around it. A ghost's physical presence was composed of water. The particles from the smoke clung to that moisture, making the forms of the ghosts become easily visible.

There were at least four ghosts. They were old, powerful beings gnarled with anger and sorrow. They flowed around the coffin. Frequently one or another would grab the coffin and shake it in a fit of rage.

Duke sighed. His knees were weak. Jericho was still dead. It was merely his ghosts shaking his coffin.

Duke took a long drink from his tankard.

Those were some severely upset ghosts. Beetle watched them shake Jericho's coffin as Cinder spread smoke through the air. He wondered if his own ghosts would be as upset when he finally died. He hoped so. He hoped they flung his whole coffin across the room.

None of the other coffins were shaking. The ghosts that had been bonded to the dead Irons were still around, though. Beetle could feel them sliding through the ether like fish just beneath the surface of the water. But after the person to whom they'd been bonded died, ghosts quickly became disoriented. They lost their focus on the real world and their ability to influence it diminished rapidly. It was amazing that Jericho's ghosts were still so strong after a week. They too, though, were losing their strength. If

Jericho had been alive, they would have torn the coffin apart.

Cinder set the brazier down and walked over to Beetle. Beetle tensed as Cinder approached. Something about that man made him uneasy. Cinder's own ghosts had collected particles from the brazier, and they clouded around him like smoke.

"Keep your eyes on me as I speak to you," Cinder said in his raspy voice. "This is very important. We must not tip her off."

"Tip who off?" Beetle said. He kept his eyes on Cinder's burnt face. "What are you talking about?"

"Lilith," Cinder said. "Jericho's friend. You need to arrest her."

"What?" Beetle was shocked. He liked Lilith. He didn't think she would do anything wrong. "Why?"

"Are you questioning your orders?"

"No. I just ... "

"Then do it. Arrest her."

Beetle thought about it. He said, "I'd like to check with Duke first."

"Don't be ridiculous," Cinder said. "Do you think I would tell you to do something like this if Duke himself hadn't ordered me to? You can't waste any time. We're afraid she might flee the city and we won't ever be able to catch her."

"Why?" Beetle hadn't meant to say it, but the word just slipped out.

Cinder shook his head like he was disappointed with Beetle.

"There are a lot of things you don't understand," Cinder said. "And frankly, you don't need to. But let me assure you, if Lilith escapes this city, she will bring this fledgling empire to ruin. This city will once again be uninhabited, its citizens all dead. You, me, Duke—we'll all rot in the cold ground."

"I don't think Lilith would do something like that."

"She might not mean to," Cinder said. "But she will do it unwittingly, I promise you. So order your men to arrest her. And tell them to kill her if she resists. Take this extremely seriously. There are things at stake here that you can't possibly comprehend."

Beetle was quiet for a long moment. Sometimes he hated being the captain of the Irons.

"All right," he finally said.

As Lilith walked home from the funeral, she was a mess of emotions. She thought about how Jericho's coffin had been shaking and how Cinder had spread the smoke to manifest the spirits. She replayed that scene in her mind over and over and every time she came to the same conclusion.

When they all lived with Flint and Thera, it had been close quarters, and they had gotten to know each other very well. Lilith knew she'd never forget the look in Claire's eyes when she was feeling the ether or the way Jericho would sometimes sit motionless for hours. They all knew each other's habits and mannerisms. That went for the ghosts they had bonded, too. Lilith felt certain she would always be able to recognize one of the ghosts that had been bonded to them. They were almost as familiar to her as her own ghosts. And yet, at the funeral, she hadn't recognized any of the spirits flying around Jericho's coffin. Not a single one.

She reviewed the facts and weighed them carefully. Yet again she came to the same conclusion: that was not Jericho's body that they had brought back.

Lilith didn't know if anyone else knew it or if anyone cared or if it even mattered at all. She didn't know what to think. Did this make a bit of difference? Probably not. She knew that Jericho had been inside that building when it burned down. She didn't see any way he could have survived it. But then, what were his coat and sword doing on someone else's body?

She was so busy contemplating the possible implications that she almost didn't notice the peculiar behavior of the ether.

In Gheistmar, the ether was in constant motion. There were so many Vagabonds present that it was stirred like the surface of a pond in a hailstorm. Only the larger waves made by the very strong Vagabonds were easy to notice.

Over the course of several blocks, Lilith noticed that she had been feeling constant ripples coming from behind her. The ripples were from a moderately strong Vagabond. She wouldn't have noticed them if they hadn't been coming from directly behind her the entire time. Someone was following her.

She glanced in the reflection of a window. It was hard to tell who was following her. There were several Vagabonds in the streets. She thought about it, and headed toward the market on the main street.

Lilith turned down the main street of Gheistmar and headed into the market. There were more people there. The market was crowded at all hours of the day. It was truly one of the most remarkable sights of Gheistmar.

Vagabonds often dressed in the attire appropriate to the era of their most powerful ghost. It was simply what they were most comfortable wearing. The market was packed with knights in full armor, pirates, legionaries, Egyptian desert warriors, Spartans, and a wide variety of ancient peoples, many long dead and forgotten in the annals of history. The most similar thing to it Lilith had ever seen was a Halloween party.

Lilith slid into the crowd, discretely picking up her pace. Most of the people in the market moved slowly as they appraised the various goods. Any Vagabonds in a hurry would avoid the market, choosing instead the less crowded side streets. She pretended to glance at a fruit stand and looked out of the corner of her eye for anyone pushing through the crowd in a hurry.

There were two Irons shoving their way through the pack of shoppers. They were closing in on Lilith, their faces grim and determined. They held their short clubs. It was better that they had clubs out instead of the swords that hung at their side, but not much better. It only meant that they intended on taking her alive.

But why come after her at all? What had she ever done? She debated about approaching them and simply asking.

She nixed that thought a second later. There were a lot of questions she had, and a great number of things didn't make much sense to her. She had a gut feeling that to get caught by these Irons was to die.

Lilith slid between a conquistador arguing with a Greek hoplite over the price of a bag of potatoes and hurried through the crowd. She pushed past a female Viking and then took off running. She looked back. The Irons weren't able to maneuver through the crowd as quickly as she had. They saw her watching them and they scowled at her. They would never catch her. She was quicker than they were, and with her head start they had no chance at all.

So intent was she at watching the guards behind her that she never saw the one who came from a side street.

The third Iron slammed into Lilith at a full sprint and tackled her. The impact carried them off the street and into a side alley. They hit the ground hard. Lilith's head bounced off the cobblestones and her vision swam. The man's weight pressed down upon her and drove the breath from her lungs.

She couldn't breath. She could barely see. The man on top of her was much stronger than she was and all he had to do was hold her down for a few seconds until the other Irons arrived. She squirmed in his grasp, but she might as well have been struggling against steel bands.

Shadows loomed in the bright entrance of the alley. Lilith blinked her eyes and shook her head. Her vision focused and she screamed and bucked futilely in the guard's arms.

The other Irons had arrived.

CHAPTER 18

Duke stood over a table next to Cinder. A paper was spread across the top of the table. It was a medical diagram.

"You're certain that this is possible?" Duke said.

"For someone with an immense will and a toleration for ... discomfort, yes," Cinder said. "The quicksilver works far better than the chains did. It is a much smoother transition. The only problem is getting enough of it."

"That's not a problem at all," Duke replied. "We received a shipment of quicksilver just yesterday from a Crossbreed coven."

Cinder nodded. "Then when do you want to do this?"

"Soon. After we do a little more research."

A loud commotion echoed in from the hall. Someone was sobbing while a stern man—it sounded like Beetle—shouted at them.

"What's going on?" Duke said.

Cinder smiled. "It sounds like they arrested Lilith."

Beetle entered the room. He half-guided, half-dragged an Iron behind him. The guard had his hands covering his face.

"What's this?" Cinder asked. "Where's the girl?"

Beetle grabbed the man's arms and pulled them away from his face. Duke grimaced. The guard's face was torn open in a long, gaping slash. The slash went across his eyes, ruining them. The sockets were filled with ugly mess. It looked like someone had poured blood over fried eggs.

"This is one of the three who caught up with her," Beetle said.

"Where are the others?"

Beetle shook his head sadly.

"Dead," Beetle said. "Both of them."

Kiev had been an Iron for several months and loved every minute of it. He was a good soldier. He was competent and disciplined and adept at most weapons. He had two ghosts bonded to him. One had been a soldier, the other a hunter. Which was appropriate, because Kiev was rather good at tracking through the ether.

The girl had two strong ghosts bonded to her and left a wide path in the ether. While two other Irons followed her by sight, Kiev trailed behind, using only the ether as his guide. When he deduced that she was going to pass through the market, he decided to take a side street. It would be quicker and he would be able to get in front of her and catch her by surprise.

It worked. As Kiev came out of the alley, he saw the girl. She was looking back at the other Irons. Perfect. He burst into a sprint and tackled her. As they fell to the ground, he used his shoulder to bounce her head off the cobblestones and grabbed her arms and pinned them to her sides.

Beetle had said the girl might be dangerous. Kiev didn't think she would be, but it was better to be safe than sorry.

Kiev's ghosts were gone! The ghosts had been ripped away from him when he tackled the girl. One of her ghosts had done it. It was holding both of his own ghosts back, keeping them from helping him. Oh well. Ghost or no ghost, he was able to hold her easily.

Another of her ghosts slid Kiev's knife from his sheath and dropped it into the girl's hand. Kiev had a split second to realize he might be in trouble and then the girl twisted just enough to stab him right below his rib cage. Kiev yelled and rolled off her and clutched his side. Gods that hurt! Kiev suddenly made up his mind that he wasn't going to capture her at all. He struggled to his feet and took out his club. He was going to beat her to death. This dark, miserable alley was the last place she would ever see. The other two Irons had arrived, he saw. Good. The bitch was tricky and Kiev didn't want to get stabbed again.

The girl leapt to her feet with the agility of a cat. She uncoiled the whip from her belt and cracked it in the air. Electricity crackled down the length of the whip and sparks slid through her hair like blue snakes.

When she spoke, her voice was as calm as the waters of a smooth river.

"You've made a terrible mistake," she said.

"Always knock an attacker's ghost away," Jericho had told them when they were training. "If you're ambushed, that is always your first action. It should be a reflex. Once your enemy's ghost is pushed away, then your own ghosts will be able to act unhindered."

They had practiced relentlessly. It was like mental wrestling. "A split second chess match in the air" was how Jericho had referred to it. Strength, speed, and cunning all played important parts in one spirit being able to push away another.

They played at this around the clock. If two of them encountered each other in the hall, they'd try to knock away each other's sprits. Normally it couldn't be done. Aside from Jericho, most of them were on the same level, so their ghosts would just kind of grapple in the air for a while. The only truly effective way to do it was an ambush.

Behind the sofa, behind the curtains, or even inside the kitchen cupboards; Lilith had her favorite hiding places. She'd curl up in her spot and wait for someone to pass by and, when they did, she'd unleash her ghosts on them. Abigail, her circus ghost, was very quick. She could dart in and out too fast for most ghosts to catch her. Even Jericho's ghosts had a hard time catching her when they played. When they did, though, Abigail was toast. She would get smacked hard and Lilith wouldn't see her again for hours.

When the Iron tackled Lilith, she ripped his ghosts away purely by reflex. On the ground and fighting against her daze, she realized he didn't have any ghosts to protect him. She used Niko to pull the man's knife from his sheath. The knife slipped through the air and into her hand. She was able to wiggle enough to jam the blade into his side.

The blade went in only an inch or so, but it must have hurt like hell. The Iron screamed and rolled off of her.

Lilith leapt to her feet and uncoiled her whip and cracked it in the air. She still held the first man's dagger in her hands. That Iron had murder in his eyes and his two companions who had just arrived didn't look any happier. Lilith was fighting for her life here and she knew it.

She told them that they had made a terrible mistake, and she ignited into a flurry of motion.

Her whip moved with the speed of a striking snake and lashed across the face of the nearest Iron. He fell to the ground screaming and clutching his ruined eyes. The other guard ran at her and she whipped his foot. He fell forward and she drove the dagger into his chest. The only Iron left was the one who had tackled her. He started to say something but Lilith wasn't listening. She stoked her ghosts and poured electrical energy into her whip. She cracked it against the man's chest. There was a loud zap and a shower of sparks as she sent a huge amount of electricity into him, stopping his heart. He dropped, dead before he touched the street.

Lilith breathed out slowly and tried to slow her own heart. She wished she had Jericho's ghost who could slow time. This had all happened so fast she could barely think.

She went to the man she had stabbed and dropped to her knees beside him. The dagger was deep in his chest and his breath came in wet, ragged gasps. He would die soon. Lilith felt incredibly sad. This wasn't the first time she had killed someone, but these men had been her allies just a week ago. They had marched against the Brutes together. What had changed in that short amount of time?

The man whose face she had destroyed with her whip was screaming horribly. A crowd was beginning to gather at the entrance of the alley. Lilith needed to get out of the area.

No, more than that. She needed to get out of Gheistmar. Killing an Iron was punishable by death. She had to leave now.

She stood and coiled her whip and tucked it back into her belt. She didn't want to push through the group of people; one of them might decide to try and be a hero and grab her. She looked for another way out of the alley. Aside from scaling a drain pipe—which she could do but it would look awfully suspicious and draw unnecessary attention—the only way out was the way she came in.

The crowd had grown to twenty or thirty people. The moon had risen, bathing the city in light. The alley, though, was covered in shadow while the street was bright. Of the crowd, not one person ventured into the shadow. Lilith felt as if she were in a tomb with a bunch of people watching her.

She could possibly fight her way out. If she attacked viciously enough, they might scatter. Then again, this was Gheistmar and she might run into a Vagabond nearly as strong as she was. Besides, those people were innocent. They were simply trying to come to the aid of the screaming Iron. How she wished he would shut up! His voice pierced her ears and made it hard to think.

She would walk out. It was that simple. She would walk out of the alley and through the crowd and if anyone so much as laid a hand on her, she would deal with them instantly and brutally.

Again, Lilith stoked her ghosts. She might have had only two ghosts bonded to her, but since she was a shallow bonder, her ghosts drew strength from any spirits in the area. Jericho had once said she was one of the best shallow bonders he had ever seen. Her ghosts were extraordinarily talented at channeling power from other ghosts, and the crackling of electricity arcing between the silver relics in her hair was nearly deafening. She couldn't hear anything else but the cracking and zapping. Her whip glowed with electricity and so too did the metal on her boots. Lilith lit the alley with a sharp blue light. Shadows danced maniacally around her like demon worshipers.

She walked toward the crowd. Each step was measured and steady. The crowd parted before her. As she walked through them, she felt like a panther striding among sheep.

One woman stepped in front of Lilith. Her mouth was open as if she were about to speak. Lilith flicked the woman's ghost away like a bug and the woman blanched. Her mouth snapped shut and she melted back into the crowd.

A few more steps and Lilith was free. She broke into a run. The moon was at her back and her shadow stretched in front of her. Maybe people were following her, maybe not. It didn't matter, really. Time was her biggest enemy now. Once the rest of the Irons were alerted, she wouldn't have a chance in hell of getting out of the city.

Lilith ran for the city gates. She ran hard. Her only hope was that she could get through them before the Irons there were told to be on the look out for her. Once those gates were closed, there was no escaping Gheistmar.

She dashed down the city streets. Even with the bizarre denizens that Gheistmar harbored, she still drew more than a few looks.

A block before the gates she slowed to a steady walk. She forced her breathing to become calm and slow. She walked to the gates slowly and steadily, like she didn't have a thing in the world to hide. Her every muscle twitched as self-preservation dictated that she take off running. The four Irons at the gates looked at her. Two guards with a rope came over to her, eager to help her cross the bridge safely. Lilith forced her pounding heart to slow and allowed the Irons to tie the rope around her waist and help her across the bridge.

Once on the other side and free of the rope and the guards,

she kept walking at the same steady pace.

The forest was a black wall that looked impenetrable. Lilith went along it until she found a meager dirt path. The path hadn't been used in a long time. Thin branches stretched across it in several places and weeds had pushed up through the dirt. There would be little traffic along this path, if any.

She took the path into the woods, finally feeling safe as the darkness enveloped her. They could track her, she knew, but at least she would have a head start. If she had any luck at all, she should be able to make it to a small coven she knew well. That group would protect her. And maybe they'd be able to explain a few things.

She was exhausted. What a horrible day it had been! She wanted nothing more than to go to sleep. The forest floor as a bed and only her clothes as a blanket would be quite fine—she had slept in much worse—and she had to ignore the temptation to lie down. Her own bed sounded so nice that the thoughts were positively indecent.

No rest for her, though. She had a long journey ahead.

She came to a wide, gentle flowing stream. An old rope bridge spanned it. Lilith occasionally came here to escape the city and be alone with her thoughts. The first few times, she hadn't dared to cross the bridge. The rope was frayed and the wooden planks looked about as sturdy as a moonbeam. Then, at some point, she had stepped onto it and, eventually, had crossed it. The bridge was in better shape than it looked.

But not for long; Lilith was going to cut the rope when she got to the other side. The stream was several feet below and the banks were steep. Anyone pursuing her would lose precious time climbing the banks and wading through the water.

A cold wind slithered through the woods. Ancient ghosts clotted the air. The temperature around her plummeted and Lilith could suddenly see her breath. The ether was so agitated it wasn't just rippling, it felt like it was shivering.

A powerful Vagabond was approaching, and approaching fast.

Lilith ran. She was halfway across the bridge when a cacophony of destruction made her glance over her shoulder. Her knees went weak and she had to grab the rope railing to keep from collapsing.

Oh God, she thought wildly. *What is that?*

CHAPTER 19

A locomotive. That was the word that flashed in Lilith's mind.

She had seen her first train when she was a little girl. The machine's amazing power had astonished her. It seemed unstoppable. It seemed as though it would have obliterated anything that stood in its way.

The thing plowing through the forest was the same way. It didn't alter its path for anything. Thick branches were snapped like brittle bones and logs were burst through with such violence it looked like they had exploded. A cloud of dirt and leaves rushed toward Lilith, looming larger than a locomotive. The rope rails of the bridge vibrated as the very ground trembled.

In front of the cloud was a massive knight in black armor. The armor was shiny and looked liquid in the moonlight. He carried a harpoon in his right hand and the harpoon had a length of chain attached to its end.

Cull. Lilith wished it were someone else. Just about anyone else. The quiet giant scared her almost as much as Cinder did.

The knight thundered forward with uncanny speed and leapt into the air. With his ghosts carrying him, his jump spanned half the bridge. When he landed, the bridge shook and swung and Lilith had to grab the railing with both hands to keep from falling down. She thought the rope would break and they would both plummet to the stream below, but it held. Even as the bridge swung, the knight came at her.

Lilith's whip was already in her hand. She stoked her ghosts and electricity crackled all around her. She charged the whip with electricity. Cull's armor might protect him against blades, but raw energy would go right through the metal. She cracked her whip, aiming at Cull's chest and hoping to stop his heart.

The whip never made it. With a burst of light and a loud pop, the whip was deflected midair. The burst of light was incredibly bright. It was like a hundred of flash bulbs of the old time cameras going off in one instant. Sparks as thick as caterpillars tumbled through the air to the dark water below.

As shocked as she was, Lilith didn't hesitate. She kept her whip in motion, lashing out at the knight repeatedly. Each time, though, the same thing happened. When it got within about a foot of Cull, it was knocked away.

She couldn't get past his special armor. Her attacks slowed his advance, but didn't seem to bother him in the least. He was walking forward while she edged back. Lilith had never moved with such speed. She was cracking her whip three times for every step she took. Her heart was racing like that of a scared little bird.

Lilith couldn't use her dagger to cut the ropes of the bridge. Cull was far too quick and would be upon her before she cut even one side. She had to do something else ...

Niko! She called her ghost forward. Niko was always the best at working with electricity. She instructed Niko to burn through the rope. The ghost zipped behind her. The smell of smoke was soon in the air.

Cull must have figured out what Lilith was planning. He plowed ahead with renewed determination. Lilith kept her whip in motion and the very air seemed engulfed in white fire as Cull's armor and her whip met again and again. So many sparks rained down that the boards on the bridge caught fire.

The rope snapped. Lilith felt it going and bounded backwards onto firm ground. She stumbled and bumped against a tree.

Cull threw his harpoon a heartbeat before the bridge flipped. Then he was falling through the air.

Lilith ducked and the harpoon imbedded itself deep within the tree. She watched Cull fall away and she collapsed in relief. Her legs were shaking so badly that she couldn't stand if she tried. Cull had nearly killed her with his harpoon. It was pure luck she had encountered him here on the bridge. Anywhere else and she wouldn't have had a chance. That armor him made him nearly invincible. Well, it couldn't protect him against water. He'd surely drown as the weight of the metal pulled him beneath the surface.

Lilith needed to keep moving. She knew that. But she was beyond exhausted and wanted nothing more than to close her eyes and drift away.

The creak of wood jolted her awake. What was that? It sounded like it was coming from the tree. A few splinters sprinkled down on her. Her gaze drifted upward to the harpoon. It was bending ... and the chain attached to it was taut.

No! Lilith realized what had happened just as Cull pulled himself up over the edge of the bank, climbing the chain hand over hand. Lilith scrambled to her feet but the knight dashed forward and grabbed her by her neck and slammed her against the tree. He held her high in the air and her feet kicked feebly against his chest. She couldn't breathe. She twisted and clawed at his hand but it did no good. Her throat was on fire. Her struggles intensified ... and then began to weaken. The knight seemed quite content to simply hold her there and watch her die. Lilith's vision clouded and then faded to black as she lost consciousness.

CHAPTER 20

Something is about to happen," Thera said. She was sitting at her desk, working on anchoring a ghost to a metal stein. Those were their biggest sellers: mugs with ghosts anchored to them to keep the liquids inside cool. Flint crafted the steins, and Thera anchored the ghosts.

"I don't feel anything in the ether," Flint said. He set down the book he had been reading and looked over to her.

"I don't either," Thera told him. "But the ghosts are acting strangely. Like something is bothering them."

Thera had become a Vagabond late in life. She and Flint were both doctors. They had lived in a human city and practiced at the hospital there. Aside from the occasional spooky thing happening—a door slamming shut at night, a disembodied voice, a feeling that someone was in the room with them—aside from those rare occasions, they lived a completely normal human life.

It was only when they moved that the trouble started.

The city was too crowded, too noisy. Thera suggested that they moved out to the country and Flint hardily agreed. They found a house on five acres of land. The house was a little old, but the land was beautiful. Thera absolutely loved it, so they moved in.

Within a week, strange things started happening. Books were flung off shelves, doors banged shut repeatedly, and windows were covered with mysterious handprints. Sometimes the lights to their house would go out for no reason. Sometimes they wouldn't be able to start either of their cars. It was frightening.

Despite all of that, neither of them wanted to move back to the city. They were doctors. They were reasonable people. There was a mystery here that intrigued them. Both Thera and Flint started taking long walks at night. They didn't know why, exactly. They just had the desire to wander.

On their night walks they noticed a funny thing: when they passed beneath a streetlight, the light would go out. It didn't happen every time, but it happened quite frequently. And again, they had no idea why.

One night Thera got sick. She was screaming and sweating and rolling her eyes back in her head. Flint didn't know what to do. He checked her all over. There was nothing physically wrong with her. And her words ... they were in a different language. Flint could only hold her and rock her back and forth as she raved. It lasted two long hours.

And then she was okay. Just like that, Thera snapped out of it. They didn't know it at the time, but Thera had just bonded her first ghost.

From then on, the streetlights always went out for Thera. So did many of the lights and machines at the hospital, and she had to quit her job. Flint bonded his first ghost a little later, and he too had trouble going into the city. After bonding his ghosts, he discovered a passion for working with metal. He had the skill for it, too, which was a complete shock to him. They would have been distraught if they hadn't already met other Vagabonds while walking at night.

It had been interesting, meeting Vagabonds for the first time. Most of them dressed differently. Some wore clothes that would have been acceptable centuries earlier. Others had a motley attire that wouldn't have been acceptable in any time period anywhere. They spoke of ghosts as casually as most people spoke of the weather.

Strange though these people were, Thera and Flint got along with them well. Guests stayed for hours or days or even weeks. They helped the sick and wounded, and sold gear to the healthy. Eventually, Jericho arrived.

Thera would always remember how everything seemed to grow darker and colder as the man in the long coat had approached their home. She had felt him approaching from a long way off, and had been nervous. Scared. There had been a handful of other Vagabonds staying at their house at the time, and they all stood outside to see who the approaching stranger was.

It felt a little like that, now. The ether was calm, but the ghosts seemed just a little jittery.

There was a knock at their door.

"Don't answer it," she whispered. She didn't know why, but she was afraid. She realized she was holding her breath. Surely they couldn't hear her breathing?

Another knock. This time it was louder and more insistent. "We know you're in there," it seemed to say. Fear pooled in her stomach, cold and metallic. The doorknob twitched and began to turn. Had she locked it? Thera couldn't remember. The doorknob turned all the way and the door moved a fraction of an inch before the deadbolt caught on the frame. She slowly breathed out in relief. She had locked it.

The door was smashed inward with such force that it nearly folded in half. Men wearing armor flooded into their home and overwhelmed them so quickly that they hardly had time to scream.

Beetle hated going to the Charnel House. He kept his eyes forward as he walked past the cells. With his peripheral vision he saw the twitching movement of the undead revenants hanging from hooks. He was pretty sure at least one of them made obscene gestures in his direction. One of the Wretched called his name. He didn't like that. He didn't like it when they talked, and he liked it even less that one of them knew his name.

At the end of the hall he descended the stairs. The air had the cool, wet feel to it that cellars and dungeons and caves all had. He knocked on the door to the operating room.

There was a pause. Then Cinder's raspy voice called out, "Enter!"

Beetle swung open the door and stepped inside. Cinder was standing next to the operating chair with a scalpel in his hand.

The chair itself was just a sturdy wooden chair with a high back and thick arms. Lined with leather straps that would be buckled around the person's arms, legs, and torso, it held the person still while the amalgam machine worked. The amalgam machine was what infused the silver mixture into the person's blood, allowing an outside ghost to control the body.

The machine looked like the concoction of some evil Victorian scientist. It was the size of a hulking piece of furniture, one made of rusty pipes surrounded by a forest of gears. It had multiple black air bladders that would expand and contract to push the amalgam through clear glass tubes that spiraled up and around and finally down into a long metal needle. The needle would be inserted into the person's arm, and they could only watch helplessly as the amalgam was forced into their veins.

From what Beetle understood, ghosts would start trying to control the body even before the person was dead. The spirits would send electrical charges through their blood, making muscles twitch and setting nerves on fire. It had to be an extremely unpleasant way to die. The person would try like hell to escape. The chair and its straps always held them, though. The corpse in the chair was proof of that.

The corpse was partially dissected. The operation must not have gone smoothly. Cinder was now trying to figure out what had happened. He would cut into the body and take a look and then dump the body into the pit. The pit was on the far side of the room. It was where they put the Wretched who didn't work out. If the amalgam mixture didn't pass into the veins properly or more than one ghost had control of the body or the person died too quickly or too slowly—well, there seemed to be a wide variety of circumstances that could ruin the operation and result in the body being tossed into the pit. Spirits still tried to use that flesh, though. The pit churned with the jerky movements of undead flesh.

The pit was deep, but it was quite full. Cinder had originally tried using chains in the Wretched. It hadn't worked well. There were many, many failures. Spools of chains still lay all over the room. Beetle was surprised Cinder didn't get rid of them. It must have reminded him of his early lack of success.

"What is it?" Cinder said. The body in the chair was struggling against the straps that held it in place. Spirits, fighting to control the flesh.

"We caught Lilith," Beetle said. He wasn't entirely sure how he felt about it. "She made it out of the city, but not too far."

"You got lucky," Cinder said.

"No luck at all," Beetle said. He couldn't keep the anger out of his voice. "I sent Cull after her. And Cull ... well, he gets things done."

CHAPTER 21

Jericho's ghost Domnul sometimes brought up a memory of a miracle he had witnessed in a battle. It had been a small thing, but miraculous nonetheless.

The battle had taken place in a field set high in the mountains. The spring rains had been falling for weeks and the ground was soft and covered with tender new shoots of grass and spattered with flowers. The warriors churned the field into black mud as they fought. When it was all over, Domnul noticed a purple flower. It was growing in the center of the field, right where the fighting had been the most fierce. Against all odds, the flower hadn't been trampled. To his dying day, Domnul would look back fondly on that memory.

As Jericho came up the steps from the basement in the servants' quarters, he had a moment similar to Domnul's. But Jericho's miracle wasn't a pretty little flower. It wasn't pretty at all.

Jericho passed by a window and looked outside. He had a clear view of the battle. The Wretched were carving the Brutes into pieces. But that wasn't what arrested his attention. It was the wagon in which the Wretched had ridden. The wagon doors were open, and the sun had moved along its path in the sky enough to shine some light inside. There, stacked inside the wagon, were clay pots.

Even from this distance, he could see them quite clearly. He could discern their shape, their tight-fitting lids, and the net-like sacks around each one. They were pitch pots. Pitch pots that were just like the ones that had been launched at their house. The memory of that first pot flying into their kitchen and breaking against the wall and showering Claire with that flammable liquid ... that memory was burned into Jericho's mind. It was as permanent and ugly as a scar, and he would be able to recognize those pots for the rest of his life.

He recognized them now. There was no doubt, no second guessing. Those were the same pots. He stared at them, struggling with the implications of this discovery.   What were they doing inside Cinder's Wretched wagon?

Jericho looked at the battle, searching for Cinder. He found him. The burned man was standing behind the lines of Wretched, shouting at them and pointing with his ashwood spear. The Wretched responded to his commands, pressing their attack where he directed.

The Wretcheds' movements were almost as smooth as a living human's. They could easily pass for human beings. Had those been Wretched attacking his home? He thought back, replaying that horrible night in his mind.

No, it couldn't have been. Jericho had killed a few of them, each with only a single arrow. From the battle here, it didn't seem like one arrow was capable of stopping a Wretched. They seemed invincible. Cinder had probably taken Irons and had them carry out the attack. That much made sense. Cinder loved his fire.

Had Duke known about any of this? Jericho didn't think so. Duke had marched with Jericho against the Brutes, and they had fought side by side. There had been plenty of opportunities for Duke to kill him, and Duke had never betrayed him. Cinder must have acted on his own.

But why? Jericho couldn't think of any reason for Cinder to destroy his home. Maybe Cinder intended to kill Duke and take control of the city. Maybe Cinder simply hated Jericho. Maybe ... hell, he had no idea.

Amazing. Claire was missing and her friend Peter was dead and Jericho's home was destroyed; all of that misery and he didn't have a clue as to why it had happened. He thought of Claire, picturing the irreverent grin that she wore when she smoked inside the house, even though she knew it upset Thera. He remembered sitting on top of the roof with her on that miserably sunny day. She might be dead now. Or she might have been frightened away from the Vagabond world forever. Maybe she'd somehow manage to suppress her ghosts enough to stay in the human world for the rest of her life. He might not ever see her again.

His ghosts swirled around him as they felt his anger. He breathed deep and forced himself to be calm.

So Cinder had used the Irons to attack their home. That made the Brutes ... well, not blameless, for they certainly weren't that. That made the Brutes guilty of fewer atrocities. Jericho didn't mourn them, but he was furious he had let his hatred of the Brutes distract him from the real culprit.

Cinder ... Liar. Deceiver.

Dead man.

Jericho would see to that. He was halfway to the front door when a roaring cheer crashed over the battle. The Brute lines had broken. Their warriors scrambled for their lives. They held onto their weapons with white knuckles and ran. Jericho thought they would scatter into the woods. Instead, they went to what must have been a pre-determined fall back position: the servants' quarters.

The entire Brute army was coming at him. The mad warriors leapt over logs and gravestones as they ran. Behind them was Cinder, looking taller than physically possible. He screamed an order to the Wretched and pointed his ashwood spear right at Jericho. The undead warriors surged forward.

Two armies were approaching. Both armies wanted Jericho dead.

He took a couple steps backward. Where could he go? Outside of the building the Brutes would cut him down. And if they didn't for some reason, he was sure that the Wretched would be happy to do it for them.

He couldn't hide somewhere inside, either. The building was large, but he would be found eventually. He pictured the Wretched fighting the Brutes, going room to room, small groups fighting for their lives. Even with the Wretched, it would be a long and drawn out battle. Surely there was an easier way ...

Cinder will torch this place, he realized. Why engage in dangerous room to room combat when he could just burn the entire building? At least that's what Jericho would have done in his place. And Cinder certainly had the pitch pots to do it.

For several long heartbeats Jericho stood without moving. He didn't know what to do. He could go out fighting the Brutes or sit in a chair and wait for the end. Either way, the final result was the same: both he and the Brutes would be roasted corpses within the hour.

The Brute army was nearly to the house, yet Jericho paid them no heed. The memory of killing Stone just minutes ago was vivid. Something about the event still tickled his mind, like a puzzle whose final piece didn't quite fit.

Stone, you beautiful devil you, he thought. A flame of hope sparked in his chest.

He ran back toward the basement. The front door burst open and Brutes flooded through. Windows shattered as Brutes jumped through them in their hasty retreat. Jericho all but flung himself down the stairs, like a stone plummeting into a black pit. He ran to the back corner of the basement, stepping over Stone's body without even looking. He went directly to the big wooden cabinet. Stone had been interested in that wardrobe in the final moments of his life. Why? Jericho had assumed some weapon had been inside. Yet the wardrobe was empty aside from a small collection of old clothes.

He grabbed the clothes and yanked them out as if they were weeds. He tossed them to the ground and felt the back of the wardrobe. Plain wood. Nothing remarkable. His heart sank. He had been hoping for a secret passageway. It would have made sense. The mansion and servant's quarters were old enough to have been used for the Underground Railroad. And Stone, seeing his army being hopelessly slaughtered, would have sought an escape.

With desperation, Jericho ran his hands over every inch of the wardrobe. There were no hidden latches or indentations. He gave it a hard kick. It was thick and solid. Even if there was a passageway behind there, he'd need an axe to chop through to it.

Jericho turned away to search the basement for a sledgehammer or axe or anything he could use to batter down the wood. He had taken two steps when something snagged at his ghost Leo. It felt like a nail catching on his clothing. Jericho used Leo to scan, feeling for that snag.

It was a silver knob on the other side of the wood. The knob contained no more silver than a small coin, and it was difficult to detect. But it was there. He used his ghosts to pull it to the side.

Nothing happened. He scanned some more and found two other knobs. His ghosts pulled those to the side and the door opened an inch. He felt along the side of the door. The knobs had been on wooden deadbolts. If they had been metal, Jericho—or any other Vagabond—would have been able to find them easily.

Jericho pushed open the door. Impenetrable blackness yawned beyond it. The passage must lead to the outside, probably to the river.

He was about to step through when an idea struck him. Cinder—and who knew who else—wanted him dead. It might be easier for Jericho if everyone thought he was dead.

Stone was close to his size ...

Everyone knew that Jericho prized his sword and coat. With a grimace, he took off his coat and put in on Stone. It was difficult to put it on the body, but at least the corpse was still flexible. He sat Stone against the back wall and laid his kilij across the body's lap.

The coat would burn, but the silver wires on the inside would still remain identifiable. The sword would be unharmed. The ghost bonded to the weapon would keep it cool enough that it wouldn't be damaged by the fire. It would still be recognizable if they dug it out of the wreckage.

Jericho stepped away with a sigh. It hurt leaving his kilij and coat behind. It was like he was leaving his old life and walking into some new and uncertain future.

He stepped into the mouth of the passageway. The Brutes wouldn't follow. Jericho doubted Stone would have shared the knowledge of a secret passage. For an added measure, he closed the door behind him and slipped the deadbolts into place.

He couldn't see a thing. It was as black as a cave. He walked slowly and carefully, taking small steps and feeling with his ghosts and his toes before putting weight on his foot. The floor was solid stone and seemed sturdy, yet he feared a pit or some other trap. The ceiling grew lower. Orion hated it. His hunter ghost didn't like closed spaces at all, and he screamed in Jericho's mind. With cold determination, he fought down both his and Orion's fear of tight spaces and pressed on.

The toe of Jericho's boot caught on something and he tripped and fell. His entire body was tense and his breath caught in his throat; he was certain that he had just triggered some trap that Stone had set. But no, there was no trap. The floor was simply uneven. Decades of moist soil freezing and thawing had cracked the stone floor and pushed sections of it up.

Jericho stood and continued walking. He was more careful to lift his feet higher so that he wouldn't trip on any more ridges.

Light was ahead! It was faint but unmistakable. It was like the glow of a quarter moon behind a cloud. He started to walk faster, anxious to get out of this damned tunnel.

With his lead foot, he stepped on a raised portion of stone. There was a crack, like some stick or other support had just broken, and the stone dropped a few inches. A rope hissed as it passed through eyelets and the wooden beams holding up the ceiling began to strain and groan. The ceiling began to drizzle dirt and small stones. Jericho had just triggered a trap!

He leapt forward, but it wasn't enough. A huge portion of the ceiling fell in, burying him deeper than a grave.

His ghosts protected him from the worst of it. They swirled around him, knocking aside stones and wood and much of the dirt that came rushing into the tunnel. When it was all over, Jericho was trapped in a small space not much larger than a coffin. He could kneel and move a foot or so to either side, but that was it. The passage was blocked both in front of him and behind.

Jericho tried to slow his rapidly beating heart. It was okay. He was still alive. There had to be a way out of this.

He felt all around him. His hands touched wood and earth and stone in every direction. He was buried completely. Fear looped its coils around his throat and constricted. Had he come all this way just to be buried alive? Orion screamed in his mind. Jericho tried to stay calm and think.

He smelled fresh air. He moved his hands around, palms forward and fingers outstretched, searching for the source of the new air. There, down near the floor of the tunnel was a small hole. It was too tight for him to fit through, though. He kept checking.

Nothing. The passageway was blocked.

Jericho let his hands flop to the ground. A humorless grin tugged at the corners of his mouth: at least he didn't have to starve or die of thirst. He still had the dagger Lilith had given him, so he could choose to end this anytime he desired.

Don't be such a baby, he chided himself. Surely there's some way to get past this.

He felt the edges of the hole. A portion of a beam had wedged against the wall, forming the little space that was just inches above the stone floor. He lay flat and tried to get through it. He was able to get his head and one of his shoulders in. That was it.

Light was ahead! Bright threads of it hung taut in the

darkness of the tunnel. Wedged tightly in the hole as he was, Jericho was just barely able to reach them. He passed his hands through them, watching as they poked at his flesh.

So close. So damned close ... The tunnel ended just ahead. It must, if light was coming in like that.

He slipped back out of the hole and felt along the floor. Maybe he could dig and enlarge the hole. No, the stone had some cracks in it, but otherwise it was solid. Maybe he could move the beam.

He maneuvered himself into a hunched squatting position. He grabbed underneath the beam with both hands and heaved. He stoked his ghosts into a fury and urged them to pull up on the beam as well. Wind whipped through the tunnel as the spirits yanked up on the beam and Jericho pulled until his knees trembled and he felt dizzy. The beam didn't so much as budge. It had tons of earth and stone pressing down on it and it wasn't going anywhere no matter what he did.

Jericho let go and dropped back down onto his knees. Well then, that was a miserable failure. He pulled out his canteen and took a drink of water. He held the canteen in his hand and shook it thoughtfully. He felt along the floor. The cracks in the stone went deep.

Hardly daring to hope, he started pouring the water into the cracks of the floor just below the hole. He had his ghosts drop the temperature. If they dropped the temperature in the tunnel, the water would run away before it froze. Instead, he focused them directly at the water.

With a sound like wind coursing over a barren tundra, the ghosts cooled the water. In seconds the water began to freeze. An eerie squeaking and grinding noise filled the tunnel as the ice struggled to expand against the rock. With a loud crack, the stone split.

Jericho felt along the floor. What had been solid stone was now large pieces. He grabbed one and pulled it out. Underneath was dirt. Precious dirt! He could dig through that!

He cleared away the rest of the stone and used his hands to

dig. A wild grin twisted his mouth as he worked. Soon he had enlarged the hole enough to slip through. The wood tore at his clothes and gouged his skin as he pushed through the cave-in. None of that so much as put a dent in his smile. He passed the cave in and came to the end of the tunnel.

The threads of light were slipping through tiny spaces around the frame of another door. Like the first one, there were three wooden deadbolts. Jericho slid them to the side. He was free! Finally free! The door probably opened to the side of the river. He envisioned the sun shining brightly and the river flashing and sparkling. He opened the door.

He couldn't have been more wrong.

CHAPTER 22

Jericho was scraped bloody and filthy beyond words after squirming through the cave-in. His clothes were tattered and he was armed only with his dagger and his bow. He was so tired that at first he thought he was hallucinating.

He wasn't down by the river at all. Instead, the tunnel door had opened to the inside of someone's house. It was a huge room, lit with candles and lined with books and paintings. A massive fireplace, cold and dark, loomed against the far wall. Luxurious couches and overstuffed chairs were strewn about the room.

The mansion! Jericho was inside the Lourde's Den itself! Fascination welled up inside him. He wanted to explore the place. So many horror stories had been told about it and he wanted to see what was true and what wasn't. It might be a dangerous place for weaker Vagabonds, but Jericho's ghosts should be able to keep him safe from whatever lurked in these halls.

No, he couldn't explore. He needed to get out of here and go to Gheistmar and warn Duke about Cinder.

The room had a single window on the far wall. Outside a thunderstorm was raging. Hail the size of stones pummeled the earth. A clap of thunder boomed so loudly it made the panes of glass shiver. Wow. Jericho hadn't been able to hear any of that in the tunnel. He wouldn't be going outside in that. Without the thick leather of his coat to protect him, the hail would beat him up badly. Besides, he was dead tired. He might was well get some rest.

He went to the nearest couch. There was a blue and black striped blanket draped over the back of it. He laid down on the couch and pulled the blanket on top of him. He closed his eyes and went into a dreamless sleep.

Almost. It wasn't quite dreamless. Like the heartbeat of a mouse hiding in a woodpile, something tiny and nearly undetectable echoed through his mind and kept him from complete sleep.

blue ... blue ... blue... The word pulsed repeatedly through his head. He was pretty sure it was one of his ghosts trying to tell him something. He tried to shut it out but it wouldn't go away. Every time he felt himself slipping into the quiet void of sleep, that little word would pull him back. *blue ... blue ...* It was like someone tapping on the side of his head while he was trying to sleep. Finally, he confronted it.

Blue. Yes, so what? Jericho's favorite color was the blue of the western sky as the sun dipped below the horizon. When he was near trees, he loved how the striking color contrasted with the absolute black of the tree trunks.

The blanket he was using had those colors. Those exact same colors ...

Too perfect. It was all too perfect. A blanket with his favorite colors, a mysterious thunderstorm that he hadn't heard previously raging outside. It was all a set up to keep him comfortable and to let his mental guard down.

Jericho wasn't sleeping, he was possessed!

Like a swimmer struggling towards the water's surface, Jericho fought toward consciousness.

Pain exploded throughout his body. He wasn't on a couch at all. He was slouched against the wall. He regained his vision an instant before a vase flew through the air and smashed into his forehead. Dazed, he tried to struggle to his feet.

A wood table took to the air and flew from across the room. Jericho tried to spin away but he wasn't quick enough and the table caught him in the side. He felt at least one of his ribs crack. Two other vases, a painting, and numerous books were scattered on the floor around him. All things that the ghosts had flung at him.

Where were his own ghosts? Why hadn't they protected him against this onslaught?

And then he saw: His ghosts were protecting him. But the room was filled—absolutely packed—with violent, ill-tempered ghosts. Strong as his ghosts were, it was the five of them against a mob. The air itself wavered. It looked like he was underwater. Angry faces and threatening silhouettes floated everywhere.

Jericho felt a stab of panic. Even in Gheistmar, ghosts weren't like this. They weren't this strong, this angry. This ... organized.

In a flash, he understood what had happened. The mob of ghosts had kept his own spirits busy and then a ghost had possessed him. As he lay defenseless, the ghosts began to hurl objects at him. He would have been beaten to death in minutes if he hadn't awakened.

He was still in the library. The couches were there, but no blue and black blanket and no window. Those had been embellishments on the part of the ghost who had possessed him, trying to make him more comfortable.

She was there, the ghost who had possessed him. She stood right next to him, a completely visible apparition. Her dress was long, but it was cut low at the top and had a slash that rose all the way up to her thigh. She was posing: chin up, leaning forward a little and knee pointed to open the slash in her dress, all of it exposing as much sensuous flesh as possible. Even now she was trying to distract him. And she was. Jericho narrowly ducked yet another vase. How many vases were in this room? He had to push these spirits back.

Jericho sent all five of his spirits against the ghost who had thrown the last vase.

He had once seen two dogs fighting. It was awful. The snarls and yips and squeals of pain had haunted his dreams for years after that.

This was much worse. The six ghosts howled and screeched as they tangled together so much that their individual forms were no longer recognizable. They became a twisted fog with angry faces biting at each other. Jericho wasn't exactly sure how ghosts fought each other, but there was always a definitive outcome.

With a loud wail, the ghost who had thrown the vase was banished. Jericho sent his ghosts against the specter of a fat man with a beard. He just looked guilty. Again, the shrieking filled the air.

The rest of the ghosts weren't throwing things anymore. They backed off some. Now that their prey wasn't unconscious and was actually fighting back, they were becoming apprehensive. Cowards. Just like most any mob of living people.

The scent of perfume ... A warm fire ... Good food ... Visions of decadence blossomed in Jericho's mind and he knew that the ghost woman was trying to possess him again. She was standing so close to him that they were nearly touching.

Instead of fighting her off, Jericho let her in his mind. Bonding was a sort of partial possession. The ghost and its memories would always occupy a part of his mind. Their emotions, too. This is what stopped most Vagabonds from bonding more than one ghost: they couldn't handle the sorrow of multiple lifetimes. It crushed their will to live, and most Vagabonds who bonded more than one or two ghosts ended up killing themselves.

Not Jericho. The sadness would bring him down, sure. He might have to spend time drinking heavily or chopping wood or pounding away in the forge to help him handle it, but in the end he never killed himself. He had a secret bit of knowledge that kept him strong and allowed him to bond more ghosts than anyone else.

He wanted to bond this woman spirit. Like a night flower

opening up to reveal its beauty, her name came to his mind: Lana. She was immensely powerful to have possessed him, and none of his ghosts were skilled in the art of possession. She'd be a valuable addition to his arsenal.

And so, as she pushed to get into his mind, he pulled her in. She hadn't expected that; he could feel how she was caught off guard.

Join me, he thought to her. *I will take you far from here and you will see many things. And most of all, I will hear you. You will be important again. You will matter.*

Ghosts almost never refused a bonding. Above all, they desired flesh again. They desired a way to influence the world around them instead of passing through it like a fading echo.

This woman, Lana, considered his proposal and agreed.

Wait, Jericho started to say. *Not yet ...*

Too late. She became part of him, joining minds. The library began to fade. Replacing it was a vision of a city. Wooden buildings, narrow streets, horses pulling wagons. Water—a lake—nearby. Chicago, Jericho suddenly knew from Lana's memories.

No. He fought it down. He hadn't been thinking. Bonding a ghost always brings on a rave. In a rush, the Vagabond experiences the most poignant memories of the ghost, including their death. Compressed like that, it's a rough thing to handle and often leaves the Vagabond semi-conscious for hours or even days. Or forever, if the Vagabond's mind snaps under the weight.

Jericho wasn't worried about his mind snapping, he was worried about the mob of ghosts pummeling him as he raved. Struggling to force down the images of Chicago, he pushed a couch into the corner of the room. He rolled underneath it so he would be protected from any other items the ghosts threw. He cried out as his ribs flared with pain when he rolled. Yes, he definitely had cracked them.

With his last bit of conscious thought, he instructed his ghosts to attack any ill-tempered spirit who came near. He started to tell them more but then Lana's memories slammed into him and the library disappeared.

Smoke burned his lungs. Fired seared his flesh. Yet, somehow, a heavy pall of despair was even more prominent as the ghost's emotions and memories joined his own.

What happened to you? The foreign memories were difficult to discern at first. Only the most heightened emotions and sensations were immediately tangible. Like water bursting out of a failed dam, the memories cascaded through Jericho's mind, impossible to catch.

A fire. Certain death. Then, against all odds, life. Undesired life. One of abject misery.

Most Vagabonds would fail here. The despair that spiked through him would have driven other Vagabonds to suicide. Raving mad, they would rip open the veins in their wrist with their own teeth, too crazed with sorrow to even remember to use a knife.

Not him. Jericho always kept in mind one of the great secrets of Vagabonding: no matter how awful a ghost's life was, if they were given a chance to live again, they'd take it. And no matter how abysmal their end was, the memories of the early years in the beginning of their lives were often quite sweet.

How lovely Lana had been when young! A real beauty. She had a perfect figure with long flowing hair. Even though she was the daughter of a poor merchant, she had been courted by many men in the city.

"An image of your mother," her father often told her. Lana liked to hear that. She never knew her mother, as she had died giving birth to Lana.

She was happy for a time. Her father was kind and she had a pleasant childhood. Later, her father was often away on business. It was a mixed blessing: she missed her father but this gave Lana the freedom to flirt. She snuck out to taverns around her neighborhood. She loved drinking and teasing the men.

She would not have been considered a good girl. Quite the opposite. More than once, one of her lovers going down the steps had passed another one coming up the steps. She used them for fun and money. Little presents were stashed all over that tiny apartment.

One day her father never returned from his business trip. Agonizing weeks slipped by as she waited to hear his heavy boots come thumping up the stairs. A letter arrived in the mail. It had no name on it, only the address. She tore it open, praying it was from her father. It wasn't. The letter was from the landlord. They were going to be evicted if they didn't pay the rent within the next few days.

Lana went through the apartment and collected some of her gifts. She sold them and paid the rent for another month. She was back to mindless waiting when another letter arrived. This one was addressed to her. Her heart fell down to her stomach. Somehow she knew what this was.

With trembling fingers, she carefully opened the letter. The letter was short and to the point. It said that her father had been aboard a ship named the *Nightingale* as it sailed across Lake Michigan. An unexpected storm had blown in and sank the ship. There were only a handful of survivors. Her father was not one of them.

Lana spent two days in blind grief. She drank her father's brandy and cried and drank some more. Her father was dead and she was alone now.

Another letter came. She was hung-over and sick when she opened it. Was it time to pay rent again already? She would be out on the street soon.

The letter wasn't from the landlord. It was from one of her admirers. The letter was sweet and sappy and full of silly things that people who are in love like to say. The young man declared his eternal love for her. He wanted to get married so they could live together. He had only a factory job now, but he didn't think that would matter as long as they had each other ...

Damn. Of all the suitors to send her a letter, it was one without a good job. His name was Lincoln Scottsdale. He was her favorite suitor, but Lana was realistic. She needed money. She had no close relatives. Her little presents might buy her one more month of rent, but that would be it. She would have to get married if she wanted to eat.

The very thought of marriage repulsed her. She was independent and rebellious. She liked to smoke and drink in public and she never gave a toss when people gossiped about her. Could she be a proper woman who stayed at home washing children and ironing clothes or whatever housewives did while her husband was out in the working and experiencing the wide world? She tried to picture herself being happy with that life.

No. That wasn't going to happen. She'd be so discontent with her narrow realm of homemaking that she'd quickly become miserable. She needed to find some other way to make money.

There wasn't an exact moment when she decided to become a whore. The process was blurred, a gray period stretching some weeks. She kept on with her immoral nocturnal dalliances. In lieu of little gifts, her lovers began to simply leave money. They knew of her dire situation concerning rent and being able to buy food for herself and they knew that she'd much prefer food and shelter to knickknacks. So they began to leave money.

A few months went by. Lana was making ends meet, but barely. She didn't feel any moral compunctious for getting paid for sex. Might as well have a job you liked, she figured. It certainly beat working in the dangerous and back-breaking factories.

Still, Lana remained realistic. She couldn't do this forever, and she wasn't making nearly enough money. She considered the problem and came up with a plan.

When night fell, she ventured into different areas of the city, speaking with various women in taverns and on the street. Nearly every night she went out, and it still took her several weeks to meet the right women.

The first two were June, a Chinese immigrant, and Rose, an Irish lass. Both had been in the country for less than a year and both were down on their luck. They were desperate and exotic and beautiful. They moved in with Lana. They bought another bed for the front room of the apartment. The front room was for working, the back room for sleeping. They slept and worked in shifts. Over the course of a year, they had enough money to purchase a small house.

When they moved into the house, Lana hired two more girls. Lana cut back on working. She spent time with only her favorite customers. This gave her the opportunity to better herself. She learned French and German and read all the fashionable literature. She visited other whorehouses and paid them to teach her sensual tricks to use on her customers.

At her peak, Lana was one of the most expensive prostitutes in Chicago. She was beautiful and cultured and highly intelligent. She moved into a large house that was almost a mansion and hired on several more girls. Lana worked less and less, taking only her favorite and highest paying customers. Among those customers was Lincoln Scottsdale, the young suitor who wanted to marry Lana while he worked in the factory. Even when it was apparent what Lana did for money, he still wanted to marry her. He ended up starting his own business and made a fortune, a substantial amount of which he lavished on her. They shared a unique romance, though Lana ultimately couldn't relinquish her independence. She loved the life she was leading and she was quite successful at it.

Then, the fire. A huge section of the city burned. The stars had been blotted out by the black smoke. Lana's house wasn't spared. Like most of the buildings in the city, it had been made of wood. The fire had raced through the building, devouring the wood hungrily. The flames moved so quickly they covered the entire first floor before anyone even knew something was wrong. The horror of it all! The screams of her girls and the smoke and the terrible heat. It hurt just to breathe. She had to crawl on the floor in order not to suffocate from the smoke. And when the fire reached her, she wished she had suffocated from the smoke. The pain had been unspeakably tremendous.

Somehow, she didn't die. When the fire was eventually put out they found her, more dead than alive, curled up in the corner.

Thankfully, most of her girls had been away when the fire hit the house. Only four girls had been in the house at the time, counting Lana. Lana was the only one who survived, though she frequently wished she hadn't.

Worse than the fire had been her life afterwards. Gone was her lovely hair. Her delicate features had literally melted; her red, flaking skin was stretched taut over a face that looked like a wax figure left too long in the sun. Only a few scraggly strands of hair ever sprouted from her scalp.

For some reason, she fought on and continued to live. She didn't know why. Each day was hell. Every look a people gave her—be it pity or revulsion—was a stab to her pride. Yet, she had struggled on. She had the house repaired and her business prospered. She didn't have clients any more, of course. Whenever she went out in public she had to cover herself completely. She dressed in all black. She had a wide black hat with veil and a black dress and gloves. She was Lana no longer. She became known as "The Madam". People who hated or feared her called her "The Crone". Lana hated that nickname, for she wasn't old at all, just hideous.

Her life was a shadow of what it had once been, but she still fought on for years before a skin infection finally killed her.

By bonding her, Jericho didn't just suddenly know all of this, he lived it. The unveiling of these memories seemed to take weeks.

In reality, it took ... what? How long had it been?

The mansion came back to him. He was still underneath the couch. His ghosts were diligently standing guard. The ghosts of the mansion weren't throwing things. In fact, the room seemed to be void of any malicious spirits. That was something.

Jericho crawled out from beneath the couch, favoring his sore ribs. They would be a painful reminder of this room for a few days more at least. He sat down on the couch. He was covered in

sweat, and started to shiver. Thirst burned his throat and he was
hungry enough to eat a rotten rat. He figured he had been raving
for at least a day, maybe two. He was sore and tired. It was going
to be a long journey back to Gheistmar.

First thing's first. He drank from his canteen and ate some
jerky. The memories of Lana were slow to fade and he waited for
them to settle, like bone dust, in his mind. Now that she was
bonded to him, he could communicate with her easily.

I am sad, she sent.

Why? Jericho sent back.

I am sad. Ghosts were sometimes like that. They were unsure
of how to express themselves or were monotonously repetitive.
This ghost was strong, though, and Jericho felt certain that he only
had to wait and she would express herself fully.

I wanted to go places with you. See things, she sent.

We will, Jericho sent. He pictured Gheistmar, trying to show
her the wondrous sights there.

No, no. She was shaking her head, he could feel. *I am sorry,
but you will not be able to leave this place alive.*

She sent her own visions. If Jericho had been standing, he
would have had to sit down. The visions were terrifying. It was a
powerful ghost, capable of not just killing living men, but ripping
them apart. He would have thought it impossible, but he could
sense her sincerity.

If she really was telling the truth, he was going to die here.

CHAPTER 23

That ghost will surely kill you, Lana told him.

So I need to leave. I need to get out of this mansion and run as fast as possible.

Lana laughed sadly.

I'm sorry, she sent. *I wish this adventure wasn't coming to an end so quickly. But no, you cannot run from here. This ghost is much stronger outside the mansion than in. Inside the house it can get confused. It is an old, old ghost and when it was alive it had never seen any building so large. The mansion doesn't make sense to it. And so it stays outside. The orchard in the back ... that is where it lives. Do you understand?*

Jericho thought on all Lana had said.

I don't like the options you're giving me, he told her. *Am I to hide in this mansion until I grow old?*

You will not grow old, she promised. *Belial will hunt you down.*

Belial. At least he had a name to attach to this ghost.

Jericho explored the mansion. He found an oil lamp and lit it and set off exploring. He didn't know what else to do. Ghosts still attacked him occasionally, but his own ghosts were able to push them away easily. With Lana bonded to him, his original five spirits were becoming stronger.

He had witnessed this before. Each time he bonded a new ghost, his old ones grew stronger. It seemed that there were a number of techniques each spirit used to manipulate the physical world. Ghosts bonded to the same person learned from one another and became more adept at performing physical acts.

With six ghosts, surely he could fend off that Belial. Right? Somehow he wasn't sure. Lana seemed so certain about Belial's power.

And so Jericho explored. The mansion was huge. It was even larger than he would have thought by looking at it from the outside. Dining rooms, kitchens, bedrooms, long halls, rooms with pianos, couches, paintings, libraries—the mansion was more a small city than a house. And it had the eerie feeling of a phantom people yet living there.

Tables were still set. Plates, glasses, silverware, carefully folded napkins—it looked like someone was about to serve dinner. Beds were made. Closets were full of clothes. Rooms would be lit with candles for no reason. The entire place had a feeling of expectation. It was as if numerous people were about to appear at any moment.

It *sounded* as if people were living there. Doors slammed, footsteps thudded across the floor, and random voices would fill the air. Even Jericho was disconcerted; this level of paranormal activity was unprecedented.

Jericho came to a staircase and started up it. It was wide enough for five people to walk abreast. Thick red carpet covered the wood, muffling his footsteps. Paintings of distinguished-looking people lined the wall.

He felt like he was being watched. Well, of course he was, he thought. Ghosts were crammed into every crack and cubby of this place. He was always being watched. Yet, this was somehow different. It felt more dangerous to him, though he couldn't say why. There was nothing to do about it, however. He just kept

walking up the stairs, the sphere of light from the oil lamp
ascending like a golden bubble in black water.

The paintings were watching him! Jericho caught a tic of
movement in his peripheral vision and saw one of the paintings
move! It was a portrait of a middle-aged man with a beard.
Before—Jericho was certain—the man had been smiling. Now his
eyes were narrowed and his lips bent into a frown. Again, the
sense of impending danger assailed Jericho.

He kept walking. All of the paintings were scowling at him.
He actually saw the transformation on one painting. With Jericho
watching, a portrait of a woman went from tight-lipped smile to a
feral snarl. How was this happening? Jericho leaned close. There
was a ghost anchored inside the painting, he could feel that. He
touched his fingers to the woman's eye. Parts of it stuck to his
skin and he rolled them in his fingers.

Silver filings. Painted silver filings that the ghost could move
as it willed.

Who could have done this? Anchoring a ghost and teaching
it to move silver filings to change the painting ... The level of
spiritual manipulation was far beyond Jericho or anyone he knew.

Run! Lana screamed in his mind. *He's here!*

Downstairs a door slammed so hard it was a wonder it stayed
on its hinges. The temperature plummeted. Jericho's breath left
his mouth in curling wisps of white.

Belial was coming.

Jericho put out the oil lamp and sprinted up the stairs. At the
top was a waist-high railing. He looked over the railing at the
floor down below. He couldn't see anything through the gloom,
but he felt a strong presence down there.

He ran into the nearest room and closed the door. He pressed
his back against the wall. He slid down it until his knees were
against his chest, trying to make himself as small as possible.
Maybe it would help him hide from Belial.

Probably not.

He hid there, scarcely breathing. The room he was hiding in
was a bedroom. There was enough starlight coming in through

the window for him to discern the shape of a bed in the corner and a wardrobe stationed along the wall. On either side of the window were curtains. Long, white, and made of a thin, translucent fabric, the curtains looked like ghosts themselves. They seemed to glow in the starlight.

Something crashed downstairs. It sounded like a table had been flipped over. Jericho exhaled softly. At least Belial hadn't come up the stairs.

I don't think you can hide, Lana sent. *You leave a large path in the ether. And the ghosts in the paintings... they will tell on you.*

Jericho didn't reply. He had nothing to say, no plan of action. He could only wait and see what—

Footsteps! Sudden and rapid, heavy footsteps pounded a staccato on the stairs. It grew louder as it came up the stairs, moving at a pace far too quick for a human. Thump-thump-thump-thump; they stopped outside the bedroom door. The presence of Belial was so ... heavy. It felt like the floor bowed with his weight.

Wood creaked and the door began to bend as Belial pushed on it. Jericho scooted away. He expected the door to shatter open. Instead, the hinges gave way with a pop that sounded like an arm being ripped out of its socket and the door fell open.

He gathered his ghosts and leapt to his feet and charged. He wasn't going to wait for this spirit to attack him.

In the dark, Belial was a massive shadow, somehow blacker than the darkness around him. Jericho had a quick glimpse of long tangled hair and then they collided.

It was like running into a wall of ice.

Belial was as cold as the artic sea and unmovable as a boulder. Jericho staggered backward, reeling from the impact. Belial grabbed his arm and flung him out the doorway. Jericho crashed through the railing and plummeted into the darkness.

With Leo slowing time, Jericho was able to right himself and use his ghosts to slow his descent before he hit the floor below. He still had a great deal of momentum, though, and he stumbled and crashed through a table and knocked over two chairs before collapsing in a heap.

Belial was stronger than he had imagined. No, not just stronger. Skilled. Jericho's ghosts had missed him completely. Like a talented boxer slipping punches, Belial had somehow dodged them and reached through to Jericho himself.

Run! Lana screamed in his head. *Run, damn you! And close doors behind you. The inside of houses confuses him.*

With blazing pain igniting through him, he pushed himself to his feet. His side ached where the table had hit him earlier. The last thing he wanted to do was to move. Gritting his teeth, he forced himself to run.

Jericho dashed down a hall and through a kitchen and through a library. He closed each door he encountered. He didn't try to be quiet, he just slammed them shut and kept running.

His flight took him to an older section of the mansion that was in disrepair. The wood was so rotten that the red carpet floor sagged and the walls curved. With his every step, the walls bent in and out as his weight shifted. It was if the building itself was breathing. With the red carpet and breathing walls he felt like he was in the throat of some giant beast.

The hall led to a huge wooden door. Instead of a doorknob, it had a heavy iron ring as a handle. Jericho heaved it open and pulled it shut behind him. He turned and ran but only made it two steps before he staggered to halt.

Keep going! Lana yelled in his head. She sent an image of Belial ripping off his arms.

Yet for a moment Jericho could only stare. He was in a blacksmith's shop. There were barrels for cooling water, a forge, anvils, and metal. A lot of metal. Steel, iron, copper, and, yes, silver. Spools of silver wire lay beside the forge. The spools were large, coming up past his knee. Farther down was a table laden with silver bars. Another table had a small pile of gold bars. There were a lot of possibilities here. Maybe he could create something that would stop Belial.

A door banged open. Belial was coming down the hall.

Go! Lana screeched.

Jericho went. Beyond the blacksmith area was an empty room that hadn't been used for some time. It was a dead end. There was a closet door, but no way out of the room. A single wooden chair in the corner was the only furniture. Two windows opened to the backyard. The orchard trees looked like hunched giants in the moonlight. If Lana was right about Belial being stronger outside ... well, Jericho would go out one of the windows as a last resort.

Belial was becoming confused. Jericho could feel the ghost's presence weakening. He decided to hide in the closet.

He pulled open the door. It wasn't a closet at all, but a narrow hall. He closed the door and ran down the hall. It led to a kitchen.

A servant's personal kitchen, he guessed. It was small and tight. He couldn't picture more than one person cooking in there.

Hide, Lana hissed.

The kitchen had one door. The door had a window set in it and it clearly led to the outside.

Hide where? He looked down at the cupboard, then opened it. A few pots were inside. He pushed those aside and crouched down and curled up in the cupboard. He pulled the door shut behind him. And waited.

Lana didn't speak. Neither did any of his other ghosts. There was none of the typical muttering amongst themselves. It was as if they were staying completely still and trying to be absolutely silent.

The kitchen door rattled in its frame as Belial tried to get in. Jericho had seen ghosts do that before: some of them just never quite understood that they could pass through physical objects.

Belial shook the door again, harder. Then, nothing. Silence fell throughout the room like dew. Jericho began to hope that the ghost was gone ...

The temperature dropped. Within the span of a few heartbeats it went from warm to just above freezing.

The floor boards creaked as something heavy moved on them. Belial had such a strong physical presence! He was coming closer to the cupboard. As the slow, pressing steps approached, Jericho coiled his legs beneath him, ready to spring.

Just outside the cupboard, the footsteps stopped ... and moved away. The door to the outside rattled. Moments later, the room grew warm again.

He's gone, Lana sent. *He couldn't resist going outside.*

Jericho said nothing. He was going to wait in the cupboard until he was sure Belial was good and gone.

Belial's in the backyard orchard, Lana told him. *He's confused and weakened from running through the mansion. Maybe —just maybe —if you hurry and go through the front of the mansion and run... maybe he won't catch you. This is your only chance. This won't happen again.*

Jericho opened the cupboard door and stepped out. He stood.

No, he sent back. *I'm not running anymore.*

Running from the Brutes, then the Wretched *and* the Brutes. And now running from some ghost named "Belial". It seemed like that was all Jericho had been doing: running.

It stopped here.

He had lost so much. Claire was ... who knows where. The life he had known was no more. And Cinder, the man who had caused all of this, was still very much alive and well. The very thought sent fire through Jericho's veins.

No more running. No more hiding. It stopped here.

With Lana screaming in his mind, he strode back into the heart of the mansion.

He had work to do.

CHAPTER 24

When Orion, Jericho's hunter ghost, was alive, he had gone on a
night fishing trip with his friends. He had a lovely wife, a young
daughter, and a son who would become a man in a few years.
Life was good: their village hadn't been raided in years and Orion
made a decent living hunting and selling the pelts and meat at a
nearby town. He was an expert shot with the bow. He hadn't lost
the village's Fall Harvest bow contest in three years.

They didn't catch anything at the lake. Of course, it would
have helped if they had put their lines in the water; going to the
lake was more of an excuse to get away from the stifling village
and drink some wine and share stories. Orion enjoyed these little
trips. The lake was small and rarely had any waves. At night, its
smooth surface reflected the stars, making Orion feel like he was
an eagle soaring over the thousand campfires of an army.

The stars were bright that night. There were no clouds.
When Orion and his friends decided to walk back to the village,
they didn't need to light a torch. It was a short walk, anyway.
One their feet knew from memory. The dirt path wound through
the woods like pale yarn.

They began to sing. They were young and it was a warm,

mid-summer night and the wine elevated their already happy mood.

The path turned a corner and they came face to face with a mountain lion. Their singing was strangled to silence. The mountain lion's eyes flashed an eerie green as it regarded them. Orion was frozen in fear. They all were. They didn't know what to do. Mountain lions were not creatures humans typically saw. Certainly not up close, unless they were about to become dinner.

The cat continued to stare at them. Finally, it rose up smoothly and slipped into the woods like a liquid shadow.

Orion's friends waited a beat and then gasped in relief. They started laughing and smacking each other on the back. What an adventure! They couldn't wait to tell the others back at the village.

Orion didn't say anything. He wasn't laughing because he had seen the crumpled form that the mountain lion had been hunched over. They had encountered the cat because it had been feeding and was reluctant to abandon its kill.

Somehow, Orion knew. He couldn't say how or why, but he did.

He stumbled forward to the crumpled form. It was his son.

His knees were unstrung and he collapsed on the ground. He shook his son. No response. The boy was dead. The blood was warm and tacky on Orion's hands.

Orion didn't remember the rest of the trip back to the village. Only vaguely did he recall telling his wife that their son was dead and setting the mangled body at her feet. Her sobbing as she clutched at him, as she told him that their son had gone to the lake to tell Orion the daughter had a fever—those were memories clouded with emotion.

He did remember, vividly, the cowbells he borrowed from a farmer. The bells were poorly made and had a flat, ugly sound. Orion tied the bells to his son's body and went back out into the night. He set the body beside the path where they had found it. The mountain lion would come back for its meal, Orion knew. And so he hid nearby behind a log with his bow and arrow and waited.

Orion was choked with rage and sorrow and he had no sense of time. Hours might have passed or perhaps only minutes before the bells began to clang. Orion rose up from his hiding spot and loosed an arrow at the glowing green eyes. An other-worldly howl pierced the air as the arrow struck home. The mountain lion dissolved into the dark woods and Orion nocked another arrow and followed.

Orion was an expert hunter, but even he couldn't have tracked a mountain lion at night. Fortunately, it was bleeding. Blood, black in the starlight, stained the leaves on the forest floor.

It was stupid, hunting a wounded predator. He had no idea how badly the mountain lion was hurt. It might be a scratch on its leg for all he knew. Yet pride goaded him on. The beast had taken his son's life and must be made to pay the price.

He should have been traveling to the town for medicine. His daughter was sick and the town was several hours away. A part of Orion knew this. A larger part of him needed to hunt this lion. He wasn't a doctor and had never claimed to be. He was a hunter. That was his entire identity. What good was he if he couldn't kill the beast that had killed his son?

Blood. The scent was sharp and tangy and strong. The cat was much closer than he had thought. He pulled back the string of his bow and spun to face the direction of the wind. A shadow detached itself from the forest and flew through the air at him with the speed of an arrow. It loomed like a mountain in front of him, blocking out his vision and Orion was certain his fate was sealed, certain that the very teeth that had torn into his son's neck were about to tear into his own.

His hands seemed to move of their own accord. Without any help from his fear-clogged brain, they loosed an arrow into the shadow. The mountain lion slammed into Orion and drove him to the ground. He put his arm back to break his fall and felt the bone snap with the impact. In pain and terror Orion cried out ... and realized he was still alive. His throat was intact. The cat wasn't tearing him to shreds. Instead, it lay motionless on top of him, a dead weight.

With his good arm, Orion pushed and rolled the mountain lion off of him. His second arrow had struck the cat through the heart, killing it.

What a shot! Triumph burst within his breast. He shouted. His voice was raw and bestial, his shout the celebration of a victory of one animal over another. It reverberated through the woods and Orion wondered if perhaps they heard it even in the village.

The village. Where his daughter lay sick. Orion still had a job to do.

He slung his bow over his shoulder. His broken arm hung at his side and throbbed with pain. It was going to be a long walk to the town. He gritted his teeth. He would endure. He had killed the mountain lion and now he would get the medicine for his daughter.

And I did, Orion had told Jericho.

There was more to the story, but the hunt was what interested Jericho now. He focused on Orion's hunting skills, reviewing them and searching for anything that would help him.

For Jericho was a hunter. And like Orion, he was hunting a dangerous predator.

No, no, no, Lana wailed. *You can't do this. You'll surely die!*

Jericho ignored her. Maybe she was right, but it didn't matter. No more running. What good was he if he couldn't handle a single ghost? Now Jericho was the hunter. His prey: Belial.

In one of the numerous kitchens in the mansion, Jericho found a meat cleaver. He picked it up, testing its weight. It was heavy enough. He rubbed his finger across the blade; the edge was still sharp. Perfect.

With the cleaver in hand, he went to the front of the mansion. He was looking for the front door, but couldn't find it. The place was like a maze! He could have asked Lana to guide him, but he kept her entirely focused on monitoring to location of Belial. So instead of using the front door, he opened a window on the ground floor. Outside, the sun was shining bright and the grass and the leaves on the trees practically glowed green. It looked like a perfect day for a picnic. Aside, that is, from the ruins of the servants' quarters and the dead bodies scattered everywhere and the graveyard that somehow still managed to maintain its fog even in sunlight.

Where is Belial now? he asked Lana.

Out back near the orchard, she sent. *But he will come after you the second you step out of the mansion.*

Jericho considered his options. The nearest corpse was about fifty feet away. How fast could Belial move? Was this even necessary? He stared at the corpse. It was a Brute who had been hacked in the stomach. Jericho guessed the man had run from the battle after getting chopped, both of his hands tight against his belly to keep his entrails in. Then, he had fallen. The man had managed to crawl several yards after that. Each painful inch was marked by his own guts, a macabre tape measure registering his progress. He had died with one arm outstretched, fingers dug into the earth to pull himself along one more desperate inch.

A fifty foot sprint. Jericho could do that before Belial got to him. Hopefully.

He swung one leg over the window sill and then the other. He dropped down to the ground and ran towards the corpse, using his ghosts to push him along so that he covered the distance in only a few momentous strides.

He's coming after you! Lana screamed. *Belial knows where you are!*

Jericho grasped the corpse's wrist and pulled the arm tight and chopped down with the cleaver. He chopped right above the elbow, hoping to sever the limb with a single blow. He would have, too, if the arm had been on a chopping block. The soft ground made for a poor cutting surface, however, and he had to strike several more times with the cleaver to break through the bone and finally cut through all of the muscle. He pulled the forearm away from the rest of the corpse. A band of skin still connected the two, and it stretched and stretched like elastic, refusing to break until he had to waste yet more time using the cleaver to slice through the skin. Finally the forearm was completely severed from the corpse and he took off running back toward the mansion, holding the arm in his hand.

The day was quiet and still, yet small trees near the side of the mansion swayed and bent as if caught in a violent wind. Other trees, ones closer to him, began to do the same thing.

Belial was coming. It was like watching an approaching tornado. The ghost tore leaves and branches from the thrashing trees and scattered a whirlwind of debris as it charged toward him.

A few tremendous strides later, Jericho reached the mansion and dove through the open window head first. He landed hard on the floor, bouncing his head against the carpet. No time for pain now. He pushed himself back to his feet and reached back and slammed the window shut and ran deeper into the mansion, slamming each and every door behind him.

He ran through living rooms and kitchens and libraries. He passed solemn paintings and gilded mirrors and antique furniture. He slammed a heavy, eight-paneled door behind him and stopped; the room he was in didn't have another way out. It was a bedroom. There was a window, but the room was kept dark by heavy curtains. A fireplace was in the corner, as black and cold as the eye socket in the skull of a long dead dragon. Silence hung in the air, the outside world was muted and distant. Jericho stared at the door, half expecting Belial to burst through it.

Where is Belial? Jericho asked Lana.

Outside. I think he respects you a little, so he might wait until nightfall to come into the mansion. That way he'll be at his full strength.

Good. At least I have a few hours to prepare.

Lana laughed.

Enjoy those few hours, she sent. *Savor them the way you'd savor the last few bites of a delicious meal.*

I know you expect Belial to rip me apart, Jericho sent. He glanced down at the arm he held. It was warm from the sun, making it feel as though it had been torn from a living man. *I look forward to proving you wrong.*

The forge had been used by a highly skilled blacksmith. The weapons and armor that hung on the walls were masterfully made. Jericho set his severed arm on top of a barrel as he looked over the collection.

Do you know anything about Belial? Jericho asked Lana. *Anything about when he was alive?*

Not much, she sent. *He was a warrior. A soldier of some sort.*

Which of these weapons do you think he used when he was alive? What would be most familiar to him?

I don't know, Jericho. She sounded tired. Exasperated. *I've spent most of my time here trying to stay away from him. He frightens me.*

A long pause. Jericho waited, hoping she'd continue. Hoping she'd have something to say that could possibly help him.

Landschette, Lana finally sent. *I've heard other ghosts—old ghosts—refer to Belial as that. I don't know what that means.*

Jericho nodded grimly. He knew that word. He took a massive broadsword off the wall. It was a two-handed broadsword with a wavy blade. It was heavy, made for smashing through the armor of knights or killing the horses of a charging cavalry.

It means, Jericho sent. *That he'll like this sword just fine.*

The sword had a stout wooden hilt wrapped in leather. He cut away the leather and then laid the hilt across an anvil. He used a heavy hammer to smash the hilt, cracking the wood. He pulled the wood apart and tossed the pieces away. With the tang of the sword exposed, he could now make a new hilt.

Using the cleaver, Jericho butchered the arm. He hacked off the hand and cut away the skin and muscle. There are two bones in the human forearm, and he tore off the smaller one. He measured the thicker bone, comparing it to the tang of the sword, then chopped through the bone near the center. The bone was flexible and fibrous and he had to saw back and forth with the cleaver before the blade cut all the way through, leaving him with two halves.

He took the larger half and cut down its center vertically. He cut the bone only partially, so that if it were spread out it would make the figure of a "Y". He jammed the bone up onto the tang of the sword, driving the tang as deep in as he could.

Jericho picked up a spool of silver wire and began wrapping it around the bone. He started at the top and worked his way down, wrapping in a downward spiral. When he reached the bottom of the bone, he started wrapping the wire upwards, cris-crossing the first spirals. He snipped the wire when he reached the top of the bone again. The two ends of the wire were next to each other and the spring of the metal pushed them tightly together.

A closed circuit.

Jericho found a small chip of wood and tied a long thread around it. He squeezed the wood between the ends of the wire.

Now the circuit was open.

He admired the sword's new hilt. It was far from his best work, but the day was growing short and he didn't have much time.

Rope. He wanted rope. The forge contained a wide variety of metals and textiles and tools, yet he couldn't find any rope. He left the sword on the barrel and went farther into the mansion to look for some.

Even with his own ghosts surrounding him, the spirits of the house still heckled Jericho. They tossed books and other small objects at him. Doors slammed in his face. He had a glass of water thrown on him.

Can't you stop them from doing all this? Jericho sent Lana.

They hold allegiance to Belial, not me, she sent. *Why? Did that water hurt?*

You think this is funny, don't you?

She didn't reply, and she really didn't need to. Jericho could feel her amusement through the bond.

It was infuriating to him. All these little ghosts—these little pests—were wasting his time. The mansion was dimming as evening approached. Shadows sprouted and stretched along the floor and climbed the walls. And still, no rope.

He decided to use bed sheets. Jericho stripped four beds of their linen and tied the sheets together. He tested each knot. They seemed sturdy enough to hold his weight. All right. Now he just had to plan his route.

He needed Belial to be disoriented. Lana had said that doors confused him. Jericho charted a course passing through as many doorways as possible. He planned to run through them, closing each door as he passed.

Because the mansion was so huge and confusing, Jericho marked his path by lighting the candles and oil lamps that lined each hallway. With night fast approaching, it seemed to take forever. He had to walk up to each lamp or candle, remove the glass cover, strike a match, then touch the match to the wick until the flame struggled to life, dancing frantically upon the wick until Jericho replaced the glass cover and the flame settled itself comfortably and became as motionless as an amber jewel.

On a whim, he decided to try to use his ghosts to light one of the wicks. One of the skills his ghosts had mastered was using moisture and cold to snuff out flame. But Jericho wondered: Could his ghosts use their electrical energy to heat the wick hot enough to catch aflame? He had Orion—arguably his strongest ghost as far as electricity was concerned—focus his energy into a tiny, pin-prick sized spot on the wick of an oil lamp. It took perhaps a full minute before the wick sparked and gave birth to a flame. Jericho nodded with satisfaction.

He tried it on a candle. Orion needed Leo's help to light the candle; the candle was more difficult since its wick wasn't soaked in oil, and it took nearly twice as long.

So, yes, he could use his ghosts to light the lamps and candles, but it took longer than simply using matches. More importantly, it took a significant amount of energy from them and he needed his ghosts to be fully rested before the encounter with Belial.

Jericho lit the remainder of the wicks by hand. He retrieved the special sword he had made and rammed it into the floor of a downstairs bedroom. He took a large mirror off a wall and set it on the floor. He used a chair to hold the mirror upright and faced toward the window. He found another large mirror and went to the front staircase where he had encountered Belial earlier. The mirror was big enough to span the entire width of the staircase. Perfect. He propped the mirror up against the wall. The mirror was heavy, but Soot was able to slide it along the carpet. Jericho had Soot slide the mirror a couple of times, practicing the movement so that it could be executed smoothly under pressure. By the time he was done with everything, the evening had faded to night. Jericho fortified himself mentally and began walking up and down the staircase.

Ghosts liked repetition. They sought order in their chaotic world and would often repeat their actions. Jericho figured the best way to lure Belial would be to do exactly what had brought the ghost after him before. And so he had gone to the stairs.

The paintings glared at him. Without a lamp it was too dark to see much, but the ghosts anchored to these paintings made them glow with a cool, pale light. The faces twisted into expressions of hate and anger as Jericho walked up the stairs past them. Before, Lana had said that these paintings would tell on him. Jericho was counting on it. He didn't know how they did it. Maybe they sent a messenger ghost to Belial. Or perhaps their consciousness was bonded somehow. He didn't know and it didn't matter. As long as Belial got the message that Jericho was here, it didn't matter.

The waiting was tense. His stomach twisted in knots as he marched up and down the stairs. The paintings seemed to grow angrier each time he went by them. Their glaring eyes followed him as he passed by.

One painting caught Jericho's eye. It was a woman holding a parasol over her shoulder. She wore a broad-rimmed hat and a long blue dress. Her eyes followed Jericho just the same as the other paintings and she certainly didn't look happy to see him, yet something was different about her. Something troubling. But what? The background of the painting seemed innocuous. It was a scene of a pleasant looking park. A rolling grassy hill sloped down to a river.

Jericho blinked as he looked closer at the river. The river water had been created using unpainted silver filings. Each filing had been painstakingly oriented to illustrate the flow of the river water. Small whirlpools spun near the shore and white water frilled the edges of rocks. The metal glowed with ghostly energy and the water appeared to be actually moving. It beautiful. A true masterpiece done by someone whose talents far exceeded even Jericho's. Yet none of that was what bothered him. He was puzzling on it some more when Lana realized what was wrong.

That bitch is trying not to smile, she said.

Lana was right. The woman in the painting had her lips pressed tightly together. She had the look of someone who knew a secret joke and was trying not to laugh about it.

Jericho didn't doubt that the joke was on him. What had happened? What had the ghosts of the house done? The hallway upstairs still glowed with the light of the candles and lamps he had lit, so that was fine. The mirror still sat near the top of the stairs, so that was fine too. Had the ghosts fooled with something else? Jericho wanted to check the rest of his route, but he never got a chance.

As one, the entire wall of paintings slid their eyes to the right, looking toward the bottom of the stairs. The temperature plummeted. The front door banged open and by then Jericho was already running up the stairs. He zipped past the top of the stairs and had Soot slide the mirror in place behind him. The mirror blocked the stairway, its reflective surface facing the stairs.

The mirror idea was a gamble. If Belial was confused by the inside of large buildings, Jericho hoped that he would be especially confused by a mirror projecting two staircases meeting in a 'V'. It might slow Belial and weaken him. Or he could push past it as easily as moving through a cobweb.

A mighty roar filled the mansion. There were words to it, yet it didn't sound even remotely human. It was more like an icy wind blasting across a barren tundra. An icy wind that preyed on wounded soldiers laying on the fields after a battle, the wind biting them and chewing away at their body heat until they finally shuddered and grew still. The roar didn't sound human, but it conveyed a very human emotion: unfettered fury. The mirror had upset Belial.

The sound chilled Jericho. It sapped his courage and made him wonder if he had been completely stupid to even try something like this. He kept running because that was the only thing he could do. He ran and then slowed to a stop and looked around in stunned surprise.

He realized what the woman in the painting had been smiling about. He realized what the ghosts of the house had done. The joke was indeed on Jericho, and it had probably damned him as surely as a knife through the heart.

CHAPTER 25

Those idiotic pests. Those imbecilic ethereal wisps of nothing. Those stupid little ghosts had likely killed Jericho with their trifling.

They hadn't extinguished his lamps. Jericho would have noticed the hallway going dark. Instead, the ghosts had lit every damn lamp upstairs. Jericho's marked route was gone, drowned out in an amber ocean of light.

The mirror at the top of the stairs shattered as Belial burst through it. Jericho ran, desperately trying to recall the route he had set. He went through a bedroom, a waiting room, cut over through another bedroom, and into another hall, all the while slamming each door behind him. Jericho was fairly certain he had followed his route correctly. He needed to pick the right door this time, too, though. It was quite important.

He counted the doors down the hall. Had it been the fifth door or the sixth?

A tremendous crash and splintering of wood shook the mansion as Belial tore through the door in the room behind Jericho, and he made a mad dash for the fifth door. He opened the door, hoping to see the bed sheets tied together like a rope and attached to the bed to form an escape out the second story window.

But there were no bed sheets. No escape. He had chosen the wrong room.

The dark form of Belial filled the hallway and Jericho slammed the door. He didn't have the option of running to the other room.

If Jericho had all of his ghosts with him, he could have easily jumped out the window. They would have been able to slow his fall enough for him to land safely. But Jericho had only Soot and Lana. The rest of his ghosts were busy, waiting to spring the trap.

The door to the room rattled violently in its frame as Belial fought to get into the room. Jericho had to take a chance. He opened the window. It was a long way down. Too far to simply fall. He'd shatter his ankles or break a leg for sure.

To his left, the rope of bed sheets dangled from the next window over. They fluttered softly in the moonlight, just close enough to mock him.

The door to the room groaned and bent inward. Its hinges popped off and Belial flooded into the room, a murderous deluge of black hate.

Acting more on instinct than thought, Jericho swung his legs over the window sill and leapt out. He had Soot grab the bed sheet rope and yank it over toward him. Jericho caught the sheets mid-fall. The silky fabric hissed against his palms as he slid down it and his momentum swung him like a wild pendulum. Jericho bounced off the side of the mansion once before he managed to spin himself around to push off the mansion with his feet. He rappelled the rest of the way down like a mountain climber, swinging in through the open window on the first floor.

Belial caught him mid-air, grabbing Jericho from behind.

Together they went through the open window and crashed through the mirror Jericho had set up earlier. Shards of the mirror cut into Jericho's skin as he skidded along the floor. He crawled next to the sword with the bone hilt. All of his other ghosts were circulating through the silver circuit, making the wire glow a bright blue-white.

Icy talons as tough as steel sunk into the flesh of Jericho's back.

No! Lana cried out as Belial prepared to rip Jericho apart.

Now! Jericho commanded his ghosts. As one, they left the silver hilt. All that ghostly energy leaving at once created an ethereal power vacuum. The bone hilt, the silver wire, and the ethereal power vacuum was too much for Belial to resist in his weakened state. His energy was pulled into the open circuit of the silver wire. He could have surged through it and been free again in less than a second, but Jericho yanked the thread tied to the wood chip that separated the ends of the wire. By pulling out the wood chip, the ends of the wire sprung together, closing the circuit and trapping Belial.

The silver wire flared brightly with energy. Its glow was reflected in the myriad of mirror shards scattered through the room, making it look as though the entire floor was on fire. The sword trembled as Belial struggled to get free.

Jericho stood up and edged toward the door.

Run now, Lana told him. *He might not be trapped for long. Go!*

Belial would get free. It was just a matter of time. If he put enough energy into the wire he'd eventually either melt the wire or burn the bone to a crisp. The weapon shook as Belial fought against his confines, and for a second Jericho was sure the ghost would break free right then. But he didn't, and the sword shook less and less as Belial tired himself out.

"Stop, you stupid spirit!" Jericho suddenly yelled.

The sword didn't stop shaking. If anything, it shook harder.

What are you doing? Lana asked in a hissed whisper. She sounded very afraid.

You shall die, you little worm! Belial cried out in Jericho's head. Jericho was shocked to be able to hear the ghost so easily. Belial's power was like nothing he had ever witnessed. *This little trick is a mere inconvenience,* Belial went on. *I am the lord of this manor. I command every spirit here. You might have trapped me for a time, but I need only watch as my legions rip you to shreds.*

Ghosts poured into the room. They kept coming. Like in the library when Jericho first entered the mansion, the air was so thick with spirits it looked as if he were underwater. There were even more spirits than before. If the library group had been a mob, this was an army. Several of the ghosts were as strong as Orion.

Jericho's own ghosts howled and bristled with anger. They flared their energy, daring the first ghost to attack.

Don't be stupid, Jericho sent to Belial.

Stupid? They are going to fight past your ghosts and tear your muscle from your bone. They are going to unwind your flesh while I watch. Tell me, how am I the one who is being stupid?

Because, Jericho sent. *They won't get to me quickly. My ghosts have worked together for a long time. Even after you minions attack, I will still be breathing for a while. And with each of those breaths, I will be destroying that which you hold most dear. I will break the oil lamps in the halls and spread fire all throughout this mansion. By the time you break free of that sword, you will be lord of nothing but a heap of ashes.*

Belial was silent. Jericho pressed on.

It doesn't have to be that way, Jericho sent. *I don't want to burn it down. This mansion and its spirits fascinate me. I want to study it and learn all I can. I want to protect it and preserve it from harm.*

What are you suggesting? Belial sounded wary. He seemed to have tapered his anger, as the sword was no longer shaking. His ghosts, though, were still pressing into the room. They were gliding ever closer, and Jericho was certain that one would attack at any moment.

The Brutes are gone. Jericho sent. *No one is ever coming back here. The mansion will eventually fall apart and you will fade way. Join me. Let me bond you. I am a worthy and powerful Vagabond. Along with me, you will see the world and experience life. Most importantly, you will matter.*

Lana couldn't possess a fellow ghost, but she could be damn persuasive. She joined in with her own speech. Jericho was too busy to be able to make it out, but he knew it was along the same lines as what he was saying.

Jericho sent the last thought again and again. *You will matter.* It was the same thing he had told Lana. Belial could either haunt an abandoned mansion or once again be able to affect the living world.

You have made a soul weapon, Belial sent. *That is impressive. You are silly and impetuous, but I doubt I will find a Vagabond more worthy. Not now. Not after the Great Death. And so I accept your offer, Jericho Toller.*

Jericho nodded. He was pleased, though worried. The ghost might simply be lying. There was only one way to find out.

Jericho used his dagger to pry apart the metal spiral, freeing the spirit from the sword. Without an instant's pause Belial bonded to him, sending Jericho into the deepest, most terrifying rave of his life.

CHAPTER 26

Lilith's cell was dark, cramped, and flooded with three feet of
dirty water. There was a big slab of stone in one corner that
served as a bed. It was hard and uncomfortable but it kept her out
of the water. She had a coarse blanket that was soaking wet and
smelled musty. Bars lined the open side of the cell while the other
walls were moss-covered stone. The lock on her door was
surrounded by metal and out of her reach. But not, she thought to
herself, out of the reach of her ghosts.

Try to pick the lock, she sent to Abigail.

I can't, Abigail sent back an instant later.

What do you mean? Did you even try?

I can't touch it at all. There was a long pause. Lilith could feel
Abigail's frustration at not having the proper words to describe
what was wrong. *The lock is like Jericho's special arrows.*

Lilith understood. This was not good news. They must have
put a magnet on her lock so her spirits couldn't pick it. She looked
through the bars at the cell door across the hall. On that lock was
the dark rectangular shape of a magnet sticking onto the lock.
They were prepared for Lilith and all her little tricks, it seemed.

Lilith slumped back on her rock and waited. Outside of her cell was a raised stone walkway. The walkway was raised just enough to be out of the water. Lilith kept her eyes on the walkway. At some point guards would come, she assumed. She hoped to get from answers from them.

Some hours later, the guards did come. There were three of them. Two had crossbows and the third pushed along a cart laden with wooden bowls filled with food. All three of the guards wore the uniform of the Irons.

When they came to her cell, one of the Irons knelt down and set a bowl in the water and nudged it so it came floating toward Lilith. The bowl contained some kind of soup with a hunk of bread stuck in it. The food looked disgusting, but Lilith was hungry enough to eat just about anything. She stepped down into the water and reached for the bowl. Before she touched it there was a splash and the bowl of food disappeared below the surface.

Lilith froze in shock. What the hell was in the water? She had a brief vision of an angry, starving woman. Lilith scrambled back up on the slab as the guards laughed. An enraged spirit like that living in the water might be able to physically attack her before her own ghosts could protect her.

She spent the next few hours staring into the water, watching the surface ripple as the ghost wormed through the murky liquid. She hated the malicious spirit for yanking her food into the water.

Finally, Lilith's eyelids grew heavy. Despite being uncomfortable and scared, she fell asleep.

Lilith was jolted awake as something grabbed her. She was yanked off her stone slab and pulled underwater. Strong arms wrapped around her and held her beneath the surface. The water was too murky to see anything, and even though the surface was close, it looked like a dim green light. The ghost in the water had her! Lilith clawed at the arms futilely. They felt like a human's arms, except icy cold. Lilith twisted wildly. If she could only stand up, she could breathe. To be drowning in only a few feet of water was maddening.

Finally Lilith's own ghosts pushed the woman spirit away. Lilith stood up. She coughed out a stream of dirty water. She gasped for air and coughed until her eyes teared. She climbed up on her slab and stood with her fists balled in rage.

"Damn it!" she screamed. "Damn all of this!" The water played hell with her ghosts' electricity and sparks burst from her hair and the metal on her dress and rained down like silver filings. After being choked unconscious and captured by Cull, her life had become one long nightmare. She had awoken to find herself wrapped in chains and bouncing on the knight's shoulder as he went back to Gheistmar. Cull had carried her through the city like that: on his shoulder like a sack of grain. It had been humiliating as people stood aside and gawked. Then she had been thrown in this miserable dungeon without any explanation.

"Why?" she screamed. "Why am I here?"

No one answered her.

Lilith wondered where her whip was. They had taken it from her, of course. But what had they done with it? Put it in some storage closet? Tossed it in the moat? If she ever got out of here, she wanted it back.

"And I will get out of here," she said aloud. To her surprise, someone spoke.

"Yes, you're going to get out." It was a woman's voice. It sounded familiar. Lilith wasn't sure where it was coming from. Then she saw the shadows stir in the cell across from her. She was startled. She hadn't even known that there was someone in that cell.

"Thera, is that you?" Lilith asked. "Why are you in here?"

"I don't have the slightest idea," Thera said. "They kicked down our door and brought us here."

"Flint is here, too?"

Thera was quiet for a moment.

"He was," she said. "As far as I know, he still is. They've let a lot of people out, but I don't think he was one."

Hope welled within Lilith.

"They're letting people out? That's good."

"No," Thera said. "It's not. The only reason they let us out of here is so they can kill us."

"That makes no sense," Lilith said. "Why would they keep us alive just to kill us?"

"I don't think you want to know."

At first Lilith thought Thera had become a shard. She thought that the woman's mind was mostly gone and she was living the life of someone long dead. But they kept talking as the days went by and Lilith realized that Thera was still sane after all. Which wasn't exactly a good thing, because what she was saying was anything but good news.

None of the prisoners had been there very long. Three months was the longest. Apparently the guards emptied the dungeons once every few months. One by one, they removed the prisoners from their cells and took them off to be executed.

Lilith was quiet for a long time after she heard this.

"Why?" she finally asked. "What did you do? What did any of us do to earn a death sentence?"

Thera didn't answer for a while. When she did, it sounded like she was about to cry.

"They asked me about you," Thera said. "They asked me when I had last spoken to you and what we had talked about and if I had spoken to anyone else after that. It made no sense. It was like they thought you might have told me something you shouldn't have."

"I'm sorry ..." Lilith said. "I have no idea what they think I know."

"Well it's got them all worked up, that's for sure. Enough for them to storm into our home and throw us in some God-forsaken dungeon." Thera was quiet for a moment. "I'm so scared ..." she said. She sounded nothing like the confident person Lilith had met at the coven house.

"It is terrifying," Lilith said. "Not knowing when they're going to come and grab us."

"No," Thera said. "We know the exact day that's going to happen."

Weeks passed in unrelenting monotony. Twice a day, guards brought food and Lilith would wade through the water and up to the bars to they could hand it to her. She was sure she was going to need every bit of strength. She was hungry and weak and couldn't let the ghost in the water ruin another meal.

She tried to communicate with the ghost in the water. The ghost woman, though, was completely insane and seemed to possess nothing more than the singular desire to drown people. The ghost was one of the malevolent spirits who hated the living. Before she went to sleep, Lilith always had to put her ghosts on guard so she wouldn't get dragged underwater again.

Days continued to slip by. The day of the prisoners' release was quickly approaching. According to Thera, a couple of the prisoners had overheard the guards speaking about removing the prisoners on Liberation Day.

This made sense to Lilith. If they wanted to move the prisoners without attracting notice, the Liberation Day celebration would be a perfect opportunity. It was one of the largest celebrations in Gheistmar. Most people would be drinking and too busy having fun to notice the prisoners.

Lilith expected that they would move the prisoners one at a time. It would be safer that way for the Irons. One person couldn't cause much trouble.

Unless ...

"Thera!" Lilith called out. "Thera, are you awake?"

"I am now," Thera said.

"When they transport us, they're going to take us out of here one at a time, right?"

"I imagine so."

"We can escape," Lilith said. "If someone could manage to pull off the magnet from my lock, I could pick the lock with my ghosts."

"We're going to have our hands chained behind our backs.

How is anyone going to be to that?"

"It's simply stuck on there. All anyone would have to do is brush up against it and slide the magnet right off."

Thera was quiet for a long time. Lilith waited awhile. Thera still didn't say anything. Lilith grew impatient.

"So will you do it?" Lilith asked.

"It's very late in my life to be tasting hope," Thera said. "But, yes, I'll do what I can. And I'll talk to the other prisoners. I think nearly all of them will agree to try to help as well."

"Thank you."

"Yeah," Thera said. "I mean, it's not like we've got a lot to lose, right?"

The Irons would probably start at the close end of the hall and simply go down the line, taking each prisoner out to transport to ... wherever they were going. As best Lilith could tell, there were over a dozen prisoners. Moving each one would take several minutes. The entire process might take an hour. She looked at the lock on her cell door. Could she pick the lock in that amount of time? Yes. Easily.

But she'd only have an hour if the first prisoner escorted out managed to knock off the magnet and she was the last one to be taken. And that first prisoner wouldn't get the chance if they never even walked past Lilith's cell. Thera had told her that no matter who got moved first, they were going to try to run from the guards. The Irons would likely be surprised by a prisoner running deeper into the dungeon, so it might work. The prisoner would brush against Lilith's lock to get rid of the magnet.

Lilith's cell was near the middle of the row, so she'd likely be moved halfway through. Thirty minutes or so. Still no problem. But again, that was only if the first prisoner was successful in dislodging the magnet, and that wasn't likely. The Irons would be extra diligent with the first few prisoners. They'd be tense, expecting some resistance. Only after several trips would they begin to relax as they developed a routine. So it was far more likely that Lilith would have only about a minute to pick the lock.

It was going to be a challenge, to say the least.

But, as Thera had said, it wasn't like she had a lot to lose.

CHAPTER 27

Months passed.

No, that wasn't right. Jericho rubbed the beard on his face and guessed at the time it took to grow that long. Not quite months. Weeks, though. Weeks since he had bonded Belial. He had little memory of that time. It had been one long terrifying nightmare.

Raves usually lasted hours. Strong ones took a day or two. Weeks ... this was unheard of. He was lucky to have survived. Trapped in the horror of the past, he could have easily died of thirst or stumbled down a flight of stairs and broken his neck. He vaguely recalled fighting to consciousness in a Herculean display of self-preservation and staying conscious just long enough to gulp some water and eat a little jerky.

Jericho hurt. His left eye was swollen. His ribs were tender. He had wrapped them tightly but it still pained him to move. Or breathe. Countless bruises and lacerations covered his skin. Some of it, he knew, was from stumbling around the mansion like a drunken blind man. Other wounds—the red lines from nails and the half-moon arcs of bite marks—were the work of the mischievous ghosts of the mansion.

He doubted he would ever bond another ghost. Each rave had been progressively worse. When a Vagabond was raving from a new ghost, any other ghosts they had previously bonded threw their memories into the stew, making the nightmares that much more severe.

Belial had been a Germanic mercenary. The sights the man had seen! The horrors he had witnessed ... and performed. His family had died in a raid or a fire or from a mountain lion ... keeping the details straight became impossible with seven ghosts. At least during a rave. Later, perhaps, Jericho would be able to examine Belial's history.

Why was Belial so strong? So physically capable?

The answer astonished Jericho. The key wasn't in Belial's old memories, but rather his newer ones. Belial had been bonded before by a rather talented Vagabond. Many years ago, that Vagabond had overseen the construction of this mansion.

According to Belial, the Lourde's Den had once been a thriving coven for Vagabonds. Belial had been their guardian, defending not only those Vagabonds but the mansion itself. When the head Vagabond who had bonded Belial died, the other Vagabonds had either moved on or died shortly thereafter. It wasn't long before Belial was left there with only other spirits for company. Not knowing what else to do, he continued to guard the mansion.

Belial never cared much for the Brutes. He allowed them to occupy the servants' quarters, but never the mansion. He had seen the Brutes break plates and glasses. They had thrown stones through windows and made campfires in the middle of a room. The Brutes had such a disregard for property it was a wonder the servants' quarters hadn't burned down years before!

But no one else came to the Lourde's Den, and the Brutes were the only living things around to entertain Belial, so he never tried to drive them away.

A vision of a cathedral flashed suddenly in Jericho's mind. The gray stone of the building rose high into the air, standing out against the sky like angry storm clouds.

The cathedral was from Belial's old memories. Jericho was slipping back into the rave.

He hurriedly drank some water. He was out of jerky. He would have to go hunting soon or find some berries or—

The rave cut off his thoughts and he once again sunk into the nightmarish dreamscape of Belial's memories.

It was a new moon and the forest was too dark to see much of anything. It was like looking at charred bones laid across black velvet. Jericho had to move slowly. A rogue branch could gouge out an eye or damage the string on his bow. It would be a shame to have the weapon break now.

It was nothing short of miraculous that his bow hadn't been crushed when he had squirmed out of the tunnel cave-in; the few remaining arrows Jericho had left in his quiver after the battle against the Brutes had been ruined. He had snapped several of them as he had pushed through the hole. The rest had their fletching all but scraped off. They wouldn't have flown straight, so Jericho discarded them. He had found new arrows in the mansion's forge. They weren't his special arrows, but they seemed well-made. Jericho shot a few inside the mansion, testing them. Yes, they would work just fine.

There! Just ahead the silver outline of a rabbit glowed. Jericho smiled. He and Orion had come up with that trick: Orion would search for game and, once he found it, would use his energy to outline the creature with light. Hunting became much, much easier.

Jericho pulled back the string of his bow. Thankfully, it was easy now. When the raves after bonding Belial had finally subsided and Jericho had first gone hunting, he hadn't been strong enough to pull back his own bow. He had needed his ghosts to assist him. The rave after Belial had weakened him dramatically. Hell, it had almost killed him.

Only now, many weeks later, Jericho felt like he was recovering. With plenty of food, his physical strength had returned. And his powers of spiritual manipulation had exponentially increased after bonding both Lana and Belial. The strength of his original ghosts had dramatically increased while Lana and Belial added their own significant amounts of strength.

Lana was a subtle ghost. Her energy was like the waters of a cold deep lake. She couldn't shoot bolts of lightning or heave boulders through the air, but she was an expert in possession. Lana could not only affect living people, but she was able to persuade spirits as well. Her skill with the spirits stemmed from her years of being a seductress. Other ghosts strived to please her. Jericho's own ghosts loved her already. Even Susha, who almost never spoke at all, hissed kind, quiet words to Lana. Lana spoke back, and soon the two spirits were having animated conversations. Susha had always been quiet, and he was amazed at how fast this transformation was.

Unlike Lana, Belial was not subtle. His energy was like the waters of a thundering waterfall. He wasn't skilled in electricity, but he was fully capable of hurling boulders through the air or ripping a living man apart. The sheer, raw power of the ghost never failed to amaze Jericho.

It took Jericho time to grow accustomed to having the power of his ghosts amplified. He used his spirits at every opportunity to practice managing the new strength. He was able to leap higher and run faster. He wasn't used to that, and he acquired some bumps and bruises from a handful of collisions before he had learned to control it better. Leo' ability with time had been enhanced as well. Everything around him moved even slower while Jericho moved quicker. His new coat worked better now, too.

That had been one of Jericho's first priorities once he had recovered: making another coat. While Domnul, his soldier ghost, had taught him how to train so that he didn't notice cold or heat, it was still nice to have a coat that was capable of regulating the temperature. Freezing to death was always a possibility, no matter how tough you were. Jericho had searched the blacksmith shop and found leather that would work. He cut the leather into appropriate pieces and began stitching them together.

Susha and Lana had sewing skills, and they never shut up the entire time he was working on the coat. They chirped their advice constantly. When they thought Jericho wasn't doing something properly, they slung insults at him. Occasionally Susha and Lana would argue when they disagreed on a technique. Their human lives were, after all, separated by centuries and thousands of miles; they wouldn't agree on everything. Their arguments were quick and quiet, held in voices so low Jericho could barely hear them. It was the only peace he received from them while he sewed.

The rest of his ghosts were silent during the process. They seemed quite content to observe the harangues from Susha and Lana. Only when he began to put in the silver lining did Soot speak up. The blacksmith ghost had some interesting thoughts on the lining.

The old coat had silver wire woven through it. Each section of wire had been several inches long, making the coat stiff and inflexible. Instead of that, Soot said, Jericho should use thicker silver wire and make it into chainmail. That would provide flexibility as well as protection. It would be heavier, but Soot assured Jericho it wouldn't be a problem.

You can handle a little extra weight, Soot had sent. *But if you're ever weak or tired, we can assist you by sort of floating the coat along. With that much silver, we won't have any problem grabbing onto it.*

Jericho had agreed with the idea. The downside, aside from the weight, was how long it took. Mail was easy to make, but it took forever. Bending each link and connecting it to the rest was a tedious process. Jericho would spend hours at a time working with the mail. The work was simple enough that he would lose himself in it, his hands moving with hardly any assistance from his mind. It gave him time to think and he took advantage of the opportunity.

Mostly he thought about Cinder and how to kill him. The difficult part would be finding him. He could be hiding anywhere in Gheistmar. If Jericho could just get close enough to that traitor, he'd put an end to his miserable, sniveling existence quicker than putting out a candle. One quick slash with a knife and that betraying reprobate would fall to his knees, clutching at his bleeding throat before falling over and passing on to whatever special hell awaited him. Jericho held that thought, polishing and savoring the image.

Soot flipped over a table. It crashed on the floor, making Jericho jump and breaking him free of his reverie.

"Quiet down!" Jericho yelled. He was so agitated that he said it aloud instead of sending it mentally. Soot was usually such a well-behaved spirit ...

When Jericho was still for too long, his ghosts grew restless. They wanted to test the limits of their new strength. They wanted to play and explore the mansion. They were harder to control with their increased power and it was frustrating to tend to them when he was trying to focus on something. If he wasn't paying attention, they would sneak off and cause mischief.

Jericho went back to bending the links and thinking about how to kill Cinder. The man was a powerful Vagabond, but not strong enough to stand up to Jericho. The biggest problem would be finding him. Oh, and the Wretched. Jericho's hopes suddenly plummeted. The fact that Cinder controlled an invincible army of undead warriors complicated matters. There was no way to win a fight against those things. Jericho would have to catch Cinder alone and by surprise.

What was Cinder's motive? He had gained control of an unstoppable army. So now what? Did Cinder want money? Land? Recognition? Or perhaps he wanted to be the king of Gheistmar himself. He could have it within hours if he made that decision. No one would be able to stop him. He could have his revenants kill Duke and then put the key to the city around his own neck.

Duke ... he had no idea one of the people closest to him was a traitor. Jericho would have to warn him, and soon. That shouldn't be too hard. As a dead man, he should be able to sneak into Gheistmar without raising any suspicions. But, just in case,

Jericho was going to go to the city well prepared.

With that thought in mind, he had redoubled his efforts at piecing together the mail.

It had taken him weeks of hard work, but Jericho finally finished the coat. He was wearing it now as he hunted. It was heavier than his last one. The leather was thicker and was layered in certain areas. It looked like armor. Which, really, it was. He probably wouldn't need the extra protection against rabbits, but he wore the coat almost constantly in order to grow accustomed to it.

Jericho loosed his arrow. It sped through the night and slammed into the silver outline of the rabbit, killing it instantly. Jericho slid his bow into the leather case strung across his back and went to retrieve the animal. The night had a chill to it, and he carefully sent some energy into the mail of his coat to warm himself.

He had learned the hard way that he had to be careful using the coat. The first time he had used it for heat, he had nearly burned himself. He was still getting accustomed to his ghosts' new power. They had surged electricity through the metal and in a second the mail was scorching his skin.

"Too hot!" Jericho had yelled as he struggled to get out of the coat. *Cold,* he had sent to his ghosts. *I need it cold.* And suddenly the mail was freezing cold. Beyond freezing, even. It became so cold that he tore off a piece of skin from his hand as he flung the coat off of himself. He had stared at the garment on the floor for a long minute, watching as icy mist flowed from the metal lining.

He had to recalibrate all of his commands. When nasty ghost slammed a door in his face, Jericho had been enraged. In a fury, he sent all of his ghosts to open the door. And they did ... in their own way. The wooden door exploded. Pieces of wood of all sizes went in every direction, including right at him. He spent an hour that night picking splinters out of his face, hands, and coat.

As the weeks went by, Jericho and his ghosts perfected their communication. He was able to convey the proper amount of urgency in his commands and they learned to understand him better. Once that happened, everything changed. The ghosts of the mansion respected him now. No glasses of water were thrown on him, no doors were slammed in his face. Jericho no longer had to set his ghosts on guard and crawl underneath a sofa to get some rest. Even the ghosts in the paintings had grown to respect him. They actually nodded when he walked past. A few even smiled at him. When he walked the halls, ghosts sparked candles and oil lamps to life to light his way and extinguished them when he was past. Jericho was the lord of the Lourde's Den now, and his spectral servants saw to his every need.

Except food. That Jericho had to do for himself.

Orion kept the dead rabbit glowing so Jericho didn't have to search through the brush. He let the silvery outline fade only once Jericho picked up the rabbit.

Jericho made his way through the woods back to the mansion. The front door swung open as he neared and closed behind him. Inside, candles and lamps blossomed like orange flowers, lighting his way. In the kitchen, he butchered the rabbit. He found a large iron pot and filled it with water to make rabbit stew.

Life was good here at the mansion. It was tempting to forget about everything else and simply stay. He could sneak Lilly out of Gheistmar and they could live here together ...

No, he thought. He was being stupid. There was no reason for these pathetic day dreams. He had to go to Gheistmar to warn Duke. He couldn't let Duke fall prey to whatever plan Cinder had in mind. He would never be able to face himself in a mirror again if he did.

Jericho spent the next day gathering together his things for the journey. Not that he had much to gather together. Most of the work entailed provisions for the trip. He stuffed his pack with rabbit and deer jerky and filled his water skins. From the armory he took a short sword that was about the same size as his kilij.

His ghosts were excited. They were far noisier than usual as they chattered amongst themselves. They were anxious to visit

Gheistmar.

Jericho wasn't. If someone saw him and alerted Cinder, he
would find himself on the wrong end of an invincible army. He
needed a distraction.

It was autumn. The Liberation Day celebration would be this
month. To commemorate the city's liberation from the Brutes,
Duke insisted on throwing a lavish party. Last year, the palace
had hosted a masquerade ball. It had been a great success, and
another was planned for this year. Only the city's finest were
privileged to attend the ball, but the entire city drank and danced
the night away wherever they were. It was perfect. Everyone
would be celebrating, not sharp on the lookout for a dead
Vagabond.

But if someone recognized Jericho, he'd have trouble. He
needed a disguise of some sort.

In the blacksmith shop, Jericho found a mask. It reminded
him of the masks that the Wretched wore. It was made of steel
and had a leather strap that wrapped around his head. The front
of the mask looked like a skull. Jericho tried the mask on. He
could see out of it all right. It was better than nothing.

The Liberation Day ball was to be held during the full moon.
Jericho waited, watching the night sky. Then, when dusk fell on
the night before the full moon, he prepared to leave. He had his
new coat, the dagger Lilith had given him, his bow, the mask and
the arrows he had found in the mansion. He was as prepared as
he was ever going to be.

The night before the full moon was a stormy night. The wind
blew in gusts and the rain fell hard. As he walked through the
graveyard, he looked back a the mansion. Even though he wasn't
far away, he could just barely make it out through the rain. He
would miss it here. He hoped he would be able to return one day.

Maybe Lilith would come, too.

With that thought to warm him, Jericho marched off into the
storm toward Gheistmar.

CHAPTER 28

The rain turned the air to iron. Thick, heavy, and punishing, it was barely breathable. There were no guards out to help Vagabonds over the moat, and Jericho walked across the bridge and through the city gates without confrontation. As he passed through the gates, he still couldn't see Gheistmar through the rain. There were only dim glows of lamps and dark, hulking shadows of buildings. The guard house directly to his left was barely visible.

This was an important moment. The guards might give him trouble. If they recognized him and they were loyal to Cinder, Jericho wouldn't stand a chance. They'd send off a messenger ghost and it would suddenly be Jericho against two dozen Wretched. They would hack him apart and toss the parts into the moat. It'd be just like Jericho really had died back at the Lourde's Den.

That was if the guards realized who Jericho was. In order to recognize him, they'd have to take a close look. Odds were, they wouldn't.

These guards were on duty while everyone else was

celebrating. The weather was miserable and they were cold and wet. One out of a hundred soldiers might find this invigorating. A challenge. They would do their duty and be especially vigilant, proud that they were the ones entrusted with this onerous charge. They'd step out of the guard house into the heavy rain and question Jericho about who he was and what business he had in Gheistmar. They'd hold a lantern close to his face and take a good, long look. That was what the top percent of soldiers would do.

As Jericho had hoped, none of the guards inside the guard house were the elite one percent. They saw Jericho walking by, sensed he was a strong Vagabond, and waved him through. They never came out to get a closer look at who he was. They weren't going to become soaked to the bone if they could help it.

Jericho raised his hand in thanks to the guards as he strode into the city. He was as wet as physically possible and so cold he was shaking. He didn't use his ghosts to heat his coat, though. He clutched his spirits tightly to him, not daring to let them do even the smallest thing. They were thrilled to be in the haunted city and they squirmed in his grasp. They wanted to explore and cause mischief.

No, Jericho told them yet again. *You'll draw attention to me if you start fooling around. Be patient. Soon you might have all the excitement you could ever desire.*

The streets were empty as Jericho walked through them. Even Vagabonds went inside to avoid a downpour this heavy. Buildings and homes were brightly lit as people celebrated Liberation day. Music floated out open windows before the notes were crushed by the rain, smothered and lost in the incessant crackling of water.

After a while he arrived at Lilith's home. He stood still, watching, as he debated knocking on the door. The windows were dark. No lamps were lit and even Jericho could sense that there wasn't a Vagabond as powerful as Lilith inside. There was no point to it.

He knocked anyway, pounding his fist against the stout wood

loud enough to be heard over the storm. He waited a long minute, listening hard for any sound of her. He pounded again and gave it another minute. She wasn't home. Probably at a feast or a dance or something.

He thought back to the time when he had given her the painting that her ghosts could light up. She had seemed to like it, and he had thought about telling her how he felt. He had stayed silent, though, and now he wondered if that had been a mistake.

This Lilly should be the least of your worries, Lana sent. There was jealousy in her voice, but she was right. Jericho stepped away from Lilith's door and walked toward the Charnel House.

The good news was that the building housing the Wretched was designed to keep them inside. It had been a jail when the Elders had been in Gheistmar, and it was like a jail now. With thick walls and barred windows, there was only one way out: the heavy wooden door in the front. The door opened outward, and multiple deadbolts locked it into its frame and two chains were strung tightly across it to keep it from opening. Duke was afraid of the Wretched breaking out and wrecking havoc on the city so he had assigned them to this jail and added extra chains and locks as precautions. Jericho was going to add some precautions of his own. He didn't want Cinder opening the door and letting his revenants out.

Several areas of Gheistmar were always under construction. Roads had to be repaired, buildings rebuilt. It didn't take Jericho long to find wagons laden with rectangular cut stones. Building stones, designed to fit together seamlessly to form a thick, heavy wall. Jericho chose the wagon that had the most stones inside.

This part was risky. He couldn't hope to move the wagon on his own. It weighed at least a few tons. He'd need multiple horses, and that wasn't feasible. He was no good with animals and the horses would fight him all the way. They weren't stupid. They'd much rather stay in their warm barn than venture out into the cold rain.

His only option for moving the wagon was to use his ghosts.

It'd create some waves in the ether, but it was a risk he was willing to take. To keep the waves to a minimum, he was going to use as few ghosts as possible.

He got behind the wagon and unleashed Soot and Leo, arguably his two best behaved spirits. They pushed against the wagon. Jericho pushed too, for all the good that did. They all strained. The wagon didn't move.

Jericho sent out Orion as well. The wood of the wagon groaned as the wheels slowly began to turn.

Let me push, Belial sent. *I'll have that wagon there in no time.*

You'd probably plow this thing right through the door, Jericho sent back. *You'd make a commotion big enough to rouse the entire city. Stay put for now.*

Along with three of his ghosts, Jericho pushed the wagon over in front of the door to the jail. Jericho stepped back and appraised their work. The door wouldn't be able to open more than a couple of inches until someone moved the wagon. Perfect.

Now, make sure nobody moves it, Jericho sent to Soot. Soot flew beneath the wagon. There was a loud crack as the back axel of the wagon broke. The rear fell and the abrupt cant sent several stones falling to the ground. It wasn't quiet, but heavy rain muffled most of the noise. If anyone heard, they didn't come to investigate.

Then came another crack as Soot broke the front axel. The front collapsed. The wheels stuck out at odd angles.

Well done, Jericho sent. Now there were tons of stone blocking the door. Even with a big group helping him, it would take Cinder precious minutes to clear the mess out of the way before he could unleash his Wretched. At worst it bought Jericho some time to make his escape.

He hoped it didn't come to that. He hoped that Cinder would be dead within the hour, his corpse cooling while Jericho and Duke sipped mulled wine and marveled over the perfidy of the burned man.

To make that happen, he had to speak to Duke. He knew where to find him.

He pushed his way through the rain. The street was

blanketed with water. It looked more like a river than a thoroughfare in a large city. The gutters gurgled and sputtered as they choked down water. The gas streetlamps ignited raindrops around them to form golden halos that shivered with each gust of wind.

Brightly lit, the palace was a jewel in a world turned to granite. Its glow pushed against the crushing gloom of the night. Every candle, brazier, and torch must have been lit. Jericho had never seen the place so brilliant. He wondered why. Perhaps the Vagabonds were afraid.

In the inexplicable fashion that animals could perceive an earthquake about to happen, ghosts could sometimes feel when someone was about to die. This fact was well known even to humans. Nearly everyone had heard of the Banshees in Ireland who would wail before someone met their mortal end. Perhaps several Vagabonds' ghosts had warned them of impending violence, of people about to die, of souls about to cross the veil. Perhaps the Vagabonds had grown uneasy at the mutterings of their spirits and had built up the fires to push back the night and their fear. They were right to be afraid, Jericho thought. Someone wasn't going to live to see the sunrise.

There were Irons guarding the front doors of the palace, set there to check invitations. Not everyone got invited to the grand Liberation ball at the palace. Only the powerful and prosperous received invitations. Jericho got one last year. This year, being thought dead, he hadn't. He had to find his own way into the palace.

He went to the side of the building. There was no possible means of entry on the ground level. The windows started on the second story. Using his ghosts, he could jump there easily. But he still didn't want to make waves in the ether. He ran his hand along the wall. There were enough cracks and spaces in the stone that he might be able to climb up. It'd be difficult, but possible. He looked up at the windows and edged sideways until he was beneath one where the glass was dark. Odds were that no one would be in a dark room while the party was going on.

The water sluicing down the wall formed a thick skin over the stone. Jericho clawed through the rippling flesh and dug into the bony knobs of stone underneath. Water rushed over his hands and trickled down his arms, twin streams bleeding off the large vertical river. He pulled himself up, held tight, then reached higher. The first few feet were easy. After that, it became much harder.

No matter how hard he kicked the his boots against the wall, he was unable to get any purchase with them. The toes of the boots were too thick to fit into any of the cracks. He had to support himself solely with his arms. Before he was even halfway up, his upper body was trembling from the effort and his fingers were growing numb. With the rain in his eyes, he was climbing blind. He had to grope around with his free hand, searching for any tiny ledge to grip. As he lost feeling in his fingers, it became increasingly difficult to find anything to grab. The wet stone was slick. He lost his grip and slipped. He slid down a few feet before he got lucky and caught onto a ledge. He swore as he was forced to painfully re-climb that bit of wall.

It seemed to take forever. It was like Leo had kicked into overdrive and stretched each second into an hour. Jericho seemed to cling to that wall forever, pulling himself up inch by inch with shuddering arms that were growing weaker. There was rawness on the pads of his fingers. He had lost some skin there. Probably when he stopped himself as he slid. Maybe he should have just gone in through the front door, guards be damned.

Then, finally, his leading hand tapped against the bottom of the stone windowsill. Numb and stupid with exhaustion, he cupped his hand around a small rounded outcrop. He pulled himself higher and released his other hand, swinging it up to grab onto the windowsill.

He almost made it.

His other hand slipped and his momentum sent him arching backwards into the air, too far away to even touch the wall as he fell.

CHAPTER 29

In the dungeon, it was impossible to judge the passage of time. They knew the night of their extraction was fast approaching, but its precise day was impossible to fix. So when the Irons came for them, Lilith was actually surprised.

She knew it was the day from the sound of them walking. The Irons' boots always thudded boldly on the walkway. It was sound she had long ago memorized and relegated to background noise. This day it was different. Louder. Normally three Irons patrolled the walkway. This time there were more. Lilith's heart began to beat wildly as she realized that their transfer was about to begin. She willed the Irons to start with the prisoners on the far end of the hall. That way each and every prisoner who was released would walk past Lilith's cell. Each one would have the opportunity to get rid of that damn magnet.

The sound of the Irons' boots grew louder. They were past the first few cells now. Lilith heaved a sigh of relief. They were going to start at the far end, it seemed. Lilith sat on her stone and put her back against the wall and rested her chin on her knees. She wanted to look as small and as harmless as possible. When the Irons walked past her cell, she didn't want them to pay her any mind at all.

The Irons came closer still. Lilith felt certain that they were going to start at the other end. But they didn't. They stopped right in front of her cell. There were five of them. They all had two ghosts bonded to them, and the ghosts weren't weak. Beetle had sent some of his best men to get her. One of them rapped a wooden club against her bars. The sound was shockingly loud in the quiet of the dungeon.

"Wake up!" he yelled. "It's time to go."

Lilith's mind raced furiously. No matter what, she hadn't figured on being the first one to be removed. Perhaps they had decided she was the biggest threat and agreed to move her first. Whatever the case, her plan of picking the lock and escaping was suddenly gone. She struggled to make a new plan. She had set up a little surprise for them, but she didn't know if it'd be enough.

They unlocked the door to her cell and swung it open. Three of them came into her cell with their clubs in hand. The other two had crossbows. They aimed them at her and stood out in the hall as the other guards approached. Lilith waited, praying desperately that one of the guards outside would step into her cell. One of the guards was right at the door and had a straight shot at her. The other would have to shoot through the bars ... a tricky shot that would have to rely on luck more than anything. Lilith hoped he wouldn't be content with it.

He wasn't. The Iron shifted to his right and left and then finally stepped through the door and dropped into the water along with the other guards.

Then Lilith made a mistake: she smiled.

The guard outside of her cell must have seen the smile and decided he didn't like it one bit. His finger tightened on the trigger. At this range, he wouldn't miss. The bolt from the crossbow would skewer Lilith and she'd bleed out fast in this miserable little room.

He never made his shot. The water near the entrance to the cell seemed to explode as the ghost woman leapt of out the water and grabbed the man and pulled him in. It was like watching a crocodile snatch a helpless animal from the shore.

Lilith hadn't been able to communicate with the insane ghost woman, but she had been able to use her ghosts to push the woman around and coral her near the entrance of the cell.

The other Irons watched in surprise and horror as their comrade was held underwater. It wouldn't last long, though. The man's own ghosts would push the woman away in a few seconds.

Lilith stoked her ghosts. Raw, electrical energy crackled around her. Bolts of electricity cracked as loud as thick tree branches snapping.

One of the guards spun toward her. For one brief moment, he and Lilith held eye contact. His face contorted in fear as he realized what she was about to do.

With her arms outspread and her chin held high, Lilith leaned forward and let herself fall off her stone slab and into the water. The sound of the electricity coursing through the water was like an entire tree breaking in half as all the voltage from her ghosts surged into the water. There was blinding light and heat and a tremendous amount of noise. It was like being in the center of the sun. It was like pouring a bolt of lightning into a glass and drinking it down in one gulp. It was rapture.

And then it was over and Lilith was drained and tired and bobbing beneath the surface the water. She stood and gasped for air. Her legs shook. She staggered through the water. One of the bodies bumped against her leg. She didn't know if they were alive or dead and she didn't much care. The effort had exhausted her and her ghosts. Instead of stepping up easily onto the walkway, she had to lean forward and pull herself up, crawling out of her room on all fours. When she was out of the water she laid on her back and pushed the cell door shut with her foot.

"Are you okay?" It was Thera.

"Yeah," Lilith said. "I guess." She felt half dead.

"Then get the hell out of here. You made quite a ruckus. Other Irons will be coming soon. A lot of them, you can bet."

Lilith didn't want to leave Thera and the other prisoners here.

Thera had been the only person she had spoken to, but the other people had been willing to try to help her escape. If Lilith had enough time, she'd be able to pick the locks to their cells. She needed to let her ghosts rest some, though.

"Get going," Thera said. "I know what you're thinking. Don't stay for us. Looking at you right now, I can tell you couldn't free me if I was trapped in a paper bag. Get out, and get help. No one even knows we're here."

Lilith was almost too tired to stand. All she wanted to do was sleep. Stoking her ghosts to that degree of severity had taken so much from her.

"Go," Thera said.

Lilith forced herself to stand. Her legs trembled but she didn't fall. She looked at Thera.

"I'll come back," Lilith said.

"Not in chains, I hope." Thera offered her a brief smile. "Hurry. And don't forget us."

Lilith put one foot in front of the other. She did it again. She started walking. She picked up her pace. Then she started running. She remembered the way out from when she was dragged in. It wasn't far. Down a few halls and up some stairs was all. She ran as fast as she could.

Stop! Abigail screamed to her.

Lilith dropped to the floor and crawled into a shadow against the wall.

What is it? she sent. *Are Irons coming?*

No, Abigail sent. *That door you just passed ... the one on your right. Look behind it.*

Lilith went back and found the door. It was a plain wooden door. There were no markings on it, and no lock. She opened it. Behind it was a dimly lit room filled with junk.

No, not junk. It looked like a wide variety of worthless items, but as she came closer she saw that some things were fairly nice. There were knives, leather purses, daggers, necklaces, pendants, bracelets, and all sorts of other things. Things that Vagabonds frequently carried on their person. This must have been where the Irons tossed the possessions of the Vagabonds they imprisoned. She started sifting through the mess. Her whip was probably in here.

It is, Abigail sent. *I can feel it.* She didn't provide any further direction, though, and Lilith could only sort through randomly.

Footsteps echoed through the hall. One man said something that sounded like a joke, and another laughed. Irons. Had to be. And they were coming this way. Lilith closed the door as quietly as she could and picked up a knife and prayed that they would simply pass on by. She was so weak that she didn't think she could fight even one guard. On the positive side, her ghosts were so exhausted that the guards might not notice any of her waves in the ether.

The footsteps came closer. The men's voices grew louder. They sounded at ease and confident. Lilith waited. She held her breath and clutched the knife in her hand. The footsteps came closer still ... and then faded as the Irons passed by the door and continued down the hall.

Then someone shouted, and the men came running back.

Jericho pinwheeled his arms as he fell. He knew he looked absurd, like most falling people do. Halfway to the ground, his ghosts caught him and launched him back up. They carried him just high enough that he was able to reach out and grab the windowsill. He grabbed it hard with both hands and hung there as he gasped for breath and wondered how big of a splash he had just made in the ether. Hopefully no one noticed. Hopefully they were all too busy drinking or dancing to feel the waves resonating out from here.

Somehow, he didn't think he'd be that lucky.

He sent Orion up to unlatch and open the windows. They were double windows, the kind that swung open like doors. They were secured with a latch in the middle. *Open them quietly,* Jericho sent.

When I was alive, I could walk on dried leaves without a sound, Orion sent back. *No one will hear me.*

An instant later the windows swung open. Jericho pulled himself up, sliding his stomach over the ledge and pretty much oozing inside like some boneless being. He collapsed on the floor, breathing hard and eyeing his surroundings even as he battled down his exhaustion. He was alone in a small room. His eyes adjusted to the dark and he saw bookshelves and a few couches and chairs for lounging. All these things orbited around a sturdy wooden table centered in the room.

This was one of the many small libraries scattered throughout the palace. Stone and his Brutes had burned most the books of the libraries for either warmth or in spite, and many of the shelves here were empty and dusty. It was a shame. How much knowledge from the Elder Vagabonds had been lost? If there was a way to kill Stone twice, Jericho would have done it.

He closed the windows behind him. With the noise of the rain shut out, the room was suddenly much quieter. The music from the ball was audible now. Lana's shimmering form appeared next to him. She wore a long gown. The front of it was scooped low.

I wish we could enjoy this, she sent. *I would love to dance all night, not stopping until the sun comes up.* She paused and cocked her head as if she were listening to something. *It won't be like that, though. I have feeling that something bad will happen.*

"Maybe." With Lana's form right in front of him, Jericho found himself speaking out loud. None of his other ghosts made themselves visible as often as Lana. Now that he thought about it, he had no idea what some of them looked like.

"As long I don't run into Cinder everything should go just fine," he continued. But something bothered him. A small thing, itching at the back of his mind. The thought was quick and elusive. Try as he might, he couldn't quite pin it down. He wasn't sure what, precisely, gave him such unease.

Not that there was much he could do about it. He had only two options at this point. He could leave Gheistmar and go back to the Lourde's Den and live out his days there in peace. No one would even need to know that he was still alive. He would practically be a ghost himself.

Or he could go into the ball room.

Like ghosts always do, he made the choice to be alive. To make an impact on the living world. He was going to the ball.

Jericho conferred with Lana and Belial, giving them strict commands. *This is very important,* he sent. *As much as you want to explore, I need you to obey me precisely.* The spirits grumbled and pouted like spoiled children but they agreed.

There was nothing else to do. Jericho put on the skull mask he had found in the mansion and went to find Duke.

Duke was leaning against a marble pillar when it happened. All the Vagabonds in the room felt it. Something impacted the ether with immense force. The waves pulsed through the room. People froze, their drinks held halfway to their lips. Dancers stumbled. The orchestra faltered, the music discordant for long moments as the ether trembled. Over a dozen Irons were posted around the room. They gripped their weapons with white knuckles and glanced at each other.

What was that? Some powerful Vagabond had just used his spirits nearby. That didn't make sense. Most of the strong Vagabonds were here in the ballroom. Cull was out patrolling the city walls. There was no reason he'd be here, much less using his spirits like that.

The waves faded away and the ether calmed. The orchestra became synchronized again. The flutes, the zithers, the drums, the string instruments all found their common beat. The music was louder, like the musicians were putting forth more effort in order to dispel the uneasiness.

This time of year was wonderful and terrifying. For the next two months the veil was at its thinnest and the ability of ghosts to influence the physical world grew. It was like the city of Gheistmar suddenly had hundreds more citizens, all spectral. Poltergeists flung items and caused such disruptions that they drove Vagabonds from their own homes. Possessions and suicides doubled. Vagabonds were always wary this time of year.

When something big disrupted the ether, they took note.

Duke found Cinder. The burned man was sitting at a table. A plate with the remains of a roasted chicken was in front of him. He wasn't eating now. He sat motionless, his eyes directed toward where the ethereal disturbance had originated.

"What was that?" Duke asked.

"Someone's here," Cinder said.

"Who? Could it be Cull?"

"I don't know," Cinder said. "But we're about to find out. They're coming closer."

Beetle appeared beside Duke. As always, he was wearing his gas mask. None of the Irons had on any masks, though. They were at the ball to stand guard, not to partake in the revelry. Three Irons were right behind Beetle. They had short swords with crossbows slung over their backs. Beetle didn't say a word. He just nodded, letting Duke know that he was ready.

But ready for what?

The music strangled to silence and the crowd churned as the interloper entered the room. Duke stood on his toes, but even as tall as he was he was unable to get a glance of the stranger. Finally the crowd parted and he got a clear view.

"Holy hells," he muttered.

The plan had been to quietly infiltrate the ball. Using a mask, Jericho would be able to pass unnoticed and approach Duke and speak to him alone. It was a simple plan, and he had felt it was a good one. Yet, thus far, it had failed miserably.

When Jericho entered the room everyone was already looking at him. The musicians quit playing and an uncomfortable silence took the place of music. Why? Why were they looking at him like this? He was holding his ghosts as closely as possible, trying to suppress them and hide their strength.

"You can't sneak around," Lilith had told him long ago. "You trying to hide your power is like trying to hide a hot coal in a paper bag." Apparently, she had been right. And that was before he had bonded Belial and Lana. Now it was more like trying to stuff an entire bonfire into a paper bag.

His ghosts swirled around him in tight orbits. Compressed as they were, they froze the water on his clothes. His coat grew fuzzy with frost and water droplets froze into beads of ice. They broke free as he moved and fell twinkling through the air before shattering on the floor with a high-pitched chime. The crowd parted before him as he walked and he was able to move through the room unimpeded as he searched for Duke. He figured the towering king would be easy to find. He was.

Duke was standing by a table. Next to Duke was Beetle and a handful of guards. Sitting at the table was Cinder.

Not exactly what Jericho had in mind. Just about the complete opposite of what he had hoped for, in fact. Beetle and Duke were clutching their weapons, so Jericho stopped a comfortable six feet in front of them. No need for this to get ugly. Not yet, anyway.

"This man is a traitor and a murderer," Jericho said and pointed at Cinder. He stared at Cinder, every fiber of his being wishing him dead. "He and his soldiers are responsible for the death of at least one Vagabond."

"Who are you?" someone said. The words were spoken in a voice barely above a whisper. It might have been Duke or Beetle.

Without taking his gaze off Cinder, Jericho removed his mask.

"You!" Cinder hissed. "You're a dead man!"

"No, I'm speaking to one."

"Jericho," Duke said. "We had thought you were lost to us. We found your remains and your coat and sword in the wreckage. Or, I should say, remains we thought to be yours. We held a funeral for you and entombed your body and weapons with honor."

Duke took a step forward, his eyes narrowing. "And now you have returned," he continued. "You have come back to us and you accuse a high ranking Gheistmar Vagabond of some serious crimes."

"Only because he committed them," Jericho said. "He and

some soldiers loyal only to him. They killed a Vagabond and burned my home. Claire is missing because of him. Our Claire, Duke."

"Do you have any proof?"

"I saw the pots of pitch he had in the wagon. They were the same ones flung at my home. The exact same ones. Think about it. You gave this man control of an invincible army that answers only to him. What did you think was going to happen? I'd wager it's only a matter of time before he tries to take your position of king for himself."

The threat to his power seemed to strike home. Duke was silent. He touched his hand to his chin like he was thinking hard.

"This is preposterous!" Cinder yelled. He jumped up from his seat. Duke's hand shot out and shoved him right back down, planting him firmly in the chair. The air was thick with spirits as everyone's ghosts circled each other, snarling like feral creatures about to scrap.

"Beetle," Duke said. "You and your Irons keep a close watch on Cinder. Keep him here. Jericho and I are going to speak alone. I'll hear his accusations and decide whether they're baseless or if there is indeed some merit to them."

Jericho squinted at Beetle. The soldier had three ghosts bonded to him, all of them fairly strong. Each of the guards nearby had one or two ghosts. Jericho counted a dozen or so ghosts total bonded to the Irons. It would have been more than enough spirits to combat against just about any Vagabond. But this was Cinder. In the blink of an eye he might possess one of the Irons and suddenly the odds would change. There was a chance he could get past this group.

The ballroom had Irons all over, though. Even if Cinder managed to get away from the table, there were plenty more guards to get past. As tough as Cinder was, he'd be lucky to make it out of the building alive.

And even if Cinder did somehow make it past all the Irons, all it would mean was that Jericho himself had to hunt him down. Jericho would be just fine with that.

"We can go to the room I came in through," Jericho offered. "It'll be quiet in there."

"Let's go then," Duke said.

They passed through the crowd. As they walked, Jericho paid close attention to the ether, feeling for any warning of Cinder launching a desperate attack. He didn't feel anything. Not that that was a surprise. It was unfortunate he was so unskilled at feeling the ether.

He and Duke made it to the room without incident. It was quiet and dark. Dim light from the streetlamps strained in through the windows. The only other light came from the arcs of electricity across the metal of Jericho's coat. The flickering blue-white light made it seem like a small thunderstorm was in the room. In the moments between the flickers, the room was black, the air as dense as wet velvet.

"Hold on," Duke said. "I'm going to light the candles."

"Oh, here. I'll do it," Jericho said. He was happy to give his anxious ghosts something to do. Orion and Susha zipped out and lit several candles along the walls. The warm glow filled the room as the ghosts lit the candles. Duke's eyes were wide as he witnessed this new trick.

"Where the hell have you been?" Duke said. "And what have you been doing? You've been gone for months."

"It's a long tale," Jericho said. "And it's not really important." He took a deep breath and arranged his thoughts. Here was his chance to plead his case against Cinder. And yet, what evidence did he really have? It seemed like so little now that he had to put it to words.

"Cinder was behind the attack," Jericho said. "I'm sure of it. He used some of the Irons. They flung pots of pitch at the house. Cinder has more of those pots in his wagons. He used some of them against the Brutes. They were the same ones. There's no doubt in my mind."

"That's it?" Duke said. "That's all you have?"

"No," Jericho said. He was silent. "Well, yes. But think about it, Duke. You've been near this man for a long time. Surely he's done some things that didn't make sense to you. He's greedy and ruthless. He's probably planning on killing you and taking your position. Hasn't he done or said something that made you suspicious?"

Duke was silent for a long time. His gaze was directed down to the floor, like he was thinking hard. Thinking back to all the things Cinder had done and said, searching for some sign of perfidy. How difficult it must be, Jericho thought, being told that someone so close to you is a betrayer.

Finally Duke looked up.

"I believe you're right," Duke said after an eternity. "Cinder killed your friends and burned your home."

Jericho's relief was sharp and ecstatic. He had been beginning to lose hope, thinking that his accusations would prove feeble and the traitor would go free.

"We need to act quickly," Jericho said. "If Cinder is able to gather together his Wretched, there'll be hell to pay. How many Irons do you have?"

"Nearly three hundred."

"Can you trust them?"

"The Irons are absolutely devoted to me," Duke said.

Jericho thought about it.

"If we have to fight the Wretched, do you think that you have enough men to kill those monstrosities?" Jericho asked.

"Maybe," Duke said. "But I don't think it will come to that."

"You're probably right. If we get rid of Cinder quickly, the Wretched might not fight us at all."

They were both quiet. The cheerful music of the ball seemed out of place. It didn't match their conversation in the least.

"Why?" Jericho finally said. "Why do you think Cinder did all of this?"

"Well," Duke said as he met Jericho's gaze. "It was probably because I ordered him to."

CHAPTER 30

"You what?" Jericho wasn't sure he had heard Duke correctly.

There was a crack of lightning. The bolt must have struck nearby, for the thunder followed immediately. It was loud, the kind of rumble that made the very building tremble from its vibrations. The kind of thunder that seemed to come not only from the sky but from deep in the earth. Like a massive battle in hell had just been joined, the two sides clashing together with such force that they sent shockwaves resonating through the rest of the world.

"I sent Cinder and the Wretched to destroy your home, kill your friends, and, most importantly, kill you."

Jericho didn't know what to say to that. He was too shocked, too confused to even feel anything. He stood motionless, silently staring at Duke and trying to figure out what was going on. Was this some kind of joke?

"For what it's worth," Duke continued. "I'm sorry. I know this isn't something I can apologize for, but I want you to understand that nothing about this was ever personal. I didn't have anything against you or your fellow Renegades. Even as I sought to destroy you, I respected you and what you've accomplished. If only you hadn't threatened to decimate this city ..."

"What?"

"I love this city. Every brick," Duke went on. He opened his arms as if wrapping them around all of Gheistmar. "You understand that, I think. You helped me drive the Brutes from here. That's even what we're celebrating here today on Liberation day. I've fought and bled for Gheistmar, and I've rebuilt it. The Brutes were destroying this place. Now it is a thriving center for Vagabonds, the one place on earth they can go in large numbers. But it's not done yet. It's still growing and developing. In few years Gheistmar will truly be like no other city in history. It will be a haven for Vagabonds, safe against even whatever killed the Elders. I love this place, Jericho. I won't let anything destroy it."

A tiny flame of hope ignited within Jericho. This might be some gross misunderstanding. Some huge botch of a miscommunication.

"Duke, I love this city too. I've never threatened this city or its citizens."

Duke looked like he was somewhere between laughing and crying.

"You really don't know, do you?" Duke said. "You don't have any idea at all. What a cruel joke. This must be terribly confusing to you."

"It is, believe me."

Duke nodded.

"I'm sorry," he said again. "I wish it wasn't this way. Understand that I have no choice."

They were both silent. Jericho's mind was processing this information, chewing on what Duke had said. It was difficult to consider him an enemy. Jericho had thought he'd be a person he could trust. And yet ... it made some sense.

"You wanted me to die when we marched on the Brutes, didn't you?" Jericho said. "That's why the one Iron tried to stab me in the back. He wasn't possessed. He had orders to assassinate me."

Duke gave a sad grin. "I spoke to that Iron myself. It was

completely secret. Even Beetle had no idea. I thought maybe one soldier might be able to sneak up on you and catch you unaware. From what I hear, it nearly worked. You're still alive only because of Lilith."

"Where is she?" Jericho said. Concern welled up inside of him. Until this moment, he had thought Lilith to be safe. He had pictured her drinking and dancing.

"Dead," Duke said. "She attacked a group of Irons. She even killed some of them before she herself died. If it's any consolation, we put her sarcophagus next to yours."

Lilith was dead? Jericho couldn't believe it. Ice cold sorrow flooded through him. It flowed through his veins, drowning out every other emotion. His poor Lilly ... If he hadn't been the veteran Vagabond that he was, tears might have misted his eyes. He felt like he had been spun around and around until his vision was teetering and his stomach threatening to upheave. His knees trembled. He wanted to sit down. Needed to, even. He grabbed hold of the edge of the table to keep from falling.

"Remember when we fought the Brutes in the city streets?" Duke said. "Edict broke apart our phalanx and a mob of Brutes descended upon us. Every moment I wondered, was this how I was going to die? Was the next swing of a sharpened shovel going to end my life? I was sure we were going to die that night. Do you remember it?"

"Of course I remember that night," Jericho said numbly. "But what does it have to do with anything?"

A ghost peeled off of Duke. It looked like a wisp of fog snared by a breeze. The ghost slid from the room.

"Every day since that night has been a blessing," Duke said. "I hope you're happy with how you've spent them. I'm sorry, but I'm sending for my guards now."

"I didn't think you would do that," Jericho said.

"Why wouldn't I send for my guards?"

"You said it yourself: you love this city. Every brick." Jericho stood up straight and clenched his hands into fists. "I don't think you want me storming through your fair city. Better an earthquake crumble the buildings. Better a volcano cover the streets and people in ash. I am worse than any disaster or army and if you provoke me Gheistmar will never be the same."

For an instant, Jericho thought Duke was going to let him go peacefully. But then six Irons with crossbows burst into the room and Duke seemed heartened by their presence.

"I apologize, Jericho. But you're going to die in this room."

CHAPTER 31

Duke clenched his hands into fists. Jericho's five ghosts were making him nervous. As Jericho began to view Duke as an enemy, so too did the ghosts. Duke's own ghosts swirled around him protectively. Five against four. Duke's were outnumbered. And Jericho's ghosts were more ancient, most furious than any spirits he had seen. Duke could see them straining to get away, straining to attack. If Jericho unleashed them, it would be an ugly mess.

But then the six Irons came into the room. Each had at least one bonded ghost. Beetle was one of the Irons and he had three strong ghosts. About twelve against five. Suddenly the numbers were better and Duke was no longer nervous. Besides their ghosts, each Iron was armed with a crossbow that could kill a man at a hundred yards. In the small room, they couldn't miss.

"Don't bother fighting," Duke said. "Even if you could get past these men, I have scores more stationed throughout the ball. And don't think about jumping through the window. There's no cover and these men would easily shoot you down as you ran. An arrow in the back would be a sorry end for you."

Jericho met Duke's eyes.

"I didn't want this," Jericho said. He took one step to the side and the world erupted.

A flurry of sound and pain knocked Duke backward. His face and entire body were sliced by what felt like a hundred knives and a massive roar filled the air. Duke fell to the floor. His ghosts were buzzing and confused and scared. The Irons were on the floor. They clutched their faces with hands that streamed blood.

His face hurt so much ... His cheeks and forehead and hands throbbed with warm, wet pain. Duke held his hands out in front of him. They were covered in blood and studded with ... what was that? ... shards of glass. Still laying on his side, he picked up a large piece of glass. His hand trembled as he held it up in front of him, searching for his reflection. When he saw it, unfettered rage tore through him. His face was marred by several long cuts.

"Damn you Jericho!" Duke shouted. His face would be forever scarred. This was too much. Jericho had gone too far.

Duke pushed himself up into a seated position. Jericho was gone, of course. So was the window. Only a jagged border of glass remained. Duke listened to his ghosts. They were babbling some story about ... no, that couldn't be true. It couldn't be possible. He listened to his ghosts more closely. Fear, cold and oily, filled him as he heard what had happened.

The impossible had happened. Jericho hadn't had five ghosts bonded to him. Incredibly, he had had seven—seven!—ghosts bonded to him. Two of the ghosts had been hiding outside the window, shrouded and silent. When Jericho gave them the command, they had burst through the window, howling and screaming and carrying the shards of glass along with them so that the very air became a whirlwind of knives.

Duke climbed to his feet and stumbled to the empty socket of the window. Jericho was nowhere to be seen. This didn't bother him. Jericho would be caught and killed. This was Duke's city.

"That bastard," said a voice behind Duke. It was Beetle. His face had been protected by his mask, but his hands were a bloody mess. "Two of my men died. They caught some glass in the throat."

It was amazing how much blood was in the human body. The two guards lay in pools of blood that continued to spread out, oozing over the thick carpeting. The rest of the men were on their knees, groaning and yanking shards of glass out of their skin. Their ghosts had been blown away like cotton in the wind.

"Alert the rest of the guard," Duke told the captain. His entire body trembled with fury. "Each and every man. The ones off duty, the ones sleeping—everyone. I want men at each crossroad and constant roving patrols. Tell them to kill Jericho on sight."

Beetle nodded.

"And tell Cinder to get his Wretched," Duke said. "Send them to the Tombs."

"What about the city gates?" Beetle said. "Won't Jericho try to flee?"

"Not yet. First he'll go the Tombs to see the coffin of his girlfriend. I told him she was dead, and I'm sure he wants to see it for himself. We'll surround the building with Irons and send the Wretched in after him."

"Nice," Beetle said. He was walking out of the room when he paused and looked back over his shoulder. "Although I think Jericho was going to go there anyway. He probably wants his sword back."

Duke hadn't thought of that. Not that it mattered. That sword wouldn't bother a Wretched in the least.

"The sword changes nothing," Duke said. Beetle gave a quick nod and left.

Duke reached up and touched his own face. His hand came away bloody. Curse Jericho! This was outrageous. It was inexcusable. It was unforgivable. Duke was going to have scars on his face for the rest of his existence. His appearance was ruined forever. Well, perhaps not ruined, but certainly less than perfect, now.

Duke was still brooding over his blemished features when

Cinder entered the room.

"I got your message about the Wretched," Cinder said with his raspy voice. "There is a problem."

"I don't want bad news right now," Duke said.

"There's a wagon of stones blocking the doors to the Wretched's quarters. The axels are broken so we'll have to remove the stones by hand. It'll be a little while before we can clear the way."

"Damn!" Duke shouted and pounded his fist on the table. This wasn't fair. It wasn't right. He didn't want to send Irons against Jericho. The Renegade would almost certainly kill some Irons before he was died himself.

Cinder chuckled. He was one of the few men who never trembled in the face of Duke's rage.

"You'll be happy to know that I have good news, too," Cinder said. "One of the Wretched isn't stuck inside the quarters. Earlier today I took Colossus to the training grounds. I wanted to see how well the ghost could work the body after the second surgery."

"And?"

"A complete success. I did extensive testing and the relic works even better than we had hoped."

Duke laughed. For an instant he forgot his damaged face.

"Well, all right," Duke said. "I'd rather have Colossus than the rest of the Wretched put together. And if the new relic works as well as you say it does, Jericho is in for a nasty surprise. Send Colossus to the Tombs."

"What if Jericho doesn't go there?" Cinder said.

"It doesn't matter. Every Iron will be out looking for him. We'll find him. Each street is death for Jericho. This mess will be resolved before dawn."

CHAPTER 32

Lilith clutched the knife so hard her hands were going numb. The footsteps of the Irons quickly grew louder as they ran back toward her hiding spot. She held her breath. The men kept running. They passed by the room without even slowing. Lilith started breathing again. That was odd. Why were they running toward the front of the dungeons? If anything, she expected them to head to the back where five bodies were floating in her cell. Strange.

She tucked the knife into her belt and resumed searching for her whip. The whip was a large item buried amongst smaller ones, and it didn't take her long to find. She grasped its coils and held it up triumphantly. She felt whole again.

Her ghosts were gaining their strength back, too. The haunted city was amazing. Especially at this time of year, when ghosts' abilities were at their peak.

Lilith went to the door and listened. She didn't hear anything. She slowly opened the door and peered out. No one was around. She stepped out. Before she closed the door, she took one last look at the room behind her. There was a lot of stuff in there. A lot of lives.

She closed the door and ran toward the entrance to the dungeons. She kept expecting to encounter Irons, yet there were none. It was only when she reached the doors leading to the outside that she saw an Iron. There was just one man there, guarding the barred doors. And he was looking outside, not back in. Lilith stole up behind him and took out the knife. She rammed the knife into his back and covered his mouth with her hand to mask his screams. She ripped out the knife and stabbed him again and again until he quit moving.

The guard had keys on his belt, but when Lilith pulled on the door it swung right open. Sloppy work. The other Irons had left in a hurry. Why? What was going on up there?

Lilith didn't spend any more time thinking about it. She had to leave before any Irons came back. She ran up the stairs to freedom.

It was night and a storm was raging. Rain pressed down like a heavy blanket. It was hard to see anything. Then lightning sizzled across the sky and lit the city in a flash.

Oh god, she thought. The city's at war!

When Lana and Belial burst through the window, Jericho didn't stay to watch the carnage. He leapt out of the broken window. Instead of going to the street below, he used his five other ghosts to shoot up several feet. He grabbed hold of the edge of the roof and pulled himself up. He turned around, orientating himself in relation to the layout of the city. The Tombs were several blocks to the north.

Reason told him to get out of Gheistmar. To make a dash for the city gates and get out and just keep running all the way back to the Lourde's Den. But he couldn't do that. He needed to see Lilith's coffin, and he needed his kilij back.

Jericho ran across the rooftop and leapt over to another building. He kept running, hopping building to building, as he made his way to the Tombs. He used his ghosts to leap over alleys and wide streets. The rooftops were lined with a variety of statues. Gargoyles, lions, and humans all watched him pass with blank stone eyes. During the day the statues were dull stone. Now, with their glazes of water reflecting the arcs of lightning, they looked like they had been sculpted out of white flame. Some of the statues spat long streams from their mouth or poured water from vases. With the shifting light and rippling water, many of the statues looked like they were moving. The city truly came alive in the rain.

The storm had arrived in full force. Lightning stitched the sky in brilliant zigzags. Puddles covered the roofs. As Jericho splashed through them, his ghosts grabbed the water he kicked up and threw it higher still. His ghosts were loving this. They felt his excitement and pride at how well they had burst through the window. They flexed their strength and flung water around to show off. Three of them used the rain to create misty human forms for themselves. They ran along with Jericho, imitating his every move.

Jericho didn't rein them in. The storm provided electricity and water and Gheistmar was a very old and haunted place. The ghosts felt tireless and invincible and their confidence motivated Jericho to push himself harder. He ran faster over the buildings and made each jump farther.

The Tombs appeared out of the gray wall of rain. It stood two stories higher than the buildings around it and was so large it looked like a mountain. If the palace was a jewel sparkling in the night, the Tombs was a black fire opal. The outside was smooth black stone. Along its walls were blood-red stained glass windows. The windows pulsed with the light of sconces and torches that were kept burning no matter the hour. The Tombs was a haunted place even for Vagabonds.

Without missing a step, Jericho sprinted and leapt through the air towards a window on the second floor. Midair, he shot a Orion forward. Orion crashed through the glass, sending knife-like shards down the hall, imitating what Lana and Belial had done earlier. An instant later, Jericho followed the Orion through the window and hit the floor and rolled and was back on his feet and running, the glass shards crunching beneath his feet.

Time was his enemy and he knew it. If Duke managed to collect a large enough group of guards, Jericho wouldn't stand a chance.

The hall was smooth, black and featureless. At first glance it looked like one long corridor. But there were breaks in the wall, open doorways that led to niches. Each niche contained at least one stone coffin. Not all the niches were filled. The ones that were had a coffin and a variety of artifacts that celebrated the life of the person entombed there. Other than one large room on the ground level that was for funeral celebrations, there were no open rooms in the building. It was all corridors and niches. "Corpse Cubbies", Lilith had once called them.

Jericho knew where his own corpse cubby was. He had purchased it months earlier. It was next to the coffin of an Elder Vagabond who, according to his epitaph, had been a warrior and an architect. The niche on the other side of Jericho's had been empty. Apparently Lilith was there now.

The walls of the building were thick, muting most of the storm. It was quiet inside. Sort of. There were several sounds that were barely audible. Someone was sobbing. Elsewhere a woman was scolding a child. An elderly man was asking if anyone had seen his watch. Ghosts, all of them. Their voices were little more than whispers, just loud enough to be heard over the steady patter of Jericho's footsteps as he ran. He turned down a different hall that led further inside.

One ghost materialized in the hallway in front of Jericho. A broad man with a bushy beard, he pointed at Jericho and yelled silently. It was a peculiar display, disconcerting in that no sound issued forth from the apparition as his mouth opened wide and his wild eyes glared at Jericho. The cantankerous spirit wanted Jericho gone from this place. He stood in the middle of the hall, blocking Jericho's path.

Unbidden, Belial zoomed forward and crashed into the man, atomizing the grumpy ghost.

Jericho barely noticed the entire interaction. He was busy

counting the niches on the right-hand side. His was the thirteenth in, a number he liked just fine. He passed the niche of the warrior architect and then turned into his own grave.

It was a nice display, Jericho had to give them that. They might have tried to kill him and everyone he cared about, but they had put a lot of effort into his memorial. Duke had probably been trying to ease his guilt. There was a large oil painting of Jericho, a book on a stand that no doubt detailed his life, and black cloth draped all over the small room. Some niches were dark. His was lit by several candles. They must have been putting in new candles every night. Very nice of them. His kilij was in a glass case next to his coffin. Many people might consider the weapon to be one of the best spirit weapons ever created, and Jericho wouldn't argue. Flint had done a magnificent job.

He lifted the lid from the case and set it to the side. He felt himself grin as he grabbed the hilt of his sword. As always, it was like holding cold fire as he felt the power of the ghost bonded to the blade. The sharp electric sensation that was almost pain bit into his hand and up his arm and raced through his body. His old ghosts were elated to have the sword back. Lana and Belial were intrigued by it.

This is a powerful weapon, Belial sent.

Getting his kilij had been his first priority. The Irons might come rushing in at any moment, and Jericho wanted to be armed as best he could. He put the sheath on his belt and sheathed the sword.

Leave the city now, Lana sent. *That girl probably isn't in the coffin next to yours anyway. That man wasn't telling the truth. Trust me, I know men. He is a liar.*

I hope you're right, Jericho sent.

He left his corpse cubby and entered Lilith's. There were no candles in there and just enough light came in from the hall to see. It was empty aside from the sarcophagus. There was nothing written on it, no decorations chiseled on its sides. Jericho put his palms on the lid and pushed. It grudgingly slid open a few inches. He used his ghosts and gave it a shove and the lid fell right off. The heavy stone boomed against the floor, making as much noise as a thunderclap in the small room.

Shadows filled the inside of the coffin like thick, black liquid. He couldn't see if Lilith was in there or not.

The floor was still trembling from the impact of the lid, the vibrations squirming through the soles of his boots. Whole seconds passed and still the floor trembled. It wasn't dissipating either. If anything, the tremors were growing stronger. How was that possible?

A tremendous crash resonated from the far end of the hall. Jericho froze. What the hell was that? It sounded like something had just exploded through a thick wooden door. Like it had run right through it without slowing. And it was coming closer. Its footsteps were shaking the very floor, the deep bass of the sound reverberating through the stone, making it seem like the building itself had a heartbeat. Steady and rhythmic. And fast. Like the racing heart of a predator closing in on defenseless prey. His ghosts flexed and swirled angrily. The thing was speeding towards them.

Jericho leaned into the coffin, trying to see if it was Lilith in there or someone else or just emptiness and shadows. He couldn't see a damn thing.

The floor was positively shaking now. Whatever it was, it was almost here and Jericho needed to be somewhere else when it arrived.

He was reaching in with his hand to feel around when something ran past the doorway.

He saw it only out of his peripheral vision. Huge and gray, it had looked like a boulder rolling by. It was so heavy that its every step boomed like a drum. Its feet tattooed a speedy rhythm on the floor as it realized it had overshot its mark and scurried to back up. Jericho leapt out the doorway. He didn't want to be caught in the tiny room with that thing.

In the hall, Leo did his trick with time and Jericho got a good look at the monstrosity. It was the Colossus Wretched. It was taller than a normal man and twice as thick. Muscle was layered upon muscle. Steel cables were used as stitching to help hold the monster together. It wore its steel mask, the black sockets making it look as if it had no eyes.

But it saw Jericho clearly enough. It burst into a sprint using its arms to run like an ape. The creature was ungainly but it bristled with physical power. This was not something Jericho wanted to fight. He ran the opposite way. With his ghosts propelling him, he was able to move faster than the beast.

But not much faster. Colossus was uncannily quick. Running on all fours, the creature thundered after him. It howled as it chased him.

Jericho ran down the hall, turned, and entered yet another hall. This was what Lilith had called the "Fancy Hall". Many of the Elder Vagabonds were entombed here. The niches were bigger and had shelves carved into the walls. Wooden benches, as long as a man was tall, lined the walls of the hall. Oil paintings and expensive cloth decorated the walls. But most importantly, this hall had windows to the outside. The distance between him and Colossus was widening. In a few moments, Jericho would have enough of a lead to take the time to break out a window and make a run for it and get away from this undead abomination.

As he ran past a window, Jericho's hope withered. A flash of lightning revealed a multitude of Irons scurrying through the streets. Through the tinted glass their armor shone like red flames. They were surrounding the Tombs. There had to be a couple hundred of them. Getting past that many would be extremely difficult. Getting past them while being chased by this Wretched ... that was pretty much impossible. Jericho had no doubt the creature would follow him right out the window, and if he slowed for even an instant to deal with a single Iron, the monster would be upon him.

The hall ended just ahead. The only way to turn was to the left. Jericho's mind raced, searching for some means of escape. Perhaps if he could make it to the large funeral room on the first floor, he'd have some room to deal with this Colossus ...

Lana shrieked a warning and Jericho instinctively ducked. A

wooden bench sailed over him, just missing his head but catching his shoulder. The impact spun Jericho to the ground. He slid along the floor and into the stone wall. The Wretched had another bench in its hands. It threw it like a normal man might throw a spear.

Jericho rolled to the right and the bench splintered against the wall. His ghosts yanked him to his feet. He had his kilij in his hand and his ghosts buzzing around him. The Wretched paused as if it suddenly had some doubts.

Then it sprung with all the feral ferocity of a starving dog. Its left arm swung like a falling tree, crashing against the floor as Jericho twisted aside. It was fast, but not fast enough. When the creature threw a wide looping punch with its right arm, Jericho ducked underneath and drove his kilij into its belly. He braced his foot against its leg and ripped the blade to the side. He yanked the sword out and leapt away.

The Wretched swayed on its feet. Silvery red blood streamed from the gash in its side. The blood ran down its leg and dripped to the floor.

Abruptly, the blood stopped. It stopped flowing from the wound. It stopped running down the creature's body. The silvery red river slowed and froze in place. Even droplets falling in the air defied gravity and froze where they were. Like a great locomotive grinding to a halt and then heaving itself into reverse with a monumental effort, the blood went backwards. It levitated in the air and ran up the beast's body and back into the wound. Somehow, a ghost was healing it. The spirit collected all the blood and pushed in back into the body. The ghost pulled the skin closed where the slash had been and the Colossus looked like it had never been stabbed.

"Shit," said Jericho.

Duke bellowed orders to his men. He wanted the Tombs surrounded. The entire Tombs. No holes in the line. No gaps in the ranks where Jericho might slip through. Bowmen stood along the roofs of the surrounding buildings, arrows nocked and ready.

Nearly every guard held a torch, turning the streets into rivers of light and exiling all shadows that could harbor the fugitive.

They had him. Jericho was trapped inside the Tombs. It was only hours before dawn. Once the sun rose, Jericho wouldn't be able to hide anywhere in the city. All they had to do was wait. Duke had considered sending the Irons into the Tombs, but that would have spread the men too thin. Instead, Duke had sent Colossus inside. He hoped Colossus would kill Jericho, but he doubted it; that Wretched simply wasn't quick enough to catch him. If it did get hold of him, though, well ... that would be that. There wasn't a chance that even Jericho could kill Colossus. Cinder had anchored a ghost to the Colossus' blood that would heal any wounds. Lop its head off and the thing would still keep going. Jericho would have no choice but to run into the arms of the waiting Irons, pleading to be saved from the Wretched.

They'd save him from being killed by the Wretched all right, with crossbow bolts to the heart and blades to the gut. Again and again, Beetle had yelled at the Irons to kill Jericho on sight.

The thunderstorm rumbled and Duke pulled his purple cloak tighter against the rain. He was wet and uncomfortable and his face burned like the devil's piss.

A guard yelped and shot an arrow. Everyone tensed and the ranks churned. No one else fired. The man had been shooting at a shadow. Duke didn't discipline him, though. He wanted them loose their bolts the instant they thought they saw their quarry.

Duke shifted his weight from one foot to another. He wanted this to be over so he could get his face sewn up. The longer he went without stitches, the worse his scars were going to be. Perhaps he should send in a handful of men to assist the Wretched ... No, Jericho would have to come out. If he didn't, so much the better. It was only a matter of time before the Irons cleared away the stones and broken wagon blocking the door of the cells. Soon Duke could send in all of the Wretched.

One of the guard's torches sputtered and went out. Then another. Like a contagion, the flames shrank and died all along the line.

"Keep them lit!" Duke hollered. "Here he comes!" More torches went out and shadows clawed their way into the street. He looked up at the windows, expecting Jericho to come crashing out of one. Duke had stationed himself on the side of the building, right below the window Jericho had broken to enter the Tombs. He figured Jericho might leave the same way he had gone in. That, or maybe he'd try and use the front doors. Duke had put extra men there just in case.

Men stationed at the front of the Tombs started yelling. Apparently Jericho had chosen the front doors.

The yelling of the Irons increased. It wasn't the disciplined roar of men in a battle, but terrified screaming of people dying. Duke grimaced. He expected something like this. Jericho would be able to kill at least a few soldiers before they got him.

The screams worsened and multiplied. Duke frowned. The bastard was killing more than just a few.

An Iron ran up to Duke. He had lost his helmet and his hair was matted flat by the rain.

"What is it?" barked Duke. "Did Jericho attack?"

"No," said the man, shaking with shock and fear. "Much worse."

Jericho leapt back, narrowly dodging one of the Wretched's fists. Blood seeped from the creature's latest wound, then stopped and oozed back into its body.

This wasn't working, he thought. Despite inflicting dozens of wounds on the Wretched, he hadn't harmed the beast at all. It always healed immediately and was as good as new. Jericho, on the other hand, was far from good or new. He was tired and his ribs hurt where the creature had managed to graze him with a punch. At this rate, it wouldn't be long before he slipped up and the Wretched caught him. One blow from the creature could easily kill him. In the narrow confines of the hall, it was becoming increasingly difficult to dodge the attacks.

The Wretched charged. Jericho spun to the side and chopped at its ankle, nearly severing its foot. The beast teetered and fell to the floor. The sound of its impact thundered through the hall. Its foot pointed at an unnatural ankle and silvery red blood gushed from the wound. Yet, in an instant, the healing ghost had twisted the foot back to its proper position and was pulling the blood back into the body. The Wretched struggled to its feet again even as its ankle was being healed.

That dammed healing ghost ... If only there was a way to get rid of it. But there wasn't. It was anchored to the blood itself. The other ghost—the ghost that controlled the body—was anchored to something else. Jericho guessed that there was an artifact buried deep within the creature's flesh that the controlling ghost was anchored to. That way both ghosts were always connected to the creature's body. There was no way to dislodge either ghost.

The Wretched took one lumbering step. It was nearly healed all the way. The last of the blood was being pulled across the floor and into the gash in its ankle. Then Jericho saw something amazing: one of the droplets went the other way. It slid several inches away from the Wretched. What the hell was happening?

Jericho felt through the ether as best he could. Another ghost, one that haunted the Tombs, had grabbed the droplet of blood and tried to pull it away. It wanted what all ghosts want: flesh of its own. Or, at least, flesh it could control like a puppet.

There was a very brief tug of war before the healing ghost snatched the droplet back and pulled it into the body.

Jericho cursed himself for an idiot. If the healing ghost could pull on the blood, so could any ghost. Most ghosts were too weak to do anything, but old strong ghosts—ghosts like his—might be able to win that tug of war.

He dashed forward. The thrill of discovery surged through his veins along with the thrill of battle. His ghosts picked up on his exhilaration and the air crackled. Leo worked his magic and suddenly the Wretched was moving as slow as a bug in amber while Jericho moved faster than ever. He slashed through the front of the beast's throat and twice across its body, his blade striking like black lightning. Colossus tried to wrap him up in its arms, but Jericho was too quick. He ducked under the arms, cut into its right leg, and sprung away.

The Wretched bled profusely from its wounds. Its entire front gleamed with the metallic blood.

Jericho urged his ghosts forward. The spirits collided into the Wretched with an audible thump. They dug their phantom claws into the blood and pulled. There was a brief moment when the healing ghost struggled against them. Then it was overwhelmed by the seven ghosts and the creature's wounds suddenly began gushing blood as Jericho's ghosts pulled blood out of it like children yanking the stuffing out of a toy. They scattered the blood across the floor, spreading it thin. Belial sent his blood shooting straight up, painting the ceiling.

The Wretched wavered. It took one unsteady step and then toppled. Jericho didn't let his ghosts stop. He continued to pull out all the blood until they had drained the undead body completely.

The hall was a mess. There was hardly a dry spot on the floor and a great deal of the ceiling had been covered. Even so, the healing ghost tried to put the blood back in the body. Jericho's ghosts swatted it away easily.

Jericho used Orion to scan the body. He found an relic imbedded in the muscles of the Wretched's back. The beast twitched feebly as Jericho drove his sword into its back and cut out the relic. It was a skeleton key. The ghost anchored to it buzzed around him in a rage, but it couldn't do anything with Jericho's own ghosts protecting him. Jericho went to the window, cracked it open, dropped the key, and the ghost went with it.

Jericho hardly noticed. He stared at the crowd of guards surrounding the Tombs. Their torches turned the streets into rivers of gold. The light of their torches reflected against the wet cobblestones and the very ground looked to be on fire. The rooftops too, were lit and heavily patrolled. Jericho could put the torches out. In a city as haunted as Gheistmar, it wouldn't be hard for him to summon up old ghosts who hated light. They could use the rain and humid air to smother the flames. It wouldn't last, though. Randomly summoned ghosts wouldn't be strong enough to continuously fight against the guards' efforts to relight the torches. At best, Jericho would have a handful of minutes before they managed to have light again. And the torches going out would warn them of his approach anyway. So stealth wasn't an option. There was no way he was just going to sneak out of here.

Nor would Jericho be able to fight through them. Not a chance. There were far too many. If he didn't get hacked by a random blade, one of the guards armed with a bow would be able to pick him off.

What a mess. Duke had really poured all of his resources into this. There were so many damn Irons. Even that colossal Wretched would have had a devil of a time pushing through the mass of soldiers.

He looked at the lifeless body. The healing ghost still hovered over the corpse, waiting for Jericho and his ghosts to leave so it could start the process of repairing the body. It didn't seem to matter to the ghost that, once fully healed, the body still wouldn't move because it had no ghost to pilot it.

Jericho drummed his fingers against the skeleton key relics that hung from his neck. Relics with ghosts that he trusted. Ghosts that, while not as strong as his own ancient spirits, were still plenty strong and longed for flesh to call their own.

It was a stupid idea. It wouldn't work. And it would be extremely dangerous even if it did work. Putting another ghost into the Wretched's body ... there was no guarantee that the ghost wouldn't turn on him. No guarantee that the ghost would even have a clue how to use the blood to make the creature move.

He almost didn't do it. Installing an relic in the creature would take time and energy that he might not have. He had to speak to the ghost, explain everything to it, tell it who to attack, and give the healing ghost time to repair the body. He debated between doing that and simply raining arrows down upon the guards and trying to leap and cut his way through them. Either way, his odds of success were dismal.

One thing swayed him to install the ghost: The look on Duke's face when one of his beloved Wretched turned against him.

Jericho took off one of his skeleton keys. The ghost anchored to the key had been a merchant. Impoverished peasants had stormed his estate and murdered the merchant and his family before taking everything they could carry. Jericho communicated with the ghost for a few minutes and then made an incision in the body and pushed the key in deep. He ordered his ghosts to collect the blood and pull it back over near the body to help the healing ghost.

With Jericho's ghosts helping, it didn't take long. The healing ghost forced the silvery blood through the veins and the dead merchant grasped it eagerly. The creature flopped around on the floor as the merchant experimented with controlling it. After several tries, he managed to stand up. He took a step and fell. Back up again. A step. Then another. It raised its thick arms and let out a roar of exhilaration. The merchant was thrilled to have flesh once again and couldn't wait to use it. It was clumsy and slow, but Jericho now had a Wretched of his own.

Jericho surveyed the streets. The guards were dispersed evenly so that every door and window of the Tombs was guarded. There didn't look to be any thin points in the line.

"The hell with it," Jericho said. "Let's just go out the front door."

He summoned ghosts to put out the torches.

CHAPTER 33

Duke was furious. His Irons' tight formation had broken apart in a matter of moments. He pushed his way through fleeing guards toward the battle at the front door of the Tombs. The guard hadn't told him much. Something about a monster attacking them. Whatever was going on there, it sounded like his men were getting the worst of it. The screams and panic were enveloping more of the ranks with each passing second.

What could Jericho have possibly done to create such havoc? How could ...

Oh no, Duke thought when he came upon the grisly scene at the Tombs' entrance. His mind fought against what he was seeing. The colossal Wretched—that invincible killing machine—was killing his own men! Its hulking form, visible as only a pale shadow in this dim light, towered over the Irons surrounding it. The smaller, darker forms of the guards would shoot forward to slash or stab, doing their best to stay out of reach of the creature. Their swords and knives did no good against the beast, as the healing ghost quickly mended each wound.

The massive Wretched didn't even seem to notice their

attacks. Again and again it charged into the guards. The tight ranks that were perfect for catching Jericho now made perfect targets for the beast. Clumsy though the creature was, it just couldn't miss. Its fists were like battering rams as it punched through their formation. It killed men with a single blow, crumbling their armor like foil. Guards slipped and fell and were crushed as the beast trampled them, the snapping of their bones audible even over their shrieks. The beast reared up high and let out a roar that rolled over the horrific din of battle. Lightning cut through the ebony sky and the steel cables in the creature's flesh flared.

Duke's knees were suddenly weak. He needed to sit down. He had witnessed the power and ruthlessness of the Wretched before, of course, but to see it used against his own men was something else entirely. He felt strangely guilty. Like he should apologize to his men for sending in the Wretched.

It was supposed to be on our side, he wanted to say. It was supposed to do the killing so you didn't have to die. Jericho must have somehow repossessed the creature. Something like that had never been done before. The possibility had never even been considered. Even now, it didn't seem like such an act could occur. This was certainly a night of unpleasant surprises.

Irons ran from the invincible beast. Bodies were dark lumps on the shadowy streets. A few wounded men crawled on the ground, begging for help or to simply be put out of their misery.

All of this to kill one man, Duke mused. Damn Jericho.

Jericho, who, Duke was sure, had slipped away in the chaos. The trap had failed. It was time to end this folly.

Duke pushed down his terror and revulsion as he waded into the fray. The stones were slick with blood. He stepped on an arm and felt it roll under the sole of his boot. The roars of the beast and screams of men he set aside. He might think of all this later, but for now he would ignore it; he had his duty to perform.

From the gold-plated sheath on his belt, he removed a knife. Its black blade looked like it was made of shadows.

Duke waited until the creature turned and then he sprang

forward and slammed the knife into the beast's back. There was an unearthly wail as ghosts screamed and then the creature fell to the ground and lay still. Duke yanked out the knife and sheathed it. He didn't spare the Wretched another glance—the thing was dead.

"Find Jericho!" Duke roared at his men as they stared at him in shocked silence. "He's in this city somewhere. Find him, or what happened just now will seem like a ballroom waltz!"

Lilith was seized with irrational fear. Gheistmar was under attack. A battle was raging over near the Tombs. A crowd of Irons yelled and the harsh clang of metal weapons pierced the air. Somehow enemies had gotten past the moat and the high walls of Gheistmar. Everyone had always thought it was impossible. Who ... or what ... had been able to do this?

She knelt in the street, struggling to recover from her shock. Her entire world had changed so much in the past few months. The rain washed over her. The chill of it made her shiver, but it helped her focus, too.

This is good, she told herself. Really, it's perfect. This attack means they won't pay any attention to me at all. I look awful, though. I look like I just walked out of the dungeons. One glance at me and people will know I'm not someone who should be strolling around free.

She stood and started walking. Other guards, in small groups or alone, ran towards the battle. They didn't notice her. The fountain in the city square was just ahead. With the rain, it was in its full glory. Water poured from the gashes in the statue's upraised wrists, and the light reflecting off the rubies dyed the streams red. The obsidian stone on the bottom of the pool around the statue turned the water as black as old blood.

Lilith stripped off her clothes and set her weapons beside them and stepped into the water. It was cold enough to make her gasp, yet it felt so good. She ducked beneath the water and scrubbed her hair. Underwater, the rain on the pool's surface was a dull rattle. Lilith came back up and shook her head, whipping her braided hair around like thin wet ropes. She scrubbed her arms and legs and all of her body, scouring the scum from the dungeon off of her. After all that time in that filthy cell, it was so nice to bathe. So nice to finally be clean. She felt alive. Reborn.

And cold. Very cold. Her teeth started chattering. Was the water this frigid when she first went in?

Something scrapped her back. It was thin and hard and almost sharp. She looked down. The water was growing a skin of ice.

Too late, she felt it. The ether was such a mess and so many Vagabonds were around that she hadn't noticed. She did now, that was for damn sure. A powerful Vagabond was approaching. He was coming down a darkened street. Abigail tossed her whip to her and she caught it without taking her eyes from the street.

Had that street been dark a minute ago? She didn't think so. Yet now it was completely dark. The air looked as solid as lead.

No, she amended, the air didn't look solid like lead. It was more like pitch, for it seemed to move like liquid. As the torches in the city square shrank and died, the darkness poured out of the street, filling the square. Atavistic claustrophobia kicked in. She could have been leagues beneath the ocean, drowning. Or suffocating under a million tons of wet earth, unable to breath as the mud and rock crushed her.

She felt the other Vagabond through the ether very clearly now. He was coming directly toward the square. They had sent someone after her, it seemed.

Lilith uncoiled her whip and stoked her ghosts. Electricity crackled around her and sent shadows dancing in harsh jerks. Blue sparks rained down on the ice around her. Her heart hammered in her chest and she prepared to strike out and then run. The cobblestones all around the fountain were glazed with ice. The approaching Vagabond was more powerful than even Cull. She wondered if they meant to kill her or if they were going to try to drag her back to her cell. Lilith didn't plan on going back to the dungeon. She was going to fight until either her hunter was dead or she had breathed her last breath.

The Vagabond was in front of her suddenly. He moved so fast it was as if the very air had birthed him. Everything behind him was darkness, the night an immense cape trailing from his shoulders. She had only the briefest glimpse of him until he closed the distance between them. Her reflexes were keen, honed over years of practice. But she had been weakened by her time spent in the dungeon, her muscles atrophied and skills grown rusty. Her arm was just starting to twitch, just starting to respond to her brain's desperate commands for action, when his hands clamped onto her. He slammed into her and drove her down into the pool. He went underwater with her, pushing her deeper until her back bounced against the bottom of the pool.

There was a tremendous noise. It sounded like hundreds of bones being subjected to great stress, creaking and groaning as they bent further and further and then finally snapping. It was an unnatural sound, and it heralded a terrifying nightmare.

The surface of the pool just froze, she realized as she thrashed in the blackness. *We're stuck under solid ice.*

CHAPTER 34

As the Irons fought the Colossus, it had been easy for Jericho to steal a dead man's cloak and slip through the Iron's faltering lines. Only one Iron had recognized him, and Susha had zipped out and stopped his heart before he could sound the alarm.

Jericho had shrouded his ghosts as best he could and ran. He had been a block away when he saw Duke's golden form dart in and stab the Wretched with a black knife. The Wretched had collapsed instantly to lay on the ground, unmoving. Dead, Jericho assumed. But how? How had Duke killed the Colossus so easily? The question vexed him. Perhaps he hadn't anchored his merchant ghost properly. Perhaps the Wretched were more complex than he understood.

Then he had turned down a street, putting the battle behind him out of sight and out of his mind. He needed to find Lilith. Her coffin was empty, so he figured that she was alive. But since Duke and Cinder had killed everyone else close to him, it only made sense that Lilith wouldn't be exempt from that death sentence. They were probably keeping her in the dungeons until they wanted to kill her. He started running in that direction.

He hadn't made much of a plan. He figured he'd have to

fight his way past the guards and inspect the dungeons and hopefully be out of there before the rest of the Irons caught up. Maybe it'd work, maybe not. But he had to try. He wasn't going to leave Lilith behind, no matter what the cost.

Time was still his biggest enemy. The Wretched would be free soon. He stoked his ghosts and ran through the streets as fast as he could, his ghosts propelling him to incredible speed. The wind yanked at the stolen cloak. Jericho unclasped it and let the wind tug it free. He didn't want anything slowing him down.

Citizens of Gheistmar were starting to trickle out of their homes. The battle had made huge waves in the ether. Jericho wouldn't have been surprised if it had woken everyone in the city. Most people, feeling that kind of disturbance, would pull the sheets up over their head and stay in bed, hoping it would pass them by. But the people of Gheistmar were Vagabonds, one and all, and a growing number of them were suppressing their fear and leaving their houses to see what was going on. Jericho passed them by without so much as acknowledging their presence. He had no quarrel with them, and they stayed well out of his way.

Lights were ahead. Jericho's spirits hadn't snuffed out all the lights in the entire city; that job was too large. They had just focused on the blocks surrounding the Tombs.

Not a problem. Jericho sent three of his spirits ahead to gather other ghosts and put out all the torches and oil lamps in his path.

It was a sight to see, the streets going dark. Like a sunset in fast motion. With the heavy clouds and steady rain, the darkness was thick and anything more than an arm's length away was scarcely visible. Jericho was one shadow among many, anonymous and untouchable.

He stormed into the city square and it suddenly hit him that he was in the presence of a strong Vagabond. The Vagabond was strong enough to be making waves in the ether that even Jericho could feel. He saw her an instant later. She was standing in the pool in the center of the city square. Naked except for a whip in her hand and sparks raining down from her hair, she could have been a warrior goddess.

Lilith ...

Directly behind her, three Irons ran into the square. They must have seen the streetlights going out and figured where Jericho was headed. They saw Jericho and raised their crossbows to their shoulders to take aim at Jericho or Lilith or both of them.

A good, well-trained soldier could be expected to identify and acquire a target and then loose the bolt of his crossbow all within the span of a single a second. Jericho had several feet between him and Lilith. He stoked his ghosts as severely as he could, urging them to draw forth every ounce of their strength to speed him along. Leo kicked in, and as Jericho leapt toward Lilith he had painfully long moments of terror when he was certain that both he and Lilith were going to skewered with arrows. He was able to watch the Irons lean forward slightly, bracing for the shot. The muscles in their hands bulged and shifted as their fingers tightened on the triggers. Mid-air, Jericho reached out and grabbed Lilith. His momentum and weight smashed them both down under the water as crossbow bolts whistled overhead.

The water in the pool was icy and black. It was so cold it took his breath away like a giant snake crushing his chest in its coils. He felt Lilith's body smack against the bottom of the pool, rebounding slightly from the impact. Then, the sound: a riot of creaking and snapping and cracking.

In the coldest winters, in the deep of night, the trees would explode, Belial sent. *Their sap would freeze and they would creak and groan like they were in pain. Then they would burst. The sound of their wood shattering would echo across the hills. This sounds like an entire forest freezing.*

The energy of Jericho's ghosts had frozen the surface of the pool! Terror assailed him. He let go of Lilith and scrabbled around, striving to brace his feet against the bottom of the pool and push up. He couldn't see, couldn't breath. Everything was slippery and he wasn't able to get any traction. He pressed his shoulders against the ice and tried to push up but his feet kept sliding out from under him. His lungs burned and the cold sapped his strength.

Belial! he sent wildly.

Most ghosts needed precise commands. Most had lost touch with the living world and were unable to understand or anticipate what a human might need. Some ghosts wouldn't even be able to understand why being stuck underwater beneath ice would be a problem for a human. After all, ghosts loved water and could be beneath the surface for as long as they liked.

Belial, though, understood. He gathered together his energy and shot upward, erupting through the ice.

Jericho stood and gasped for air. All around the square, chunks of ice rained down, exploding wetly against the cobblestones. Along with those explosions was something else:

Crick-crick, crick-crick. It was the sound of crossbows being cranked back.

The Irons ...

Jericho spun around. Two of the Irons were hastily cranking their bows. The third had never shot his first bolt and was now calmly taking aim.

Jericho half-rolled, half-fell out of the pool as the Iron pulled the trigger. Just before he hit the stones, Jericho felt the breeze of the bolt as it zipped past him. He dug his fingers and toes into the glaze of ice on the cobblestones and launched himself forward. The two Irons cranked their bows faster while the third unsheathed his sword and stepped ahead of his comrades.

Jericho unsheathed his kilij in a wide arc that clashed against the Iron's blade. The soldier was a learned swordsman. Instead of pushing back against Jericho's weapon, he let the power of the impact send his sword into its own arc. He leaned back to get out of the range of Jericho's blade while he aimed his swing at Jericho's throat, forcing Jericho to step backward to avoid the attack.

One of the crossbow men finished cranking. He slid the bolt into place.

The Iron with the sword came at Jericho with quick, short attacks designed to put Jericho on the defensive. Jericho was able to parry each swipe, but time was slipping by ...

Jericho feigned a clumsy cut at the Iron's midsection, hoping the soldier would take the bait.

He did.

With visions of glory likely dancing in his head, the Iron swung his sword high to cut into Jericho's neck. The blade met only air as Jericho ducked down and cut into his opponent's leg. The Iron let out an ugly, pain-laced wail. His face contorted horribly and he dropped to the ground. Dead, it looked like. Which didn't make sense. That was far from a mortal wound, much less an instantaneous kill.

The Iron who had finished reloading first was bringing up his crossbow. Jericho swung his blade downward. The chop severed the crossbow's string and knocked the ruined weapon from the Iron's hands. Jericho slid to his right and cut the other Iron's throat before the man even managed to get his bolt loaded. The Iron was still standing, his throat just beginning the show its bloody smile, when Jericho shifted his footing and continued with the momentum of his slash to drive his blade into the chest of the Iron whose crossbow he had ruined. The dark blade sheared through the man's ribs and cleaved his heart. Jericho twisted his kilij and yanked it free. Both men hit the ground about the same time. There was a certain symmetry to it that made Belial chuckle.

Those last two died normally enough, Jericho wondered. *Why not the first one?*

He froze to death, Belial sent. *The ghost in your sword is even stronger now that you've bonded more ghosts.*

The ghost was able to chill the man's body that quickly?

Instead of an answer, Jericho got pain. Out of nowhere, electricity coursed through him. Every muscle in his body tensed. Each nerve was on fire. He stood there for a long instant, rigid and frozen. Then he fell, his muscles twitching in spasms. A scorched smell wafted through the air. Like burnt flesh, but not quite. More like burnt leather.

My coat, he thought. His coat had kept him alive, the thick leather insulating him from the electricity and the chain mail dissipating it. The charge might have killed him, otherwise. It might have stopped his heart or burned him horribly. Only his coat had saved him.

Saved him from what?

Jericho fought against his malfunctioning muscles, fought to roll onto his side to get a view. And what a view it was.

"Gods be good," he said to Lilith. "You look like the devil's wife herself."

Vagabonds don't cry. Weaker Vagabonds might, occasionally. Or Vagabonds deep in some horrific rave. But not strong ones. And certainly not Renegades.

Lilith and Jericho weren't crying as they held each other in the square. It might have looked that way, though. The rain slid down their faces like a thousand tears and their eyes pinched shut with emotion. Their arms were wrapped around each other. Lilith was standing on top of Jericho's boots so her bare feet didn't have to be on the ice. His coat was wrapped around her like the wings of a demonic god.

She had so many questions about where he had been and how he had managed to stay alive. He probably had more than a few questions for her, too. Yet neither of them spoke. There would be time enough for that later. Maybe.

Just down the street, armor plating clanged together and rasped across chain mail. Soldiers, running toward the city square. Their voices echoed off the buildings.

"We have to leave," Lilith said.

"Yes," Jericho said.

Neither of them let go.

"We need to leave this city," she said. "They'll find us if we don't leave."

Jericho said nothing.

"What's wrong?" Lilith said.

"We can't go together," Jericho said. "They can track me wherever I go. They'll follow my path through the ether and kill both of us."

It was Lilith's turn to be silent.

"And they might have closed the city gates already," Jericho said. "If they did that, then we have to stay here."

The noise from the soldiers was getting louder as they approached. Lilith stepped off Jericho's boots and put on her clothes. She tucked her whip in her belt and sat on the edge of the fountain to put on her boots.

"Can you make it to the gate before they close it?" she asked as she slipped on her boots. "Can you make it there and keep them from closing it for about ten minutes? Just shoot an arrow into every Iron who touches the gate wheel or something?"

"I suppose."

"Good." Lilith hopped to her feet. "I'll meet you at the gate in ten minutes. We're leaving together, Jericho. Don't worry about them tracking us. I'll take care of that. You just make sure to keep that gate open."

Jericho flew through the streets, his feet hardly touching the cobblestones. He passed by several guards so quickly that they never saw him. One guard walked into Jericho's path and Jericho slashed his sword and the man was in the gutter bleeding to death without ever knowing what had killed him.

The main gate was just ahead. Jericho figured that a significant force would be guarding it. A large number of Irons, probably. Many of them might have multiple ghosts bonded to them. This wasn't going to be an easy fight. Jericho was going to have to take them by surprise and hit them hard. If any of the Irons went for the gate wheel, he would stick them full of arrows, just as Lilith said.

They needed that gate to be open. The walls of Gheistmar were four stories high and topped with iron spikes and the moat was on the other side. Even Jericho couldn't jump it, much less carry Lilith over it along with him.

The Irons would probably try to close the gate the instant Jericho attacked. Fortunately, the gates were massive, ponderous things. It took three strong men to turn the wheel that opened the gates. If Jericho rained arrows down around the wheel, it would be difficult for three Irons to coordinate together and close the gate.

Of course, if the gates were already closed, then Jericho and Lilith were in a world of hurt.

The gates were shut tight and guarded by twenty Irons. Beetle paced back and forth. The battle at the Tombs sent shockwaves through the ether that shook the entire city. The lamps all around the Tombs went out and that area of the city descended into darkness. What the hell was going on there? Jericho's last stand, hopefully.

But then other flames started to go out. A wide swath of black was cut from the Tombs through the city. Jericho was on the move. He was probably going to come to the gates. Well, let him. Beetle was ready.

The first thing Beetle had done when he arrived at the gates was to order them closed. With nearly two dozen men guarding the gates, it was improbable that anyone would slip through. But Beetle didn't like to take chances.

It was still raining hard, just like it had been the entire night. The drops ticked and popped against his goggles. His men were wet and miserable, but he was glad for the inclement weather. It meant that Jericho wouldn't be able to see them from as far away. He'd have to get much closer before he could start to shoot arrows at them.

"He's coming." Cull's voice rumbled from the cavern that was his armor. Beetle felt comfort in the knight's presence. The special breastplate that Cull had won in the sparring tournament protected him from any weapons. Beetle had seen Cull wade through battle, calm and unhurried, as knives and swords and shovels were turned aside like waves dashing against rock.

The only thing that bothered Cull was the Wretched. No surprise; the Wretched bothered just about everyone. Beetle, too, felt some apprehension at seeing those monstrosities at work.

The lights continued to go out and the path of blackness was almost upon them. One thing—a small, tiny, insignificant thing—happened that worried Beetle. As the darkness approached, Cull took a step backward. A small gesture, one that Cull probably wasn't even aware he had done. But Beetle saw it. And he knew what it meant: even Cull was scared.

Beetle gripped the hilt of his sword and gritted his teeth.

"Come on now, you bastard," he growled at Jericho. His heart was pounding like never before. If this was Jericho approaching—and who else could it be?—then how in the holy hell had he gotten past the Wretched and Duke and the majority of the Irons?

The oil lamps and torches around them sputtered. Ghosts were wrestling down the flames. The flames shrunk and went out and the main gate was suddenly draped in velvet darkness.

"Get ready," Beetle told his men. "This is going to be a wild ride."

CHAPTER 35

The gate was just ahead. Its black shape loomed, darker than
even the murky night. Jericho pressed against the side of a
building to hide in its shadow and peered ahead. Though he
couldn't see anyone, he knew the gate was well guarded. He
could hear the creak of leather straps and the clink of metal
buckles.

Jericho continued to listen. There were a lot of men there.
Too many. He couldn't just walk up and start fighting. It'd be
much better to pick them off with arrows. He couldn't shoot what
he couldn't see, though.

Unbidden, Orion slid ahead to check things out. He zipped
back. *Big trouble,* he said. Jericho tried to get more out of him, but
the ghost couldn't elaborate. Something about a metal man was
all Jericho could understand. Jericho asked Orion if the gate was
open. The ghost was hardly interested in the gate. He was all
worked up about something else, and Jericho had to ask him
several times before he finally received a reply: The gate was not
open.

Jericho slumped. Despair pressed down upon him. With the

gate closed, there was no way he and Lilith could get through. They couldn't get over the walls, and they couldn't open the gate by themselves. They had to find somewhere to hide, and soon. Dawn was swiftly approaching. With the sun, it would be just a matter of time before the Irons searched the bright city and found them.

Nor did Jericho have the protective cover of the storm. It had spent itself out. No more lightning and thunder, just heavy dark clouds that pressed down upon the city. And those were thinning. A stiff wind might rip away the protective blanket of clouds, letting moonlight flood the streets. He had to do something, and fast.

Men were approaching. An Iron patrol was coming down the street towards him. Noisy soldiers. Jericho slipped down a side street to avoid them. The side street ran alongside the newly built building. The freshly cut wood of the structure stood out against the dim stone and weathered wood of the other buildings in Gheistmar.

He made it halfway down the street when he heard the creak of leather and realized another patrol was just ahead. This group of Irons was stationed at the intersection. Damn. If the moving patrol happened to turn down this street, Jericho would be sandwiched between the two.

They did turn down the street, of course. It was just Jericho's luck. The patrol sounded like five or six guards. They were chatting nervously amongst themselves. High strung and on edge, it would be difficult to kill them without making any noise. The group stationed ahead would certainly hear the commotion.

Jericho had to hide. But where? The street was narrow and contained nothing aside from a few trashcans. Each side of the street was lined by buildings. No alleys or side streets to run down. The rooftops wouldn't work, as Duke had covered the roofs with archers and guards.

The sewer? Jericho ran to one of the steel gratings and grabbed hold. Water trickled below. Water and darkness. Jericho and Lilith might even be able hide during the day down there. He pulled on the grating. It didn't move. He pulled harder. The guards were almost upon him. A few more steps and they would be able to see Jericho. Safety was so close and yet unobtainable! He pulled with all his might. Sweat beaded on his face. His vision started to go black, he was pulling so hard.

Nothing. The grate didn't so much as wiggle.

Jericho fell to one knee, gasping for breath. Damn it all to hell! He gripped the hilt of his kilij and drew it out of the scabbard. He was going to make those Irons sorry they caught him, that was for sure.

As he turned to run towards the guards, something caught his eye. The empty socket of an open window gaped from the new building two stories above. Black even in the dark night, the open window was a lovely as any jewel to Jericho. He gathered his ghosts and leapt, sailing through the night air without a sound. He caught hold of the windowsill and vaulted over inside, bending his legs so he landed silently. He peered over the edge and watched the Irons pass by below. He expected them to feel the waves in the ether, but they never even looked up. There was probably too much going on, and they didn't notice the extra waves.

Jericho eased back into the concealing darkness of the room. Someone was in the room with him. The person was sleeping. Steady, rhythmic breathing came from the corner. It was a small room, and he closed the distance between him and the sleeper in a few strides. He stood over the man, his sword ready. The man didn't awaken.

Amazing! Didn't this man at least have a ghost watching over him while he slept? A ghost to wake him if trouble neared? Jericho scanned. No, the man had not one ghost protecting him.

As Vagabonds go, the man was extremely young. He had almost no weight in the ether. He had probably never even seen a rave, much less experienced one. Why, he could scarcely be considered a Vagabond at all. What was he even doing in Gheistmar? Less than a year ago, only talented and experienced Vagabonds could step into the city. Quite literally. The weak

Vagabonds couldn't make it across the moat bridge. And only the very most talented and experienced were permitted to actually reside inside Gheistmar. Jericho wondered why Duke was letting Vagabonds like this—humans, practically—enter the haunted city.

Perhaps the man was an aberration. Maybe he was simply the friend of someone important and had been granted access through them.

No. That wasn't it. Jericho's ghosts were roaming through the building and none of the people staying there had any power. Odd. Perhaps it was housing for new Vagabonds or something. It didn't matter, really. Jericho was running out of time and he had to find a way out of the city.

He moved to the window and was about to go back outside when he heard Lana sigh in relief. Most Vagabonds wouldn't have even heard such a soft sound. And if they had, they wouldn't have been able to detect the extreme emotion that filled the faint expression. But Jericho was one of the very best at listening to ghosts. He possessed patience and empathy and had earned the loyalty of some of the most recalcitrant ghosts.

Why? he asked Lana *Why are you so happy to be leaving here?*

This building is all wood, she sent. *If there was a fire, we'd be roasted.*

Jericho thought about Lana. He thought about her special talent of possessing people. He stoked her. Lana gathered water and energy together and appeared at his side. Oh, she was beautiful. She wore a long dress that looked modest enough until she moved and the fabric betrayed the long cut that went nearly all the way up. She took a step, flashing the bare skin of her leg as she did so. Ever the flirt.

How do you feel? he asked her.

Strong, she sent. *This city is amazing.*

Good. I want you to do something for me. Jericho told her what he wanted. *Can you do it?* he asked.

Lana giggled and curtsied, bowing low and letting the front of her dress fall forward.

Of course, she sent.

Thank you, my dear, Jericho sent. He leapt out the window, using his other ghosts to slow his fall. The instant he landed on the cobblestones, he was off and running. Time was short. There was a lot of killing to be done before dawn.

The city gates were just ahead. Once again, he could hear the noise of the undisciplined soldiers. He couldn't see them in the thick night, though. And they couldn't see him.

Excellent.

He stoked Orion.

Do you remember hunting the rabbits in the woods at night? Jericho asked him. *You would outline them with light, allowing me to shoot them in the dark.*

Yes, Orion replied. *Yes, I remember.*

Jericho readied his bow and nocked an arrow.

I want you to light up the men ahead, Jericho sent. *Make those scared little rabbits glow for me.*

Orion shot over toward the main gate. A second later, the faint outline of a man was sketched in silver. It was just strong enough for Jericho to see. He pulled back his bow.

This is it, he thought. This is either going to work or we're never leaving this city alive.

He loosed his arrow.

The first three men went limp and dropped to the ground before anyone knew something was wrong. Then the Irons realized they were under attack. They yelled and raised their shields to protect themselves. Where was the attack coming from? As men fell screaming, the soldiers didn't even know which direction to face. For an instant, Beetle thought it was the wind. His terrified mind conjured the image of a wind carrying hundreds shards of glass, each sharper than any knife. Then his addled brain recognized the centuries-old sound of arrows zipping through the air.

Beetle raised his shield and crouched down. Nothing much to worry about here. The night was far too dark for even Jericho to shoot arrows with any degree of accuracy. He might get a couple of lucky shots, but ... Wait, no, this wasn't right. Every arrow was finding its mark. His own archers shot in all directions. Their arrows disappeared into the night, clattering against stone buildings and skipping along the street. They were hitting nothing and they knew it. Yet they continued to die. How was Jericho doing this?

Beetle's men ... Dear holy god his men were glowing! They looked as if they were outlined in strands of glowing silver wire. They were bright, easy targets just begging to be picked off.

A thought suddenly occurred to Beetle. He glanced down at his own hand. Yes, he too was glowing.

Beetle found Cull in the chaos and dove behind the giant knight. Cull was glowing too, but no arrows hit him. Every time an arrow came his way, there was a sharp crack as the ghost of Cull's armor slapped the arrow away. That was a good thing, too, as a strong bow would pierce even plate armor.

"This Jericho thinks he's very clever, doesn't he?" Cull rumbled.

"He's a right bastard, he is," Beetle said. He felt like a coward crouched behind Cull like that, but the alternative was hardly palatable. Most of his men were dead or on the ground dying. The few left were laying flat on the ground, making impossible targets.

"He's not going to be very happy when he meets me," Cull said. He laughed as another arrow was slapped away.

Beetle didn't reply. Something else was happening. The sound of screaming people reached his ears, rising even above the din of his dying soldiers. Beetle peeked out from around Cull to see what the source of the commotion was.

Scores of terrified people came running out from the gloom of the streets. They had feral panic in their eyes, running with complete abandon. Anyone who slipped on the slick stones either clawed their way back up to their feet immediately or they were trampled. The human stampede was headed directly towards them.

Beetle understood instantly: these frightened people wanted

out of the city.

"Guard the gate wheel!" he shouted to his few remaining Irons. Only two stood up from the ground to obey. They didn't even make it a step before each was rewarded with an arrow through the chest for their effort. Their bodies collapsed on the pavement, shuddering and then going still.

When the mass of screaming people was almost upon them, Beetle dashed to the gate wheel. He planted his feet and held his sword ready in his hands. He stoked his ghosts, goading them into a fury. If he was going to die, he hoped it wasn't at the hands of weak little Vagabonds like these.

It was almost a game, shooting down the glowing soldiers. Jericho had never used Orion like this against people before, and he couldn't help but be delighted that it worked so well. With his incredible speed, he loosed arrow after arrow. Each arrow found its target. The Irons scurried wildly and shot their arrows in all directions. Not a single arrow came even close to hitting him.

One of them, though, he couldn't hit. He didn't understand it at first: the man was huge and unmoving, yet Jericho's arrows didn't kill him. Hell, they didn't even seem to bother him! Then he realized that the man was Cull. The black knight must have been wearing Edict's old armor.

Jericho grimaced. He didn't have any of his magnet arrows. He wasn't going to be able to shoot Cull. Well, he had killed as many of the guards from a distance as he could. Time to open the gates. He ran back to the apartment building and kicked open the front door.

"Fire!" he yelled as loud as he could. "Fire! Fire! Get out now! The city's on fire! We have to get out!" He ran down the hall, banging the hilt of his sword on each door he passed.

The response was almost violent. Dazed Vagabonds ripped open their doors and stumbled out of the building and ran for the main gate. They were more animal than human as they ran. Their screams of terror sent a chill down Jericho's spine. He never liked possessions, but this was a thing of necessity.

His ghost Lana had done well with the ruse. Instead of possessing just one person entirely, she had visited each person in the building. She had taken her fear of a burning city and sewn that kernel into their minds. It had been a simple thing for her, really. The Vagabonds were weak and she hadn't even had to possess them. She had merely influenced their thoughts and stoked their atavistic fears of fire.

Jericho grabbed an unlit oil lamp from its wall mounting and flung it against the back wall of the hallway. He used Orion to spark the oil into flame.

A few people's minds had fought off Lana's possession. Now, as they smelled the smoke and saw the flames, they joined the mass egress.

The flames were spreading. Fire licked at the ceiling with a relentless rhythm. Jericho followed the last trickle of people out of the building. He didn't care if the entire building burned down. The new construction didn't fit in with the rest of Gheistmar.

He ran towards the gate. He could only hope that the terrified Vagabonds had managed to open the gate. The ten minutes he and Lilith had agreed upon were up.

Beetle beat the first few Vagabonds away with the flat of his sword. He couldn't bear to kill them. These were citizens of Gheistmar, after all! He fought off as many as he could but the horde soon overwhelmed him. They pushed him down and Beetle fell on his ass. He rolled aside to avoid being trampled as scores of people rushed to the gate wheel. Frantic hands grabbed the wheel and pulled. Usually three strong guards rotated the wheel; a dozen terrified people worked just as well. The massive gates swung open and the crowd poured across the bridge. The moat ghosts attacked them, mercilessly dragging several of them off the bridge.

"Damn you!" Beetle cried out at the Vagabonds who had made it across the bridge unscathed. "Damn you all! You don't know what you've done!" With the gates open, there was nothing stopping Jericho. Beetle's men were dead or scattered. Only Cull remained.

Only Cull. Beetle nearly laughed. "Only" was not the proper word to use. Cull was an army himself. If there was one man in Gheistmar who could cut down Jericho, it was Cull.

Suddenly Jericho was there. He materialized out of the gloom, moving an amazing speed.

Jericho didn't pause for even a second. He must have seen the way to freedom and seen Cull blocking that path and made his decision that very instant. He leapt to attack, his spirits propelling him forward and making the leap a fantastic one that spanned some thirty feet. Cull barely had time to raise his harpoon to parry Jericho's slash.

The battle between them was truly something to see. The air wavered and sparked as their ghosts struggled against each other. Their weapons rang as they clashed again and again. Jericho's kilij trailed cold mist as he stuck at Cull repeatedly. Each time, Cull's special armor protected him. The big knight swung his harpoon as though it weighed less than a pound, but Jericho had room to move and was able to dodge the attacks.

A woman on a horse rode past.

It was so incongruent that Beetle nearly rubbed his goggles in disbelief. Where the hell had that come from?

Jericho didn't seem surprised. He leapt back and away from Cull and ran after the horse. He vaulted onto the horse and put his arms around the woman. The woman—it was Lilith, Beetle realized—flicked the reigns and the horse took off running. They went through the open gates and were soon swallowed by the dark night.

Beetle followed for a few steps and then stopped. It was stupid to think he could catch them on foot. Instead, he stared off after them. He could discern groups of Vagabonds wandering around out there. They were probably wondering how they had gotten there. Beetle thought about closing the gates and making the idiots wait outside the city for a few days. It would serve them right.

He stood there for a long while, watching the night beyond

the city. The eastern sky was starting to lighten. Dawn would be there soon. Something was burning nearby. The sharp scent of smoke pushed through the air. It wasn't a small fire either. Great. Beetle figured they should at least be thankful that Jericho had left any part of the city still standing.

Groups of Irons arrived. They came from all over the city. Too late, of course. Far too late to stop Jericho. Duke came, too.

Duke looked furious. His face was a bloody mess. His hands were fists and his teeth were clenched.

"Did Jericho get away?" Duke hissed.

"Yes," Beetle said. "And Lilith, too, I'm afraid."

"We need to find them. Now. Get every Iron on their trail. Stop at nothing. They need to die. If they don't, Gheistmar is done for."

"I don't know if my Irons can catch them," Beetle said. "They have a horse."

"They have to stop sometime," Duke said. "Just follow their trail in the ether and kill them when you catch up to them. Tracking them shouldn't be hard. A person with even one bonded ghost leaves a decent path through the ether. Someone like myself who has four bonded ghosts makes a wide path. Jericho has seven ghosts. Following him and Lilith will be as easy as tracking an entire army."

"And just as easy to kill."

"I'm not asking that they die easy. I just want them dead."

CHAPTER 36

Jericho had one arm wrapped around Lilith while the other hand was clenched tightly to the saddle beneath him. He had hoped this would get easier as the miles passed, but it didn't. He felt certain he was about to fall off the horse with every step it took. How did people ride these things? Of course, he had the added challenge of keeping his ghosts suppressed. Lilith had been quite adamant in her insistence that he keep his ghosts as tightly suppressed as possible.

It wasn't easy. Suppressing one or two ghosts wasn't hard. But seven? That was tough. The ghosts constantly struggled to break free and explore, and he had to use every ounce of his will to keep them under control. He had his eyes shut and his teeth gritted together and he was so busy suppressing his ghosts and trying not to fall off the damn horse that he never even thought to ask where they were going. He was in a sort of trance, stoically enduring his lot as best he could.

He was snapped out of his reverie by a sound he hadn't heard in years. It sounded like an angry wind tearing through pine trees. Like a swarm of upset bees. It rushed right beside them and he was so startled that he couldn't help but open his eyes.

"Good god!" he cried out in surprise.

A horseless carriage had just roared by them, missing them by mere feet. Lilith was riding Wisp along the side of a human road. The street was bright with electric lights. Human homes were everywhere, illuminated by their cold, efficient lights.

Jericho's ghosts took advantage of his momentary lapse in attention and slipped free from his grasp. They radiated out from him and the streetlights snapped out. A second later, the lights in all the homes went out. So too did the red lights on the back of the horseless carriage. The entire area was suddenly black.

"Damn it, Jericho!" Lilith turned in the saddle so she could glare at him. "Control your ghosts!"

"Where are we? Why are you taking us into human territory?" He was suddenly painfully aware of the feel of her against him.

"We need a safe place to hide," Lilith said. "There's a coven here that I know rather well. They're just outside the big city, and all the electrical wires really muddle the ether. Duke won't be able to follow our path at all. That is, if you manage to keep your ghosts suppressed."

Jericho fought to get his ghosts back under control.

"What's a coven doing by the big city?" he said.

"They specialize in training Crossbreeds," Lilith said. "Most of them can walk among the human population without ever being detected. The head of the coven has helped me get a lot of stuff I needed from human stores. Gears and glass tubes and all kinds of other things that I couldn't find in Gheistmar."

"Good. I'm sure I'll like him, then."

"No," she said. "You're not going to like him. And he's going to absolutely hate you."

On average, Jericho was able to easily discern most Vagabond houses. They just had a certain look to them. They were usually older than the houses around them and were isolated from their neighbors by trees or a hill or some other geographical feature.

And Vagabond houses tended to look spooky. They looked like haunted houses which, of course, was exactly what they were.

The house that Lilith rode Wisp to, however, didn't fit that mold. It looked like a normal, two-story human house. There was nothing spooky about it. It had a long driveway and was surrounded by woods, but even the woods weren't ominous in any way. It might have been because the trees stretched for only an acre or two before they were cut off by the property line of the next house's grassy yard.

Not only did the coven house look like a normal human home, but, as far as the ether was concerned, it felt like one too. Most Vagabond houses were easy for other Vagabonds to find. They left a large imprint in the ether. Similar to a heavy rock set on a soft blanket, the houses created an impression in the ether that attracted both Vagabonds and spirits. Ghosts, relics, large quantities of silver, antiques, and Vagabonds themselves all attracted more Vagabonds. The larger and more populated a house, the deeper the impression in the ether and the stronger the attraction. If coven houses were rocks on a blanket, the city of Gheistmar was a boulder. Any full-fledged Vagabond could close their eyes and point in the direction of Gheistmar. The attraction was always there. Even at great distances, Gheistmar called to the nighttime wanderers.

This house, though, wasn't even a pebble on the blanket. It made no impression at all. As Lilith rode up the long driveway, Jericho couldn't feel the house in the ether in the least. Lilith had chosen a perfect hiding spot, it seemed. Duke's minions could march right past and they wouldn't so much as turn their heads.

The Vagabonds of the house were standing outside to meet them. There were six of them. They stood in a line, watching. Lilith guided Wisp in front of them. She tugged on the reins and brought Wisp to a stop. With effortless grace, she swung her leg over and dismounted. Jericho followed her lead and dismounted as well, but without much grace. It was more of a controlled fall.

"Hello, my dearest Lilith," one of the Vagabonds said. He wore good fitting dress clothes. He stepped forward out of the line and hugged Lilith with a big smile on his face. Then he looked at Jericho and his smile died. "Who's this?" he said.

"Tim, this is Jericho," she said.

Jericho nodded. He tried to look friendly.

"Jericho Toller?" Tim asked. A few of the Vagabonds back in the line murmured amongst themselves. Their eyes were wide and they looked afraid. Jericho wasn't sure what his reputation was, but he could guess that it wasn't good.

"We need to stay here for a little while," Lilith said. "We can pay, of course. We have plenty of silver. But we're hiding. Duke has decided to murder us, and we don't know why."

"So you came here?" Tim seemed disquieted by the notion. "What if they follow you?"

"They won't," Lilith said. "They can't, and you know it. This is the one place that they can't track us through the ether. I'm sorry ... this was the only place I could turn."

"Lilith, I like you," Tim said. "You're always welcome here. But Jericho ... I mean, I heard about what happened in Gheistmar with the clock tower."

"If he can't stay here, then I won't either," she said.

Everyone was quiet for a long moment. Wisp snorted, and Lilith rubbed him on the nose. The line of Vagabonds shifted nervously. Most of them were very weak Vagabonds. Jericho doubted any of them could survive for long in Gheistmar. Tim was the strongest of the group. Jericho was able to discern three ghosts floating around him, though the ghosts were so small and pale that he could scarcely see them at all.

"Come in," Tim finally said. "We've just made dinner. I'll set two extra places."

Dinner was strange. The food was different. Jericho was ravenous, and he ate several plates' worth. So too did Lilith. The food tasted good because Jericho was so hungry, but it also tasted weird. It wasn't like what he was used to eating. Nothing tasted quite like it should. He couldn't describe it. It had a sort of chemical taste to it. Not poison or anything like that. Just ... not fresh. Not quite natural.

"We bought this food in the city," Tim said. "There's a big store full of nothing but food right in the center of the human city, and we can go there without anyone noticing that we're Vagabonds." He continued talking about the progress his coven was making, how his Crossbreeds were able to venture into just about any human location without detection. Tim kept looking at Lilith and smiling at her as he spoke, and Lilith kept smiling right back. Jericho felt a spike of jealousy, and he felt guilty about it. Lilith had been his student, and nothing more.

The table went quiet as Lilith told of how she was caught and imprisoned. Everyone listened with rapt attention, Jericho included. She hadn't told him anything of their months apart. She spoke of the watery dungeons and her escape and how she met Jericho in the streets and how they fled the city.

"I had thought Jericho was dead," Lilith said. "I can't describe how happy I was to see him."

"We heard about the Brutes," Tim said. "How they've been killed, each and every last one of them. We heard that Jericho died trying to wipe them out. Obviously, the last part of that doesn't seem to be true." He didn't sound all that happy to discover Jericho was alive.

Dinner was over. One of the younger Vagabonds started clearing away the plates.

"You two must be exhausted," Tim said. "If you like, I can show you each to your room."

Jericho was given a room upstairs. Lilith's was downstairs. Before they parted ways, Jericho grabbed Lilith's arm and pulled her close.

"You were right," he said. "I don't like this guy. I don't know why, but I don't like him. Can we trust him?"

"Does it matter?" Lilith said. "Where else could we go?"

Jericho didn't have an answer.

CHAPTER 37

Jericho slept very little. He expected Duke to attack at any moment. After a few hours' rest, he went back downstairs and stationed himself in the front room of the house. He sat in a chair by the window with his bow across his lap and an arrow already nocked. He kept the room dark so he could see outside. The only light was the cold blue glow of the wolf's eyes on his bow. He was neither fully asleep nor fully awake, resting as much as he could while keeping watch. His ghosts helped him. Orion in particular was of great assistance. The hunter ghost patrolled the yard and the woods around the house, watching for Irons or Wretched or perhaps even Duke himself.

Nothing came. Jericho kept sentry in that front room for five days, leaving only for brief periods of time when Lilith kept watch in his stead. If Duke was able to track them, he'd come after them right away. Jericho was sure of that. The Gheistmar army would descend upon them soon ... or not at all.

After five days, Jericho decided that they weren't coming. There was no reason Duke would wait that long. If they hadn't been able to track him and Lilith by that time, then they couldn't do it. Jericho finally relaxed. He went up to his room and slept for several hours.

Jericho awoke to the sound of Lilith's laughter bubbling up from downstairs. It was dinner time and everyone in the house was probably eating at the table. They did that each night around sunset. Jericho had never gone. He had always sat in the front room, watching the outside. Lilith had brought him his food. Now that he wasn't standing guard, he considered sitting with them. He went down the stairs and to the dining room.

When he got there, the room was dark. He could just barely see the shadowy forms of the people sitting in their chairs.

"Why are you eating in the dark?" Jericho said.

"We weren't," Tim said. "The candles all went out when you arrived."

"Sorry," Jericho said. "Here, I'll have Orion light them." He sent Orion zipping around the room lighting the candles. Numerous candles were on the dining room table and they filled the room with a warm, comfortable glow. The dinner looked very nice. There was even a vase filled with flowers in the center of the table.

I'll bet Tim bought those flowers for Lilith, Lana sent.

Maybe, Jericho sent back. *And if he did, I don't care. I can't care.* He looked at Lilith. She was wearing strange clothes. She had on some sort of thin shirt with writing on it and trousers. Modern clothes, he supposed. The clothes were strange but she still looked breathtaking.

One of the candles on the table suddenly flared with light. The candle bent and shifted as the wax melted and broke apart. It was as if the entire wick had been ignited at once. Within seconds, the candle was a messy puddle of wax on the tablecloth.

"I'm sorry," Lilith said. "That was Niko. I think he was jealous of Orion lighting the candles like that and wanted to show off a little."

"If your ghosts are done being assholes," Tim said. "Can we get back to eating our dinner?"

"Of course," Lilith said.

Jericho looked at what was on the table. It was more of the strange human food from cans and boxes. The colors of the vegetables were too bright, too artificial. They had been dyed. The meat looked like gray mush. Its texture had been ground away. And all of it would have some funny chemical taste to it.

There's rabbits in the woods, Orion sent. *Plenty of them.*

"I'm going to eat out," Jericho said.

His bow was already slung across his back in its leather case so Jericho just walked right out the door and into the woods. Wisp, corralled with a makeshift fence in the backyard, whinnied nervously as Jericho passed. Orion flew ahead, searching for prey. It wasn't long before the glowing outline of a rabbit appeared. Jericho shot it and gutted it. He dug a little fire pit in the back yard and used two Y-shaped sticks along with a straight stick to create a spit. He gathered wood and started the fire and began roasting the rabbit. It smelled good. Hell, it smelled great. He was sitting on the ground waiting for his meal to finish cooking when Tim came out of the house. He walked over to Jericho. He held a cookie between his thumb and forefinger. He bit into the cookie delicately. Jericho stood and pointed to the rabbit.

"Do you want any?" Jericho asked.

"No," Tim said. "But that's very civil of you to ask. I'm pleasantly surprised, actually."

"What? Why?"

"You're a mindless killing machine," Tim said. He took a bite of his cookie. He politely waited until he was done chewing until he spoke again. "All your skill with bows and arrows and knives ... what can you possibly offer the members of the Vagabond community aside from an early termination?"

Jericho wasn't prepared for this conversation. The past few days he had been concerned about Duke coming to kill them, not what he could offer the community.

"The weapons are good for protection ... " Jericho said slowly.

Where was this all going?

"Protection?" Tim laughed and dabbed his mouth with his napkin. "Protection against whom? Other people like yourself, I suppose. Don't take this personally, dear Jericho. I'm not criticizing you in particular, I'm criticizing the type of person you are."

"I don't follow."

"I'm sure you don't. People rarely find fault with the great Jericho. They see that you've bonded seven ghosts and they bow down and kiss your boots. They never stop to look at the kind of ghosts you've bonded. An assasin? A mercenary? A whore? They're garbage."

Jericho's blood pounded in his ears as rage overtook him. His ghosts were very dear to him. And calling Lana a whore was uncalled for ... no matter how accurate it may have been.

"My ghosts are the youngest ghosts ever to be bonded," Tim said. "They were all children when they died. The oldest was two. They are the epitome of purity. And then we have your ghosts. All your ghosts do is hurt people. They contribute nothing to the community."

"I also bonded a blacksmith, an astronomer, and a hunter," Jericho said. "Let's not forget them."

"Ah, yes. A ghost who knows how to make—surprise!— weapons. Another ghost who spent his nights alive staring up at the sky, completely unconcerned for his fellow man. And the last goes out and kills creatures that had been living peacefully. Look at this beautiful night in front of us. How could you ruin it with death?"

"Sometimes you either have to kill something or go hungry," Jericho said. "In the world I live in, people don't hand you meals that have already been cooked and stuffed into boxes."

"My point is: your ghosts offer nothing positive. I'll go further and say that they're evil. You should break the bonds and toss the spirits back into the pits of hell or wherever you found them."

"And do what? Bond baby sprites like you have?" Jericho

squinted at the little puffballs floating around Tim.

"If you could, yes. Though I seriously doubt a child would agree to bond to a soul as tainted as yours."

"You keep speaking of what I can offer the community. What does a baby offer? They bring nothing. They're empty vessels, waiting to be filled with the experiences of life. Hell, children can't even go near Gheistmar. A ghost would possess them before they came within miles of the city."

"My little lambs offer innocence," Tim said. "They're pure and unsullied by this cruel world."

"What good could that possibly do for the other Vagabonds?"

"We're not talking about me here," Tim said. "We're talking about you. You and all the other simple-minded Vagabonds who still cling to the morals of the cavemen. Who believe that violence can solve anything at all. The only thing you fear is those like you: other Vagabonds obsessed with weapons and killing. You're out-dated. You're little more than an antique curiosity. You think that you're respected in the Vagabond world. That people look up to you and your achievements. They don't. They respect me. I made this coven what it is. I have helped change the admittance policies of Gheistmar itself. I, who have bonded only three ghosts—ghosts you undoubtedly consider weak—I command respect and admiration.

"You, on the other hand, don't. People don't respect you, they fear you. There is a difference. You'd do well to learn it."

Jericho struggled with his anger and considered Tim's words. He remembered the way the other Vagabonds in the house looked at him when he walked in. There was fear in their eyes, no doubt about it. What about Lilith? Did she respect him, or was it something else? The very idea of his dear Lilly being afraid of him hurt Jericho's black heart.

"I'm not trying to be flippant with you," Tim said. "Just honest. I'm well aware you could snuff out my life like a sputtering candle."

"Then why even speak to me like this?" Jericho said. He noticed his fists were clenched.

"Because I don't think you would hurt me. Not for my sake—heavens no. But for the sake of the one person you care about. Her happiness depends on my well being, and I think you want her to be happy."

"You ... and Lilith?" Jericho spoke slowly.

"How can you be surprised? She loves to create, to build. She's been teaching me about ghosts and electricity. She focuses on life, and so do I. It's a natural union."

Jericho nodded. He gritted his teeth and tried to smile. This was a good thing, really. Lilith was his student. He had no business thinking of her in any other way. He stared out into the night, looking at nothing. At some point, Tim walked away, but Jericho hardly noticed. He stayed standing there, as motionless as the worn statue of a civilization long dead and forgotten.

The next day was bright and sunny. Birds chirped in the trees and a gentle wind made the long grass sway like thousands of drunken dancers. The day was perfect and beautiful and it annoyed the hell out of Jericho. He would have much preferred a grim rainy day to match his mood.

You should have let me kill him, Belial sent. *Did you hear what Tim called Lana? I could have taken him apart piece by piece. That little fop is hardly a Vagabond. The ghosts he bonded couldn't haunt a washtub.*

Lana was silent. She was so angry she wasn't speaking to Jericho.

Orion sent simply, *I didn't like that man.*

Jericho didn't respond to his ghosts. He just walked through the yard, contemplating his next move. He wasn't staying here for long, that was for sure. If he ever saw Tim holding hands with Lilith, he'd probably retch ... and then cut off Tim's hand and feed it to him.

Stop being stupid, he told himself. You have more important things to think about. Claire is missing, her friend Peter is dead, your home was destroyed, the entire city of Gheistmar is trying to kill you; all of that and you have no idea why. Maybe you should

be considering that instead of pouting around like a lovesick
school boy.

But when he saw Lilith come out of the house, all thoughts of
anything but her flew from his mind. She was wearing a black
dress that ended just above her knees. He had never seen her in a
dress before. She looked amazing. She glided up to him with a
crooked smile on her face and looked him up and down.

"You look out of place walking through flowers in the
sunshine," she said. "It just doesn't fit. Like a wolf wearing a bow
around its neck."

"Tim told me you're teaching him how to use his ghosts to
create electricity," Jericho said.

Lilith laughed. She seemed just full of laughter.

"Sure," she said. "I'm 'teaching' him." She used her fingers to
put quotes on the word "teaching". "He contacted me by letter
back when I was living in Gheistmar, and we've been at it off and
on ever since."

Well, there that was. Jericho made the instantaneous decision
to leave the next night. He wasn't sure if he'd venture into the
wilderness or go back to the Lourde's Den, but either way he'd be
on the road.

"I'll be back," he told Lilith. "I have to go hunting. I don't
want to eat another meal of that artificial human food." He strode
off into the woods.

Jericho stayed in the woods until long after sunset. He
skipped the house dinner, opting instead for a modest meal of
roasted rabbit and some wild carrots. He had been hoping to
shoot a deer, but there didn't seem to be many in these woods.

It was just before midnight when he came back to the house.
A handful of Vagabonds were in the front room. He passed them
by with a curt nod and headed to the stairs. He had to walk past
Lilith's room to get there, and, in a quirk of piss poor timing, he
encountered Tim.

"Have a good night, Jericho," Tim said with a smile. He
winked and opened Lilith's door and went in, shutting the door

soundly behind him.

Jericho about punched the wall. He had to remind himself that he was a Vagabond who could control his emotions, not some idiot kid. He ground his teeth together and marched upstairs. He undressed and lay on his bed. He was perfectly still. In a flash of embarrassment, he realized he was straining to hear some sound coming from Lilith's room. Stop thinking about it, he told himself. He rolled over on his back. He willed sleep to come to him, but it didn't and it was silly for him even to try. Thoughts of Lilith clouded his mind. He tried to think of something else—anything else—but it was useless. It was like his brain was filled with nothing but Lilith, his very language alchemized into her, each word melted down and forged into her name.

He felt stupid for even thinking like this. He should have been focusing on figuring out why Duke had put out a death warrant for him, and why they had imprisoned Lilith. That should have been priority number one. Or maybe he'd never know why. Duke was sometimes petty like that. Maybe he should focus instead on some way to kill Duke.

No sounds from downstairs that he could hear. That was good.

Duke. Killing Duke would be hard, if not impossible. Jericho should have killed him when he had confronted him at the ball. But he hadn't done it and now they knew Jericho was alive and that same chance would never come again. All of Gheistmar would be alert and on the lookout. He had blown his one opportunity.

What could Lilith possibly see in Tim? Granted, the man was extremely well dressed in modern clothing, had excellent manners, and was a good looking guy. But ... somehow it just didn't fit. Not with Lilith. Tim had said that Lilith focused on life. That much was true. Lilith was never afraid to go after something she wanted. She had certainly proved that when she decided to live in Gheistmar. She had proved it again when she clawed her way out of the dungeons.

Tim, though ... he didn't seem like loved living at all. If

anything, it seemed like he was afraid of living. His most prized value was innocence, a blank slate that was the complete opposite of a life well lived. His baby ghosts were the perfect example. It was true to say that they had done nothing wrong, but it was also just as true to say they had done nothing at all.

Jericho had made many, many mistakes in his time. Yet, he couldn't call them regrets. He had always done what he thought was best. And if the ghosts he had bonded were miscreant renegades, then so be it. His ghosts were great at what they did. He would never apologize for them, and he would certainly never apologize to a man who had never risked anything, had never done a damn thing with the time he had been granted.

Lilith herself was a Renegade, and Jericho knew she was proud of that moniker. It made absolutely no sense that she would want to be with Tim.

Jericho got out of bed and put on his pants, boots, sword, and dagger. He wasn't going to miss this opportunity. He left his room and went downstairs. The Vagabonds in the parlor were still talking. They went silent was he walked into the room. They stared at him with wide, shocked eyes. Were they staring at the myriad of scars that crisscrossed his bare torso or were they startled by the dark look on his face? Jericho didn't know and he didn't much care and he passed them by without saying a word. He had living to do.

Lilith's door was closed. The skeleton key hole glowed with orange candle light from the other side. Had she locked it? Jericho didn't turn to knob to find out. Instead, he had his ghosts drop the temperature of the lock. In less than a second, the door knob was furred with frost as the ghosts plunged the temperature of the mechanism far, far below freezing. He smacked the door with the palm of his hand and the brittle metal shattered and the door swung open.

Lilith was sitting on the edge of the bed. Tim was sitting next to her. Their legs were touching. That was bad. But they were both fully clothed. That was good.

Tim stared at Jericho with unmasked horror. Lilith, though,

didn't seem horrified. She looked at Jericho with eyes narrowed like a cat and her mouth hinting at a smile.

Jericho had his ghosts fling her off the bed toward him. She yelped in surprise as she flew through the air. Jericho caught her and spun and pressed her hard against the wall. He held her underneath with one arm. Her dress had slid up and the heat of her thighs radiated against his skin. He trailed the fingers of his free hand along her face and down across her throat, marveling at the smoothness of her skin and the feeling of the breath moving through this beautiful little creature that was entirely his now whether she wanted to be or not.

He reached behind her head and took a handful of hair, clenching the braids in his fingers, crushing them as mercilessly. He pulled Lilith to him and kissed her long and hard. Hot lines of pain seared across his back as she tore her nails into his skin from either pleasure or rage and he not only didn't care which but actually enjoyed the thought of either. When he finally stopped kissing her, he still didn't let her go. He simply held her, their faces close and their foreheads resting together as they both trembled from the sheer intensity of the moment.

With speed that belonged to Lilith alone, she ran her tongue quickly along his lips and kissed him before he could even respond.

That was it for Jericho. He carried her over to the bed and laid her down. Her hair fanned out behind her head and she absolutely glowed with beauty.

Then they were kissing again. He pinned her arms above her head with one hand while his other hand moved along her body. She was amazing, this contradiction of firm, hard muscle and soft female curves. She smelled like frosted wildflowers and the very scent of her drove him beyond thinking, beyond sanity.

He was yanked back into the harsh, cruel reality of the world when a blast of cold air hit his skin. Was a powerful Vagabond nearby?

He rolled off the bed and unsheathed his sword all in one fluid movement. He was going to destroy whoever was ...

Oh. The window was open. Regaining some capacity for thought, he realized that Tim was no longer in the room. Instead of trying to push past Jericho and Lilith to go through the door, he must have opened the window and left that way. Jericho smiled at the thought. Then his attention went immediately back to Lilith. She was on the bed with her legs coiled beneath her, an animal ready to spring at whatever threat Jericho had felt.

He slammed the window shut and walked back toward the bed. With a flick of his wrist, he flung his kilij down. It stuck into the wooden floor with a thud. He unsheathed his dagger and flung it into the floor as well. The blade crackled with electricity and the light flickered across Lilith's face. Her eyes were dark and fluid and followed his every movement. Jericho approached the bed, a predator closing in on wounded prey.

He grabbed Lilith by the shoulders and pressed her back down, a relentless force as unstoppable as the glaciers that had slid across the land, knocking aside trees and pounding rock into dust.

"I've always hoped that you might like me like that," she whispered as he took off her clothes.

He didn't answer. Not with words. But the candles had burned low and guttered out long before he was done showing her just how much he liked her.

Lilith's arm was draped over Jericho's chest and she was pressed against him. He watched the gentle rise and fall of her steady breathing and couldn't help but smile as he marveled at her. He thought she was sleeping, but then her eyes snapped open.

"Your ghosts," she said as if a sudden realization had just occurred to her. "Were they ... ah, did they watch?"

That was lovely, Lana sent. *If a man had done me like that, I wouldn't have charged him a dime.*

"No," Jericho said. "They didn't watch."

"You almost never lie," Lilith said. "But when you do, your eyes slide down and to the left." She grinned and slapped him on the stomach.

"I hope you weren't upset about me interrupting your 'teaching' session with that little fop."

"You know, I thought about that," Lilith said. "I was curious why you were upset that I was teaching him."

"You noticed I was upset?"

"You can't hide your emotions any better than you can hide your path in the ether," she said. "When you're angry, you go out and kill things. I didn't need a psychic to see that I had made you angry. So I thought about it. Why would that have bothered you? Finally it came to me that you thought I was having sex with Tim."

"Well, yeah," Jericho said. "I mean, you put 'teaching' in quotes. And you looked so damn happy about it."

"Because it hardly qualified as teaching. He's a smart enough person, but without stronger spirits, he's hopeless. Those ghosts of his couldn't make a spark. He always insisted we study somewhere private so no one would see how weak he was."

"So why were you wasting time on him?"

"I love science and learning," Lilith said. "I'd do anything for it. I've been away from my family and living in a scary city; studying how ghosts interact with electricity and machines was something I could focus on to keep my sanity. It's such an unexplored concept and I'm fascinated by it. And it's something you can't do well. Something I can beat you in."

A realization dawned on him. The gap that he thought had been growing between them ... perhaps it wasn't what he had thought. Maybe she had been trying to distance herself from him, trying to stand on her own. Trying to graduate from being merely a student.

"You're quite competitive, aren't you?" he said.

"Of course," she said. "But you're a hard person to compete against."

"In some things. You've certainly surpassed me with machines and electricity, though."

"Thanks," she said and smiled. "I can't get enough of the

subject. If anyone else wants to learn, I'm happy to try to help them. Tim might not be able to do much, but he could popularize the idea of it. He could get a lot of people interested in it, and some of those people might be quite talented."

Someone knocked on the bedroom door. Since the latch had been frozen and shattered, the door swung open. One of the female Vagabonds of the coven came in the room. She looked at the pieces of the door latch strewn about. She looked at Jericho's sword and dagger imbedded in the floor, and at Jericho and Lilith in bed together.

"This was on a telephone pole a few blocks over," she said. She tossed a crumpled piece of paper onto the bed.

Jericho smoothed it out. The paper read:

LOST DOG
NAME IS "JERICHO"
REWARD: EIGHT HUNDRED DOLLARS

The reward was actually eight hundred rooks. Vagabonds coded their public messages so that humans wouldn't become suspicious. Jericho considered the reward. It was substantial.

"They've posted them all over," she told him. "They want to find you bad."

"Would you feel better if I left your coven?"

"I'm afraid you have to. Tim left sometime last night, and he took his traveling gear. I'd wager he's going to turn you in."

Lilith sat up suddenly. The sheet slid down and Jericho couldn't help but eye her trembling breasts.

"After all I've done for him!" Lilith said. "I've spent many long nights trying to teach him the basics of spectral electricity. And I was the one who helped him endure his third rave. He wouldn't dare betray us like that!"

"He never liked Jericho," the woman said. "And I'm guessing that after whatever happened last night, Tim would turn him in even if there wasn't a reward." She started to walk out of the room, but stopped and turned back. "You could have stayed here, you know," she said. "Tim didn't like Jericho, but he would have managed to get along with him for Lilith's sake. It didn't have to be like this. I hope it was worth it." She left, pulling the door shut behind her.

Damn right it was worth it, thought Jericho. His morning wasn't tainted by a single iota of regret. Tim's betrayal created a lot of problems, though. He and Lilith sat in bed, both of them contemplating their dire situation.

"How long do we have?"

"Not long," Jericho said. "If they believe him, they'll send out a force right away."

"They'll believe him," Lilith said. "He's actually respected in Gheistmar."

"It amazes me that anyone would listened to that little peacock." Jericho shook his head. "Do you know what he said? He told me that he helped change the admittance policies for Gheistmar."

"He did. He helped convince Duke to allow Vagabonds of all abilities into Gheistmar. The rule that any Vagabond had to tie a rope around their waist as they crossed the bridge over the moat? That was Tim's idea. And he sent dozens of letters to Duke, telling him that he should construct new housing for weak Vagabonds, as the older structures were far too haunted and dangerous."

"Duke would never be swayed by a fool like Tim."

"Obviously, he was," Lilith said.

"No, I don't think so. I think it was something Duke wanted to do already. He just gave credit to Tim so no one would wonder why he was doing it."

"So let's say you're right. Let's say that was something Duke wanted. Why would Duke want to allow large numbers of weak Vagabonds into Gheistmar?" Lilith asked.

"I have no idea."

Lilith's face went white.

"What's wrong?" Jericho asked.

"I know why," she said.

CHAPTER 38

"**Think about it,**" Lilith said. "What does Duke need to keep his army going? For his Irons, he needs food and water. For the Wretched, he needs quicksilver and bodies."

"He said he raids human graveyards ... "

"He lied. Did you see how good of condition the bodies are in? Not one is old or sickly or has suffered from some dramatic physical trauma. How many people look healthy when they die? A very small percentage. I'm telling you, he's using the weak Vagabonds for bodies to make the Wretched. Vagabonds come and go from Gheistmar all the time, especially weak ones. No one would even notice they're missing. And if they did, well, people die or disappear mysteriously in Gheistmar rather frequently." Her eyes widened. She said quietly, "The Vagabonds in the prison were all weak. Duke is going to turn them into Wretched. He was going to turn me into one."

"But you're not weak," Jericho said. "Not even close."

"Aside from Thera and Flint, I was the only one in the dungeon with more than one ghost bonded to me."

Jericho was silent. It made sense. All of it made sense except for them going after Lilith.

"So why'd they come for you?" he said. "And why Thera and Flint?"

"I have no idea."

"Think about it," Jericho said. "You lived in the heart of Gheistmar for months and Duke never had a problem with you. Then, suddenly, the Irons come to arrest you. What had changed?"

"I spoke to you."

Her words were like cold water splashed in his face. Lilith was right. She had been just fine until he had come back into her life. Then Duke had come for not only Lilith, but for the people closest to her, too. He felt guilty even though he didn't know why.

"I have to go back," Lilith said. "I need to go back to Gheistmar and free Thera and Flint and the other Vagabonds in the dungeon. They were willing to help me escape. I can't let them suffer the fate of being turned into a Wretched."

Jericho stared into space. Lilith's words "I spoke to you" resonated within his skull. He was missing something here. Why would it have mattered whether he had spoken to her or not? What was so poisonous about his words? He mulled over everything he had said or thought or written, searching for some venomous bit of information that had caused Duke to sign his death warrant. Duke had to know the information too, right? Otherwise he wouldn't be aware that he had to act. So what did both he and Duke know that could be significant? Jericho's brain churned, his thoughts clicking into place like the tumblers of a lock.

"Will you go back to Gheistmar with me, Jericho?" Lilith asked.

"No," he said.

Lilith was surprised by his answer. She had never known him to back away from a fight.

"Gheistmar would be a death trap," Jericho said. "You know

that. They'd feel me coming from a mile away and wait for us to walk across the bridge and then they'd close the gates behind us and surround us with the Wretched. We wouldn't last two minutes. "

They were quiet for a long moment as they both envisioned dying like that.

"You're right, I guess," she said. "I feel awful about leaving them to that fate after they were willing to help me."

Jericho got out of the bed. He put on his pants and tore his kilij from the floor board and sheathed it. Then he ripped his dagger free. The dagger crackled with light.

"Is there another Crossbreed here?" he asked. "One almost as good as Tim?"

"Yes," Lilith said. "His name's Brandon. He can even drive a car."

"I need him to go to the human store for me. And I need maps of the city."

"Why on earth would you want those?"

"Since I embarrassed the Irons in Gheistmar, Duke will send the Wretched after me. I'm sure of it. He's not going to take any chances. And I'm not going to fight them here. I'm going into the human city."

Lilith nearly laughed. The idea of Jericho entering a human city was ludicrous. His ghosts wouldn't trot at his heels like tame puppies. They were wild things and would wreck unimaginable havoc. Belial could probably stop a human's heart on accident if Jericho walked too close. And the electronics his ghosts would short out, the flammable gasses they might ignite ... he would be a walking apocalypse. The image of it was so crazy it was nearly comical. But she didn't laugh. Not only did she see that Jericho was completely serious, but she noticed that he had said "I" and not "we".

"You don't want me to go into the city with you?" She was hurt.

"I have a plan," he said. "A tremendous gamble. If it works, I'm going to destroy the Wretched. But if I'm wrong, I'm going to

be in some serious trouble. Alone, I might be able to escape. I can
run quicker than the Wretched. Together, we'd be trapped." He
held her by the shoulders. "Lilith, I really care for you. I can't
bear the thought of you being ripped apart by those undead
monsters. Or being captured and turned into one of them. Please,
when I go into battle against them, I need to know that you're
somewhere safe. Otherwise I might be distracted and make a fatal
mistake."

She was silent for a long moment. She cared deeply for
Jericho. Perhaps she even loved him.

"We could run," she said.

"For the rest of our lives? They won't stop. They want me
dead. They *need* me dead. Because I know a secret. A secret so
big I didn't even know it was a secret."

"You're not making any sense."

"To put it simply, this won't end until either I'm dead, or
Duke is."

Lilith got out of bed. She was naked, and she stood
unabashedly in front of Jericho.

"Then go kill that son of a bitch," she said.

The kid Brandon had one weak, young ghost bonded to
him—a teenaged girl who had slit her wrists for some reason—
and he was the perfect Crossbreed. When Jericho asked him to
buy some items at the human store for him, the kid listened with
wide eyes and then smiled eagerly and dashed off.

"Are you sure about all of this?" Lilith asked.

"Sure enough to risk my life," Jericho said. "But not certain
enough to risk yours. I need you to be somewhere safe. Promise
me that."

"And where would that be?" she said. "This was the only safe
place I knew. The only place they couldn't find us."

Jericho frowned. He had ruined the one place that Lilith had
been beyond Duke's grasp.

"Is there no where else?" he said quietly.

Lilith sighed.

"There's a coven to the south where I might still be welcome," she said. "It's hidden like this one."

"Will you go there? For me?"

"If that's what you want," Lilith said. "But you should know that I'm not happy about it. You should also know that we don't have much time. Tim didn't walk to Gheistmar, he drove."

"He ... what ... what did he drive?"

"What do you think? His car."

"It won't take him the entire way," Jericho said. "It will die miles from Gheistmar. But you're right, we don't have much time." He looked at her and held her eyes. "Leave now," he said. "Take Wisp. I need you to be safe."

She stepped close to him and slid her arms up along his arms and around him and held him tight. He held her back as tightly as he dared. She seemed so small sometimes, so fragile. Then they kissed. It was a long tender kiss. The kind a soldier gives his girl before going to war. The kind two lovers give when they don't expect to see each other ever again. Then Lilith had stepped back, her eyes large and wet and locked onto his as she stepped backward out of the doorway.

"We'll meet again," she said. "This will all be over soon."

"I hope so," Jericho said.

Then she was gone. Without her, the room suddenly seemed large and empty. Jericho stood there for a minute, wondering if he was making the right choice. Then he shook away his doubts and found one of the coven Vagabonds to ask for maps of the city.

The maps weren't a problem. The coven had been there for years and the Vagabonds ventured frequently into the city. They had several maps of varying sizes.

The first map Jericho examined encompassed the surrounding area. The city was roughly in the shape of a kidney bean. It ran along the shore of Lake Eerie. Someone had used a pen to draw a spot just outside the city, marking the location of Tim's coven house. The city was only a few miles away.

Jericho found another map. This one showed only the city.

Its narrower focus allowed it to be much more detailed. Nearly all the streets were clearly labeled, even short side streets that ran for only a block or two. Jericho scanned the shoreline, searching for a location that would suit his purposes. After a few minutes he found what looked to be the perfect spot. He was studying the map and planning his route when Brandon returned.

The kid had three shopping bags. Two of them were full of arrows. Jericho still had some arrows left from the ones he had found in the mansion, but he wanted more. He took out one of the arrows the kid had purchased. It was composed of a modern material he didn't recognize, but looked to be well made. He figured they would work just fine.

It was late afternoon. The sun would be touching the tops of the trees already. He wanted to be in the city by nightfall, and he still had a lot to do.

"Can I help?" Brandon asked.

Jericho tossed him two rooks.

"See if you can put together some food," Jericho said. "I'll be eating on the road tonight."

Brandon flashed a smile and ran off, eager to please. Jericho started working on the arrows. It would have been nice to have some help, but his life was going to depend on these arrows and he wanted them done exactly right. He worked as quickly as he could, continually glancing out the window to check on the sun. The day was dying, and his time was running out.

Tim was most helpful. Beetle watched, amused, as the flustered man ranted about how evil Jericho was. Tim pointed out the exact location of the coven where Jericho was hiding. He repeatedly jabbed the spot on the map with his finger. Off to the side, Duke loomed. He observed the display in silence, his arms crossed as he considered the situation. Finally, Duke looked to Beetle.

"What are you waiting for?" Duke said. The red wounds on his face bunched and crinkled as he spoke. "Take your men hunting."

"How many do you want to go?" Beetle asked.

"All of them," Duke said. "Spare a few to guard the gates of the city and take the rest."

"Are you sure?" Beetle said quietly. The Iron Guard had never marched en masse.

"Damn right I'm sure," Duke said. "We're taking the Wretched too. Every last one of them that's here. Either Jericho dies, or we do. It's time to end this silly game."

Milestones in the form of twisted, burning wreckage littered the streets behind Jericho. Every time a car came close enough to him, all of the electrical components of the vehicle would cut out. Occasionally the driver would be able to pilot the vehicle safely past. Other times—most times—the drivers didn't maintain control of their cars. He lost count the number of accidents he caused. After so many, he didn't even turn at the sound of screeching tires and crunching metal. Thankfully, it seemed no one had correlated the man in the black trench coat with the car crashes. Night had finally fallen, and the traffic had lessened and then all but disappeared, leaving Jericho alone on his march to the city.

Like nocturnal flowers, the streetlights had blossomed into light. The moist air shaped their light into white pedals that orbited the lights. Now, one after another, the streetlights blinked out as Jericho passed beneath. He grimaced each time, like person accidentally stepping on delicate blossoms. He was trying to keep his ghosts contained, but it was difficult.

Shrouding one or two ghosts wasn't hard. He could suppress them and they were typically obedient. But suppressing all of his ghosts ... that was like trying to flex every single muscle in his body and still move around. It was simply unsustainable. He could only do it for short times. So he just gritted his teeth and battled forward, step by step, into the city.

CHAPTER 39

The bartender was trying not to look over at the corner of the room.

He picked up a dirty glass, giving it his full attention. He used a small towel to wipe the glass. There was a half moon shape of lipstick on the rim. It was translucent, hardly visible unless he turned the glass just right. He rubbed the smudge of lipstick away. He turned the glass in his hand, going over the rest of it. His hands were shaking so badly that even this familiar motion was difficult. That man in the corner ... what was so wrong about him? The bartender almost glanced up. He caught himself just in time, forcing his eyes elsewhere—anywhere—but toward that man.

The bar was decorated for Halloween. Because the building was already a dark, dingy place, they hadn't gone with silly decorations. There were no cartoon cutouts of goofy-looking monsters or foam gravestones with funny names or bubble-lettered signs proclaiming "Happy Halloween". None of that childish stuff. This was an adult establishment and they wanted something properly grim. So the bar staff had scattered pans of water around the room and dropped blocks of dry ice into them to carpet the floor in fog. They had turned off all the lights—even the neon beer signs—and lit the room only with candles. Chains draped the walls and a full sized mannequin hung by a noose dangling from the ceiling.

The bar staff had dressed in costume. The waitresses were devils and the bouncers were executioners. The bartender had an executioner costume too, as he sometimes had to jump over the bar to help out with unruly customers.

The customers were well behaved tonight so far. It was early though. Plenty of time for drinks to be drunk and people to become stupid. The bar was about half full. Not busy, not slow. Just enough action for the bartender to keep sufficiently occupied so that he didn't have to look over at the corner.

Then a waitress came up to the bar. She was pale and her eyes were wide.

"That guy," she said. "You've got to get him out of here."

"Why's that?" The bartender didn't have to ask which guy she meant.

"He bit me."

The bartender set down the glass he had been cleaning.

"What?" he said.

"I know," she said. "Sounds crazy, right? I spun around when he bit me and he was sitting there like nothing happened. He must be quicker than lightning. I thought maybe he pinched me. But I'm positive it was a bite. I went in the bathroom and checked. There are teeth marks."

"Um ... where, exactly, did he ... ?"

"My ass, okay? Right on my ass. So can you do something about this guy? My boyfriend's gonna be pissed when he sees those marks on me."

"All right," the bartender said. "We'll get him out of here." With reluctance, he looked over at the corner.

Like most everyone else, the man in the corner was dressed for Halloween. He looked like one of those Greek Spartans. But

instead of a cloak he wore dark clothes and a thick leather trench
coat that looked almost armored. And he wore several keys. The
keys were the old-fashioned kind. Skeleton keys, the bartender
was pretty sure they were called. The man wore them hanging
from leather cords looped around his neck.

That was all right. The bartender thought that was a good
costume even if he wasn't sure what, precisely, the costume was.
But there were two problems. The first was that the guy might
have a weapon underneath his coat or in that leather case slung
across his back. The bartender had been in this business a long
time; he had a feeling for these things and he felt certain that the
guy had some sort of weapon on him.

Really, that was all right too. The bartender and a few
bouncers could rush the guy and grab him before he had a chance
to reach for his weapon. The bartender signaled to the bouncers
and pointed to the biting guy. The bouncers nodded their heads
and started moving toward the corner. The bartender stepped out
from behind the bar to go join them.

The waitress was still standing at the bar . "Hey," she said
and touched the bartender's elbow as he walked past her. "Am I
crazy or is something weird about that guy's shadow?"

No, she wasn't crazy. Something was very wrong about the
shadows dancing in the corner. That was problem number two.

It was the kind of thing you might not notice right away, but
once you did notice you couldn't stop puzzling over it.

There was one candle at the man's table. The man was sitting
alone. Behind him was the wall. It should have been simple:
candle, man, man's shadow. But it wasn't. Instead, it went:
candle, man, and seven or eight shadows. The shadows weren't
still, either. They moved constantly while the man himself sat
motionless. There looked to be an entire crowd of shadow people
having a party on the wall. This made no sense to the bartender.
More than that; it scared the hell out of him. He made a sudden
decision not to grab this guy in the dark. He motioned the
bouncers over and they all huddled together, a team ready to

make a big play.

"I'm going to turn on the lights," the bartender shouted to the three bouncers over the music. "Then we'll grab him." The bartender pushed through the customers and went to the breaker box. He opened the box and put his fingers on the switches for the lights. He paused. Was he doing the right thing? This would ruin the mood and upset customers. Some of them might even leave. The bar would lose money if he turned on the lights. Was it really necessary? He looked back over at the man in the corner. The man was as unmoving as a stone while his shadows danced like tongues of flame.

Easy decision.

The bartender flipped the switch to turn on the lights.

Jericho's journey into the city had been breathtaking. He stared in silent awe at the massive buildings. How could they be so tall? They loomed on either side of him like rectangular mountains. The sun had gone down a few hours ago and the glass of the buildings was a shiny obsidian. The buildings could have been shells of monstrous sea creatures, their many legs and tentacles long decayed until only this enormous husk remained. Their vast size made Jericho feel infinitesimal.

His ghosts were astonished at the city, too. They ceased their chatter and pulled tighter to him. Even Lana was impressed.

I've never seen anything like this, she sent.

I thought you lived in a city, Jericho sent back. *One even larger than this.*

Larger, yes. But not so high. These buildings touch the stars themselves.

It was convenient to have his ghosts amazed by the city, as it kept them close to him. He was holding them in as best he could—which really was not very well—and he needed every bit of help he could get. The walk into the city had gone smoother than he had expected. Aside from automobile accidents and knocking out the lights of a handful of buildings, he had passed into civilization without disrupting it.

He checked his map. The lake was just ahead. He went a couple more blocks and then came to the shore. There were numerous buildings along the waterfront. They were much smaller than the other buildings. These looked to be restaurants and shops and they were all closed at this late hour. They held no interest for Jericho. He turned left and walked along the waterfront street for perhaps a quarter of a mile or so before he found what he was looking for: docks.

Docks had changed relatively little over the centuries. There simply wasn't a better system yet devised for allowing ships to interact with land. Here were several small docks for boats slightly bigger than the automobiles. Two people could walk abreast down one of these docks. Ropes were looped around poles to allow the boats to tie up. There weren't many boats tied to the docks, however. Aside from a couple of beat-up row boats and a single medium-sized boat with its sails furled, the docks were empty. Jericho guessed that it was too late in the season for casual sailing. The only people braving the cold, autumn storms would be merchants willing to risk their ships in order to sell their wares at increased prices. These merchants would have larger ships for the rough weather and they would need larger docks than these. Jericho kept walking. He passed a few more closed shops before he came to another dock area.

It was perfect.

There were several medium-sized docks and one that was positively huge. It stretched boldly out into the water, an arm of the city itself. Jericho stepped out onto it. The dock was made of wood. Large timbers had been sunk vertically into the water. Wide boards had been laid horizontally and secured to the timbers with heavy rope as thick as Jericho's arm. Five or six men could easily walk abreast without any of them falling into the water.

Jericho walked the length of the dock. There wasn't a single boat tied up. He guessed that these places were reserved for only the largest ships. He kept walking. It was cooler out here over the lake, and the air smelled fresh and clean. When he reached the end of the dock, he turned around and took out his bow. This dock was long, but was it long enough? He nocked an arrow and pulled back the string. He aimed at forty-five degrees, trying to get as much distance as possible out of the shot. He let it fly. The arrow zipped off and he heard a distant thud. He walked back toward shore and found the arrow stuck into the dock. It was still about a third of the way from land.

Jericho smiled. The dock was long enough. No one from the shore could hit him with arrows.

He went back to the area designed for smaller boats and brought a few things back. He set up everything how he wanted and admired his handiwork.

Everything was done. He had only to wait for the arrival of the Wretched.

He wasn't going to wait here, though. He didn't want to tip off Duke that he was going to make a stand on the dock. Duke was sneaky and smart. He might think of something that Jericho hadn't. This spot needed to be a surprise.

Instead, Jericho was going to find a more populous area of the city. He needed people around for his plan to work.

He walked away from the water and farther into the city. Streetlights blinked out as he passed. Electric signs that flashed words in bright colorful letters sparked and went black. Jericho tried to pull his ghosts in tighter. It was difficult. Their awe of the city was wearing off and was being replaced by curiosity. They wanted to go investigate this exciting new place. Jericho had to put forth enormous effort to keep them reined in. When he walked too close to a large store window, the glass frosted over. It was surprisingly loud. The frost crackled and creaked as it spread over the glass in long white branches. Jericho redoubled his efforts to keep his ghosts close and hurried along.

A few blocks over, he found a particularly wide street. It was twice as wide as the other streets. It must have been a main thoroughfare or perhaps even the main street of the city. Automobiles, silent and cold, lined the sides of the street. Small groups of humans walked along the sidewalks. About half of them were in a costume of some sort and Jericho's attire didn't seem to draw any unwanted attention. Good. He didn't want anyone to notice him. Not yet. Later, once Duke attacked, he wanted the entire city in an uproar. The humans would come rushing in, forcing Duke and his army to flee.

Jericho—just one man—could hide from searching humans. There was no way a large group could hide. And Duke wouldn't fight the humans. Not only would it make the entire populace aware of the existence of Vagabonds, but Duke and his army might actually lose the fight. Ghosts shorted electronics and sparked gunpowder, rendering most of the human's technology useless. The ghosts had a limited range, however, while there were some human weapons that were effective from a considerable distance. The outcome of a battle between Vagabonds and humans was uncertain at best.

Duke would flee when the humans came. Jericho was sure of it.

As Jericho walked farther along the street the buildings changed. They went from towers to constructions of a more modest size. Most were two to four stories high. They were pressed tightly against each other like peasants huddling together in fear. The flat rooftops touched except when the buildings were separated by an alley or street. Jericho judged the distance between the tops of the buildings. If the Irons closed off the streets, he'd still be able to get away by hopping roof to roof like he had done in Gheistmar.

There was a cluster of people gathered outside of one of the buildings. As he passed by, he heard music, the clink of glasses, and smelled the unmistakable scent of beer. It was a tavern of some sort. A perfect place to wait.

He sent Orion in to scout.

Be careful, Jericho sent. *Don't play with the electronics or do anything to draw attention. Walk on those dry leaves without making a sound.*

Orion zipped off. Jericho tried to look casual while he waited.

A few of the people looked at him, their faces mixed expressions of curiosity and fear. One or two opened their mouths as if they were about to speak, but then changed their mind. He looked back at them, equally curious. Was that what people were wearing these days? No one said anything, and the silence grew long and awkward. When Orion returned, Jericho heaved a sigh of relief.

It's a tavern with about thirty people inside, Orion sent. *There's a rear door as well as stairs that go up to the roof. There are windows, but they have bars over them.*

Jericho thought about it. The place was ideal. There were a sufficient number of humans around to cause a panic when the fighting started, there were multiple exits, and he would arouse minimal suspicion while he waited.

He pulled his ghosts as tightly to himself as he could and went inside. Music, loud and angry and brooding, hit him like a wave. The inside of the bar was darker than the street. He let his eyes adjust. They had used candles to light the place. It looked nice. Almost like it could have existed in Gheistmar.

He made his way to a corner table and sat down. A single candle was on the table. He watched the flame and felt through the ether. The Gheistmar army was coming. The pull was so unmistakable even he could feel it.

A waitress came by and asked him what he wanted to drink.

"Give me the strongest stuff you have," he said. He had no idea what this tavern might serve. He didn't want to bring attention to himself by ordering something that hadn't been brewed for centuries. She went up to the bar. Jericho watched which bottle the bartender poured the drink from, hoping to see the label so he could order it by name next time. He couldn't make it out the name from this far away, though. All he could see was that it had a red label with black letters on it. The waitress came back with a small glass with about an inch of clear liquid in it.

She told him the price and he thought she was joking. Back when he consorted with humans, drinks cost cents, not dollars.

But she wasn't joking. The look on her face made that clear. So Jericho dug out the appropriate amount and gave it too her. She looked at the dollars with a funny expression on her face and for a second he thought she wasn't going to take them. They were very old, after all. But she took a good look at them and slipped them into her pocket. As she was turning to go, the trouble started. Jericho felt Lana zip out and bite the waitress. The poor girl yelped and stared back at him in fury.

Damn it, Lana, Jericho sent. *Be good! The last thing I need is trouble with the humans!*

Oh, calm down, she sent back. There was rage and hate in her voice that surprised him. *That little slut liked it.*

Jericho watched the waitress. She stomped back to the bar. As he watched the girl, he took a sip from his drink. Gods in heaven and hell! The stuff was almost pure alcohol! He could clean paint brushes with it. He set the drink back down and grimaced both from the taste and what he saw: the waitress had approached one of the men working in the bar. From the look on her face, Lana was wrong. The little slut hadn't liked that at all.

Taverns hadn't really changed that much throughout the centuries. As the man working at the bar looked over at him, Jericho and all of his ghosts agreed that trouble was coming.

CHAPTER 40

Beetle smiled. It was amusing and a little sad to watch the humans scurry before them. Then again, what did he expect them to do? The Irons were marching down the street in full armor. The army was in perfect time. Each step they took was like a clap of thunder as hundreds of studded boots stomped on the paved street. They encountered dead cars whose electronics had shorted out while they were still blocks away. The Irons' columns split and realigned as they flowed around the unmoving vehicles. The few humans who were outside to witness the march either stood watching, frozen with awe, or simply ran like animals before a storm. Most ran.

The humans weren't afraid just of the ancient-looking army, they were also afraid of the ghosts the army brought with them. Even humans who were nearly deaf to the spirit world could still sense the sheer magnitude of ghosts as the electrical power went out and the temperature dropped. The air was heavy with the wailing and grumbling of disembodied voices.

To Beetle, this was pure joy. The Irons had never looked so intimidating. The men were angry and eager to avenge their earlier embarrassment in Gheistmar. They looked ready to tear Jericho apart with their bare hands. Their eyes were narrowed and their mouths were set in straight, hard lines. Their armor was polished brighter than the harvest moon. They looked invincible and righteous. They looked like arch-angels going to war.

Except Cull, of course. In his black armor and carrying the harpoon with the chain, he could have been a grim pagan god who had clawed his way up from hell for a taste of blood.

All of these valiant warriors were marching behind Beetle. His chest was bursting with pride. Not with pride of himself, but pride of his soldiers. They were well trained and ready for this. The men who had died at the battle in Gheistmar were going to be avenged.

Jericho was just ahead. It had been effortless to follow the path he left in the ether. Almost too effortless. Jericho had to know that they were searching for him. The thought worried Beetle. When they came close to where Jericho was hiding, Beetle ordered his army to a halt as he considered the situation.

They were on a main street in the city. Parked cars lined the sides of the street and numerous vehicles were stalled haphazardly across the lanes. The buildings were set close together and none of them were particularly high compared to the towers farther in the city. Beetle closed his eyes and felt through the ether. Jericho was inside the building with people gathered out front. It was a bar of some kind. Surely he didn't think that he could hide amongst humans? Beetle looked around. There had to be more to this. What would he do if he were Jericho? Would he make a stand inside the bar? Would he try to flee to the open street? Beetle stood there, chewing on the problem.

A minute later, he had it. The roofs. That's where Jericho was going. The building must have roof access and Jericho was thinking he could hop rooftop to rooftop just like he had done in Gheistmar.

Well, he was wrong. There would be no repeat of the Gheistmar disaster. Beetle would make sure of that. He turned to his men.

"I want guards on top of every building around here," he said. His voice was confident and loud. "Be ready, because I think Jericho will try to take the high road out of here."

Many of the humans on the street had run away. The few that hadn't run watched the Vagabonds in amazement. They pointed and chattered amongst themselves as the Irons dispersed. Beetle wondered what the humans could be thinking as they watched the soldiers climb ladders on the sides of buildings with crossbows slung on their back. At least three Irons went to each building in the area. If there wasn't a ladder or fire escape on the side, they broke down the door and used stairs inside to gain access to the roof. On some of the shorter buildings, they used a grappling hook and a rope to get to the top. It was quite a sight, watching them scale the buildings like mountain climbers.

Finally, Beetle's avenging archangels had ascended into the heavens. If Jericho tried to escape on the rooftops, he'd be shot full of arrows and cut to pieces. If he ran out into the street, the Irons could rain arrows down upon him.

Beetle had kept a dozen Irons down on the ground with him. They all had crossbows loaded and ready to go. He sent half of them to the back door of the tavern. The other half went to the front door. The group of humans scattered like startled birds as the soldiers approached. Beetle was in the lead, and he glared at the humans as they retreated. He wanted the humans scared and out of the way when this began. He didn't want to kill any of them if he could help it.

Beetle paused in front of the door. He had sent four Irons to the top of this roof. Was that enough? Jericho would probably try to escape by that route. Beetle wanted some assurance. He turned to Cull.

"Head up to the roof," Beetle said. "When I shoot up the signal arrow, we'll all go in at the same time. I'm guessing that Jericho is going to try to run up your stairs, so be ready."

The black metal mountain that was Cull nodded once. He crouched down and leapt. His ghosts grabbed hold of him at the top of his leap and yanked him twenty feet into the air. He caught a windowsill with one hand and dangled for a brief instant. He dug his feet into the side of the building and leapt again. This time his ghosts carried him high enough that he was able to grab the edge of the roof and pull himself up onto it.

Beetle blinked dumbly. He had expected Cull to take the fire escape. It was astonishing to witness the raw power of that man's ghosts. If Jericho made a run for the roof, he was going to have a very nasty surprise on the way up.

Now there was nothing left to do. All bases were covered, all contingencies taken into account. Beetle took a deep breath. In spite of it all, he was nervous. For a brief moment, he considered waiting for Duke and the Wretched. Then he quickly squashed the thought. The Irons had demanded that they be the first ones to confront Jericho. They wanted—needed—to atone for their failure in Gheistmar. Beetle saw the anger in their eyes every time he looked at them. The Irons' honor was at stake, and Beetle refused to deprive them of the opportunity for redemption. Besides, this was a delicate job. Killing a specific person in a room crowded full of humans might be beyond the Wretched. The Irons didn't just deserve this job, they were the best ones for it.

Everything was in place. It was time.

Beetle unslung his crossbow and reached into his quiver and took out his signal arrow. The tip of the arrow was wrapped in strips of cotton fabric and had been soaked in pitch. He held it out at arm's length and one of the Irons ran over and lit it. The arrow flared with orange flame so bright it made Beetle squint. He nocked the arrow and put his finger on the trigger. He leaned back and shot the arrow straight up. The arrow flew over the buildings, racing upward like a star trying to return to the night sky.

Before the arrow reached the apex of its flight, Beetle and the Irons surged into the building through every door.

The bartender's blood was pounding in his ears as he flipped the light switch. His muscles tensed as he prepared to dash at the creepy guy in the corner. He took half a step and stopped. The lights hadn't come on.

He reached back and checked the switch. Yes, he had flipped it. Why hadn't the lights come on? He flipped the switch up and down several times. Nothing. Man, of all the times for the breaker to flip ... He really didn't want to deal with this guy in the dark.

The bouncers were looking back at him expectantly, probably wondering what the hell was taking him so long to turn on the damn lights.

He clicked the switch a few more times in blind hope. No dice.

The bartender shrugged and gestured to the bouncers to grab the guy. They were going to have do this thing without lights. They all moved forward, pushing around other customers. They were within a few feet of the table when the damnedest thing happened. It made them all freeze. The bartender blinked slowly, uncertain if he was seeing things correctly.

Kiki, the waitress who had complained about being bitten by the creep, came over and sat on the guy's lap. She wrapped her arms around him and kissed him on the cheek. This made no sense at all. The bouncers looked over at the bartender, wondering what they should do. The bartender was wondering the same thing. He watched Kiki and the guy chatting. The two seemed as close as grade school chums. Kiki had a big smile on her face. The guy was frowning.

What on earth was going on?

Jericho frowned as the waitress came over and sat on his lap. She put her arms around him and kissed him once on the cheek.

"I was prettier than this girl," she said. Her voice was different. Not the sound of it, but the manner in which she spoke. Her pronunciation of every word was precise, her tone formal. Outdated.

"Lana," Jericho said. "Get out of that poor girl."

Ghosts could be amazingly petty. Something as small as an open door or a crooked mirror could engage their attention utterly. They might fixate on that one thing so much that it might grow to define their entire existence. They would focus all of their energy on slamming a door shut or straightening the mirror. They wouldn't care about anything else. These types of ghosts were perfect for anchoring to items.

Lana was different. Like most powerful ghosts, she still had a fairly human thought process. Talking to her was usually about the same as talking to a live person. Usually. Sometimes, though, memories of her old life crept in and she got distracted. Jericho guessed that she had always been accustomed to being the prettiest girl in the room. This waitress—a lovely girl certainly— had caught Lana's attention by being too attractive. Before Jericho could stop her, Lana had slid away and possessed the girl.

Her timing was atrocious. The ether was quivering with the sheer number of Vagabonds in the area, and all of those Vagabonds wanted Jericho dead. He needed Lana.

"Get out of her," he said again. The music cut out and the air had a sudden chill to it. The Gheistmar army was right outside. A few humans yelled their irritation at the sudden silence. Others, though, looked around in alarm. The humans could feel that something bad was about to happen. Some of them backed into corners or ducked under tables, seeking shelter from whatever was coming their way.

"Oh Jericho," she said as she put her arms up and stretched like a kitten laying in the sun. "You don't understand. It's so pleasant to have flesh again. This girl has a very nice body. It's not nicer than mine was, though." She pulled open the top of her shirt and looked down. "My teats were much better and this bony little ass has just got to be digging into your leg." She wiggled for emphasis.

"Lana ... "

"Still, I think this girl could make some money on her back."

"I need you right now," Jericho said. "Now, not later. I can't do this without you."

"That's good to hear," she said. She placed her palm against his face. "Don't worry, I won't let you down. But I want you to

promise me one thing. Someday, I'd like to fully experience
having flesh again. I'll get a nice girl like this and you can show
me the pleasure, the sheer joy of being alive. Can you promise me
that?"

"I ... " Jericho was taken off guard.

"Promise me, Jericho, and I'll be oh so good." She gave him a
smile that was somehow wounded and hopeful and seductive all
at once.

"Well?" she said. "Do we have a deal?"

The bartender edged closer as Kiki stood up. She walked
over to a chair and sat down. For one long second she was
motionless, then her eyes rolled back in her head and she fell
forward. One of the bouncers sprang over and caught her just
before she hit the floor.

The creepy man stood up. He moved smoothly, like he had
the balance and poise of a boxer. His coat fell open and there, on
his belt, was a sword. A real goddamned sword!

Before the bartender could say anything, several men rushed
in through the front door. They wore metal armor and were
carrying bows and arrows. The bartender made a sudden
decision. He grabbed Kiki from the bouncer and tossed her over
his shoulder.

"Come on," he called to his bouncers. "We're getting the hell
out of here!" He ran for the back without looking to see whether
they were following or not. Kiki's dead weight bounced up and
down on his shoulder as he ran. He was almost to the door when
the bar was hit by a tornado.

Beetle burst into the bar with six of his Irons right behind
him. His finger was hooked around the trigger of his crossbow
and he had the weapon raised; Beetle expected Jericho to attack
immediately and wanted to put a bolt through his heart before he
could do any more damage.

The room was full scurrying humans and it took Beetle a
fraction of a second to find Jericho in the crowd. It was a fraction

of a second too long.

Jericho unleashed his ghosts. Their raw power was breathtaking. Tables, chairs, and even humans were flung toward Beetle. It was an impenetrable wall of debris that crashed against them with mind-numbing force. The edge of a table caught Beetle on his shoulder and knocked him flat to the ground. Furniture shattered against the wall above him. The sharp cracking of wood mixed with screams from both humans and Vagabonds.

Beetle raised his head in time to see Jericho dash across the room and up the stairs ... and right into Cull's fist. Cull timed it perfectly. He caught Jericho full on in the face, sending Jericho back down the stairs to land in a heap on the floor. Jericho lay motionless, completely unconscious.

Cull jumped into the air. He held his harpoon with both hands, the tip pointed down. He was going to pin Jericho to the floor like a bug ...

The misty form of one of Jericho's ghosts swirled around Jericho and harshly yanked his body out of the way. Cull landed right where Jericho had been, driving his harpoon into the floor. The entire building seemed to shake with the impact.

Jericho's body rolled across the floor and crashed into some chairs. The collision seemed to wake him. He got up on all fours and shook his head like he was trying to clear the cobwebs there.

Beetle got to his knees and then forced himself to stand. He ached where the table had hit him, but he didn't think he had any broken bones. He looked over to his Irons. They had all been knocked down. Four were getting up. Near the back door, three Irons were struggling to their feet.

Cull gripped his harpoon and pulled. Splinters of wood flew into the air as he tore the weapon free. He strode over to Jericho and swung the harpoon downward, looking to split Jericho's head like he was chopping a piece of wood. Jericho somehow managed to roll to the side and the harpoon thundered against the floor, sending more splinters into the air. As Cull lifted it from the floor, he swung it horizontally. Beetle was certain it was a homerun swing, sure to send Jericho's head flying.

In a motion so smooth and liquid that it seemed to have superhuman speed, Jericho drew his blade and blocked the swing. The brute force of the impact slid him back nearly a foot. Jericho looked dazed and worried. How could he not be? He'd just been knocked unconscious and woken up to find himself suddenly fighting the strongest Vagabond in Gheistmar. Beetle didn't think Jericho would last much longer before Cull caught him. One solid hit from the harpoon would put any man down permanently.

It wasn't enough for Beetle. Jericho was too dangerous.

Beetle lifted his crossbow to his shoulder.

"Shoot him!" he cried out loudly to the Irons. "Don't worry about Cull, you can't hurt him. Shoot Jericho!"

Like the well-trained soldiers they were, the Irons shook off their stupor and raised their crossbows. Every Iron able to stand—both those in the front of the room as well as those in the back—sighted in on Jericho and let their bolts fly.

CHAPTER 41

Jericho woke up to find himself fighting Cull. It was quite possibly the worst way to wake up ever.

He vaguely recalled running up the stairs and getting hit. The knight's black armor had blended in with the dark of the stairwell and Jericho had seen Cull just in time to get slammed in the face by one of his massive fists. The next thing he knew, he was rolling away from Cull's harpoon. He stood on wobbly feet and drew his sword to block a swing of the harpoon. The two weapons clanged together and the jolt hurt Jericho to his bones.

From what sounded like far away, he heard someone shouting "Shoot him!" The Irons raised their crossbows and Jericho knew he had less than a second to live.

In an idea born of desperation and sheer craziness, Jericho sprang forward and wrapped his arms around Cull's waist. The crossbows twanged. Immediately after came the sharp crack of Cull's armor ghosts slapping the arrows out of the air. The deflected arrows rattled across the floor. Not one had penetrated the ghostly barrier.

Jericho heaved a sigh of relief. He hadn't really thought that would work.

Cull brought his fist down on Jericho's head and Jericho fell the floor, dazed. He was seeing double and barely managed to roll to the side as Cull's massive harpoon crashed into the wooden floor right where he had been.

Jericho staggered to his feet. His knees were still unsteady. A duel with Cull was about the last thing he wanted to be doing.

With a crack of wood, Cull pulled his harpoon free of the floor and swung again. Jericho blocked the blow with his sword and the impact numbed his arm. Again and again Cull attacked and Jericho parried. The man carried the heavy harpoon like it was a toothpick! Jericho was quicker, but he had nothing to aim for. The knight's armor was practically seamless. There wasn't any weak spot that Jericho could discern, even if he could get past the protective ghosts.

In a fair fight with plenty of room to move, Jericho felt he would have won. Either he could have simply shot Cull with one of his magnet arrows or, if he didn't have the time and room to use his bow, he could have used one of the arrows like a dagger. He could have danced around Cull until the knight grew tired and Jericho could stabbed with the arrow to get in a cut here and there at the joints in his armor and slowly bleed him out. But in the cramped room, the odds were not in Jericho's favor.

The Irons stayed where they were and hastily reloaded their crossbows. The crik-crik of their cranks sounded like a group of giant insects. In a handful of heartbeats, they'd be ready to shoot again. And this time, Cull would be expecting Jericho to dive forward. That trick wouldn't work twice. Jericho was about to have his ghosts put out the candles so that the Irons couldn't see him when a thought occurred to him.

Jericho clashed weapons with Cull again, maneuvering until he was able to jump over the bar. He looked for the bottle of the stuff he had ordered. There it was, the red label with the black lettering. He grabbed the bottle and flung it at Cull. Cull's armor ghosts slapped it out of the air, breaking the bottle. The high proof liquor splashed all over the front of Cull's armor.

The black knight looked down at himself. When he realized what had happened, he held one hand up like he was saying "Wait."

Jericho didn't wait. He jumped back over the bar. He unsheathed the dagger Lilith had given him and clashed it against his kilij. The ghost bonded to the dagger responded, and the blade crackled with brilliant blue sparks that cast trembling shadows across the walls. He feinted a straight thrust and, as Cull moved to block it, Jericho spun and delivered a backhand slash. The armor ghosts knocked the dagger away, but not before the electricity ignited the fumes of the liquor.

Cull roared as flame covered him. He tried to pat it out it with his free hand, but only smeared the flames. The entire room was bathed in the glow. It was bright inside the bar now.

Cull roared again, this time higher and more frantic. The heat was getting to him already. The knight tugged at straps on his armor. He couldn't get them undone. He dropped his harpoon and used both his hands. The front chest plate of his armor came loose and dropped. He frantically undid the clasps to his flaming breastplate, getting first one side free and then the other.

Before the armor even hit the floor, Jericho drove his sword in a powerful straight thrust that pierced the leather Cull wore and sunk into his flesh.

Cold! Jericho commanded the ghost bonded to the blade. The ghost obeyed. In the span of one second, the ghost pulled tremendous amounts of heat from Cull. Enough to kill two men through hypothermia. Jericho yanked the blade out and Cull fell to the floor and didn't move. Frost crusted his leather armor, covering the scorch marks.

The Irons had finished reloading. A couple of them were already taking aim. Jericho flung himself toward the stairs and dashed up them. Crossbow bolts thwocked into the wall behind him. His ghosts sped him up the stairs so fast he was practically flying.

What the hell had Jericho done to Cull? Beetle wasn't sure, exactly. The stab with the sword hadn't looked fatal, yet Cull's limp body was laying on the floor. Beetle was upset. He had liked Cull, even if the man hadn't said much. Now that he thought about it, maybe that was why he liked him.

So what had happened? Beetle didn't have a clue. He hated these little tricks from Jericho. Why couldn't the man fight fair and die properly?

Beetle didn't follow Jericho up the stairs. It would do no good. Jericho was too fast. Besides, Beetle knew where Jericho was going. The situation was acceptable. They had planned for this.

"Outside!" Beetle shouted to his men. "He's taking to the roofs!"

Jericho prepared himself for a confrontation. He figured Beetle might have another nasty surprise waiting for him on top of the roof.

When he passed a window, he stopped and went back to look out. Maybe he didn't have to go to the top of this building at all. The roof of the next building was close and just slightly higher than the window he was looking out of. The window didn't have any bars on it because it was so far above the ground. He used his ghosts to blast out the glass. As the shards fell tinkling through the air, he climbed onto the windowsill. He sheathed his sword and dagger and jumped out the window to the other roof. It was a short jump and he didn't even need to use his ghosts. He caught hold of the edge of the building and pulled himself up.

Four Irons were on the roof. Like a reflex, Leo did his trick with time and suddenly everything was moving in slow motion, allowing Jericho to take in every detail.

All four of the Irons carried crossbows. Jericho shot two of them before they even saw him and the third before he could raise his crossbow. The fourth managed to raise his crossbow and fire, but he was nervous and his aim was off. The bolt missed its mark by several feet. Jericho lunged forward and unsheathed his sword. He used that momentum and kept his weapon moving in a smooth arc that slashed across the last Iron's neck. The Iron tumbled backward with gouts of blood spurting from his wound.

Time snapped back to moving quickly and Jericho saw that he was far from alone up here. Irons stood on every neighboring rooftop. Some had seen him. They aimed their crossbows. A handful of hastily fired bolts flew and clattered against the building.

The rooftops weren't an option. The moon was out and far too bright. Jericho didn't have the element of surprise. He'd be shot down before he made it two blocks.

Another bolt zipped by. It missed by only a few feet. The next one might not miss at all. He had to get off this roof. Now.

He ran to the edge of the building. Two stories below, the street was clogged with stationary automobiles. In the moonlight, their metal shone like the dark polished wood of coffins. From this high up, they looked like little shiny insects. He picked one and leapt.

Beetle swore as he watched Jericho jump from the building. Jericho's long black coat fluttered behind him as he fell through the air. His ghosts swirled around him, slowing his fall. Their pale forms trailed him like a misty comet tail.

He landed on the roof of a car, crumpling the thin metal and lacing with car's windows with a webbing of white cracks. The impact drove him to one knee.

Jericho rose up. His face was contorted into a feral snarl. He seemed to be glaring at Beetle, at the Irons, at the entire world, daring them all to just try and kill him. The raw determination in his every movement sent knives of fear into Beetle's spine.

But there was something else. As Jericho jumped off the car and onto the pavement, he stumbled a little. After he took a few steps it was apparent that he was favoring his right ankle. Jericho was wounded.

Like a long distance runner finally sighting the finish line, Beetle felt relief and excitement that the end was approaching. The Irons had this area of the city completely surrounded. Jericho had nowhere to go. Any running he did would only delay the inevitable. And with him wounded, the hunt would be that much easier.

The clop of horses' hooves echoed through the street. Duke was coming, and he was bringing the Wretched.

Jericho's ankle hurt. He had twisted it on the crumpling car roof. He jumped down to the street and tried to run. He couldn't. It felt like a spike had been driven into his ankle. He hobbled a few paces. This was slow going. Far too slow.

A crossbow bolt tore through the edge of his coat and skipped across the pavement. Irons stood along the edge of the buildings lining the street. He had to get moving or he was going to be skewered where he stood.

He ducked down and pressed his back against an automobile. He cut a strip of leather from his coat and tightly wrapped his ankle with it. That would help some, at least.

A few blocks down, someone shouted. Jericho leaned and looked down the street. The black carriage that transported the Wretched was approaching. Six massive armored horses strained at the reigns and Duke sat in the driver's seat. He cracked the whip above the horses, his face twisted in an unnatural combination of rage and joy.

Jericho didn't know what to do. If he ran for the alleys, the Irons could easily shoot him down. There was no possible way for him to outrun the wagon, not with his hurt ankle. And taking on both Duke and the Wretched that were surely inside the carriage was beyond even Jericho.

Lana was beside him. Her appearance was sudden. One second she wasn't there, the next she was. She had her back pressed against the car, mimicking Jericho. Her mouth moved like she was talking, but Jericho couldn't understand her. He was too distracted by the arrival of the carriage. What was Lana trying to say?

The wagon passed Beetle and the tavern where Jericho had been ambushed. Duke made eye contact with Jericho. His blue eyes seemed to be glittering with joy. The horses' hooves sounded like cannons firing as they resounded against the pavement. The air was filled with the wails of ghosts. It sounded like an out of tune violin.

It was a cacophony. Jericho had to focus completely on Lana to understand her. And even then, he was able to make out only two words.

Those two words were enough. Jericho understood.

Duke had one hell of a surprise coming.

CHAPTER 42

"**Horses**" **was one** of the words Lana was trying to say. Another word was "fire". Jericho was fairly certain she was saying that horses hate fire.

Jericho's knowledge of modern technology was extremely limited. He couldn't explain how electric lights worked or how buildings were so high or how a car ran. But he did remember one of the basic aspects of a car: it was powered by a flammable liquid.

He tried to recall where, exactly, the liquid was held. Somewhere near the rear of the vehicle, he thought. He nocked an arrow and aimed at the side of a large vehicle close to him. He picked a large one on the reasoning that it would hold more flammable liquid. Gasoline. Yes, that was it. He figured the large car would be full of gas.

His bow was capable of piercing the heavy armor of knights; at close range the thin metal of the car was almost like paper. His first arrow ripped through one side and out the other. His second lodged somewhere in the car's guts. He kept shooting, hoping to hit the gas by sheer luck.

After six arrows the car was leaking. The fluid trickled across

the street, passing right in front of him. Jericho hoped it was the
gas. The pungent smell seemed right, at least.

Fire was a tricky business. It was unpredictable. And he
wasn't sure just how flammable that gas was. Jericho wanted to
get as far away from the car as possible. But there wasn't any
time. If he wanted to create a flaming barricade, he had to do it
now.

He had Susha spark the stream of gas and flame snaked
lightning fast toward the car.

The plan had been simple: set a car on fire to spook the horses
and buy Jericho some time. It didn't work out quite right.

The flame gobbled up the gas that leaking from the car and
burrowed into the vehicle. The car exploded with a boom. Parts
of the vehicle shot everywhere, whistling through the air before
careening off buildings and pavement and other vehicles. Jericho
fell and rolled beneath another car. A wave of heat pressed down
and sizzled the hair on the back of his hands. The street was
brighter than day as the fiery explosion soaked the city in oily
orange light. The horses whinnied in terror and jerked hard to the
left. The wagon teetered on two wheels, balanced there for a
moment, then fell on its side.

The scorched ruin of the car crashed down onto the
pavement, bounced once, and was still. The bright light from the
explosion faded, leaving a night that seemed darker than before.

Jericho scrambled out from underneath the car and started
running again. His trick had worked better than he thought, but
he still didn't have much time. The Wretched would be out of the
wagon and on his heels in moments. And so he ran. He tried his
best to ignore his ankle. He tried to ignore the commotion behind
him as Gheistmar' best warriors gathered together and pursued
him. He focused only on putting one foot in front of another.

It was time to make his stand, and he needed to be in just the
right place for it to work.

The horses were dragging the wagon on its side. Beetle ran
over and started cutting the reins. As each horse was set loose,

they galloped down the street and to be swallowed by the night.

Duke had leapt free as the wagon tipped. Now he stood looking off in the direction of Jericho. His entire body shook in rage.

The heavy doors of the tipped wagon flung open and the Wretched began to climb out. With a jerk of his head, Duke sent them running off after Jericho.

"Where can he go?" Duke growled.

"Nowhere," Beetle said. "This street dead ends into a pier. Beyond the pier is only the lake."

"Can he leave the street, cut through some alley and escape the city?"

"Not without getting stuck full of arrows from Irons. I have them on the top of every building."

"And if he fights through them?"

"More Irons," Beetle said. "We have everything committed to this operation. Unless Jericho can walk on water, he has nowhere to go."

They were both silent. Beetle was pondering if there was any way Jericho could indeed walk on water, and he knew Duke was wondering the same thing. The very idea was preposterous and Beetle hated Jericho for making them even consider the possibility.

"So there's nowhere he can go," Duke said quietly.

"The only place he's going," Beetle said. "Is to his grave."

Jericho somehow made it to the pier without being skewered by an arrow. Those bastard Irons were everywhere! He wondered if they had left any of them in Gheistmar.

He ran down the dock that was wide enough for five people to walk abreast. He ran to the end of the dock, far out over the black water. He stood on the edge. The stars were reflected in the water and it seemed as if he were standing in space, surrounded by nothing but distant planets and stars.

The illusion was shattered when a shudder ran through the pier. Footsteps. A lot of them. Jericho turned. There were the

Wretched. They ran onto the dock and formed lines.

Behind them, on the land, came the Irons. They lined the shore. Jericho was out of bow range for them. A couple tried anyway. Their arrows arced high in the air and came down and slipped into the water with hardly a sound. The Irons were simply there to guard against the slim possibility that Jericho got past the Wretched.

The Wretched weren't moving now. They had formed up and then gone still.

Jericho wondered what they were waiting for. Surely they didn't expect him to just charge them. Then Duke arrived on the shoreline. And there was Beetle, right by his side. Duke made a quick motion with his hand and the Wretched began to advance. As one, they took a step. Their discipline was impressive. They were working as a perfect unit. Although their bodies were different sizes, their masks made them all look the same. They each held a gladius. The short sword, perfect for thrusting and slashing in close combat.

This style of fighting had been effective for hundreds of years. The Romans had perfected it. The Roman legions had been nearly unbeatable in their time. Countless barbarians had launched themselves against that machine of death and been processed into lifeless piles of flesh. Jericho could feel the helpless terror of those barbarians, as they knew even before the battle began that they had already lost and the only task left to them was to die well.

Jericho breathed deep, inhaling the night air. The night was cooling and thin wisps of mist curled on the lake's surface. The pier felt good beneath his feet. Solid. The air tasted clean and wet. He had few regrets in his life, if any.

Jericho breathed out.

He was ready.

Duke started chuckling. His amusement gathered strength until it was a full out laugh.

"What?" asked Beetle. He was happy too, but it was far too early for laughter. Not with Jericho still alive.

"We've been idiots," Duke said. "Jericho doesn't need to walk on water at all."

Beetle squinted at him.

"What do you mean?" Beetle said.

"Think about it," Duke told him. "How do people normally get across water?"

Beetle considered the question. He stared out at the end of the pier where Jericho stood, taking in every detail.

He saw it. A shadow in the shadows, it was practically invisible.

"That cheeky bastard," Beetle swore. He glanced at Duke. "So why were you laughing?"

"Because it doesn't change a damn thing," Duke replied. "I just wish I could see his face when I ruin his little plan."

The pier shuddered as the Wretched advanced. Their slow, steady steps resonated through the wood.

But that wasn't what Jericho was listening to. From underneath the boards came a thumping in time with the waves.

Tucked underneath the dock was a row boat. It was tethered with a short rope to one of the dock's wooden beams. The waves knocked it gently against the beam and the rhythmic thumping comforted him. He had tied it there before going to the tavern, and he had feared that the rope would somehow break or someone would take it. But nothing had happened. The boat was there and Jericho could escape. There was no way the Wretched would be swimming after him. With metal for blood, they would sink straight to the bottom.

Jericho nocked an arrow. He gauged the distance between him and the Wretched and was about to fire the first shot when the ruse hit him.

The ruse was powerful, and it evoked a spark of terror in him for an instant. *The ship is sinking. Everyone is drowning. Get into a boat! Get into a boat!* Images of a sinking ocean liner flashed in Jericho's mind. The screaming people were nearly audible and he could almost feel the slippery deck as it canted to an angle that grew steeper with every passing second.

Jericho was stunned. The ruse had came from Duke, that much was for certain. But why?

The water beneath the pier rippled and splashed, and Jericho had his answer.

Damn, he thought. My boat!

CHAPTER 43

Ghosts saturated everything. They soaked into spooky old houses and ancient jewelry and even people themselves. Lake Eerie was no exception. Numerous people had drowned in the lake and the ghosts were attracted to water anyway. Duke's ruse roused the sleeping spirits and goaded them into a thrashing fury. They were drowning! They needed to get in the boat!

The boat was yanked out from underneath the pier as though a giant fish had grabbed it. It stopped suddenly as the rope snapped taut. The water roiled beneath the boat as several ghosts all fought to climb in.

There was plenty of room for them all, of course. How much space did a ghost take up, anyway? But the ghosts didn't know they were dead, and the ruse made them panic. They acted just as drowning humans would act. Dozens of pale watery hands shot out of the water and grabbed onto the sides of the boat. They clawed for purchase against the slippery wood. Drowning! Drowning! The boat rocked one way and then the other. Back and forth it went until the ghosts on one side pulled harder and the boat tipped and flooded with water and sank.

Jericho watched it go. It was like accidentally dropping a gold doubloon in a pond and being able to do nothing but watch as it faded from view.

Even when it was underwater, the ghosts continued to struggle over it. The boat jerked back and forth as unseen hands played tug of war with it. There were so many ghosts down there that the surface of the water above the boat glazed over with a thin film of ice. That had been one hell of a ruse! Jericho was impressed. If this was the end, at least he wasn't losing to an unworthy adversary.

The ice broke apart and the waves scattered the few remaining shards. The boat was no longer even visible. A single oar floated up from the depths and bobbed on the surface. For some reason, he felt like it was mocking him.

Nothing to do about it. The boat was gone. The Wretched were still there. And he hadn't expected to come out of this anyway. He had hoped to somehow escape, certainly. But deep down inside he had always known that the odds of him surviving were miniscule.

Like the barbarians knowing that they had already lost, Jericho had only one thing left to do. He drew back the arrow and took aim. He told Orion to help guide his arrows into the small areas of exposed flesh.

The Wretched continued to march toward him, an unstoppable wall of metal and cold flesh. They were incapable of feeling pain and had no concept of mercy. These unbeatable soldiers were supposed to chop him apart while Duke and Beetle enjoyed the show from the safety of the shore.

Cold rage surged through him. They had tried to kill him and forced him into hiding. They had taken everything from him.

Now it was time for Jericho to take something from them.

He loosed his arrow. It zipped through the air and struck the neck of the Wretched on the far right side in the front line. The Wretched howled and stumbled and then fell and lay still. Jericho loosed another arrow and dropped a second Wretched. This one tumbled into the water and disappeared beneath the surface.

Again and again Jericho fired. Each arrow found its mark and dropped an undead soldier.

On some level, Jericho was happy. He was happy that his arrows were working. The magnet arrows that he had designed for the Brute's special armor worked just as well to drive the ghosts from the Wretched. The magnets disrupted the ghosts' electricity and took away their ability to control the undead body.

He had solved the puzzle of how to kill the Wretched. He remembered when Duke had dropped the Colossus simply by stabbing it with the knife outside the Tombs. How that had puzzled him! Much later he had realized that Duke's knife must have had a magnetic blade. The blade on Cinder's spear probably magnetic as well. That was how they were able to control the Wretched. Jericho was almost embarrassed that it had taken him so much time to figure it out. And even then, using magnets to kill the Wretched had been just an untested theory. Now, he was sure. And despite the awful circumstances, Jericho experienced a small splash of happiness.

The magnets arrows changed everything. This was why Duke had been trying to kill him. This was why they had destroyed his home and tried to kill everyone close to him. They were trying to erase the concept of magnet arrows, as that was the one chink in the armor of the otherwise invincible Wretched. It turned them from unstoppable soldiers to fragile mortals.

Of the twenty or so Wretched, Jericho had already killed half. The remaining ones charged. Their only hope was to overwhelm him before he could shoot them all. He loosed arrow after arrow furiously. The Wretched were dropping, but they had closed the distance fast. If he slipped up or missed with even one arrow, they would be upon him.

A massive creature pushed through the back of the Wretched ranks. Its heavily muscled flesh strained against the steel cables that held it together.

They had put a new ghost into Colossus.

Jericho shot an arrow that caught the beast in its thigh. The new Colossus roared and staggered as the ghost fought for control of the body. The ghost lost its grip, though, and the creature collapsed and didn't move.

These arrows sure would have made the Tombs battle a lot easier, thought Jericho. A pang of regret echoed through him. He really should have figured out all of this a long time ago.

Two Wretched remained. One of the Wretched's mask had been knocked off in the fray. It was Peter. Poor Peter. He and Claire should have been holding hands and watching the moon rise. Instead, she was missing and he was an undead revenant.

Yet one more person who had died because they knew Jericho.

He shot the other Wretched in the chest and the kid leapt through the air at him, his sword poised to ram through Jericho's chest.

Instinct more than thought made Jericho react. He sent all his ghosts out in one concentrated force against the Wretched. They clawed into the creature's silver blood and yanked with all their might. Their strength was ferocious, and the air was filled with a dense cloud of silvery mist as they tore the blood out of it.

When the Wretched collided with Jericho, it was only a lifeless husk. It fell to the boards and lay still. Jericho slammed an arrow into the corpse just to be sure.

Jericho stood tall, breathing heavily. The bodies of the Wretched lay scattered along the pier. Several had fallen into the water and sank into the depths. The fish would eat the flesh and Cinder wouldn't ever be able to install new spirits into the bodies.

"It's over!" Jericho screamed out to Duke.

"You're right," Duke called back. "It is over."

The Irons were scurrying around on the shore. They carried red containers full of liquid that they spilled across the dock.

Gasoline. It had to be. They had probably looted it from one of the stores in the city and now they would set the dock on fire.

They did. Someone nicked a piece of flint and with a whoosh, the front section of the dock was carpeted in flame.

The fire ate into the wooden pier and began to spread. It was excruciatingly bright. The rest of the night became impenetrable blackness compared to the inferno. Jericho could no longer see the men on the shore. Standing alone above the dark water, he felt isolated from the rest of the world.

The fire was coming for him quickly. The wood of the pier had been baked dry by the sun, and it burning very fast. Like the Wretched, it advanced steadily. But now he had no special arrows, no surprise up his sleeve.

The fire reached the first bodies of the Wretched and their flesh began to cook and then burn.

There was a loud crack near the shore and the boards beneath his feet shifted as the fire burned through the ropes holding the dock together. The front section of the dock collapsed. The burning boards hit the water and sizzled in a cloud of steam.

Jericho wasn't going to burn. He knew that. Before the flames got to him, he would jump in the water and swim for shore. The problem was that the entire shore was lined with Irons. They would shoot him full of arrows before he even got a single foot on dry land.

He sat on the end of the pier. He cursed himself, wondering why the hell he had decided to make his stand so close to the water. If he had to die, he wanted to die on land. Surely he could have figured out a way to do all of this and stay dry.

Nothing to do about it now. He stared at the dark water. The flames were getting close enough to feel their heat. He wondered fleetingly just how big of a fire his ghosts could put out. This was far too large, he knew that. But a bonfire? Maybe.

It was getting hot. Rivulets of sweat trickled down his forehead. He didn't have much time left. The heat clawed at his back, penetrating through even the thick leather of his coat.

Another section of the pier fell away and the boards Jericho was sitting on suddenly canted backward, flinging him toward the flames. He rolled down the dock, which was now simply a ramp. His few remaining arrows spilled out of his quiver and rolled along with him. He clawed at the boards, desperately seeking purchase.

Like a reflex, Leo worked his magic and Jericho seemed to fall in slow motion. He could discern the sharp tips of the individual flames as they rose up from the glowing embers. Where the dock met the water, the surface of the lake was a chaotic mess of hissing steam and boiling water.

The fingers of his left hand caught in a crack between boards, stopping his decent only a few feet from the fire. The heat was brutal. Even with his ghosts cooling the metal in his coat, he could feel the heat tearing at his skin. One of his arrows rolled past him, and he shot his free hand out and grabbed it. He slipped it back in his quiver. It probably didn't matter. Not now. But he would need it if there were any more Wretched about.

The dock shifted again. The entire thing wobbled unsteadily. Jericho had waited too long to go into the water and now it was all about to collapse.

With a groan, the final supports to the dock gave way and it broke apart. An angry tower of steam and sparks broiled up from the surface of the lake as the burning wood met the cold water.

"Eyes open!" Beetle yelled to the Irons as he paced the shore. "Bows at the ready! If you see anything in the water, don't hesitate to shoot! Jericho will be coming soon."

They waited. The seconds oozed by, slow and sluggish. The Irons were as tense as their bow strings. Every other minute one of them thought they saw movement in the water and shot an arrow into the lake, prompting half a dozen other guards to do the same, unleashing a small flock of arrows. There would be a pause as they looked to see if they had shot something. So far, nothing.

Jericho had to come out of the lake soon. The cold would sap his strength and he would drown. No part of the pier was left standing, so Jericho was definitely in the water. Beetle had Irons spaced out to line the shore for a half mile in either direction. There was nowhere for Jericho to go. The nearest island was miles away. Even if Jericho could swim that far, the water was too cold. He had to make his attempt at an escape within the next few minutes.

This was a delicate and dangerous waiting game, Beetle

knew. While they were waiting for Jericho to try to escape, Jericho was out there treading water and hoping that the humans would come and force the Gheistmar army to flee. Beetle thought it was a clever but foolish gamble on Jericho's part. Sometimes the humans investigated, other times they waited until the Vagabonds and their haunts were long gone before venturing from the illusionary protection of their homes. Beetle felt certain that if they had enough patience, it would all be resolved. The odds of the humans coming were slim and with the wall of Irons, Jericho wouldn't be able to slip past unnoticed. Like Duke had once said, Jericho left a path through the ether as wide as an army. He couldn't sneak by.

A banshee began to wail. It was a long, drawn-out wail that was unbroken as if the banshee never needed to draw breath. The wail echoed off the buildings and reverberated in Beetle's very bones.

That wasn't quite right. The wail wasn't from a banshee. No, it was something different. Beetle had heard it before, but he couldn't place it.

"Sirens," Duke muttered. He frowned and looked toward the city. "Police sirens. So the humans here have more starch in them than I would have thought."

"Damn!" Beetle said. "We're so close."

"Give me your best estimate," Duke said. "How much longer can Jericho possibly survive in the water?"

Beetle considered the question.

"Well, I can't see that coat of his working in the water," Beetle said. "And I'm not even sure he could wear it. With all that metal, I think it'd drag him right to the bottom. So if he's not dead yet, I'd guess he couldn't last more than a quarter of an hour more. And that's being optimistic for him. In all likelihood, he's already fish food."

"We have to be sure," Duke said.

The sirens grew louder. They were very close now.

"Should I give the order for the men to disperse?" Beetle asked. "The human guards will be here any moment."

"We're not leaving," Duke said. "Not while there is even a remote possibility that Jericho could still be alive. Take some Irons with you and deal with the humans. I'll keep watch here."

"You want me to 'deal' with the humans? How? I'm no good at possessions."

"Kill them, Beetle. Simply kill them."

Beetle couldn't believe what he had just been ordered to do.

"Kill them?" Beetle said. "Are you sure?"

"Kill half of them, and let the survivors get a good look at you." Duke grinned. He took off his coat and held it out. "And wear my coat while you do it."

Beetle understood at once. In the dim light, Duke's dark purple coat looked a lot like Jericho's. The police would scour the city, searching for Jericho and ready to kill him on sight.

"Attack them without mercy. Send them running," Duke said. "That will buy us the time we need. The humans will send more, of course. Once they realize they are dealing with a serious threat, they will send their best soldiers with their best weapons. By then, though, we will be gone."

Duke leaned closer to Beetle before he continued. "Maybe Jericho somehow tricked us. Maybe he hid a second boat somewhere or he's walking on water or whatever. I can't tell if he's alive or not—the ether's a complete mess right now. But I can tell you that Jericho planned for us. He planned to face the Wretched and the Irons. Foolishly, we obliged him. But he couldn't have planned to deal with humans and their technology. Humans who are furious at having several of their fellow men killed. They will track him like a beast and kill him from so far off he'll never know he was in danger. Land, sea, air—Jericho will have nowhere to hide."

Beetle nodded slowly. He didn't like it, but he saw the wisdom of what Duke said. He cast one last glance out toward the dark water of the lake.

"Your goose is right cooked, boyo," he muttered.

Jericho watched the shore. Duke and the Irons still hadn't

left. They had lit torches, making the shore bright and impossible for him to slip by unnoticed. How much longer were they going to wait? The humans were coming. The piercing wail of their vehicles ripped through the air and drowned out all other sounds. The wail sounded desperate and urgent as the humans rushed to get to their destination.

Jericho wasn't in a hurry. He was warm and comfortable and almost dry. Before leaping into the water, he had used his ghosts to focus all of their energy on the water and drop the temperature. In mere seconds they had created a raft of ice thick enough to support his weight. He had grabbed the lone paddle from his boat and paddled himself out farther into the lake. He was far out enough that they couldn't see him in the dark. His coat kept him warm and his raft kept him dry. Now all he had to do was wait for Duke and the Irons to flee from the humans.

The sirens cut off abruptly. Jericho smiled. They must have come too close to the Vagabonds and the electronics on the vehicles died. With the sirens stopped, all the other sounds of the night came back. The whisper of the wind, the chattering of the waves. It was peaceful. Then, screams. A lot of them. Numerous small explosions cracked through the air.

What was happening? Who was fighting? The torches were put out and the Irons' shadowy figures on the shore scurried about and faded away. Lilith must have ambushed the Irons from behind! Jericho was angry at her for not listening to him. She was placing herself in danger. He started paddling wildly toward the shore. When he came within bowshot range, he slowed. Beetle was crafty. He wouldn't be surprised if there were a few guards left behind. He sent out Orion. An instant later, three figures were outlined in glowing silver. Two were to his left and one was to his right. Jericho had his bow, but only one arrow. He drifted on his ice raft for a few seconds, debating how to get ashore without being shot.

The screams of battle continued. It sounded like the fight was just a few streets away. Jericho had to get there to help Lilith.

The figures shifted. They had seen him. Jericho crouched flat and arrows hissed above him. There came the ominous crik-criking as the Irons reset their crossbows. He had only seconds before the guards nocked their next arrows and loosed another volley. Jericho was nothing more than a bobbing target out here!

He dove into the water. It wasn't the best idea he'd ever had. The water was so cold that it shocked the breath from his lungs and his coat and boots and weapons pulled him down into the murky depths of the lake. He flailed his arms and kicked frantically but it hardly slowed his decent. He could only watch as the dim light of the water's surface faded away.

Even in dark water, he could see their shapes. Domnul, Orion, Soot, Susha, Leo, Lana, and Belial were all half-formed lambent figures. In the water, they were nearly as physical as Jericho himself. They swirled around him, watching with curious eyes.

Get me out of here, Jericho sent. *Take me to the Iron on the far left.*

All seven of his ghosts grabbed him and Jericho was sent rocketing through the water like the bolt of a crossbow. Going this fast through the water hurt. It felt more like going through solid rock than water. His entire body was taking a terrible beating from this. It would be nothing short of a miracle if he didn't break any bones. Hell, his ghosts just might end up flinging his battered corpse out of the lake.

The sandy bottom came rushing up toward him, a dark beige ramp. His legs churned and he ran along the bottom for a few steps and then his head broke the surface and even as he gasped for breath, he pushed off the bottom with all his strength. With his ghosts still pushing him, he sailed through the air and was just barely able to right himself so that he slammed into the Iron with his boots, smashing the man to the ground with a satisfying snap of bones.

Jericho radiated death like a feverish man radiates heat, and his ghosts took their cues from him.

Hundreds of water droplets still tumbled through the air from Jericho's explosive burst from the lake. Belial turned the droplets to ice and hurled them with tremendous speed into the nearest Iron. The man spun around and was thrown off his feet as the ice pellets tore into his flesh, shredding his cloak and nearly skinning him in the process.

Jericho ran toward the Iron on the far right, hoping to reach him before the man could shoot an arrow.

The man was already on his knees! Susha was choking him. Amazingly, the man was smiling. His eyes were glazed with happiness and his mouth was stretched into a wide grin. Lana had possessed him so the man didn't even have the option of attacking Jericho before Susha killed him. The guard was dying and he probably thought he was in front of a warm hearth next to a woman he loved. He didn't so much as make a sound as he expired.

Jericho was awed by his ghosts. Not only were they taking initiative and doing things without him having to directly command them, but they were working together. Spirits tended to be fickle beings who often didn't even recognize each other's existence, let alone cooperate. This had to be Lana's doing. She had organized the ghosts in the Lourde's Den. He was proud of her and very glad he had bonded her, even if she had almost killed him in the mansion.

And Belial ... Jericho glanced down at the ripped up corpse of the man. Ice pellets littered the ground. Turning the water to ice and using it as a projectile was something Jericho had never thought of.

A favorite trick of the last Vagabond who bonded me, Belial sent. The ghost was a wispy form in the air. His features were visible enough to discern that he was grinning. Jericho grinned back.

You're one scary bastard, Jericho told him. *Now let's go help Lilith.*

It wasn't until he got to Main Street that he realized he had guessed wrong. Lilith wasn't in the city at all. The whole thing was a trap.

CHAPTER 44

The humans were clustered around a police van. Several of them were on the ground, dead or dying. Crossbow bolts jutted from the bodies of the fallen police. When they saw Jericho, they ran and crouched on the other side of the van, using it for cover. They didn't try to use their guns—from the ruined hands on some of the fallen bodies, it looked like ghosts had been playing with the gunpowder and making the bullets explode.

The battle hadn't been Lilith, it had been Duke attacking the humans. Was Duke crazy? What was he thinking?

There was a crack of a gunshot and the front window of the car next to Jericho burst. He dropped to the ground, unsure of what had just happened.

They're hunting us, Orion sent.

Who? Where? Jericho vaguely understood that he had just been shot at, but that was all. It hadn't come from the police hunkered behind the van. Not only were they in no condition to be fighting, but they were too close to him to use guns. He was certain the electrical field of his ghosts would prevent it. If they ignored their guns and didn't touch them or even think about

using them, the ghosts might not notice them. If the spirits'
attention was drawn in any way to the bullets, though, they
would go right for the gunpowder.

So it was someone far away. Jericho looked at the rooftops,
expecting to see a human with a gun. No one was up there.

The air had a heartbeat. That's what it felt like. A rapid but
steady thub thub thub pulsed through the air. It wasn't a sound
Jericho had ever heard. He couldn't place it. Something machine-
like. Something modern.

He listened carefully to the murmurs of the local city ghosts.
He tried to focus on the youngest ones, the ones who understood
the technological advances of the present day. Listening to their
voices was like listening to a distant, mumbling crowd and trying
to make sense of what they were saying. He could discern only a
few words here and there. One word was repeatedly spoken,
though: hell-a-chopper.

Hell-a-chopper. What on earth was that? The word meant
nothing to him.

Another crack of a gunshot. This time the bullet ripped a hole
through the metal of the car. Fragments from the blacktop
sprayed as the bullet went through the car and into the street
beneath it. Jericho did a quick judgment of the trajectory: the
shooter was somewhere up high.

Again he checked the rooftops. He took in the metal stairs
that zigzagged up the sides of the buildings—fire escapes, he
heard from modern ghosts. It wouldn't be difficult for him to use
those stairs to climb to the top of the buildings and get at the
shooter. He just had to figure out which building the shooter was
on.

While looking at the buildings, he noticed something
different. It snagged his peripheral vision and he focused on a
spot he hadn't looked before. There, in the sky: some sort of
machine hovered in the air like a low hanging cloud. He ran
across the street and pressed his back to a building, putting the
structure between him and the mysterious shooting machine. He
peeked around the corner. The machine was nearly motionless. It

didn't drift with the wind or zoom across the sky. It simply hung there like an evil moon. He could barely see it against the night sky. The only thing making it visible was a scattering of colorful lights that clung to the exterior of the machine, glowing like jewels.

There was a flash of light from the hell-a-chopper. The bullet impacted inches from his head, hitting a spot on the side of the building and sending cement chips tearing through the air. The actual sound of the gunshot reached him just as one cement chip bit into the upper part of Jericho's leg. Gods that stung! He ducked back behind the building and slid to the ground.

His leg was bleeding. The cut wasn't deep, but it was long. Blood was welling up from it and dripping onto the ground. He took out his dagger and cut away part of his shirt and tied it around his leg as a makeshift bandage. In a few moments the rag was soaked through and blood continued dripping. He cinched it as tight as he could, putting more pressure on the wound. There, that seemed to slow the blood.

Jericho considered his position. Even though it was still night, the people in the flying machine could see him easily and shoot accurately. The police down the street were becoming braver. A handful of them had left the shelter of the police van. They dashed from the cover of one vehicle to another, closing the distance between them and Jericho. Pretty soon he would have to fight them or flee into the open where the hell-a-chopper machine would gun him down.

His biggest problem, though, lay to the east. The eastern horizon was fiery orange; the sun would be up in minutes. When it came up, the strength of his ghosts would be significantly weakened. Not only would all of their abilities be weakened, but the sphere of their electrical influence would greatly diminish. The people in the hell-a-chopper already somehow knew to stay far enough away so that their electronics wouldn't be affected. When his ghosts' sphere of influence shrunk, they'd be able to get much closer. The police on the street might even be able to simply to shoot him! He had minutes before sunrise. He had to act now.

Jericho stood up ...

... and fell right back down. His wounded leg was completely
numb from the bandage. He had cinched it far too tight, making
it a tourniquet. It had slowed the bleeding, but he couldn't walk,
much less run or fight. He untied the rag. His leg tingled with
pins and needles as circulation was restored to it. Immediately
blood rose up from the wound and made a small crimson stream
that ran along his leg before tumbling to the ground in trembling
fat drops.

"He's hurt!" one of the policemen shouted. The small, brave
group of them was about twenty feet away. They were behind a
car, but not really using it for cover. They didn't seem too
concerned about him attacking them. Maybe they saw that he had
only one arrow left. The police carried short clubs in their hands.
Other police ran up to join the brave group. There were too many
people to hide behind the small car and the sight was almost
comical.

"Come on!" one of them yelled and lead the charge. They ran
at him in two lines, one from each side of the car. They yelled like
primal warriors, holding their clubs high.

On the ground with his back against the building, Jericho had
to lean to unsheathe the dagger Lilith had given him. He
whacked it against the cement sidewalk. He hit it again, then
sawed the dagger back and forth against the cement. The edge of
the knife lit up as the anchored ghost poured energy into it. The
blade grew so hot that it felt as if he was sitting next to a fire.

The police were only a few steps from him.

He took a deep breath ... and pressed the flat of the blade
against the wound on his leg.

The pain was incredible. Jericho jerked his head back,
smacking it hard against the building. He didn't even feel that
impact, as it was blotted out entirely by the burning. He gritted
his teeth and pressed harder. There was an ugly sizzling sound
and the smell of cooking meat. His vision was clouded until it
looked like he was viewing the world through two tiny holes as
he cauterized the wound on his leg.

With a roar, he leapt to his feet and crashed against the closest policeman.

Jericho was half insane from agony and he fought with the feral ferocity of a wounded predator. His dagger cut dazzling swaths in the air. The light threw their shadows along the pavement and against the surrounding buildings, making it look like a larger battle was being fought by dark, stretched nether creatures.

His rage and the burning pain in his leg kept Jericho on his feet as blows from the clubs rained down upon him. One man caught him flush on the head and Jericho staggered, clinging to consciousness only through sheer will. As the man jumped forward for a follow up blow, Belial grabbed the man and flung him several feet.

With the presence of multiple humans so close to him, Jericho's ghosts were weakened. Weakened, but far from helpless. They tossed several police into the air or against the building. The unexplained force of the ghosts, more than anything, broke the humans' attack. They became terrified and the survivors ran back toward the relative safety of their van.

Not the man whom Belial had flung. Crazed with battle rage, the man dashed toward Jericho yet again. The man was a true warrior. Even after flying through the air, he hadn't lost his grip on his club. He swung it, trying to crush Jericho's skull.

Jericho parried the swing so hard the man was visibly jolted. He sent Lana into him and suddenly the man's eyes were empty and glazed. His expression melted from rage to contentment.

Jericho's expression changed, too. Feeling very much like a tiger bearing his teeth, he smiled.

The pilot eased the helicopter forward. He kept one eye on the street below, watching the police car that coasted up the street with its lights flashing. The guy they were after was able to short out electronics. Some sort of electronic magnetic pulse device, they figured. It'd play hell with the systems on the helicopter, to say the least. But the EMP thing had limited range. The pilot figured out the range by having a car drive just ahead of them. If the car's lights cut out, that the was edge of the EMP's effects.

The car kept going, coming increasingly closer to the building behind which the man was hiding. The helicopter followed. In a few moments, they'd have an unobstructed view of the bad guy. When that happened, the sniper riding behind the pilot would be able to take care of business.

"There he is!" the sniper's voice radioed into the pilot's helmet. "He's making a run for it!"

A man in a long black coat dashed across the street. He was running toward the lake.

The pilot calmly rotated the helicopter to give the sniper a better shot. They were flying low—about even with the tops of the buildings—making the shot a fairly easy one. The pilot nodded to himself. He had done everything he could. Now it was up to the sniper to do his job.

CHAPTER 45

Lilith approached the gates of Gheistmar on foot. She had dismounted and walked the final two miles. When she and Jericho had made their escape from Gheistmar, she had left the city riding a horse. Her braids had been flying in the air and electricity had been crackling all around her. She wanted to distance herself from that image as much as possible. No horse, no braids, no electricity.

She cloaked Niko but left Abigail visible. She was wearing jeans, a T-shirt, and a hooded sweatshirt. With her human clothes, she looked like a young Vagabond who had one ghost bonded to her. Her leather Vagabond clothes were in her pack. Her whip was underneath her jeans, coiled around her leg. If the guards saw the whip, they'd know her identity instantly. She figured they might search her pack, but they probably wouldn't feel her all over.

Lilith didn't want to fight them. She might be able to kill all four. If she was able to surprise them, she'd manage it. But it would make a ruckus. Far better to be sneaky.

Two of the Irons had crossbows. The other two had swords

on their belts. They all watched her approach. None of them came out with the rope to tie around her waist. She guessed the city was on high alert, and all typical niceties had been abolished. The Irons just stared at her, watching her carefully. She stared back without smiling. She even glared at them like a young Vagabond who was trying to make an impression, trying to show that she was worthy of entering the haunted city.

As she crossed the bridge, she walked close to one edge and looked down. Vagabonds new to the city did that sometimes. They were intrigued by what was down in the moat, and didn't appreciate the danger. She pushed Abigail away from her. Without her ghosts close by to protect her, she was practically taunting the ghosts in the moat to come grab her.

One ghost took the bait.

A murky gray form shot up from the moat and wrapped around her leg and pulled. Lilith fell flat on her stomach and screamed. The ghost pulled her a few inches closer to the edge. She made a big show of scratching at the bridge with her fingernails like she was trying to claw her way back to the center of the bridge. Abigail was practically doing back flips in the air. She wanted to come help her, but still Lilith held her off. This was going perfectly.

One of the Irons came out onto the bridge. His ghost attacked the moat ghost. There was a quick struggle, one of those split second chess matches in the air. Then the moat ghost was pushed back and Lilith was able to kick free of its clutches. She stood up and wrapped her arms around the soldier.

"Thank you," she said.

Her apparent savior patted her shoulder.

"You have to be careful," he said. "The ghosts are especially strong this time of year. We've lost five Vagabonds to the moat just this month."

"Oh, thank you," she said again. She didn't let go of him as they walked across the bridge. When they passed through the gates, she looked around, gawking as if she was seeing Gheistmar for the first time.

In reality, she was watching the Irons carefully through her peripheral vision. She was watching for some sign that they recognized her. The instant she saw any indication that they recognized her as the death dealing Renegade that she was, she would strike. Her hand was near the knife on her belt and her ghosts were poised and ready.

The Irons would either let her into the city or try to kill her. It was one or the other. Black and white with no shades of gray. They had either believed her little show or not. It was a coin, flipped in the air deciding her fate. She could only wait and see which way the coin landed.

The pilot waited impatiently for the sniper to shoot. Each second felt like an hour. The man in the black coat was running fast and would be behind cover in a few steps. They couldn't let this guy get away. He had attacked cops, which was pretty much the same as writing his own death warrant.

"Hurry!" the pilot said. He spoke to himself, though. He didn't say anything over the radio because it might distract the sniper. What was taking so long?

Then, finally, the sharp crack of the rifle sounded and a cloud of red mist spouted from the fugitive and he dropped to the pavement. He twitched slightly, but was otherwise motionless.

The pilot eyed the police car below them. It was still moving forward, its lights yet flashing red and blue. Perhaps the EMP device had been used once and then depleted. The pilot played it safe, though, and didn't move ahead of the car.

The sniper sent another round into the man in the coat. The body jerked from the impact, but that was the only movement. The man had to be dead.

The police car pulled up beside the body. The officers got out and stood over the dead man. Even from here, the pilot could see something was wrong. The two officers were arguing. He eased the helicopter forward for a better view.

One of the officers knelt and rolled the corpse over onto its back. The dead man was wearing a cop uniform! Fear twisted its icy coils in the pilot's gut like a python roused from its slumber. They had been tricked, and he had a feeling that there would be a steep price to pay.

The helicopter was even with the top of one of the buildings and a flicker of movement caught the pilot's eye. There was a man on the roof of the building next to them! He had been hidden behind an air conditioning unit and out of the pilot's view until the helicopter had flown forward. The man had neither a gun nor anything even remotely resembling an EMP device. Instead he had a sword and dagger hanging from his belt and what looked like a bow slung across his back. The man wasn't holding any of those weapons. He stood rooted in place with his arms crisscrossing his chest and his hands crushed into fists. The man's entire body looked clenched, like he was flexing every single muscle. Sweat made his face shine as though it was sculpted from scorched porcelain. His eyes were squeezed shut and he didn't move at all.

The movement that had caught the pilot's eye came not from the man, but from the air around him. The very air seemed alive. Dark figures swirled around him and blue bolts of electricity arced from figure to figure.

Then the man opened his eyes and the churning mass of darkness and electricity burst outward.

The pilot barely had time to scream before the helicopter rocked like it had been hit with a huge gust of wind and all the lights and dials blinked out.

Jericho clutched his ghosts tightly to him. They fought wildly, struggling to escape.

After Lana had possessed the police officer, Jericho had put his coat on the man. He sent the officer off running as a distraction while Jericho climbed the fire escape to the top of the building and hid behind a big metal box. He wanted to be as close to the flying machine as possible to ensure that it would be inside his ghosts' sphere of influence. He had pulled his ghosts in, suppressing them as much as he possibly could to allow the helicopter to come within range without any warning. He didn't want them to notice a few small electrical problems and pull away.

As usual, Jericho's ghosts fought being suppressed. They squirmed in his grasp and he had to wrestle with them. It was a little easier with Lana gone. With her down there possessing the police officer, Jericho had one less ghost to contain.

The machine came closer. Its steady beat pulsed through the air. Wave after wave of sound crashed against him in a relentless assault. He couldn't see it, as his eyes were screwed shut with the effort of holding his ghosts. The sound of the machine was increasing as the hell-a-chopper moved ever closer.

The gun from the machine fired. Even with his eyes closed, he was sure they had just shot the officer wearing his coat. After a space of time, the gun fired again. The second shot sounded almost casual, like the shooter hadn't been in any rush to make the shot. It was the type of leisurely shot a person would make on an unmoving target. An extra bullet, just to make sure the target was dead.

With the man dead, Lana would be free.

Uh oh, thought Jericho.

Lana came rushing back to him. It was like trying to catch a glowing hot coal. He mentally bounced her from one hand to the other and then gave up. He couldn't hold them anymore. His ghosts were too anxious and too excited. They wanted to go create mayhem.

He didn't just release them, he pushed them away and stoked them. He gave them every ounce of energy he could, pushing himself and them to the farthest possible limit.

They exploded outward with a roar of thunder. A sizzling sphere of energy expanded from him, engulfing the hell-a-chopper and radiating further and further before finally fading away into the distance.

The hell-a-chopper's lights died and the machine plunged downward. It had been moving forward when he let his ghosts go, and its momentum carried it into the tall building across the street.

The blades on the top of the machine bit into the building first, sending glass and metal shrieking through the air. Then the main body collided with a huge, dull crunch. As the hell-a-chopper slid down, the blades kept trying to spin, sending the entire machine into a thrashing frenzy. It tore down the side of the building, disemboweling the structure. The building's guts of glass and metal and plaster poured out, flashing and burning as they fell behind the hell-a-chopper. Like a crazed, feral animal fighting for its last breath, the hell-a-chopper ripped at the building all the way down until it slammed into the street and erupted in a fireball. A mushroom-shaped mountain of smoke and flame shot upward, as huge and angry as the fist of a burning giant rising into the air, defying the world even as he died.

The explosion roiled the air. Jericho covered his face with his arm against the heat. Stray pieces of metal whined as they went spinning past.

Above all the noise, Jericho could hear Belial. The ghost was laughing. Laughing so hard it sounded like he might never stop.

CHAPTER 46

Even from miles away they heard the explosion and felt the ether ripple. Duke looked at Beetle. Beetle was looking right back at him. Everyone turned and glanced back toward the city. What was happening back there? Jericho hadn't died in the water, that much seemed certain. Was he dead now? What the hell had blown up?

"We must assume the worst," Duke said. "We must assume that Jericho somehow killed all of the humans. We must assume he's escaped the city and is now coming after us." The idea of one man chasing an entire army should have been funny. No one smiled. More than a few Irons peered nervously at the shadows around them.

"What do we do?" Beetle said. "Do you want us to set up an ambush?"

Duke thought about it.

"No," he said. "There are too many roads to Gheistmar. There's no way to be certain he'll take this one. He could take a parallel road and cut over and surprise us by coming from a different direction."

"We'd feel him approaching," said Beetle. "To catch up with us, he'd have to unleash his ghosts."

"True," Duke said. "But this area is flat and wooded. It's not a great defensive position. I'd much rather have the high walls of Gheistmar and the haunted moat between us and Jericho. With the gates closed, Gheistmar in impregnable."

Beetle nodded.

"So it's a race back to the city, then?"

"Yes," Duke said. "That's exactly what it is."

And the race began.

Jericho, Lana sent. *I didn't want to tell you this, but Lilith was lying.*

Jericho was running down the metal steps on the side of the building. More humans would be coming after the hell-a-chopper's crash, and he didn't want to be anywhere around when they arrived.

What are you talking about? he sent.

I didn't want you to be distracted, so I waited to tell you, Lana sent. *But Lilith was lying. She didn't go to some safe coven to the south. She was lying when she spoke those words.*

Where would she go?

I have no idea, Lana sent. *But I'm certain she wasn't telling the truth. She wanted you to think she was safe, so she lied to you. Trust me, I know women.*

Jericho paused. He froze, right there on the steps and thought about Lilith. He thought about everything she had said and what she wanted to do. And suddenly he knew where she had really gone. He started running down the steps as fast as he could.

Duke marched the men at double time. They never stopped to rest or eat or piss. Some of the men were falling behind, but there was nothing to do about it. It might even be a good thing. Maybe it'd slow Jericho to fight the stragglers.

That is, if Jericho was even coming. Duke was paying close

attention to the ether and he didn't feel any waves that could be from Jericho. The waves would have been large and unmistakable. Like Beetle had said, in order to catch up to them, Jericho would have to unleash his ghosts. Those ghosts of his made waves in the ether like a whale splashing in a swimming pool. Even if Jericho was taking a parallel road, and even if that road was miles away, Duke would know.

So far, nothing. Still, Duke didn't slow the march. He wasn't going to stop until they were safe behind the high walls of Gheistmar.

When Gheistmar came into view, the army picked up its pace. It was a subtle thing, yet noticeable. No order was given to hurry, but the Irons' steps grew longer and quicker. With safety in sight, the men would have run if Duke had let them.

The last quarter mile was hell. If Jericho was going to strike, it'd be soon. Each tree, each shadow, was a possible hiding place for the Renegade.

An Iron shouted and shot his crossbow into the woods. An unearthly scream came out of the woods, prompting more soldiers to shoot. The army was close to panic. Ghosts flew through the air, wailing and fanning the flames of chaos.

Duke pushed his way back through the ranks. What was going on? Had Jericho found some new way to hide his ghosts? Was he now able to move without agitating the ether?

No, it was none of that. Duke actually laughed. It was a horse. It was dead now, skewered by dozens of bolts. The horse was one of Duke's own, one of the large black horses that had pulled the wagon. Cut free of its reins, it had wandered back toward Gheistmar.

"Calm down, gents," Duke called out. "Jericho's nowhere around. You can feel the ether yourselves. We're fine. We're safe." He pointed to the city. "And we're going home."

They found four dead men at the gates of Gheistmar. Duke stared down at their bodies. He ground his teeth. His old wounds felt tight on his skin as his jaw moved.

"How did this happen?" he hissed. Was Jericho already inside the city? How had he beaten them back?

It was Beetle who solved the mystery. He checked the logbook of the gate's guards.

"The last person the guards logged was a young woman," Beetle said. "They wrote that she had long, dark hair and pale skin."

And suddenly, it all made sense.

"Lilith," Duke said. "She decided to sneak into the city while we were away dealing with Jericho."

"Why?" said Beetle. "Why would she risk coming back to Gheistmar?"

Duke thought about it. It was a good question. What could possibly motivate Lilith to return to Gheistmar? Had she left something important behind? What could be worth risking her life? No, not "what", but "who". Lilith had come back to save Flint and Thera.

The Irons filed through the gates. They looked tired and beaten and scared. They looked nothing like the proud men who had left the city to hunt down Jericho.

When the last Iron had entered the city, Duke ordered the gates closed and the bridge raised. As the gates shut with a thud, more than one person blew out a sigh of relief. They had won the race. Even Jericho couldn't jump over the city walls. The moat ghosts would interfere with his bonded ghosts. If he tried to make the leap, he'd end up in moat where the ghosts would rip him to shreds.

"Post new guards here and tell them that the gates are not to be opened for any reason," Duke said to Beetle. "Put extra guards on the wall, and tell the remainder of the Irons to get some rest."

"What about Lilith?" Beetle said. "Don't you want the Irons to search the city for her?"

Duke shook his head.

"No," he said. "I know where she is. She made a mistake. A fatal miscalculation. She thought we would take Cinder along with us."

Beetle's eyes widened behind his goggles.

"So Cinder has her?" Beetle said.

Duke nodded.

"If Lilith's not dead, she's wishing she was."

The sun was fully up when Lilith killed the two Irons guarding the dungeon. She snuck up on them and stoked Niko. The ghost surged energy into the whip. When her whip connected, there was a bright burst of light and a sharp crack. She attacked fast, her whip striking one Iron and then the other. Crack, crack! Just like that, they were on the ground twitching, their hearts stopped. Their bonded ghosts hadn't diffused any of the charge. Lilith hoped that the rest of the Irons who had been left behind were just as weak.

She removed the keychain from the belt of one of the dead men. She fumbled with the keys, inserting one after another into the lock before getting the right one. She unlocked the door and swung it open. Her stomach flip-flopped as she stared down the steps into the dungeon. This was about the last place she wanted to be. The unpleasant memories of her time spent here rose up in her mind like corpses floating up to bob on the surface of a lake. She really didn't want to go down there.

Someone was crying. The sound was faint but unmistakable. It gave Lilith courage and reminded her why she had come here. She'd never be able to meet the eyes of her own reflection in a looking-glass if she allowed these people to die.

She started down the stairs. She moved slowly and quietly. Her ghosts were unleashed and her whip hummed with electrical charge. She expected another Iron to be guarding the prisoners. She moved down the corridors ready to spring. She passed the door that led to the room full of the confiscated possessions of the prisoners. Still no Irons. She kept going until she finally came to the hall where she had been held.

There were no guards. The hall was empty. The cells lining either side of it were not. There looked to be even more people imprisoned than when Lilith was here. They looked miserable.

Cold, hungry, and huddled on their slabs of stone to stay out of the water, some of them were barely alive.

Lilith started with the first cell on her right. Once again, she went through the tedious process of trying several keys before finding the right one. She unlocked the door and swung it open. The prisoner inside was a middle-aged man. He was sitting in the water and watching her with tired eyes. He made no move to leave his cell.

She kept moving down the line, unlocking one cell after another. Some of the prisoners dashed out, greeting her with hugs and tears. Others were like the first man. They just sat in their cell, waiting to die. Most, though, were elated to be free. They were hysterical with joy. Ghosts, pumped full of emotion, flew around the dungeon. The spirits splashed water and threw rocks, metal cups, and any small objects they found. Lilith was smiling herself.

Then she came to Thera's cell. It was empty.

"Where is she?" Lilith asked. Her heart beat faster. Some small part of her knew the answer already.

"Gone," said a man in a cell across the hall. "Your ghosts must have shown hers a thing or two, because she used them to pick the lock to her door. To get the magnet off the lock, she soaked her shirt in the water and then twisted it like a rope and froze it so it was like a long stick and used it to scrape the magnet off the lock. After that, her ghosts could touch the mechanism. It took her ghosts a long time to pick it, but they finally succeeded."

"So she's free?"

The man didn't say anything. He just turned his gaze downward and shook his head.

"What happened?" Lilith said quietly. She unlocked his cell.

The man stood, waded through the water, and stepped up out of his cell.

"They caught her in the hall," he said. "It was a case of unfortunate timing. She wasn't out of her cell for more than thirty seconds when she ran into a group of Irons. They beat her bad and took her away."

Lilith didn't have to ask where they had taken Thera. There was only one place the prisoners from here went: The Charnel House. It chilled her to think of Thera being turned into a Wretched.

"How long ago did this happen?" she asked.

"Last night," he said. "A few hours before dawn."

Lilith handed him the key ring.

"Unlock the rest of the cells," she told him. Maybe Flint was down here somewhere, maybe not. There wasn't time to look for him. She had to rescue Thera. She turned and ran down the hall. She ran up the stairs and past the two guards she had killed. If only a few hours had passed since they had taken Thera, Lilith might not be too late. She might still be able to save her. Since Cinder was out with the rest of them hunting Jericho, Thera was probably just strapped down in the chair. They wouldn't try to make a Wretched without Cinder. Only he had the skills to properly integrate the amalgam into a person's veins.

Lilith ran through the streets of Gheistmar toward the Charnel House. She passed through a small market. She passed through an area built in the manner of the ancient Romans. She passed the hulking, ominous red and black building that was the Tombs. She kept going deeper into Gheistmar, towards the unsavory area near the back.

There weren't many Irons in the streets. It seemed like almost all of them were out hunting Jericho. There weren't many other Vagabonds, either. Since most Vagabonds kept late hours, the city didn't really wake up until late in the day.

As she came closer to the Charnel House, the buildings around her grew decrepit. Shards littered the street corners and huddled in alleys, their faces as blank and confused as their minds. One man was staring straight up at the sun without even blinking. Some of them glared at her as she ran past. It was like they knew that she didn't belong in this area. None of them dared approach her, though. She was like an eagle soaring above sparrows.

The short structure of the Charnel House squatted in front of her. The double doors had a thick lock on them. She sent Abigail to work on the lock's tumblers. She could only stand there in front of the doors, waiting for Abigail to pick the lock. The shards and other miserable denizens of the area stared at her. Some stood and moved closer. They clustered in groups, muttering to each other and gathering their courage.

Hurry, Lilith sent to Abigail. *This could turn into a mob at any second.* She narrowed her eyes and stared at the growing crowd like she was daring one of them to do something stupid.

One of them did dare. He was a droopy-faced man whose jowls hung down and jiggled like a hound dog's. His face was red, probably from drink. He was squinting in the light but it was still easy to see that he was angry and spoiling for a fight. He stumbled across the street towards Lilith. One of his hands was upraised like he had something to say.

Abigail ...

Almost there, she sent back.

Lilith could deal with the drunk man, of course. But then the entire crowd might attack her. If they rushed her, she would have to run. Even as strong as she was, she couldn't kill them all before one got to her. She'd have to run away and lose precious time.

The drunk man was only a few yards from her now. His shuffling footsteps kicked up clouds of dust in the dirty street. Lilith tensed, ready to fight or flee as the man drew closer.

There was a loud click and it startled Lilith so badly that she nearly lashed out and killed the drunk man.

Got it! Abigail sent.

Lilith spun on her heel and took off the lock and pulled open the heavy door. The drunk behind her stopped. There was no way he was going in there. No one went in the Charnel House of their own accord.

Lilith went in and pulled the door shut behind her. Even with oil lamps lining the hall, the interior was astonishingly dark after the bright sunlight. Lilith gave her eyes a moment to adjust and then strode into the gloom. It was so cold inside! She wrapped her arms around herself and walked quickly. She passed rows of empty cells where the Wretched used to hang on their hooks. Some of the hooks still gleamed with dark, metallic blood. Lilith kept moving, glancing in the cells to confirm that they were indeed unoccupied.

She reached the door that led to the operating room. She paused. Someone was on the other side. She felt their bonded ghosts in the ether. Three ghosts, all of them fairly strong. She stood very still. She could hear the rhythmic sound of the Vagabond's breathing. The Vagabond probably sensed her too. He was probably waiting for her to open the door. But he didn't know whether she was a fellow Iron or an enemy. He would take a split second to look at her and then make a decision on how to respond. She didn't need that split second. She knew he was an enemy.

Lilith uncoiled her whip and stepped back. She used Abigail to rip open the door and sent her whip streaking toward the figure on the other side.

It was a large Iron. He was heavily muscled and had a mean face half hidden by a dark beard. Lilith's whip wrapped around his thick neck. Niko wasn't able to send voltage through the whip right away, though. The Iron's ghosts saw that their Vagabond was in danger and tried to fend off Lilith's ghosts. It became a dangerous contest. The Iron's ghosts tried to push Lilith's away while the Iron tugged at the whip in an effort to free himself.

The contest didn't last long. Lilith's ghosts were older and stronger and better trained. Voltage surged through the whip and the Iron jerked and twisted as he fried. His hair and his beard smoked and the smell of burning flesh wafted through the air. It was far from the quickest death Lilith had ever delivered. The Iron fell forward, pinning her whip to the floor with his corpse.

Lilith yanked on her whip in an effort to try and free it, but it was wrapped around him. She stepped into the room so she could roll him over and untangle her whip.

The room lit up in a brilliant flash of light. It was like a bonfire had suddenly whooshed to life. Right next to her was

Cinder. His dark cowl was thrown back and his fiery robe radiated light as he unleashed his ghosts.

Lilith hadn't felt Cinder in the ether. Not at all. He must have felt her first and been waiting—hiding—with his ghosts shrouded and his cowl wrapped around him.

Cinder's ghosts attacked her ghosts with the ferocity of starving wolves. The spirits shrieked hideously as they fought. Cinder stalked toward her, his ashen spear poised to thrust. Lilith gave her trapped whip a longing glance and let it go. She backed away. As Cinder moved, the room's shadows twisted and contorted. The operating chair, the amalgam machine, the spools of chain; their shadows thrashed like burning men.

Cinder was one skilled Vagabond. He must have directed his ghosts to focus on attacking Niko. Her poor electricity-loving ghost was getting the worst in the spirit battle. She couldn't let him get banished. Without Niko, Lilith would be practically helpless.

Like a reflex, her hand dipped and grasped the handle of her dagger. But she didn't unsheathe it. It wouldn't do any good. Cinder's spear had a much longer reach and he was damned quick with it. There was no way she'd get in close enough to cut him. She needed her whip, but Cinder was keeping himself between her and her whip. Besides, even if she was able to reach it, there was no way she'd be able to free it before he got to her.

Lilith looked around, desperately searching for something she could use against Cinder. She noticed something she hadn't noticed before: the operating chair had someone strapped in it. It was Thera. Thera's eyes were open, but her gaze was blank and she wasn't moving. Cinder saw Lilith looking at Thera and he laughed.

"That one wasn't a success." Cinder had to shout over the shrieking ghost battle. "She fought too hard against it and the spirit wasn't able to get a good grip on her body. Now she's ruined. She's like a puppet with only one string. The ghost can jerk her around some, but that's about it. As soon as you die, she'll go into the pit with all the other failures."

Cold rage filled Lilith. Her beloved Thera was dead. Thera, who had taught her so much and been so patient with her. And being turned into a Wretched ... that was a horrible death. Lilith hated Cinder more that she had ever hated anybody. And yet, what could she do? Not a thing. She thought furiously, searching for some way to hurt him. No ideas came to her, and she had to continue backing away as Cinder kept coming closer.

She heard wordless murmurs behind her. They were low groans, like the speech of people whose tongues had been ripped out or who were missing their lower jaw. Lilith glanced over her shoulder. Cinder was maneuvering her toward the pit filled with the failed Wretched. The undead flesh churned as they sensed her. Hands reached up, their fingers crooked like claws. Lilith planted her feet in her fighting stance. She could back up no further. She had to fight now, or die.

It was hard to judge the progress of ghost battles, but Lilith was quite sure her ghosts were losing. They were outnumbered, after all. And Cinder's ghosts were strong and organized. They fought cohesively, all of them focused on Niko. She had only seconds before Niko was banished.

Lilith thought of something Abigail had told her long ago. Something about being in the circus. Something about how to surprise people. And she had an idea.

She leapt over to a spool of chain that was sitting on the floor. She unwound a length of it and began spinning it over her head. It wasn't her whip, but it would conduct electricity just fine. Cinder must have had the same thought. His eyes widened and he backed up.

Lilith took a few steps forward while spinning the chain over her head. Then she ducked low and released the chain, aiming for Cinder's legs.

Shock him, Niko! She sent. But there was no answer. Instead, an unearthly scream ripped through the air as Cinder's ghosts banished Niko. The chain bounced harmlessly against Cinder's leg.

Niko was banished. Lilith couldn't shock Cinder. And the

ghost battle was suddenly very lopsided. Then Cinder's ghosts were upon her.

Cinder's ghosts hit Lilith like an avalanche of scalding hot rocks. They dug their ghostly talons into her and shoved her to the floor, biting and scratching and digging into her skin. The pain was terrible, and Lilith screamed. She bucked and writhed in pain.

"They won't kill you quickly," Cinder said. "But don't worry, you'll get there. Eventually they'll open up a vein." He came closer and stood over her, watching with a grin stretched across his burnt face. He leaned forward and pressed the point of his spear against her throat. Lilith tried to force herself to stay still, but she couldn't, and the tip cut across her skin in lines of scorching pain.

"You know what?" Cinder said as he pressed harder on his spear. "I think I might just help my ghosts along."

CHAPTER 47

Insane, maniacal laughter echoed off the walls.

Amazingly, Lilith recognized it as her own. Cinder's ghosts were tearing into her and she was in severe pain, yet she was laughing.

Because this was fine. This was all just fine with her.

Cinder's ghosts were able to get to her because her own ghosts couldn't protect her. Niko had been banished. And Abigail couldn't protect her because she was busy.

Misdirection. That was what Abigail had told her was the secret to surprising people. Make them look in one place while you work your magic in another. Cinder had only been concerned about Lilith using the chain to shock him. And it had been a valid concern—Lilith would have done it if she had been presented with the opportunity. But she had been very much aware that Niko was about to be banished. So she thought up a backup plan. One that didn't involve Niko. Cinder was right to be worried about Niko, but he should have been watching Abigail, too.

She had told Abigail to do one simple thing while Cinder's

ghosts were distracted, and she did it now. It was a simple task, one that took less than a second: Abigail wrapped the chain around Cinder's leg, passing the end through the loop and cinching it tight to make a knot.

Cinder felt the chain on his leg and looked down. He dropped his spear and reached down to undo the knot while his ghosts went after Abigail.

But Abigail was quick, and she zipped out of there before the ghosts could smash into her and send her to ghost limbo. She flew over to the spool of chain and smacked against it at top speed. The spool tipped over. Abigail hit it again to send it rolling.

Cinder's ghosts chased after Abigail, trying to stop her.

They were too late. Abigail gave the spool one final push to make it roll faster ... and into the pit.

"No!" Cinder screamed as the spool went over the edge. He clawed at the chain around his leg. It was a very simple knot. He should have been able to untie it in a few seconds. Right after the spool fell into the pit, though, the chain went taut and untying it suddenly became an impossibility.

The chain went taut because undead hands were pulling on it. Only one or two at first, it seemed. Then more of the revenants noticed the chain. They gave it a good yank and Cinder was pulled off his feet.

"No!" he screamed again. His ghosts gave up chasing Abigail and rushed over to help him. They grabbed hold of him and pulled and Cinder became the rope in a tug of war. He hovered inches above the ground, stretched tight and screaming. There was a loud pop as his leg was pulled out of its socket. His ghosts let him go and he dropped to the floor. The ghosts grabbed at the chain, but they were no match for the purely physical presence of the Wretched, and Cinder was dragged along the floor, slowly and inexorably, toward the pit.

Lilith stood. Her skin burned from a hundred cuts, bite marks, and scrapes. She spat with contempt.

Cinder was begging her now. Begging her to untie the chain,

or at least cut his throat to spare him an ugly death. When she didn't move, he cursed her. He called her a whore in several languages, most of them long dead. He flopped all around, like a landed fish.

Then he went over the edge and into the pit. A moment later, his screams redoubled. His voice seemed much louder. He became hysterical. He wailed, unable to form words. His voice was accompanied by the wet, ripping sound of flesh and the cracking of bones.

How long his screaming went on for, Lilith couldn't say. She stood motionless, her heart pounding wildly as she listened. Her stomach twisted. If she hadn't been a Renegade, she would have thrown up in disgust.

Finally Cinder's voice stopped. His ghosts floated around the room aimlessly and then faded away. Most ghosts tended to stay near the body of their bonded Vagabond, but it seemed like these wanted to be nowhere near the failed Wretched.

Lilith walked over to the edge of the pit and looked down. Cinder was all over. The failed Wretched had torn him to pieces. Scraps of his fiery robe made his body easy to discern amongst the rest of the flesh. His torso was right below her. His head was near the center of the pit. His eyes were gone and the empty sockets gaped black. His mouth was open as if he was still screaming.

The Wretched never stopped. Undead hands grabbed at the torso, trying to pull it apart. They bit into it, pulling of chunks of flesh with their teeth. Some spat out the flesh. Others swallowed it. They had managed to rip a hole in the skin near his stomach. They shoved their hands inside the tear and pulled out his intestines and flung them around like party streamers.

They saw Lilith standing above them and reached up for her. They would do the same to her if she fell in, she knew. She stepped back and turned away from the pit. The operating chair loomed in the corner, its needles and syringes stuck into Thera's body. It looked like a giant metallic insect feasting on her. Lilith shuddered. What an awful fate. Tears clouded her eyes as she walked over to her friend. Thera's face was slack. Her mouth was open and moving very slightly. She was staring at nothing at all.

Lilith started to undo the straps, but stopped. This wasn't Thera anymore. It was Thera's body, but another spirit was controlling it. A cruel, greedy spirit. If it suddenly managed to operate Thera's body, it might attack her. Lilith stood there for a long moment, unsure of what to do.

Thera's eyes suddenly locked onto her. It was like the ghost had just become aware of her. The eyes stared hard at Lilith. They narrowed, glaring. Then they slid to the side and widened, like she was looking at something behind Lilith. Something frightening.

The Wretched was scaring her. She decided that she should just go.

Lilith took a step backwards ... and bumped into something hard and unyielding. She spun around. It was Duke. She stared up at him in confusion. Had she been so preoccupied that she hadn't felt him approaching through the ether?

Duke smiled as he looked down at her.

"I knew you'd come here to free your friend," he said. "I think you'll find she's beyond help. And so are you."

CHAPTER 48

Lilith couldn't move an inch. She couldn't even wiggle. Her eyes were the only part of her body that possessed any degree of freedom. She rolled them left and right. Everywhere she looked, metal needles and syringes pointed at her.

With Niko banished, she hadn't been able to do much against Duke. Just her and Abigail against Duke and his ghosts ... not a fair fight. Although she had fought, that was for sure. She had fought like an alley cat. She had even managed to stick her dagger into Duke's thigh, driving it all the way in until just the hilt was sticking out. As she drove it in, he had caught her with an open-palmed smack on the side of her face. He put a lot of power into the blow. If it had been a closed fist, it would have broken bone. As it was, it sent her reeling. He hit her again and again, beating her until she didn't know up from down. She was only vaguely aware as he carried her over to the operating chair.

Duke held Lilith with one arm while he undid the straps holding Thera with the other. He grabbed Thera and dragged her over to the pit and tossed her in. Then he carried Lilith back over to the chair and shoved her into it. He tightened the straps around her arms, legs, body, and head until she couldn't move at all. He stepped back and admired her.

"You will be a very pretty Wretched," he said. His gold-plated armor sent yellow light dancing along the walls.

Lilith wasn't really listening to him. Her mind was racing, trying to figure a way out. Duke's ghosts were keeping Abigail away, keeping him from undoing any of her straps. Niko came back from being banished. It felt good to have him back, but Duke's ghosts kept them away too.

"This won't be pleasant," Duke said. "Feeling another spirit enter and control your body is going to be like a rape of your body and soul. But all you have to do is endure it. The hard part's on our end. We have to keep the injections balanced so your heart keeps pumping as long as possible. If you die too early, your heart won't push the amalgam through all of your veins. A ghost could move you, but it'd be limited, awkward movement. If it happens with you, your body will go into the pit with all the others. You shouldn't worry, though. Cinder has become very good at this." He looked toward the door.

"We'll begin as soon as Cinder gets here," he said.

Lilith never quit tugging on her restraints. She kept pulling, hoping that some buckle might give way or a strap would stretch. No luck so far. None at all. The chair had proved sufficiently sturdy to contain people much stronger than she was. If the man who had been made into the Colossus Wretched hadn't been able to break free, what hope did she have? Still, she never quit trying.

Duke paced back and forth. He looked like he was becoming impatient. He kept glancing at the door, waiting for Cinder to enter the room. Lilith prayed Duke didn't think to look into the pit. If he discovered Cinder was dead, retribution would be swift. His inexpert hands would jam the syringes into her and pump her full of the amalgam until she was either possessed or just plain dead.

"We already picked out the ghost to inhabit your body," Duke said. They had been silent for minutes. When he spoke, his voice startled Lilith.

Duke opened a wooden chest and took out a skeleton key on a leather cord.

"She's perfect for you," Duke said with a grin. "She was a nurse. A very bad one. She tormented patients who were unable to speak out against her. The elderly, the sick, the weak—they were her prey. When she came stalking down the hall, patients filled their bedpans in terror." Duke dangled the key in front of Lilith's face, and the image of a pretty woman flashed in her mind. The ghost woman had a lovely face, but there was something about her that was chilling. She had a certain sadistic gleam in her eyes and a cruel twist to her lips. Or maybe Lilith was just imagining those aspects about her, trying to force the woman's image to fit what Duke was telling her.

The nurse ghost was greedy. There was no doubt about that. The sprit was already attempting to dig through Lilith's aura to possess her.

"I'm curious," Duke said. "After the operation, will your spirit linger? Will you be able to watch as your own body moves without you? Try and stick around. I'd love for you to see what I'm going to do to your body later."

"Jericho will kill you for this," Lilith said.

"Jericho is dead," Duke said. He paused. His mouth twisted into a frown. Then, "And even if he's not dead, he can't help you. We left him back in the human city. The gates to Gheistmar are shut. Between the high walls and the moat, not even Jericho can get in."

"He'll still kill you," Lilith said. "You might just have to wait awhile. Jericho won't give up. He'll spend the rest of his life hunting you."

"Jericho's too late," Duke said. "He's too late to save you, and too late to kill me. You should let your hope go of being rescued. The only thing you have to hope for is a clean death."

The temperature dropped. A powerful Vagabond was right outside the room. The candles' flames shrank as though they were cowering in fear. There were only a few Vagabonds strong enough to affect an entire room like that.

"Oh good," Duke said. "Cinder has finally arrived." He rubbed his hands together like a greedy child.

"Cinder is already dead, you fool," Lilith said. "And so are you."

The door was flung open so violently that its top hinge snapped, and Jericho strode into the room with his sword in hand. He stared at Lilith, his eyes wide as he saw that she was strapped in the chair. With a cry of feral rage, he launched himself at Duke.

Their ghosts clashed like two thunderstorms colliding. Electricity crackled and the air twisted and distorted. Disembodied voices shouted at each other in rage and hate. Outnumbered and overpowered, Duke's ghosts were strictly on the defensive. They condensed close to Duke and were barely able to protect him against an assault from Jericho's spirits.

They could do nothing about Jericho himself, though.

Duke managed to draw his mace and parry Jericho's first few swings. He was giving ground, being pushed backward with each attack.

With Duke focused solely on staying alive, his ghosts were no longer blocking Lilith's own. She set Abigail to pulling on the straps so she could get free of the chair. Her whip was right there on the floor, wrapped around that dead Iron. If she could only get free ...

Jericho knocked Duke's mace to the side. Time seemed to freeze. In the frozen moment, everyone in the room seemed to know exactly what would happen next. And it did.

Jericho drove his kilij into Duke's chest, cleaving his heart. Duke's mace fell from his hand, landing with a heavy clang and rolling away. Jericho twisted the blade of his sword and ripped it out. He spun around and lopped off Duke's head with a backhand cut.

Duke dropped to the floor. His body hit with a heavy thump, like a sack of grain. His head landed with a higher sound, more like a wooden bowl being dropped.

Jericho rushed over to Lilith.

"I can't stand to see you in that thing," he said. He tugged at the straps.

"How are you here?" Lilith said. "Duke said he left you back at the human city. How'd you get over the city walls?"

"I entered the city before they closed the gates. Lana told me that you had lied to me, that you weren't going to a safe place. Then I knew you were coming here to rescue Thera and Flint. I knew I had to beat the army back here, and I knew that I couldn't use my ghosts to travel fast because they'd feel the waves in the ether. So I just did what you and I did when we traveled in secret to Tim's coven."

"You rode Wisp?"

"Well, not Wisp. But a horse. I saw one of Duke's wagon horses running through the streets and realized that riding it was the only way I'd make it back in time. Riding it was a nightmare. It threw me twice before it started to behave. The rest of the trip was easy. Even I could feel where the Gheistmar army was in the ether, so I stayed clear of them. I killed the guards at the gates. That was easy, too. There were only four of them."

Jericho pulled one of the straps on her arm loose and started working on a second one. Abigail was still trying to undo a strap on her other arm. Working the leather strap through the buckle was hard for the ghost. With four straps on each limb, it seemed to be taking forever to set her free.

"I'm glad you ... " Lilith trailed off as her ghosts hissed a warning to her.

Right behind Jericho was Duke. He had a knife in his hand and his arm was drawn back, poised for the thrust.

"Jeric—" Lilith started to scream. Her words were cut off by the sound of Duke's knife ripping through leather and snapping chain mail links like metallic twigs before driving into Jericho's back. Jericho cried out in pain and fell to the floor. Duke bent over, grabbed the last arrow in Jericho's quiver, and flung it across the room.

Lilith screamed and thrashed in the chair. Her voice echoed

off the walls, long and drawn out like the wail of a banshee. She had been scared before, but she had clung to the hope that Jericho would come for her and save her from Duke. Now, though, despair choked her as she realized how Duke was still alive.

"I was afraid of you," Duke said to Jericho. His voice was raspy, but otherwise he looked completely unharmed. "I was afraid your silly magnet arrows would ruin everything I've worked for. I had an invincible army, Jericho. And you managed to stumble upon their one weakness."

Jericho pushed himself up on one elbow. His breathing was labored.

"I tried to keep the arrows a secret," Duke said. "I gave orders to have everyone you might have told about the arrows killed and your books and manuscripts burned. And you, of course, were supposed to die. I knew you would never agree with our process of creating Wretched."

"I just ... cut your damn head off," Jericho said. He spoke slowly, like every word was a struggle. "How are you ... alive?"

"Isn't it obvious? I sat in that same chair your little Lilith is sitting in right now. I did it right after you both fled Gheistmar. Now I'm invincible. You can cut me to pieces and my healing ghost will pull me back together, good as new."

"You're ... a Wretched?"

"That was my desire from the very beginning. The Elders died, Jericho. They all died and we don't have any idea why. What good is it being a Vagabond if we're not truly immortal? History always repeats itself. Whatever happened to the Elders will eventually happen to us. As a Wretched, I will be able to survive it. That's all this ever was about. Simple survival."

The air around them crackled and flexed and distorted as their ghosts battled. Now, though, Duke's ghosts seemed to be getting the better of Jericho's. The condensed thunderstorm had been pushed from around Duke over to near Jericho. It was Jericho's ghosts who were on the defensive.

Jericho looked to Lilith. He was trying to tell her something, trying to get her to understand. Understand what? What did he want her to do?

Jericho looked back to Duke and gave him a chilling grin.

"I killed ... your precious Wretched," Jericho said. "They're not ... invincible. With my arrows, they died like pathetic humans."

"Lab rats, all of them. Having an army of Wretched was nice, but in the end they were nothing more than an experiment. I needed to learn how to become a Wretched myself, a Wretched that my own spirit controlled. It took us a long time to perfect the process. Not only did we have to make the amalgam just right, but we had to inject it in a precise manner as well. The trick was to pace the injections so that the heart kept pumping as long as possible. If the person died too early, another ghost could claim the body. It was necessary to keep the original spirit in there long enough that it started learning how to use the amalgam while the person was still alive. It was a difficult thing to do and it took us many attempts before we got it right. The final reward, though, was well worth it."

Duke stepped closer to Jericho. His ghosts advanced, too. The ghost battle was now right above Jericho.

Lilith stoked her ghosts. She was about to send them over to assist Jericho's. But what would that accomplish, really? Maybe they'd manage to push the battle back over near Duke, but they'd never banish his ghosts. So what did Jericho want her to do?

It hit her suddenly. She felt stupid for not realizing it earlier. She knew why Jericho was losing the ghost battle. And she knew what he wanted her to do.

CHAPTER 49

Counting the number of ghosts in a fight is next to impossible, yet Lilith was sure that not all of Jericho's ghosts were fighting against Duke's. It didn't make sense that Jericho would suddenly be weaker than Duke when it came to spiritual manipulation. Jericho had at least one of his ghosts focused on doing something else: keeping him alive.

Jericho must have listened to Lilith months ago back at her apartment, because he was using one of his ghosts to hold his body together. By closing the wound from Duke's knife, he was able to keep from bleeding out.

That's what Duke was probably waiting for, Lilith thought. Even now, he seemed to fear Jericho. Duke was talking and stalling because he wanted Jericho to pass out from blood loss so he could kill him. Jericho was trying to buy time because he was waiting for Lilith to act.

Bring Jericho his arrow, Lilith sent to Abigail.

Abigail zipped off and was back within a second.

I can't, she sent. She sent her an image of a man trying to pick up water with his hands. The ghost couldn't touch the arrow because of the magnet.

"When you two escaped from Gheistmar, I thought my chance to live forever was destroyed," Duke said. "Standing at the open gate and staring out into the night, that was my darkest moment."

Jericho looked over to Lilith. There was desperation in his eyes. Without the arrow, he couldn't do a damn thing to hurt Duke.

"You might think this right now is your darkest moment, but I assure you, you have far worse times ahead," Duke said. "Take this moment, for instance. Before you die, you can watch your woman be turned into a soulless puppet for a malevolent spirit." He turned to Lilith and covered the distance over to her in a few long strides. With no hesitation whatsoever, he pulled back the lever to release the weights.

Gears clacked and purred against each other as they started to turn. Air bladders puffed and wheezed as they expanded and contracted, each one beating like a black, misshapen heart. A needle slid into her arm and the clear glass tube connected to the needle flared red as it filled with her blood. Her blood raced through the tube, whirling through the loops before dripping into the mixing beaker. The other tube leading into the beaker was already dripping the silver amalgam, and her blood mixed with the amalgam to form a shiny, dark red liquid.

Jericho coiled his legs beneath him. Lilith knew he was going to spring at Duke, and she was certain that it would do no good. Even if Jericho, injured now, was able to get the best of Duke again so that he could free her, the fight between Jericho and Duke earlier had lasted over a minute. She had seconds before the amalgam went into her. Jericho needed that arrow. And Abigail couldn't touch it.

Then again, maybe she didn't need to.

Take the arrow to Jericho, she sent to Abigail. *Use a chain. Wrap it around the arrow like you wrapped the chain around Cinder's leg. Then just drag it to him. And hurry!*

Abigail zipped off and grabbed a length of chain that was a

few feet long. It was a bizarre sight, the chain sliding across the floor and seeming to pounce on the arrow like a hungry metal snake. It looped once around the arrow and then Abigail pulled it over toward Jericho.

Jericho didn't seem at all surprised as the chain and arrow slid to him. He grabbed the chain and removed the arrow. In one smooth motion, he rose to his feet, unslung his bow, and nocked the arrow.

Duke started to yell something. It might have been an exclamation of surprise or profanity or a curse—he didn't get more than a syllable out before Jericho loosed the arrow. Quicker than the eye could follow, the arrow flew and smacked right into Duke's chest. The impact was solid. A heavy, wet thud, like a stick puncturing a bass drum covered in water. Duke dropped his knife. His legs trembled and he dropped to his knees.

Jericho was beside her suddenly, frantically undoing the straps on her right arm. The amalgam mixed with her blood was already flowing down the tube. There were two straps still holding her arm down. Jericho unbuckled one.

Duke stood up. He ripped the arrow out of his chest and tossed it aside.

Jericho spared a quick glance over his shoulder as he tried to unbuckle the last strap. Duke lunged and grabbed hold of Jericho and flung him across the room.

Lilith looked down. The last strap was unbuckled, but her arm was still pinned by the needle. It was pinned tight to the arm of the chair. She couldn't move it at all.

The mixture flowed down the last few inches of glass tube and entered the needle.

Duke picked up his knife and advanced toward Jericho with a wicked grin. He was between them, keeping Jericho from going to her.

Lilith gritted her teeth. This was not going to be pleasant.

She jerked her arm upward with all her strength, ramming the needle through the center of her forearm. All the way through. Right between the two bones. The tip of the needle stuck out the bottom. An instant later, the first drop of the mixture dripped from the needle like a fat red bead.

It hurt. Gods be good, did it hurt. Her ghosts roared as they felt her agony. Her arm felt like it was on fire. But she was alive. At least for a little longer.

Lana and Susha were holding Jericho together. They were pushing the severed muscles in his back together and holding shut the skin. He had chosen Lana and Susha for the task because, of his ghosts, they were the most capable of using their strength delicately. Soot or Orion might cause more damage than they prevented. Belial might inadvertently kill him.

Stay still! Lana sent as Jericho forced himself to his feet.

I can't, he sent back. Duke was coming towards him. The magnetic arrow was on the ground between them. He needed to make it to the arrow before Duke. He took a single, lurching step. His knees were unsteady and he was dizzy.

You're bleeding a lot, she sent. *If you keep moving around, I can't stop it.*

Try as best you can, Jericho sent.

We're good at taking people apart, Susha sent. *Not holding them together.*

Just do what you can.

On his way over to Jericho, Duke casually bent and picked up the arrow. He held it eye level and used his thumb to snap it in half. He flung both halves across the room. The pieces skipped and rolled along the floor and then fell into the pit.

"I told you," Duke said. "With my own spirit controlling my body, I'm far stronger than the other Wretched. You'd have to shoot me with a whole quiver of your arrows to kill me." He bent down and picked up his mace.

Jericho didn't have another arrow, much less an entire quiver.

Duke lunged toward him suddenly, swinging his mace viciously. Jericho parried the blow, but just barely. Duke had been plenty strong when he had been alive. Now, as a Wretched, he was even stronger. When their weapons collided, Jericho almost lost his grip on his sword.

Stay still! Lana or Susha sent. Jericho didn't know which, because he was engaged in a desperate struggle for survival. Duke pressed the attack, his mace flashing bright golden arcs through the air. Jericho was able to keep from getting hit, but just barely. He was tired and weak and he had only half his ghosts. Duke, on the other hand, seemed just fine. It seemed like he could swing his mace all day and not become fatigued. More than fine, he looked happy. At ease in his body. Perhaps he had been concerned about fighting Jericho as a Wretched, and now he was finding out that he had nothing to worry about. He seemed to be enjoying it. He grinned as he swung his mace. His attacks were almost casual. One slash was downright sloppy. Jericho took full advantage of it.

He ducked under Duke's slash and drove his sword into Duke's chest.

Cold! Jericho sent to the ghost in his sword. The ghost started to pull warmth from Duke.

Ideally, the ghost would lower Duke's temperature low enough that his blood would freeze. Jericho had no idea of the freezing temperature of the amalgam, but he did know that the ghost in his sword could make it damn cold. If Duke's blood froze, then he wouldn't be able to move and Jericho could cut him up to buy some time, free Lilith, and then get the hell out of there.

Duke's own ghosts were fighting the sword ghost, though. They weren't letting the spirit rip much warmth from Duke. The air rippled as the ghosts battled. Duke's spirits were winning. The reason was simple: the battle was in Duke's body. That was home turf for his spirits. This wasn't going to work.

Duke twisted and sprung backward, tearing himself free of Jericho's blade in a spray of blood. His blood beaded together on the floor and scurried over to him like beetles, each one shiny and perfectly round. They quivered as they bounced and rolled along the floor before they scurried up Duke's leg and under his clothes to reenter his body.

"Your stupid tricks ... will do you no good," Duke said. He

staggered a little. He seemed stunned. Injured, even. That wouldn't last long.

Jericho looked around. He needed something to stop Duke. There had to be some way ...

Jericho didn't have much to use. He had his usual weapons. And there on the floor, wrapped around the neck of an Iron, was Lilith's whip. That was all he had.

He thought about it.

He had enough.

CHAPTER 50

The book was ash now. It had been burned when they torched his home. But Jericho could still picture it perfectly. It had a worn leather cover with pages as soft as velvet. The book had smelled a little musty, kind of like the smell of a freshly overturned log in the woods.

Ghosts were electricity and water, so Jericho had set about acquiring all the books he could on the nature of those components. This book was about electricity. A fascinating book. Electrical power was capable of some very interesting things.

Jericho sent out a command and Soot grabbed Lilith's whip and pulled hard. The Iron flipped into the air and spun as Soot pulled the whip free. Soot tossed Lilith's whip to Jericho. Jericho caught it and coiled the whip tightly around his left forearm.

Leo kicked in and the next three steps Jericho took seemed to take an eternity. The searing pain in his back was astonishingly acute in his senses. He was moving as fast as he could and he was tearing his wound open. All around the wound was the warmth of his own blood as it seeped out of him and soaked into his clothes.

Duke was two steps in front of him, still looking dazed from the icy blade. His eyes widened as he saw Jericho dashing towards him.

The light in the room was flickering. It was like there was a lightning storm inside. And there was a smell of something burning. Jericho took a fraction of a second to look over at Lilith. Her ghosts were wrapped around the buckles on the straps of her left arm. They were sending electricity into the metal, heating the buckles until they burned into the straps.

He looked back to Duke. Duke was moving his right arm, trying to bring his mace up.

He was too slow.

Jericho slashed his kilij across Duke's gut. It was a forceful cut that bit deep, parting layers of skin and muscle.

Along with the momentum of his dash, Jericho used every last bit of strength in his legs and body to slam his left fist into Duke's gut, right where Jericho's sword had cut. His fist and the first half of his forearm pushed past the opening of the wound and into Duke.

Jericho used all of his ghosts to create electricity. Even Lana and Susha, who had been keeping him alive. Domnul, Orion, Soot, Susha, Leo, Lana, and Belial all sent electrical energy into the whip. The coils of the whip wrapped around his arm—and around the chain mail of his coat sleeve—became a magnet.

Duke tensed. He started to twitch. His teeth chattered. His fingers twitched like he was playing an invisible piano and his mace fell to the floor. His ghosts battled Jericho's. It was a near thing. They had the home turf. And Jericho's ghosts had never been good at creating electricity.

Then Lilith was beside him. She looked exhausted. She had bruises on her face. The dark blotches stood out against her pale skin. Her right arm was bleeding and swollen and her left had burn marks. But she was smiling.

"See you in hell," she said sweetly. She put her hands on the handle of the whip and sent some serious voltage through its coils.

More than anything, the sound was what Jericho remembered as Duke's spirit was forced from his body. It was like a bitter winter wind howling mournfully across barren hills. It was a cold, lonely sound. And it was loud. Loud enough to drown out the electric crackling of Lilith's whip.

The mournful howl resonated through the room. As the sound still echoed, Duke went limp and dropped to the floor. Jericho ripped his hand and arm out of the body with a disgusting sucking sound.

They both stared down at Duke's body, waiting.

Jericho wasn't sure what he expected to happen. He didn't know if Duke had bonded the healing ghost to his blood or to himself, and he didn't know if the ghost would remain behind and continue trying to heal the body like the healing ghost bonded to the Colossus had.

It seemed not. Duke's body didn't move. The blood didn't flow back into the body. No spirits were orbiting around the corpse at all.

Still, it didn't hurt to be sure.

"Could you find me some pitch?" Jericho asked Lilith.

"There's some oil lamps in the hall," Lilith said. "Could you make do with that?"

"I believe that will work just fine."

While Lilith was gone, Jericho cut Duke to pieces. It was hard work, cutting a body apart. Even with a razor-sharp blade the human body didn't come apart easily. Especially with metal for blood. Lana and Susha still shouted at him to stay still, but there was no way Jericho was going to rest with Duke looking even close to alive. He hacked away relentlessly. In the process, he became covered with sweat, his own blood, and Duke's blood and amalgam mixture.

When Lilith came back, she stared at the mess. Jericho had thrown a few pieces of Duke into the pit. The rest he had piled in the corner in a macabre pyramid. Duke's head was on the very top, his empty eyes staring into nothing.

"Well," Lilith said. "You've certainly been enthusiastic." She handed him an oil lamp.

Jericho unscrewed the top of the lamp and dumped the oil over Duke's body. He took a candle from a table. The candle's flame reminded him of something.

"Cinder wasn't in the human city," Jericho said. "We need to find him!"

"He's dead," Lilith said.

"You're certain?"

"He's in more pieces than Duke. I sent him into the pit. The failed Wretched tore him apart."

Jericho stared at her.

"You killed Cinder? He was one tough Vagabond."

"Yeah," she said. Her eyes seemed to flicker with electricity and hate. "He was."

"For what it's worth, I'm impressed." She had certainly come a long way from when he had first met her.

Jericho looked at the heap of Duke's body. The mess glistened with metallic blood and oil.

"This is it, then," he said. He moved closer with the candle. Before he could touch the flame to the oil, though, Lilith put her hand on his chest.

"Wait," she said. "Let me borrow this for a moment." She grasped the hilt of his kilij. She looked at him, waiting for him to nod before she unsheathed it. There wasn't another person alive Jericho would let use that sword. It was a deeply intimate gesture, and she seemed to understand that.

Lilith unsheathed Jericho's sword and stood over Duke's body. She poked around a bit, and then dug in with the point. When she brought it back up, the necklace with the key to Gheistmar dangled from the blade. The key weighed down the cord, forcing it into a long, thin oval. With a quick jerk of the sword, she flipped the necklace over to Jericho.

Jericho caught it one-handed. It was slick from Duke's blood, and it was still warm.

"That's yours now," Lilith said.

The key was heavy. So too were the implications. The responsibility of leading an entire city. An entire people, really. It was intimidating. Something he didn't know if he could do, or if he even wanted.

"I don't know what's ahead," Jericho said. "I can't even begin to imagine. But I do know that this is over."

He dropped the candle onto Duke's remains, igniting them. He and Lilith stood there, watching the flames and the shadows dance.

The waves in the ether were huge. Something was happening in the Charnel House. Beetle ran through the streets, gathering Irons to him as he went.

The door to the Charnel House was wide open. Beetle ran in, dashing past the empty cells. Down at the end of the hall was the operating room. That door was open as well, but Beetle couldn't see inside. The operating room was completely dark. Not so much as the light of a single candle radiated out from it. It was like a Cyclopean stone had been placed in the entrance.

Beetle stopped. So did the Irons behind him. No one wanted to enter the room. Whatever had caused the waves in the ether was in there, though. Beetle drew his sword and eased forward. He walked on the balls of his feet, moving as quietly as he could. His breathing was quick and shallow. The air whistled softly through his sharpened teeth.

He was still a few feet from the entrance when a strong spirit pushed past his ghosts and grabbed hold of him and yanked him into the room.

Beetle sailed through the air. He heard the door slam shut behind him with a boom. He hit the floor and rolled to stop. He laid there with his heart hammering in his chest. The room was as black and as sightless as the inside of a coffin. He stood. He had somehow maintained his grip on his sword, and now he held it out in front of him with trembling hands. The Irons pounded on the door. They were trying to get in, but the door was held shut by a powerful spirit. Beetle was very much alone right now.

Light! A candle on the far side of the room sparked to life. Then another, and another. All of them were on the far side of the room, leaving Beetle still cloaked in shadow. Two figures stood in the center of the room. They were backlit by the candles, and he could discern them only as dark silhouettes.

More candles were lit, revealing a horrid mess of burned, smoking flesh. There was very little of the corpse that was recognizable, but Beetle was fairly certain that it was Duke.

A ghost flew around the room, sparking electricity to light the remainder of the room's candles. As the light flooded the room, he was able to see the figures in front of him. He inhaled sharply when he saw who it was.

It didn't make sense. It shouldn't have been possible. And yet, somehow, Beetle wasn't surprised.

"You have a choice to make, Beetle," Jericho said. He wore the key of Gheistmar around his neck. "A very important one."

Jericho was hurting. His back screamed pain. Susha and Lana both chided him for every small movement he made, breathing included.

I can't stop breathing, he sent.

Do the best you can, Susha sent back.

He wanted nothing more than to lie down and have a stiff drink of whiskey against the pain. The possibility of that drink was far away, though. If it ever came at all.

The Irons pushed and pounded on the door to the room and Soot was still able to hold it shut against them, but it was only a matter of time before they and their ghosts managed to open it.

"Duke is dead," Jericho said to Beetle. "So is Cinder. I now wear the key to the city." He watched Beetle. He expected some reaction. Surprise, fear, panic ... something. But Beetle's facial expression didn't seem to change. Not that Jericho could see much because of the gas mask Beetle always wore.

"You can stay loyal to Duke," Jericho continued. "I won't

punish you for that. You'd have to leave Gheistmar, of course, but I wouldn't kill you. I respect loyalty. In fact, that's precisely what I'd like from you. You're a good and dedicated soldier, and your men stand by you even in adversity. It seems that I now have a city to run, and I'd like you and your Irons to help me."

No one spoke for a long moment. Jericho wondered if they were going to have to fight their way out of the Charnel House. He wondered just how well Susha and Lana would be able to hold him together.

"Duke made me kill humans," Beetle finally said. "And Cinder ordered us to do much worse. I'll follow you. I just have one condition."

"What is it?" Jericho said.

But Beetle was looking at Lilith.

CHAPTER 51

"I hope they both die," Jericho said. He looked out over the
railing of the palace balcony. The city was laid out before them. It
was past midnight, and the streetlamps made the streets pulse like
veins filled with glowing amber blood.

"You can't say that," Lilith told him.

"Not even if it's true?"

"No," she said. "Especially not then. Tim might deserve
many things, but I don't think death is one of them."

"That little prick betrayed us," Jericho said.

"Yes," Lilith said. "And it cost him dearly. Coming to
Gheistmar cost him his sanity. You saw how he was. He just laid
in bed and jabbered. Some nasty ghost got ahold of him and sent
him in a real bad rave. He's a shard now."

"What about Cull?" Jericho said. "He nearly killed you when
he captured you and carried you back to the city. And he came
damn close to killing me, too."

"Cull frightens me," Lilith said quietly. "But a deal's a deal. If
Beetle's one condition for loyalty is that we save his friend, we
can't deny the request."

"I just can't believe he didn't die. I set him on fire and ran my blade into his chest ... "

"I think when you used your sword to draw heat from him, you put out some of the flames," Lilith said. "He's a big person. His body is capable of surviving significant amounts of trauma. We'll see, he still might not make it."

They both watched the city. A cold wind blew and Lilith pressed close to Jericho. Her hair smelled faintly of flowers.

"Do you think we'll ever see Claire again?" she asked him.

"Yes," Jericho said. He had thought about it many times, wondering if she was lost to them forever. But he didn't think so. "She'll come back to us."

"I almost wish she wouldn't," Lilith said. "I wish she could stay safe and live a happy normal life. Away from this horror."

"Her ghosts won't let her. You know that. And there is too much beauty and wonder here for her to stay away." He wrapped his arm around Lilith. "We've seen only the surface of what this city has to offer."

Lilith pushed away and stared at him with wide eyes.

"You're thinking of opening up more of the abandoned buildings, aren't you?" she asked him. "Like what you did with the clock tower."

"I am," Jericho said. "Who knows what we might find in there? Maybe we'll finally find out what killed the Elders."

"What if Duke was right?" Lilith said. "What if history repeats itself and whatever killed the Elders comes for us?"

"With you by my side," Jericho said. "What can I possibly fear?"

Lilith didn't have a special coat like his. The night was cold, and she was starting to shiver. Jericho picked her up and carried her inside.

Erik Kreinbrink grew up in Ohio and wrote Vagabonds while working nights as a security guard in an abandoned convent set deep in the woods. He has a bachelors in Creative Writing and attends Thriller Fest regularly.

www.ingramcontent.com/pod-product-compliance
Lightning Source LLC
Chambersburg PA
CBHW021436240626
47153CB00001B/169